all the colours in between

A novel by Eva Jordan

URBANE
Publications

urbanepublications.com

First published in Great Britain in 2017 by Urbane Publications Ltd
Suite 3, Brown Europe House, 33/34 Gleaming Wood Drive, Chatham, Kent ME5 8RZ
Copyright © Eva Jordan, 2017

A CIP catalogue record for this book is available from the British Library.

ISBN 978-1-911583-28-8
MOBI 978-1-911583-30-1
EPUB 978-1-911583-29-5

Design and Typeset by Julie Martin
Cover by Author Design Studio

Printed and bound by 4edge Limited, UK

urbanepublications.com

The publisher supports the Forest Stewardship Council® (FSC®), the leading international forest-certification organisation.
This book is made from acid-free paper from an FSC®-certified provider. FSC is the only
forest-certification scheme supported by the leading environmental organisations, including Greenpeace.

To Mum and Dad, thank you for always encouraging me to reach for the stars, and Steve for helping me touch them ...

"The purest and most thoughtful minds are those which love colour the most."
– **John Ruskin**

"Let me, O let me bathe my soul in colours; let me swallow the sunset and drink the rainbow."
– **Kahlil Gibran**

"Colour directly influences the soul. Colour is the keyboard, the eyes are the hammers, the soul is the piano with many strings."
– **Wassily Kandinsky**

PROLOGUE

...and so they left home, my daughters that is. Grew up, sort of, spread their wings and flew the proverbial nest. The hard years were over. At least, that's what I told myself. I'd navigated the terrible twos, which, for all intents and purposes, is much akin to negotiating with a walking, talking middle finger; a mini dictator with the uncanny ability to know just how far to push you, often precariously towards the precipice of insanity. Where simply asking your small child to put their shoes away or giving them the blue cup instead of the yellow one often results in the most spectacular and colourful meltdown.

Then came the challenges of single parenting, later followed by the blended family including that age old universal enigma, otherwise known as the teenage daughter, which, in my case also included a step daughter; "I hate you, you've ruined my life", their default reply to most things. Be prepared for large amounts of eye rolling, emotional outbursts and thoughts of running away, and that's just the parents. Demotion is swift with these beautifully strange and incongruous creatures; one minute you are their best friend, the next, Satan himself. Don't get caught out by their words either. If your teenage daughter tells you she is fine, she is most definitely not. If they tell you they'll be five minutes, add another fifty-five to that. "Thanks" is a rare but legitimate apology; "thanks a lot" is NOT.

Nonetheless, I weathered the storms, took the rough with the smooth and at the end of the day, family is family. Whether it's the one you start out with or the one you gain along the way. Don't get me wrong; there have been a few minor casualties, a few near misses but thankfully no fatalities. And yes, I know I'm not out of the woods just yet, after all, I still have a teenage son to contend with but somehow his angst-ridden journey to adulthood is somewhat quieter than that of his siblings. There is still plenty of eye rolling and heavy sighing but unlike the verbose high-pitched ramblings of his sisters, verbal communication with my son is usually carried out via a series of unintelligible grunts and nods. And, although, like his sisters before him, my son also carries the weight of the world on his rather stooped shoulders, as long as there is a Wi-Fi signal to his bedroom, food in the fridge and hair gel in the bathroom, I hardly know he's there.

So, on the whole life has been good. I've survived it thus far, usually with poise and decorum but mostly with copious amounts of cheap wine and good friends and I've embraced my colourful life. I remember though, as a small child, how very black and white my world appeared. Not in terms of my surroundings or for that matter the clothes my mother dressed me in, it was the 1970's, after all, polyester was the material of choice and bright colours reigned supreme, but in terms of life itself. I quickly came to the conclusion that human beings were annoying, contradictory creatures. An opinion that, I must confess, hasn't changed much over the years. However, I gradually learned there were no easy answers to anything in life, especially when it came to the questions and actions of my own children.

So, I took all that life had to throw at me and I learned the subtle differences. White represented a new day and relief from a dark night and scary dreams, which differed from the effervescent glow of snowflakes and the promise of adventure, which in turn differed from the porcelain white lies I found myself telling, and still do, from time to time. I felt the iridescent pink flush of desire reflected in the magenta sunrise of childhood holidays along the Cornish coast and I picked out the coral pinks of friendship that tasted so different to the cranberry passion of first love. Sulphur was the colour of intense pain that quickly transformed into the earthy greens and pastel yellows of new life tinged with a touch of the baby blues. I heard the buttercup yellow of my children's laughter and remembered how the Tuscan sunset differed so greatly from my flaxen fear, especially when I found myself as a newly divorced single parent. I also understood that the obsidian skyline, which at times weighed me down like a great cloak of depression, also provided the perfect backdrop for the stars to shine. Stars, like scattered moon dust that my children loved to count. I learned that rose tinted glasses had distorted my bright orange suspicions and while the rusty taste of my crimson blood reminded me so much of my scarlet anger I also understood it was a million miles away from the apple blossom red of true love. I gradually learned that life was not black and white; that there are in fact, many colours in between.

Why then, is everything fading to grey...

Part One

Chapter 1

FOUR-TWENTY

Lizzie

I descend the stairs and except for the slight feeling of nausea washing over me, I feel reasonably well and at ease with the world. Hovering mid-step, I listen, enjoying the sound of silence. How quickly things have changed in the years since my recovery. Instinctively, I reach up and touch my head. Fingers poised like the legs of a spider, I search and find one of several raised scars amongst freshly washed strands of hair and as always, I shiver. I prefer to think of them as battle scars, a constant reminder of both the strength and fragility of life. I danced with "the gloomy shade of death" but lived to tell the tale and for that I'm truly grateful.

Letting my hand fall to my side again, I quickly push the memory aside and find my gaze resting on the collage of framed memories adorning the stair wall. Examining the frames for dust, I linger on a photo of Cassie and Maisy before Maisy left for Australia. Both girls have their arms around each other and are laughing. I can't remember what the occasion was but I love the photo because it's completely natural. A spontaneous moment caught on film and not a selfie pose or pout in sight. I tap the glass affectionately and smile at my girls. Life was so noisy whenever these two were around, especially Cassie. In fact, I swear if I listen hard enough, I can hear an echo of the raucous comings and goings of her angst ridden teenage years bouncing off these very walls. It was hardly surprising the stair carpet needed replacing. Maisy, the Goth, my sulky, surly stepdaughter was less theatrical, less verbose than her sister but still as troublesome in her own way, like the time she went off, without permission, and got a full leg tattoo of a tree. I'll never forget the look on Simon's face when he first saw it.

As my gaze wanders, prompted by snapshots of the past, I find myself excavating old memories; Mum and Dad, first married and unbelievably young; Sean and I as children; Sean and Natasha getting married, he with his dreadlocks, she with her white Doc Martins; Sean and Natasha after the arrival of my niece, Summer; Simon, my man and one of my very best friends; Ruby, my other best friend, standing next to Andy, lovely, kind, generous Andy, taken from us in the mere blink of an eye.

Sniffing, I wipe away a lone tear running down my cheek, immediately cheered when my eyes fall upon a photo of Connor, pre-pubescent and still my little big man, so very different to my Connor of late. Far less emotional than his sisters were at sixteen years old, he is nonetheless chartering his own angst-ridden journey to adulthood. I miss our great big bear hugs. At least he has a nice group of friends though. I envy him in a way. Fast approaching the end of his GCSEs, his only major concerns in life appear to be having the correct gel for his hair, his phone, and earphones, and how much food he can consume. Actually, come to think of it, it's less about consumption and more about inhaling.

I shake my head and laugh, realising time is getting on. I need to get some work done. 'I am a writer, you know,' I shout playfully to my rather quiet, rather empty house. And it's true; I am. Who'd have thought it, me? Lizzie Lemalf, blogger extraordinaire and writer. I still have to pinch myself from time to time to believe it is actually true. But it is nonetheless. I still can't believe I have an agent and a publisher and, as well as finding me ensconced for months on end in my writing cave, I can also occasionally be found swanning around the country attending book festivals and signings.

Feeling a vibration in my pocket I look down. It's my phone and it's a text from my agent, Michelle.

Hi Lizzie. Just checking you are all set for the meeting with the publisher a week on Monday? Oliver and I will meet you off the train at Kings X. Nothing to worry about but if you have any concerns we can discuss further when we meet beforehand at your Author Q&A session at the Haversham Literary Festival on Thurs. If that's ok?

It is okay; at least it should be okay, except the text clearly states that Oliver, Michelle's personal assistant, will be with her. Oh god, why does he have to come? Just the thought of him has robbed me of speech and has my stomach performing tiny, slightly panic induced somersaults. Not that there is anything wrong with the man. As far as personal assistants go, Oliver is lovely, but that's the problem, he's actually *too* lovely. To look at I mean. The man is stunning. Perfection on legs. Reaching over six feet tall with a chiselled chin, a clearly defined, taut physique (especially when he takes off his jacket and rolls up his shirt sleeves) and piercing blue eyes, I'm barely able to think straight whenever he appears. I swear to god the song 'Take My Breath Away' by Berlin plays on a loop in my head every time he enters a room. I kept asking Michelle to please turn the music off at our last meeting, until I realised it was literally in my head. I also, somehow, lose my ability to talk when I am around Oliver. My words become jumbled and fall out in reverse order so that I always sound like I'm doing some terrible impersonation of Yoda from *Star Wars*.

"Hi Lizzie, how are you?" Oliver will ask.

"Oliver! Fine, am I. You are, how?" is often my ridiculous reply.

It's not a sexual attraction either, well, maybe it is a bit, but it's not like I'm having some crazy mid-life crisis and want to run off and have mad, passionate sex with this beautiful man. I love Simon and I've even told him about Oliver and the effect he has on me, which met with a raised eye and a wry smile, followed by an exaggerated patting of his slightly expanding waistline. 'I'd better get back to the gym then, eh?' he said. 'Or I'll be losing you to a younger, fitter man.' To which we both laughed.

Fingers hovering above my phone, I consider asking Michelle not to bring Oliver before dismissing the idea. I tap out a reply telling her I'll be there and am very much looking forward to it (as long as I avert my gaze from Oliver).

My thoughts about managing my meeting with Oliver are interrupted by a soft, warm sensation weaving between my ankles. I look down and spy Romeow. He looks up, his face a little craggier of late, and lets out a rather pathetic meow. I bend down and he allows me to pick him up, nudging my cheek, purring loudly. I talk to him for several minutes, like a baby, and again he allows me to, before deciding enough is enough and jumps from my arms. His landing is silent and graceful and, with a flick of his tail, he swaggers towards the back door. He waits, patiently. I laugh and grab the back-door key from the kitchen drawer.

'Oh … I see … you want to go out do you, Romeow?' I ask.

Romeow responds with another weary meow. I fiddle with the key and the lock before finally opening the back door, whereupon, much to Romeow's disgust, I scream, very loudly. Someone is languishing on one of the garden chairs. His hands are shoved deep into his jacket pockets and his head is leant skywards, mouth wide open. The large, motionless body is snoring. I step out of the door and walk cautiously towards the sleeping individual. On closer inspection, I realise it is Connor.

Why on earth is Connor sleeping outside at 6.00 a.m. on a Saturday morning?

Connor

This is it; I'm going to die. And I'm only sixteen years old. I haven't even lost my virginity and now I never will because I'm going to die. I grab my chest with both hands, desperate to stop the pounding against my ribs. My heart is beating so hard and so fast I swear it's going to explode, leaving nothing but a gaping bloody mess as the life drains out of me.

Bending forward I try and breathe, slowly. It doesn't work. I stand up keeping one arm locked across my chest. Tight. I'm scared. Really scared. It all seemed like such a good idea yesterday. "It'll be a laugh," Jake had said. I didn't expect to feel like this, though.

Struggling to focus I look for Jake. I see him, rolling all over the floor in hysterics, pointing at me. Bastard. Still keeping one arm closed against my chest, I throw the other one forward, pleading, without words, for help. But there's none coming. Gripped by fear I turn in the direction of another sound. Running water, I think? I see Robbo standing against the churchyard wall. Maybe he's having a piss or maybe, just maybe, it's the sound of my blood pumping through my veins. Yes, that's what it is. *My* blood surging through *my* veins feeding *my* pounding heart that is beating waaaaay too fast. This is not right, not normal. What the hell am I going to do? I turn away and look at Jake again.

'Help me Jake,' I beg. 'This is really serious man. I'm dying, I'm actually fucking dying.'

Jake, clutching his stomach and still pointing at me, laughs even harder. Double bastard. He doesn't get it, or doesn't give a shit, but I swear to god I'm going to die. I'm going to die, in front of my best friend. And he doesn't even give a shit!

Thinking of Mum, I try and remember the way home. She'd kill me if I died like this. That doesn't make sense, except it does, coz if I died, like this, Mum would find a way to find me, even though I'd be dead, and kill me all over again!

I start walking in the direction I think is home and focus on the sound of my footsteps instead of the pounding noise of my heart that won't leave my head. I walk fast, I think. My feet feel mushy and twisted, though, so it's hard to tell. I look over my right shoulder and see Jake, still laughing. I look over my left shoulder, and freeze. The Tracer, the evil soul sucker character from my computer game, hovers high above me, and he's looking straight at me. His twisted face is evil, and he's looking straight at me. Not Jake. Not the others, but me. ME!

Somewhere in the distance a girl screams, or is it me? I try and run but it's not easy with mushy feet. A terrifying whooshing sound tells me The Tracer is behind me, chasing me. Oh no! He's gonna reach right into my rib cage, pull out my live beating heart, then he's gonna eat my soul.

I tell myself this is not real. Keep repeating it over and over again, unsure if I'm saying it out loud or just to myself, but I keep saying it anyway. Like a mantra.

This is not real. This is not real.

But still I can't get The Tracer out of my head.

Think of something else, you idiot, something funny.

Again, I try and distract myself by listening to my footsteps. Think, you idiot. Think. Cassie jumps into my thoughts, but shit, that's really done it now coz instead of focussing on Cassie, my brain is taking me to the last conversation I overheard her having with Mum. They were discussing the right for women to have hairy fannies. And they're right of course. Women should be allowed to be hairy down there, if they want. Or they can shave it all off too, if they want to, but they shouldn't feel like they *have* to have a bald fanny, like in the porno movies. Cassie says too many boys watch porn on the internet and think that's how women should be and how sex should be, and it's degrading. Cassie says if too many boys mistake porn for real life then boys will expect girls to look and act like the women in those films. I don't. I've never thought real life was like any movie I ever watched, porno or not, and, if Hayley Patterson ever went out with me (which she wouldn't coz she doesn't even know I exist, except to help her with her maths, sometimes) I wouldn't mind if she had a hairy fanny. Don't get me wrong, I wouldn't want it to be *really,* really hairy, like hanging down her legs hairy. But a bit hairy would be okay. Jake thinks girls should be bald, says he'd dump a girl with a hairy fanny. Jake's a knob, even though he is my best friend. I can still hear him behind me, laughing, instead of helping me escape from The Tracer.

Petrified, I look over my shoulder to see if The Tracer is still there. I'm relieved to see he's gone. But now something worse has taken his place. A giant fanny, cloaked in never ending, wiry, black hair with one huge, pulsating red eye, hovers above my head. Pointing, I let rip a terrifying scream, as the glaring, one-eyed, bearded clam gets even closer.

'Hairy fanny, hairy fanny!' I shriek.

Again, I'm not sure if I've said this out-loud or to myself but right now I don't give a shit.

The hairy minge gives chase and, screaming all the way, I run for my life. Run for home, I think?

Chapter 2

LIAR, LIAR, PANTS ON FIRE!

Cassie

I hug Honey goodbye, press the buzzer on the door and step back inside the small reception area. I hand Jaz her change and the cheese sandwiches and Frappo she asked me to get for her.

'Thanks Cas,' Jaz says.

'No problem, babe,' I reply. The door buzzes again and I walk off towards the stairs, leaving Jaz to it but Jaz calls out to me to come back. The person buzzing at the door is Honey. Jaz releases the door and Honey pushes it open. She's panting like she's out of breath.

'God, I'm unfit. Too many fags. I need to quit. Here,' she says handing me my phone, 'you left this in my bag.'

'Shit. Thanks, hun!'

Honey smiles at Jaz then looks up, scanning the entrance of my workplace. 'So, this is where the magic happens is it?' she asks.

'Well, not here. Up there,' I reply pointing upwards, 'where the studios are.'

'I'd love to have a loo-ook,' Honey sings, all wide eyed and smiling.

'Not today, babe,' I reply shaking my head. 'The boss is in and –'

'Really! Hunter Black is actually in this building right now? Pleeeease introduce me. I promise I'll behave.'

'Honey, I've told you before,' I whisper, 'I can't do that. He gets really pissy about that sort of crap.'

Honey throws up her hands. 'It's not bloody crap. I'm a

singer, a good one, who just happens to be your friend and all I want is for him to listen to me. See what he thinks?'

'I know, babe. Leave it with me, to pick the right moment, eh? Please, trust me. He can be really weird at times. I know what I'm talking about.'

Honey sighs and sticks out her bottom lip. She looks disappointed but says she understands. She kisses me goodbye for the second time and says she'll see me later at home. 'Oh yeah,' she adds, 'Carmel just phoned me back.'

'Who?'

'The landlady of the flat?'

'Oh yeah, weirdo.'

Honey laughs. 'She said she wasn't telling you to shut the door.'

'But she did,' I protest. 'One minute we were talking about rent charges in London compared to home and the next she was telling me to shut the bloody door. Crazy woman.'

'And I thought I was the dippy one! It's just the way she talks, you silly cow. She's an Essex girl.' Now I really am confused. 'Shut the door,' Honey continues, 'is just another way of saying "No. Never. Really."'

'Really?'

'Yeah, really.' We both laugh, then Honey whispers in my ear telling me she thinks Jaz is fit and asks me to pass on her phone number. I laugh and tell Honey I think Jaz is straight and Honey assures me she isn't. 'At the very least she's bi,' Honey replies.

Jaz, who is now on the phone, releases the door with the buzzer thing behind her desk and Honey disappears again.

'Yep, will do,' Jaz says into the phone as I once again pass her desk and head towards the stairs. 'That was Hunter,' Jaz shouts to me, 'he wants you go to his office before you go back to the studio.'

My tummy flips. Oh no, now what? I pass the studio on the second floor and head towards Hunter's office on the floor above. I get a whiff of him even before I reach the third floor. He wears the same aftershave all the time and I can smell it a mile away. I reckon he baths in the stuff. It's not cheap but I hate it all the same. The door to his office looks closed but as I get nearer, I realise it's slightly ajar. He has someone with him. I can hear his and another man's voice and they're both laughing. I put my ear to the door and listen.

'Yeah, but let's be honest, women are just not cut out for it. They don't think like men. Far too bloody emotional for a start,' Hunter says. They both laugh again and the other man says something I can't hear. 'I've told you before, put it in their coffee in the morning,' Hunter replies and both men laugh even louder. I'm not sure why but the back of my neck prickles. I don't know what the hell they are talking about and if I'm honest I don't really give a shit. I can't be arsed to listen to anymore. Taking a deep breath, I knock on the door.

'Come in,' Hunter shouts.

A fat man with a huge neck and squinty eyes sits opposite him. He looks me up and down then screws his face up like he's just stepped in dog shit or something. 'Thought you said she was pretty,' he says.

Hunter looks at the man then looks at me. He starts at my feet then slowly his eyes climb upward, sometimes lingering longer than they should. He's doing it on purpose, of course, trying to intimidate me, and it's working. I feel my cheeks burn and have to look away, shifting uncomfortably from one foot to the other. Hunter says my name and I look up again. Our eyes lock. 'If I'd have known you were going to dress like a fucking bag lady all the time I wouldn't have hired you,' he says.

As usual Hunter smiles, as if it's a joke. He has a row of perfectly straight, perfectly white teeth and like me, he has a big nose but it's flatter looking than mine. His eyes are dark, really dark. So dark, in fact, you can barely see his pupils. He kind of reminds me of a shark when he smiles. I swallow hard and feel my throat tighten. What the hell has what I wear got to do with how I do my job? I'm nervous but I have to say something. Shoulders back, I take a deep breath.

'What ... exactly ... has what I wear got to do with my job?'

Hunter smirks and rolls his eyes. 'Don't mind her,' he says looking at the fat-faced, fat-necked man, 'I think she's had a humour bypass. Lighten up Cassie for fuck's sake. I have got a reputation to keep.'

'Yeah, for making good music,' I protest.

The fat necked man raises his eyes and coughs. 'Ahem, among other things,' he says, laughing.

I choose to ignore him but can't help smirking when the fat man's laughter turns into violent coughing and a spray of spit gushes from his mouth. Repulsed, I look away from the now red, fat-faced man as Hunter passes him a glass of water. 'Besides, I like wearing jeans and a T-shirt, they're comfy when you spend hours and hours in the studio.'

Hunter's eyes fall to my feet again. 'Well at least get yourself some decent footwear. Those trainers look as though they belong in the bin.'

He's not wrong. My battered old Converse have seen better days. But I wore them all through uni and I hate to part with them. Hunter's fat friend, who has stopped coughing, is now looking at me again.

'Mmmm,' he says licking his lips, 'a nice pair of black patent, knee high, leather boots would be just the ticket.'

Hunter laughs but I don't. As usual, he thinks it's just a bit of banter, having a laugh. I want to tell his fat, disgusting, pervert friend he's a sexist pig but I don't want to lose my job, so I decide silence is golden.

'What was it you wanted, Hunter?' I ask, 'I really need to get on.' Hunter smiles at me and my tummy performs a little somersault. I'm both surprised and annoyed at the same time. His dark eyes match his really dark hair. He's old, late thirties

I think and although I don't fancy him, at least I'm pretty sure I don't, I can see why women do. He reeks of money, which is attractive to a lot of people, I suppose, but there's something else about him too. Something sort of charming but dangerous.

There's another knock at the door, it's Adam, the intern. He's wearing black skinny jeans, a vintage Jimi Hendrix T-shirt and trainers. I wait for some comment about his appearance but of course there is none. 'Hey all, I'm just making a cuppa, anybody want one?' he asks.

I tell Adam I'd love a coffee but Hunter tells Adam to get back to work because Cassie will do it. 'But, I don't mind,' Adam replies looking at me, 'I could do with a break anyway?'

Hunter shakes his head. 'No, Cassie can do it. Cassie does as she's told, like a good little girl, eh Cas?' he says winking at me. Adam shrugs his shoulders, says "okay" and disappears again. Hunter leans back in his chair and looks straight at me, twisting his wedding ring around on his finger.

'So, Cassie, who was the girl in reception?'

'Oh, what just now?' I swing round and point to the door. 'Do you have cameras downstairs then?'

'I have cameras everywhere, Cassie,' Hunter replies as he and his fat friend start laughing again.

I have a sudden urge to pee. 'That was just an old friend. Someone I used to know. She had some business in London so asked if I could meet her for lunch.'

'Where do you know her from?'

'College.'

'Music College?'

'Yeah.'

'Does she sing?'

I shake my head. 'God no.' Hunter looks confused. 'She went to the same college as me but was on a different course,' I explain. 'Business, I think it was,' I say, cringing inside. I hate lying.

'Shame. She's very pretty. What does she do?'

'I dunno,' I reply waving my hand dismissively. 'Works in a call centre I think.'

'Get her on the phone for me, now.'

'Can't. Don't have her number.'

Hunter's black eyes narrow in disbelief. 'How the hell did you arrange to meet up then?'

'Through another mutual friend, there was a few of us. We all met up together.'

'So, ring one of them.'

'Okay,' I smile through gritted teeth. Shit. How the hell am I going to get out of this? I reach into my back pocket and slowly pull out my phone. I swipe the screen but nothing happens. Yes! 'Erm, sorry but the battery is dead,' I continue, waving the blank, dead screen of my phone for Hunter to see.

Hunter shakes his head and sighs. 'I suppose it's too much to suppose you know her number?'

I shrug my shoulders. 'Don't know anyone's numbers, except my mum's, I know my mum's number.'

'Fat lot of good that is. What's her name?'

'Who? My mum?'

'No, for fuck's sake. The girl, what's the girl's name?'

'Ho-nnah. Her name is Hannah.'

'Hannah what?'

'Smith. Hannah Smith.'

'When will you be seeing her again?'

I shrug my shoulders. 'God knows. Probably in another two years.'

Hunter covers his mouth with his hand. Quiet for a minute, he looks thoughtful. 'Hmmm, well, next time you meet up, bring her here. I'd like to meet her. It would be a shame to let looks like that go to waste. Even if she can't sing, we can always make it sound like she can, eh Cassie?'

Hunter winks at me again and his ugly fat friend, who hasn't taken his piggy eyes off me, continues to stare. I cough. I feel really uncomfortable but I don't want to show it. 'Yeah … sure … whatev's,' I reply in a voice at least an octave higher than my natural one. 'Now, if you don't mind, I need to get some work done.'

'Coffee first,' Hunter reminds me. His grin is almost as wide as the fat man's neck and I still can't believe how white Hunter's teeth are. I wouldn't be surprised if they actually glow in the dark. I shiver. The thought of Hunter in the dark sends a tingling sensation down my spine.

'Of course,' I reply.

'Good girl. A woman's work is never done, eh Cassie?'

I force a smile and turn to leave and as I do I ask the universe to forgive me for sabotaging my best friend's chances with one of the biggest music producers in the industry.

Chapter 3

GOD OF CHAOS

Lizzie

Thank you, god of chaos, as if today hasn't been stressful enough. Thanks to the shat-nav in my car, I arrived at Haversham Hall, historic stately home of the notable Haversham family, an hour later than anticipated. An annual event, now in its tenth year, the Haversham Literary Festival is, apparently, the brainchild of the current Lord of the Manor, Henry Haversham. When the family fell on financial hard times, leading to the possibility of losing their beautiful home and gardens, it was the rather forward-thinking Lord Haversham that could see the potential of sharing the family's grand house, and equally grand gardens, with the general public; for a generous fee, of course.

After parking my car in the allotted space, where a large wooden stand displayed my name, I jumped out of my car and headed for the door. Somewhat flustered by my lateness I then spent ten minutes trying to push the pull door in to the main entrance, only to be saved by someone who looked remarkably like Stephen King. I thanked the stranger, who held the door open for me and walked on. However, the stranger, who may or may have not been one of the world's most successful and prolific authors, insisted on opening a succession of other doors for me as he, too, headed towards the main hall, bringing me out in a cold sweat as I realised I was quickly running out of ways to say "thank you." Having deployed; thank you, cheers, ta, thanks, and nice one, I quickly scuttled off in search of Michelle but hopefully not Oliver.

I found her hovering by the main stage where a couple of

comfy looking chairs and a small coffee table had been placed in readiness for a number of Author Q&A's and interviews that had been booked over the next four days. I swallowed hard and felt my legs turn to jelly as I looked around and realised how fast the hall was filling up with people who had come to listen to me talk. I had attended this major literary event many times in the past, as a reader, this time I was here as a writer. With a little less than ten minutes to go (shielding my gaze from Oliver) Michelle draped a lanyard with a name badge attached, my name emblazoned in bold, black letters, over my head and introduced me to Michael, the appointed compére for my Author Q&A session. We shook hands and I followed him onto the stage. Somehow I managed to trip and head-butt him straight in the mouth as he turned to show me my seat. This saw us both flying across the stage, with me eventually lying astride my traumatised presenter when we both finally skidded to a halt. And, just to add insult to injury, Michael gained a fat, bloody lip to boot. Poor man. It was obvious he was in pain because he winced every time he asked me a question.

Forty minutes (and several hundred apologies to Michael) later, listening to a playback of my Q&A session (kindly recorded by Michelle) I have now decided, upon hearing my recorded voice, it would be criminal for me to ever talk publicly again. And now, mid-afternoon and having a book signing to attend to, I find the familiar waves of nausea, which are far too familiar to my person of late, wash over me with uncomfortable immediacy.

I look up and see a snake-like line of people politely forming an orderly queue in front of me. I sit down in front of the desk provided and take several large swigs of water from the complimentary bottle provided. A streak of yellow sun streams through the entrance to the marquee and a noisy throng of people gather to look at various bookstands or commissioned works of art by local artists. Looking down the line of readers eager to purchase a signed copy of my book, I am both overwhelmed and forever grateful to those willing to spend their precious time and money on the half-crazed ramblings of a middle-aged woman, such that I am.

I feel a hand on my back and turn to see Michelle smiling at me. 'Are you okay?' she asks. 'Only you look a little peaky?' I admit to feeling a little queasy and Michelle assures me it's probably just nerves. I nod my head just as my stomach performs another sea churning somersault. I feel both hot and cold at the same time. Taking another sip of water, I reach up for my reading glasses, slightly annoyed when they become entangled in my hair. I hear the twanging of individual hairs as they snap and break in my attempt to rescue my glasses from the top of my head.

Stupid, bloody glasses.

I look up at the sea of anxious faces in front of me and wonder if I've spoken out loud. Their smiling expressions assure me I haven't. I put a hand up behind my damp neck and realise I'm sweating. This is more than nerves; I actually don't feel well. Michelle puts her cool hand on my hot forehead and informs the ever-growing queue that I'll be ready to start in a couple more minutes.

'You're really not well are you?' Michelle whispers urgently.

'I think it may be the stuffed mushrooms I ate at lunch, I thought they tasted a bit funny.'

A child, a young girl, about four or five years old breaks free from the hand she has clearly been holding of someone half way down the queue. Stepping away she cocks her head sideways. She has a head of untamed, beautiful, brown curls and skin colour to match but even from this far away it's her stunning eyes that catch my attention. Not blue exactly, azure or cerulean would be a better description. She smiles when she sees me return her stare and raises a small chubby hand to wave at me. I smile and wave back at her before the hand of her guardian reaches out from the queue and gently pulls the young girl back.

'Right,' Michelle says assertively, 'let's get through this as quickly as possible then you can head back to the hotel for a lay down. If worst comes to worst, we've already got a pile of signed books, we'll just have to use those.'

Michelle calls out to Oliver and I vow not to look at him. He passes her a bag that she reaches into. 'Ah hah,' she says pulling out a small, elastic hair band, quickly gathers my hair together and ties it loosely away from my face.

Free of wet, sticky hair, I notice a cool breeze blowing through the entrance of the marquee dancing across my damp neck, for which I am extremely thankful. The young girl with the brown curls sticks her head out of the patiently waiting queue again. With chubby arms forming an arch above her head, she attempts to stand on her toes and twirl herself around. She loses her balance and crumples to the floor, giggling. A dark-haired woman bends down and scoops the laughing child into her arms. I can't see the woman's face but the child seems familiar. She catches me looking again and gives me another dazzling smile. I'm suddenly reminded of Cassie and wonder where all the years have gone. Taking me unawares, a bouquet of jasmine and vanilla droplets splash onto my skin and waft up my nose as Michelle blasts me with several squirts of perfume.

Taking a deep breath, I wipe my clammy hands on my dress, pick up my pen and smile. After all, it's the very least I can do for these wonderful people, who prove to be as equally enthusiastic about my writing, if not more so, than me. Some readers chat to me at great length while others appear slightly dazzled, almost star struck, which I find endearing but highly amusing. I wonder if they realise that I am as much in awe of them as they appear to be of me. I love meeting my readers, love knowing how much they enjoy my work but as for the rest of it, fame and all that malarkey, well, you can just stick it up your arse.

'I beg your pardon?' a voice filled with mock disapproval declares. I realise I've said my thoughts out loud again but am relieved to see it's with the lovely Alexina, one of the first people to read and review my book and recommend it to others in her online book group. My biggest cheerleader in fact. We chat like old friends, talking about everything from our kids, other writers we like and even the weather. I agree to try and meet Alexina and a few others in the bar for drinks later, although, at this rate, I suspect my still churning stomach has other plans for me.

As Alexina bids me goodbye, I feel my tummy begin to contract. I barely have time to turn away before I begin violently heaving. Romeow, when he has a fur ball stuck in his throat, immediately springs to mind. I hear tiny gasps of horror as people attempt to jump out of my way. I endeavour to stand up, make a run for it, but it's too late and I projectile vomit on a rather distinguished looking gentleman wearing black-framed glasses and a rather expensive looking tweed jacket. He looks as mortified as I feel. I hear Michelle's voice and feel someone's arms folding around me, guiding me away.

Sick dribbling from my mouth I turn to look at the now dispersing crowd. 'I'm sorry,' I shout. 'So, so, sorry everyone.'

I think I hear someone calling my name, a woman, 'Lizzie!' she calls. Once again, I look over my shoulder only to be met by a swarm of scattering faces. Some wear a look of revulsion, some pity, others mild amusement. I hear my name being shouted again but can't see where it's coming from. I do see the little girl with the brown curls, though. With downturned lips, her smiling face has now morphed into one of sadness. I raise my hand in farewell and, somewhat reluctantly, the child also raises her hand. Her disappointed eyes bore into me as her limp wristed hand waves back and forth. Then, turning away, I allow myself to be swept along by the entourage, eager to remove me lest I vomit on anyone else.

I'm troubled by the steely blue eyes of the small girl though.
I know her. I'm sure I know her.
But how?

Chapter 4

BAD NEWS TRAVELS FAST!

Connor

The boys are waiting for me at the school gates and I can already hear them sniggering. Jake lifts his arm and something dangles from his hand. I can't make it out but whatever it is, it catches the light and flashes at me as it swings from his finger. As I draw closer, I realise it's my bloody front door key. The very same one I managed to convince Mum I'd lost when I went out early Saturday morning to give Robbo some exam papers for revision. Don't think she believes me though.

'When do you ever get up before twelve o'clock on a Saturday?' she asked.

'It was like, important. He needed them. To revise.'

'And he couldn't wait until some civilised hour?'

'Dunno,' I replied, shrugging my shoulders and staring at my feet. It's much easier to lie to Mum when I don't have to look her straight in the face. Especially when she looks like she's sucking on lemons.

'Connor, can you please look at me when I'm speaking to you,' she said. I looked up, cautiously. I wasn't wrong. Cross-armed and squinty eyed she was definitely sucking on at least three whole lemons. 'And why didn't you just ring the doorbell instead of sitting outside?' she asked.

'Didn't wanna wake you up.'

'Hmmmmm,' she replied. 'Well, as you're up you can make yourself useful. The kitchen floor needs cleaning and the dishwasher needs unloading.'

I opened my mouth to protest but by this time Mum was

now sucking on four lemons so I quickly changed my mind and closed it again.

Little did she know I'd sneaked out to try a bit of puff with the lads in the churchyard and little did I know what my bloody reaction would be trying it for the first time. I started off okay, in fact we all were pretty chilled, it was only when the paranoia set in that the trouble started. That's when I started to believe The Tracer, who then morphed into, of all bloody things, a huge bearded clam that actually chased me down the bloody road, was stalking me. That's when I lost my key. I'm surprised I didn't lose my phone as well. Or my mind, come to that.

I draw closer and Jake continues to dangle my key from his finger, swinging it in front of my face.

I cough. 'Jake,' I declare.

'Conman,' he replies. 'Or should that be … hairy fanny?'

Jake, Robbo and the Rickmeister all burst out laughing as raspberry blown snorts spew from their mouths.

'Piss off,' I mumble, snatching my key out of Jake's hand but I can't help laughing too.

Robbo is laughing so hard he's actually bent over, holding on to his knees. 'Where the fuck did you get a hairy fanny from?' he asks in between gulps of laughter.

'It's bloody Cassie's fault,' I reply. I saw The Tracer first, who scared the bloody shit out of me–' this is followed by more howls of laughter '–I knew he wasn't real,' I continue, 'but he scared me bloody shitless anyway.' Jake, Robbo and the Rickmeister are now laughing so hard they are no longer capable of speech and neither, for a brief moment, am I.

'I still don't get how you jumped from Cassie to hairy fanny, though?' Jake asks.

'He's a perv,' the Rickmeister replies. 'Conman has been spying on his big sis' getting out the shower or something.'

'Piss off,' I say. 'Why would I wanna see my own sister naked?'

Jake sniggers. 'I would … if I had one,' he replies.

'Pervert,' Robbo, the Rickmeister and I all say at the same time.

'Have to put a cushion on my lap every time I'm at your house and your sis' is home,' Jake continues.

'Urrrrrgghh, shut the fuck up Jake.'

Jake winks at me. 'I'd do your mum as well. Bit of a MILF your mum is, Conman.'

I shoot him a sarcastic smile. 'Shame that Jake, coz my mum ain't interested in little boys.'

Jake grabs his crotch with his hand. 'Ain't nothing little about this, Conman,' he replies, shaking his balls in his cupped hand.

'Wanking yourself off again Jakeman?' a familiar voice asks from behind us.

We all turn around to see Maximus Kray (self-christened Max, The Snatch Catcher) the school's biggest tosser but also the school's biggest hard man. Tall with blonde hair and dark eyes, he looked about twenty years old by the time he was five. He's already slept with a ton of girls, or so he says, and if you don't do as he tells you, you get punched. Simple as.

'Jakeman, give me your fags. Conman, give me some money,' he orders.

Oh fuck off, Maximus Anus, I say. In my head, of course. I'm not completely suicidal.

'Oh, for fuck's sake,' Jake says, sighing and reaching into his rucksack. He pulls out a brand new, sealed packet of fags. 'I ain't even opened 'em yet.'

Max snatches the packet from Jake's hand.

'At least open 'em and leave us a couple for the week?' Jake pleads.

Max thrusts his face into Jake's. 'Ain't no-one told ya, smoking's bad for ya?' Max laughs. He then pushes Jake, hard. Jake loses his balance and almost falls but his pride saves him.

Max then turns his dark eyes towards me. He sneers, cocks

his head to one side and shows me his empty hand. 'Money, NOW, Conman,' he orders.

I stare at his sneery face and wish I had the guts to ram his teeth down his throat.

'Don't have any,' I reply. I do, but I'm pissed off with this wanker terrorising everyone.

Max's dark eyes grow darker still. 'What?' he replies, walking towards me.

'Max. Max. Did we tell ya about Conman seeing a giant, hairy fanny?' the Rickmeister suddenly interrupts.

Max's expression changes to one of confusion. He turns away from me to look at the Rickmeister. 'What the fuck...' he begins to ask but before he can finish, the Rickmeister is spilling the beans about my first experience of puff. By the time he finishes explaining, Max is in fits of hysterical laughter and in between those fits all I can hear is Max's voice telling everyone that I'm a hairy fanny man. Everyone walking past us looks confused but they laugh anyway, including, much to my total and utter embarrassment, Hayley Patterson.

I hang my head, swearing to beat the Rickmeister to a pulp when this lot leave. Mr Longthorpe, our head of year, wanders out, and I'm more than relieved when he calls everyone in. 'Stop loitering at the gates, you lot, haven't you got exams to get to?' he shouts. Max and his cronies finally leave with loads of loud whooping and shout-outs about me being a hairy fanny.

I turn and look at the Rickmeister in disbelief. 'What the hell were you thinking, Rickmeister? Telling Maximus Anus of all fucking people?'

He says he did it to distract Maximus from asking me for money. 'Worked, didn't it? He totally forgot about the money, didn't he?'

I roll my eyes and sigh heavily. 'Well, thank you very much Rickmeister. Because of you, my last remaining days at school are going to be bloody unbearable.'

The Rickmeister, who has now stopped smiling, thrusts his hands into his trouser pockets. His voice is sulky. 'Well, piss off if you're gonna get all menstrual about it. I was only trying to bloody help.'

'Well, do me a favour next time and DON'T.'

We head towards the main entrance and all around me I can hear sniggers of laughter and talk of hairy fannies.

'He's right though, Jake, you know?' Robbo suddenly pipes up.

'Who's right?'

'Maximus Anus.'

Jake scrunches up his nose in disgust. 'About what?'

'Smoking. It's bad for you coz ...' Robbo pauses for a moment and screws up his face like he's constipated but clearly he's trying to think. 'Coz,' he continues, 'you can get ...'

'Girls?' Jake interrupts. 'And if you get girls, you get sex?'

'No you bloody idiot! You can get tumours and brain damage and cancer and stuff.'

Jake starts laughing. 'Well s'cuse me if I don't give a shit.'

My phone vibrates in my pocket. I look at the screen and see it's a call from Nan. That's strange? Nan hardly ever calls me, not on a school day anyway. Robbo and Jake are still arguing. 'Will you two just shut the hell up for a minute,' I shout swiping the screen of my phone to answer the call.

'Hey, Nan. What's up?'

Nan sounds upset and is asking me if I know where Mum is. I tell her I think she's in London having a meeting with her publisher. Then I remember that she's also going to meet Cassie afterwards for lunch.

'She's probably turned her phone on silent, Nan. What's wrong?'

Nan tells me not to worry and get to school but her voice is shaky. I'm worried. Something is definitely wrong. I push Nan to tell me and eventually she fesses up. Grandad has been taken to hospital.

'He's had a fall,' Nan says. 'Possibly a stroke. I'm worried Connor, really worried.'

No. Not Grandad. This doesn't make sense. I know who Grandad is, who he *really* is (although I've never admitted it to anyone). How can Grandad be ill? It just doesn't make sense?

'I'm coming Nan,' I yell down the phone. 'I'm coming to the hospital.' Nan starts to protest but I cut her off before she can say anymore.

'I have to go, boys,' I say, turning to look at the lads.

Jake looks puzzled. 'But you have an R.E. exam in an hour?'

'I know. Fuck religion though, my Grandad's been taken into hospital.'

'Shit man,' Robbo says. 'Hope the old bugger's okay?'

The boys all gather around me and take it turns to pat my shoulder. The Rickmeister reaches into his pocket and gives me his half-smoked fag and Jake presses a ten-pound note into my hand.

'Thanks boys,' I say.

'Go,' they reply.

And so, I do.

Lizzie

After my disastrous Author Q&A session and book-signing event at the Haversham Literary Festival, I was determined the meeting with my publisher today wouldn't go the same way. As promised, Michelle and Oliver met me off the train at Kings Cross, and as usual, I did everything in my power not to look at the beautiful Oliver. Michelle asked me if I had any questions beforehand but there was nothing I could think of and I was happy for her to talk and negotiate on my behalf.

I walk away from the meeting with my publisher no more the

wiser than when I first arrived. I may have, for all I know, signed away all the rights to my next book. The only thing I am certain of is that Oliver is *the* most beautiful man in the world and Berlin's 'Take My Breath Away' has, once again, been playing in my head during the whole meeting.

I wasn't the only one affected by Oliver's presence, though. Even as we entered the building one poor woman became entangled in the glass revolving doors when she spotted Oliver. The security guard, whom I assume was going to her rescue, only made matters worse, so mesmerised was he by Oliver when he looked up and spotted him. I floundered, unsure whether I should try and help, but as Michelle and Oliver trotted on unaware of the carnage unfolding behind them, I felt compelled to follow them, leaving the young woman and security guard trying to escape their semi-revolving glass cocoon. Then there was the young man on reception who, like me, began to speak fluent Yoda, as did the beautiful woman who came to collect us. She now, unfortunately, has a rather large egg-shaped lump smack in the middle of her forehead. Instead of actually looking where she was walking, her gaze (along with her gaping mouth) remained firmly fixed on Oliver and she walked into the very door she was meant to be showing us through. Even Bernard, my publisher, although far more composed than I and able to maintain comprehensible speech, nonetheless found it impossible to avert his gaze from Oliver.

Oliver, I have now decided, should be against the law. Although, he appears to be blissfully unaware of the impression he makes on others. Whereas Michelle, however, I'm pretty convinced, does have some inkling. She is a wily young woman. Passionate about books and her work, and very confident in her own abilities; she never appears particularly perturbed by anyone or anything, not even Oliver. Maybe Oliver is her secret weapon. Maybe Oliver is the real reason Michelle is so successful. People are so bewitched by Oliver on meeting him, they simply agree to Michelle's proposals, for the privilege of looking at such a beautiful man for a while.

I managed to thank Michelle and Oliver (although god knows what I was actually thanking them for, I can only hope Michelle worked out a deal that was good for all involved) and am now heading towards Greenwich. It's a beautiful afternoon and I've decided to forgo the two stops on the underground and walk instead. I'm pleased to be away from the air-conditioned offices we were in. I appreciate it probably makes for a more comfortable working environment but I felt cold. My feet, in particular, were like blocks of ice. Now, as I walk along the busy street, the warmth of the mid-day sun has a pleasant thawing effect.

It's 1.00 p.m., lunchtime for most, and I am carried away with the rush. A swarthy sea of people of all races, all colours, some smartly dressed, some not so, are in hot pursuit of a place to relieve their hunger or otherwise heading for meetings or appointments. Passing a number of shops, my eye is drawn to stylishly clad mannequins in window displays and every now and again I pass a restaurant where I hear the stacking of plates, the clinking of glasses and my rather sensitive nose detects the strong smell of food. Pan fried fish, sizzling steaks and a familiar fusion of onions, garlic, peppers and spices, along with the industrial waft of diesel from black cabs and red buses make for a potent combination, causing my tummy to perform an Olympian somersault.

I feel nauseous again. Why? I am also beginning to perspire a little and tiny beads of sweat form a moist moustache above my lip. I use the back of my hand to wipe it away and have a sudden yearning for the air-conditioned office I've just left, as I'm forced to stop at yet another pedestrian crossing. I wait patiently, along with a body of others, until the green light tells me it is safe to cross and, with barely any exertion at all, I am practically lifted off the ground by the mass exodus of bodies. It's such a different experience to using the small-town crossings at home. Far less busy than those in the city and regardless of whether they are controlled by lights or not, drivers feel obliged to stop and pedestrians feel obliged to semi-run and wave in thanks.

The spring sun, pleasant though it is, beats down on my head and I feel another wave of nausea. Maybe those health websites were right, maybe it is something sinister, like cancer. Then again, some of the dodgier looking sites did suggest a stubbed toe could be cancer. I wave my hand manically about my face like a fan as the heat within me rises. Then it hits me like a blow to the head. I'm hot because I'm having a hot flush. That's what this nausea is all about; I'm going through the bloody menopause. It all makes sense now. That's why, despite not putting on any extra weight, my clothes are too tight around the waist. It's middle-bloody-age spread! Great, as if pregnancy, labour, giving birth, breastfeeding, stretch marks, saggy boobs, and cellulite weren't enough! The menopause must be nature's last laugh at women.

My buoyant mood drops and I suddenly feel old. I can hear Dad's voice in my head, *you're only as old as you feel, Lizzie my gal*. That would be about one hundred and ten years then.

Oh, shut up Lizzie Lemalf, life is good. Life is very good. Don't ever forget that!

'No, you're right,' I respond to myself, out loud (I still don't seem to be able to break that habit but then again, it does help when I need expert advice!) but my one-way conversation is broken by the sound of another familiar voice.

'Mum! Mu-um?' I look up and see Cassie waving at me. Smiling, she walks towards me. I smile back but my parental alarm bell is ringing far too loud for comfort. She looks skeletal. And tired. It's only been a couple of months since I last saw her but she looks terribly thin and terribly tired. Why?

We hug for a few seconds before Cassie pushes me away. She looks me up and down and studies me as if looking at a shop mannequin.

'Wow, looking good Mum. I'm loving the naked skirt and shoes look.'

Somewhat alarmed I look down. 'Naked?' I reply.

'Yeah, your matching shoes and skirt.'

The penny drops. 'Ahh ... right. I think you mean nude.' For one dreadful moment, I visualised myself naked from the waist down in response to the brain fog of my newly realised menopausal state.

'Yeah, whatev's. Naked, nude, it's all the same.'

I shake my head and laugh. 'Oh Cas, I don't think it is but thanks anyway.' Cassie, still the queen of malapropos and Spoonerisms, although nowhere near as bad as she was in her teens. 'I wasn't sure, if I'm honest,' I continue. 'Didn't know if it was a bit mutton dressed as lamb?'

Cassie's wrinkles her nose and shakes her head. 'Nah, it suits you, and besides, you'd best make the most of it, you'll be sixty before you know it. Now that really is old!'

Unsure whether to feel grateful or mortified, and as if on cue, another wave of nausea washes over me. Beads of sweat now form around the back of my neck, as well as my top lip and I'm acutely aware of my uncomfortably moist armpits. My internal thermostat appears to have only two settings: hypothermia or the eternal fires of hell. Suddenly the idea of being naked seems like a remarkably good one. Oh god, is this what I have to look forward to? Ten years of hell followed by death? If I didn't know any better I'd say there was steam emanating from every menopausal pore of my body right now.

'You okay?' Cassie asks.

I waft my hand in front of my face like a fan. 'Just a bit hot.'

'Oh okay, well yeah, anyway, I was only joking. You look great.'

'You think?'

'Yeah, defo. You look, I dunno? What's the word?' Cassie

clicks her fingers in a bid to find the word she's looking for. 'Glowing!' she declares. 'Yeah that's the word. Bloody glowing!'

She's not wrong there! Only when I asked for a smoking hot body, this wasn't what I had in mind.

Wearing faded jeans with holes at the knees, a pair of Converse trainers that have now seen better days and the Arctic Monkey's' T-shirt Connor bought her for Christmas, I wish I could say the same for my tired looking daughter. The fake lashes, hair extensions and teetering heels of her teenage years have long gone. And if I'm honest I quite like this grungy look, but not the weight loss.

'Thanks love. You look, tired?'

Cassie rolls her eyes. 'Cheers Mum. I thought I looked pretty good.'

'You do. You do. Just a bit tired and, well, if I'm honest, a bit thin.'

'Mum, please ... I have lost a bit of weight, but only because I've been working hard. Working like a ray gun, or whatever the bloody saying is.'

I laugh. 'It's Trojan,' I correct her. 'Working like a Trojan.'

Cassie waves her hand dismissively. 'Okay, okay. You know what I mean! And because I started this job before I officially finished uni, I've only just finished my dissertation. It's been manic!'

I can't fail to notice the landmark buildings, some of the largest in Europe, that sprout up behind Cassie and fill the skyline. It brings a smile to my face. Located in Tower Hamlets, East London, I remind Cassie of the time she referred to Virginia Woolf as Canary Wharf. 'During your English exam, I think it was?'

Cassie rolls her eyes. 'Oh god, Mum. Please!' she replies. Thankfully, though, she is laughing. She points to a building up ahead and links arms with me. 'C'mon, let's walk. I'm taking you to Billie's, the Jazz Bar I was telling you about, for lunch.'

We walk and talk. 'How's things then? How's the job going?'

Cassie shrugs her shoulders. 'Okay, good mostly. They usually get me doing all the crap non-music things, making teas and coffees, stuff like that, but I did get to work with Dezi No–A the other day.'

I have no idea who Cassie is talking about and clearly it shows on my face. Cassie laughs. 'Oh, never mind,' she says. 'Si will probably know who he is. And Grandad, he'd know.' Cassie and I both laugh. Dad has always loved music, almost as much as he loves books but the idea of Dad being down with the kids and their music is always a source of amusement, less so when he attempts to sing, though.

'And your boss, what's he like?'

Cassie's face drops. 'A wolf in cheap clothing, and no, I haven't got that saying wrong, that's what he is! Except his clothes are not cheap, he just makes them look cheap.'

Her tone is acerbic and makes me slightly uneasy but she smiles again so I choose to ignore the disgruntled, disquiet voice in my head.

Cassie and I are seated at a small table by the window. A young man who nodded at Cassie as we walked in is effortlessly moving both hands across the keys of a polished black, Baby-Grand piano. The lighting is low but the room still manages to feel light and airy. I pick up one of the menus given to us on arrival and am more than a little surprised at the price of a bowl of pasta. I pull my reading glasses down then back up to check and double check that I am actually reading the menu correctly.

You could feed a family of six for those prices!

Cassie laughs, as if she's read my mind. 'I don't normally eat here,' she says. 'But sometimes when they're stuck for a piano player,' she nods in the direction of the Baby-Grand, 'you know, if someone can't make it or calls in sick or whatever, they have my number and if I can help out I will. Sometimes I get paid and sometimes I accept food as payment.'

'Oh, I see. I hope they don't take advantage of you?'

Cassie laughs again. 'It's not very often and I don't mind. I'd probably do it for free anyway. I love getting the chance to play the piano. No room for one in the flat, that's for sure. Anyway, I told them I was bringing my mum today and they said we can eat for free if I play later, so order what you want and don't worry about the prices.'

Alex, a nice young girl who Cassie appears to know, takes our order. 'Ray says to offer you both a glass of wine each, too?' she offers. 'Or are you still not drinking Cas?'

Cassie looks up, her expression one of slight alarm. 'No, wine would be good, thanks. A glass of white for me please. Mum, the same for you?' I nod yes. 'Two glasses of white then. Thanks Alex, and thank Ray for me.'

Alex smiles at Cassie and walks off towards the bar.

'Who is Ray?'

'He's the bloke who manages the place,' Cassie replies, but she doesn't look at me, her eyes remain firmly fixed on Alex who is mouthing our drinks order to a young man behind the bar. The barman nods and Alex disappears to the kitchen to place our food order, I assume, before quickly returning to the bar again. Cassie temporarily averts her gaze from the bar to look at me. 'He's quite nice, a bit old, about your age,' Cassie continues.

'Thanks!'

'But nice enough.'

'Why did Alex ask you if you were still not drinking?'

Cassie waves her hand dismissively, her eyes once again fixed on the business at the bar. 'Had a bit too much to drink the other week. Was a bit sick. Well, a lot sick actually. Put me off for a while. But I'm okay now,' she adds.

I'm not sure she is though. Cassie watches intently as the bartender produces a pair of clean, vintage wine glasses that remind me of the ones Mum and Aunt Marie used to drink Babycham from during my childhood, before reaching behind him for a new bottle of wine. He pulls out a corkscrew and effortlessly pushes it into the neck of the bottle. After a couple of manly turns the cork is withdrawn with a familiar squeak and to my surprise, Cassie jumps up and strides towards the bar. 'Back in a sec,' she shouts over her shoulder. The bartender fills the two empty glasses and Cassie swiftly returns with them. Taking a couple of large swigs from one glass as she passes me the other, her rigid shoulders relax and she immediately appears more settled. 'Wow, I didn't realise how much I needed that!' she declares smiling at me. Dark circles frame her large brown eyes and her pale, tired looking skin would make most vampires proud. 'What?' Cassie asks, touching her nose. 'Are you looking at my nose?'

I'm confused. 'Why would I be looking at your nose?'

Cassie sighs. 'Of course you're not, it's just something I've got into the habit of asking.' She rubs her finger up and down the bridge of her nose pausing at the slight bump in it. 'I hate it, it's big and I hate the bump in it.'

'It's the same as mine, a Roman nose. We can thank Grandad for that. I never used to like mine when I was younger, but I grew into it and so will you.'

'I dunno about that,' Cassie snorts. 'People, well, boys mostly, laugh at it. I feel bad not liking it because it's kind of like insulting you. Sort of. But ...' She trails off for a moment, staring intently at her wine glass.

'But what?'

She taps out a beat with her fingers on the side of her glass before looking up again. 'Whatev's,' she sighs, shrugging her shoulders. 'It doesn't matter. I just wish it wasn't so bloody big!'

'You're lovely Cassie, just as you are. Besides, I thought you'd got past all that silly nonsense.'

Cassie shifts uncomfortably in her chair and wrinkles her nose. 'What nonsense?'

'Getting caught up in placing a higher premium on shallow

things. 'Surely you don't want to be the same as everyone else, anyway? Do you?'

'I dunno. No. Yes. Maybe?'

'It's okay to be different you know? No one is perfect. Besides, your nose suits you, gives you character.'

Cassie sighs again and rolls her eyes. 'You don't understand Mum,' she says dismissively.

'What don't I understand? Is it that despite having far more liberation than they've ever had, women are *still* objectified? That low-level sexism still exists and the difference between the way women and men are portrayed in the media is stark, to say the least? Or is it that the images of women that saturate our magazines, movies, adverts, and the internet in varying stages of undress, arguably for the male gaze, is only a fraction of the objectification of women that permeates our world?'

Cassie holds her head in her hands. 'Oh god. Not the women's lib speech again, Mum, please.'

'Look, you go on all these protest marches in a bid to stop making young women feel like they have to conform to an ideal image, an image that often entails bags of money and hours of surgery, and yet you worry about a little bump in your nose? It's crazy. At least when I was younger the only surgery a woman might consider was a facelift and a boob job whereas now, well, it's everything. The lips, the eyes, the arms, the knees, the hair, the boobs, the bum, especially the bum. Why? What is this ridiculous need for huge baboon like bottoms? Berdinkadonks, are they called?'

Cassie laughs and shakes her head. 'Badunkadonk. It's pronounced badunkadonk.'

'Its madness is what it is. I mean, it's fine if you're genetically pre-disposed to such a look, but filling your butt with shots of god knows what and risking your health for it in the process is, well, as I said, madness. Utter madness. Then there's the other extreme of course, the stick insects of the fashion industry, where women are not allowed to have breasts or hips or thighs because designer clothes don't look good on real women, apparently! I was reading about an ex-model the other day. Lived on one apple a day and loads of bottled water. She nearly died. Had the good sense to get out of the industry, though.'

'Oh, whatever Mum. You're old, you don't understand.'

The irritation in Cassie's voice tells me I've gone too far. Determined not to ruin what little time we have left together before I catch my train home again, I immediately drop this particular topic of conversation.

Our food arrives and Cassie doesn't allay my fears about her recent weight loss. She barely eats, spending most of her time talking and pushing her food around the plate. Her glass of wine however, is empty, tipped back in three large, easy gulps. I feel agitated and wrung with protective fear, unsure if I should say something or not.

To hell with this tiptoeing around, just ask her.

'You are looking after yourself, aren't you? You've lost an awful lot of weight.'

Cassie slams her fork down on her plate and her brown eyes bore into me. If I didn't know any better I'd say something supernatural has just transpired. Cassie is possessed. No longer do I hear the voice of my wiser, slightly calmer twenty-one-year-old daughter, instead I am confronted by the teenage angst of her former, moody sixteen-year-old self.

'Oh for god bloody sake Mum! I'm fine. I'm not doing drugs, I'm not an alcoholic and I *am* eating enough. So, no, I don't have a bloody eating disorder if that's what you're hinting at. 'Kay?'

Sitting back, I hold my hands up in surrender. 'Okay. I'm sorry. I was only asking. You are my daughter after all.'

Cassie sighs and the angry teenager makes a quick exodus. 'I know, I'm sorry. I'm just tired. I got this job before finishing uni and it's been mad. I haven't really had a break. Not that I'm complaining because I love it, but sometimes I'm a bit crap at remembering to eat. But I'm fine. I'm honestly fine.'

I'm not convinced but the intonation in Cassie's voice tells me loud and clear this subject is now closed. My phone vibrates on the table. Picking it up and swiping the screen, I click on a couple of messages. Cassie sighs, loudly. Looking up, I am met by the steely glare of my slightly irritated daughter. Her head cocked to one side, both arms locked across her chest, she wears a look of disgruntled amusement. 'How did your meeting go then, with the publisher?'

My eyes flit back towards my phone as I attempt to type and speak at the same time. 'What? Oh yes, publisher. Erm, just give us a sec, will you?' I reply, hammering out a reply across the tiny keyboard. I love my phone, my portable office, but it does put a strain on my eyes. I read somewhere that people have written novels on their phones. God knows how they manage that!

'Mum!' Cassie yells. 'For god sake, put your bloody phone away, will you!'

Slightly taken aback, I look up again, met by Cassie's scowling face and impatient drumming fingers tapping the table. I consider myself well and truly told off, which is a little galling to say the least, considering all of my children appear incapable of breathing without their mobile phones. Too afraid to finish my email, I click my phone off, lift off my reading glasses and offer Cassie my full and undivided attention. 'Sorry, was just checking a couple of emails about the book.'

'Well. Do. It. Later, please. God, when I think about how you used to moan at me and Maisy for using our phones and now you're a writer, you're actually way worse!'

I recoil a little at Cassie's truthful observation. 'Well, it is different, for me. This is work and I have to stay connected. Reply to the publisher, respond to my readers. You know what I mean?'

'No, Mum, I don't, this is me and you time. You can put your bloody phone away for an hour or so, can't you?'

Her words of wisdom carry with them an echo from the past, to a time of sulky, angst-ridden, teenage daughters, only it was the other way around then and I was the one doing the telling off. Folding my arms across my chest, I'm more than a little irritated to find they rest quite nicely on my slightly expanding belly.

Definitely middle-aged spread.

'So, the meeting, how did it go?'

I think back to my meeting, which was less than an hour ago, and shrug my shoulders as the gorgeous Oliver once again repossesses my thoughts. I feel myself blush, or maybe it's just another hot flush. 'Okay, I think?'

'Good news?'

'Errrmm...I don't know? Think it was.'

Somewhere in the room 'Take My Breath Away' is playing. I look across at the Baby-Grand. Is it the pianist or is it in my head again?

Cassie looks amused. 'Why are you laughing? And what do you mean *you don't know*? Was it good news or not?'

I swat Oliver from my thoughts and regain my composure.

'Yes. Yes of course, it was all good.'

At least, I hope it bloody was!

We leave the Jazz Bar and step into the warm afternoon. I shield my eyes with my hand as they adjust to the bright sunlight. The roar of the city once again penetrates my ears, replacing the mellow tinkling of the Baby-Grand piano. Then, like a trapped bee, my phone vibrates in my hand. Sheepishly, I look towards Cassie. She rolls her eyes. 'Go on, for god bloody sake, answer it.'

'Oh, it's Connor,' I reply as I look at the screen. 'What's he doing ringing me?' I press the accept call button and am surprised to hear the agitated voice of my youngest child explain that Dad has been rushed into hospital. Connor doesn't elaborate much but does beg me to get there as quickly as possible.

'What? What is it?' Cassie asks.

'It's Grandad, apparently, he's been rushed to hospital?' The words have slipped from my mouth before I've had time to censor them and I can already see the panic etched in Cassie's face.

'Right, I'm coming home with you.'

'No, no you're not. I'm sure it's nothing. Besides, you can't just up and leave, you're expected back at work. I promise I'll ring you as soon as I get home and if it's anything serious you'll be the first to know.'

Cassie isn't convinced at first but thankfully she comes around. We hug one another goodbye and Cassie holds me a little tighter and little longer than usual. She tells me she loves me and I detect a slight quiver in her voice. She seems upset and although I know she's worried about Dad, I'm convinced there's something she's not telling me. I ask her once again if she's sure she's okay and she does her level best to assure me she is.

Cassie walks away in one direction, I in another. When Cassie is well and truly out of sight, I stop for a moment and rest against a wall. I feel hot and nauseous again.

Damn these hot flushes.

Cassie

Wow, Mum looks good. Looks better every time I see her. Especially for an old woman. Can't believe she's almost fifty! She's put on a bit of weight but it suits her. Means she's not worrying about stuff. She can't eat when she worries, like me. It's funny really because it's like she's old, but her life is just beginning. Being a writer suits her. It was so good to see her though, well, except when she had her bloody head in her phone.

How rude! She needs to learn to reply one handed while talking at the same time, like me.

I hope Grandad is okay? I'm even gladder I didn't tell Mum now. She doesn't need to be worrying about me *and* Grandad. I feel so weepy at the moment, though, so god knows how I kept it in. I nearly let it out at one point, when Mum looked at me like she does when she's worried, her forehead and nose both wrinkling up at the same time, asking me why I looked so thin. It was there for the telling, sitting on the edge of my tongue. Waiting to flick out and hit her right between the eyes. But I knew it would ruin the day, our few hours together. Besides, although I know she wouldn't judge me, would she think it was my fault anyway? That I could have done more to stop it from happening? Would she think I should have made different, better decisions? That I should have protected myself more? Would she secretly think I am a bad person?

Great, here come the tears again. I normally tell Mum everything, even that time we played beer pong in our uni dorm and everyone ended up virtually naked. She seemed a bit shocked, at first, but eventually saw the funny side and laughed. So it felt strange not telling her. Not talking about it. I love my job and living away from home but lately it feels like a blanket of loneliness has wrapped itself around me. How is it possible to live in a huge city bursting with people, but still feel so lonely, even though I have Honey and so many other friends? I'd like to stop the world and get off, just for a while.

Looking down the road I realise Mum has long gone but I have an overwhelming urge to run after her. Taking my phone from my pocket I swipe the screen and find her number. I let my finger hover above the call button but I can't do it. I wipe away my tears with the back of my hand and put my phone away. Telling Mum, telling anyone, is not an option. Besides, what can she do to help me? What's done is done.

Oh god, please let Grandad be okay. I think of him, old and

poorly instead of big and strong, and my tummy turns. I cup my hands around my belly to try and stop the fear rising up inside me. Memories of the last couple of weeks and thoughts of Grandad become all mixed up in my head.

'Please let Grandad be okay,' I shout out loud. Several people pass me by but no-one stops; no-one gives a shit. People in the city are way too busy to care. And now the tears are falling, again. Hot and salty; they really sting. How many tears have I cried these last weeks? Surely I'm all cried out?

Maybe I should go into work and tell them to stuff their job. To catch the next train "home" and tell Grandad everything will be okay. Put his mind at ease. What I really want, though, is for Grandad to put my mind at ease. I imagine everyone fussing around him and how much he'd hate it. How he'd be telling them all to "fack orf." Thinking of Grandad swearing makes me laugh. I feel my fear disappearing and hear Grandad's voice in my head reminding me, like he always does, always reminds everyone in fact, whenever things don't go to plan, not to worry because "it's not a life, it's an adventure!"

I breathe in deeply and out again, slowly. My head feels woozy but I feel calmer. I suddenly remember Dezi is coming into the studio again this afternoon and I immediately feel the blackness disappearing. I love his work and how he puts his music together and I love that he trusted my ideas with one of his tracks. It only happened by accident, when he came to the studio a couple of months back and everyone went outside for a fag break. Can't believe he smokes but then again, so do I. The difference being though, I don't have a voice like his. The man is a legend. Abso-fucking-lutely amazing vocals. I was pissed off because Hunter was treating me like a bloody skivvy again, which I know is part of the job but he always seems to give me the shit stuff. Adam gets way more studio time than me. I was ready to walk that day, chuck the whole the thing in, so when they all went out I thought, why the hell not?

I started playing with the track they were recording. Dunno what got into me really, because I knew Hunter would have a shit fit when he caught me, but I just didn't care. Dezi came back before the others. I didn't know he'd been watching me, jumped so high I nearly peed myself when he spoke. He said he really liked what he heard, said I was talented, that I had an ear for music. So, he let me help produce the whole track. You'd think it would have made Hunter happy, that he would have been proud of me but no, he told Dezi he'd taught me everything I know, which is a bloody lie. Then, when no one else was looking, Hunter cornered me. Leaned in, so close, I actually thought he was going to kiss me. He stunk of fags and booze and that godawful aftershave he always wears.

'Don't you EVER do that again,' he said. He was smiling as he said it but his voice was really threating. I'm not ashamed to say my legs went a bit wobbly and not for the first time, I wondered again why I keep working for him.

Then I remembered why. Dezi has actually asked for me in person this time. Says he's even going to credit *my* name, not Hunter's, on the last track I did. Of course, I'm not going to leave. I love my job. Even though I work way too many hours for shit pay. It's the music. It's all about the music.

Back to work Cassie. Back to work.

12 Jan/8

Chapter 5

WORRY, MOTHER'S RUIN

Lizzie

I try and remain calm, reminding myself Dad is in the best possible place right now. I also try and convince myself that Cassie did look okay.

She didn't though, did she?

'Actually, no! Let's be honest, she looked bloody awful.'

'What's that love?' Simon responds to my mutterings.

'Cassie,' I reply. 'She looked, not well? Gaunt. And thin. I've never seen her that thin.' My thoughts bounce from one insane idea to the next. 'Oh my god,' I gasp. 'What if she's taking drugs? She does live in London, after all?'

Simon shoots me an amused quizzical look. 'She wouldn't have to be living in London to obtain drugs. You can get hold of most drugs anywhere these days. Even this sleepy little town.'

I raise my eyes. 'And how would you know?' I reply, mock disapproval in my voice. We both laugh, knowing full well Simon would be the last man on earth to be found partaking in the use of illegal drugs. I can barely get him to take a couple of paracetamol for a headache. 'Anyway, don't be so pedantic, you know what I mean,' I continue, waving my hand dismissively. 'She is probably more readily exposed to them in London. Plus, she *is* working in the music industry,' I add.

Simon laughs again. 'And? You work in the book industry, don't you think they have their fair share of addicts of one sort or another?'

I roll my eyes. Is he purposely trying to wind me up? 'Don't be an arse; you know damn well what I mean. A writer's life is hardly rock and roll.'

'Plenty of tortured souls though, eh?'

I purposely choose to ignore the sarcasm in his voice. 'But Cassie is young and impressionable and living in a big city and...'

I tail off and Simon sighs, heavily. He walks towards me placing his hands on my shoulders. I hadn't noticed before but he looks tired, very tired. Like me, he works long hours, which is crazy, really, because with both girls gone I thought life would be easier. But what with my new writing career and Simon and I scraping enough money together to pay Ruby for Andy's share of the company so that Simon now co-runs it alongside Dean, in Andy's place, we never seem to have a moment, at least not with each other.

Raising his hand, Simon gently tucks my hair behind my ear and looks at me. 'Look, maybe Cassie is doing drugs, maybe she isn't?' I open my mouth to reply but before I can, Simon places a finger across my lips to silence me. 'But,' he continues, 'we have to trust her, trust that she'll make the right choices. I hate to point it out, Lizzie, but Cassie isn't your little girl anymore, she's all grown up and unless she asks us for help or our opinion, she has every right to live her life exactly as she wants to.'

I want to tell him to piss off but Simon is right, of course. His words don't offer me any comfort, though. Does a parent ever really let go of their child? I'm glad the girls have spread their wings but a part of me still wants them close by so I can keep a watchful eye on them, notice the day to day changes and nip the little problems in the bud so they don't develop into big ones. Is it wrong to want that much control?

I feel a lump form in my throat and stupidly want to cry. However, I suspect this has more to do with my lack of sleep. Wide awake and fretful at 4.00 a.m., I spent most of the early hours of this morning worrying about Dad, after visiting him at the hospital last night. I drove straight there from the train station after arriving back from London, after lunch with Cassie, and to be honest he looked fine. Better than Cassie at least. I'm not particularly concerned about the fall he had, either; the damage, thankfully, was minimal, despite being caused, according to the consultant, by a mini-stroke. It's the extra tests the hospital insisted on doing that really bother me.

"They're purely precautionary Ms Lemalf," the very nice doctor had said. "Better to be safe than sorry." Why don't I believe him then? The hairs on the back of my neck stood on end, not unlike when I was first introduced to Harvey, Ruby's new partner. He seemed nice enough, very charming and attentive, athletically handsome and well dressed, the polar opposite of Andy, in fact. Mum was totally bowled over by him, all giggly and smiles like a love-struck teenager. Good job Dad's not the jealous type. He just raised his eyebrows and shook his head before going back to reading his newspaper. I, on the other hand, I'm now ashamed to admit, wasn't so sure about Harvey. My intuition has never let me down thus far but I have to concede I'm a worrier, especially about the people I love, and I also have to concede that as far as Ruby is concerned my niggling doubts appear to be totally unfounded.

Harvey adores Ruby, and little Andrew. He's not Andy of course, and never will be, Andy's are huge shoes to fill, but he's good for Ruby. I do wish he'd relax a little more, though, and extract the stick stuck up his arse from time to time. As an only child, with no children of his own, I do find some of his views a bit antiquated. Then again, my noisy family is enough to overwhelm anyone. Ruby is happy, which is all that counts really. The bottom line is, despite his slightly conservative views, I was wrong about Harvey. So maybe, hopefully, my fears about Dad will be baseless too.

I sigh and wrap my arms around Simon, snuggling my cheek against his chest. I'm just tired and worrying for nothing. 'Thanks. I know you're right,' I mumble.

Simon lifts my chin and smiles at me. 'That's better,' he replies. 'I love to see you smile. And you know what?' he adds. 'At least Cassie is only a train ride away, not like Maisy, living on the other bloody side of the world!'

Sheepishly, I nod my head. I can't argue with that. I think of Maisy and Crazee and the last time we visited them. Their business, a tattoo shop, was thriving and they both looked positively healthy and happy. They have a wonderful set of friends and when they're not working, they're on the beach, even on Christmas Day. The outdoor life clearly suits them both.

I smile at the memory, until I remember something. 'Actually Simon,' I say, feeling a slight wave of concern wash over me, or is it just another bout of nausea? 'I've just remembered that Maisy didn't call us last week? Do you think she's okay?'

Simon shakes his head and starts laughing. 'Lizzie, for god bloody sake, will you stop worrying!'

Simon's amused but somewhat vexed tone pops my anxiety and like a balloon; I feel it deflate and whittle away.

Life is good. Life is very good and I must not forget that.

'What am I going to do with you, Lizzie Lemalf?' Simon asks, pulling me towards him again and kissing the top of my head. 'Now, I don't know about you, but I'm starving. I was just about to cook up some eggs, want some?'

My stomach flips in revulsion. They haven't even been cooked yet but already the smell of eggs is making me feel sick. I decline Simon's offer and decide there and then to make a doctor's appointment. I know I'm going through the menopause (a little early at forty-nine, if you ask me) but surely feeling sick all the time isn't a symptom, is it?

Chapter 6

ABSENT FATHERS

Connor

Shit, shit, shit! Why did I agree to skip the party that me and the boys were invited to so I could see Dad instead? He wanted us to have a "boys' night" in with him at his new flat. Sharon, the step-monster, has kicked him out. Which is bloody bad karma if you ask me, considering he walked out on us, all those years ago. Sharon's let him keep his beamer but she's not letting him have any money, which is double karma coz he never gave Mum a penny for us. Not even after she came out of hospital. Why do some men do that? Think they can have kids then walk away and never pay a penny? Loads of 'em do it, the Rickmeister's dad for example. Although, to be fair, his dad is worse than mine coz at least my dad took me and Cas out once a week. The Rickmeister's dad can't even be arsed to see him. We were never allowed to stay at Dad and Sharon's house, though, coz Sharon said they didn't have the room, even though it was the size of a bloody mansion. Didn't want us is more like it, cow.

The problem for Dad, though, is he hasn't worked, not for years. Sharon made him stay at home and look after Harriet, my spoilt brat of a half-sister, while she worked in some high-flying job. That's how they worked it so they didn't have to pay Mum any maintenance. Now the step-monster has found some new bloke and is going for sole custody of Harriet. She says Dad will have to fight her, in court I assume, if he wants the house or money or anything. Karma or fucking what?

The flat is a dump. Stinks of stale air and booze, like Dad's breath. He shows me into what must be the living room, which is rank. It has a dodgy looking sofa and chair, an old TV, and a dirty brown coffee table scattered with empty beer cans and an ashtray full of fag butts. Bet that lot didn't come from John Lewis. Dad coughs and looks embarrassed when he spots me staring at the coffee table. He waves his hand like the teachers do at school when class is dismissed.

'Oh, don't mind them,' he says, scooping up the empty beer cans into his arms. 'I've only had one or two a night, just haven't got around to clearing them up. Been a bit busy,' he smiles. 'You know, what with moving out and having to find somewhere to live and everything.'

'Okay,' I reply.

'So, what do you think?'

I shrug my shoulders and wish I could find something nice to say. 'S'kay, I suppose. A bit …'

'A bit what?' Dad replies.

'Different … to what you're used to. But okay.'

'Bit of a dump, you mean?'

'If I'm being honest then, yeah, it is a bit of a dump.'

Dad looks hurt. I feel bad, but he asked. What does he expect me to say? I've given up a Saturday night out with the boys to spend time with him, in this bloody hole. And I heard Hayley Patterson might be going to the party. Even his TV looks shit. And he doesn't have a satellite box or a games console.

'So … what's the plan?' I ask trying really hard to keep the annoyance out of my voice. 'What are we gonna do all night?' My phone vibrates in my pocket and when I pull it out I see it's a text from Robbo.

Hayley Patterson's here. Looking well fit!

I groan and put my phone away again. When I look up I see Dad staring at me or into space. I'm not sure which. He looks sad and pathetic which only makes me feel more pissed off. 'Well?' I ask flinging both my arms out. 'What are we going to do all night?'

Dad hunches his shoulders forwards and somehow seems smaller. He points a half-stretched arm towards the TV. 'Thought maybe we could watch some TV?' he replies. Great, I gave up seeing Hayley Patterson for this. 'And I've got a bit of money,' Dad continues, reaching into his jeans pocket to pull out some notes. 'We could get pizza? I've made the second bedroom up for you.'

'Really?' I snort. Now I have a bedroom! Never had one for all those years you were with the step-monster, coz she didn't want me and Cas, and you went along with it. NOW she's kicked you out, and you live in a dump, you tell me you have a bedroom for me. Wanker.

I feel my phone vibrate again. It's another text from Robbo.

Get your arse over here Conman. Ant is playing his Decs and he wants you to help him. HP is still ere ;)

That's done it for me. I don't owe this bloke anything. He's never really been there for me and Cas, and now he's on his own and has nothing, he wants me.

'I tell ya what Dad, some of my mates are at a party and they want me to go DJ for them. Give us the money for a taxi, I'll go and spend some time with them, then I'll come back and stay here the night with you. How does that sound?'

Dad smiles, sort of. 'Yeah, you go, son,' he says pressing some money into my hand. 'I understand, you go and spend time with your mates. I'll be waiting up for you.'

I take the money, quickly before he changes his mind. 'Cheers, Dad,' I reply. 'I'll erm … see you later then?'

'Yeah, see you later son,' he replies.

I head out of the front door, relieved. Relieved to get away, relieved to get some fresh air.

Chapter 7

CANTANKEROUS TIMES

Lizzie

Simon and I look at one another, partly out of concern, mostly out of confusion. A number of voices radiate vociferously through the walls of Dad's hospital room, including a number of "fack orfs" from Dad.

'Where are we? Where are we going?' Uncle Teddy asks, again. Simon shakes his head and I can't help wondering if this was a good idea after all.

'I told you we shouldn't have brought him with us,' Simon mouths to me. 'Not to the hospital. It's too confusing. We should have waited until your dad was home.'

I sigh. 'I know,' I whisper, 'but Aunt Marie needed to go out and there was no-one else to watch him. Besides, it does him good to get out and it gives Aunt Marie a well-deserved break. She looks absolutely worn out lately.'

'Who's worn out?' Uncle Teddy asks.

Simon and I are either side of Uncle Teddy. Arms linked we steer him towards Dad's room. 'No-one. It's nothing Uncle Teddy, don't worry,' I reply.

'Where are we? Where are we going?'

As we approach the door I hear another angry "fack orf" and wonder what has Dad so riled up. 'We're at the hospital Uncle Teddy,' I remind him. 'To visit your brother, Salocin. He's had a stroke. Remember?'

'Has he? Did he? When was that then? I didn't know?'

'Yes, it was the other day Uncle Teddy. Remember, I told you?'

'Oh yes. Yes, of course, I remember.'

But he doesn't though, bless him. At least not all the time, and he seems to be getting worse lately. Poor Uncle Teddy is suffering from Alzheimer's. He didn't seem too bad at first, after his diagnosis a couple of years ago. But just lately, he seems to have deteriorated somewhat. I did suggest to Aunt Marie that she should perhaps think about having him admitted to a care home, something I'd never imagined myself saying and never want for my parents, but Alzheimer's is exhausting for the carer of the suffering individual. Uncle Teddy has already wandered off twice during the night and last week he burned himself. But Aunt Marie is not having any of it. She and Uncle Teddy, like Mum and Dad, have been married for years. 'I'm not about to give up on him yet,' Aunt Marie had said. 'I married my Teddy for better, for worse, in sickness and in health, and that's exactly what I intend to keep on doing.'

I open the door and find Mum ensconced in a corner of the room. Red faced, she is shaking her head from left to right. Dad spots us and waves his good arm dismissively at the young woman standing bedside.

'Tell her to speak blady English or fack orf,' he yells.

'Dad! Stop it now!' I reply.

'Where are we? What are we doing?' Uncle Teddy asks.

Simon and Mum roll their eyes. 'We're at the hospital Uncle Teddy, to see Salocin, over there.' I point at Dad lying in the hospital bed.

'What's he doing in bed in the middle of the blady day?'

'He's had a stroke Uncle Teddy.'

'Blady haven't,' Dad replies. 'Nothing blady wrong with me.'

'Has he? Did he? When was that then? I didn't know?'

Uncle Teddy walks over towards Dad, eyeing him up suspiciously. The uniformed young lady, oriental I think, turns to speak to me but is temporarily interrupted by the ranting of

Uncle Teddy who is now waving an angry finger at Dad and shouting.

'Whachu bleedin' doing in bed in the middle of the bleedin' day? Pull yourself to-bleedin'-gether.'

Simon starts to laugh, indicating with a flick of his hand and a nod of his head that he'll deal with the grumpy old buggers fighting bedside, if I talk to the young lady wearing the frustrated smile.

The young woman, who introduces herself as Ting, is the occupational therapist assigned to help Dad. She's pleasant enough and speaks good English but she does have a bit of an accent, making it slightly difficult to understand what she's saying.

'I simply ass your farter to wiff his wef weg,' she explains.

'See! What's she bleeding goin' on about?' Dad interrupts. 'Wiff wag weg? What the bleedin' hell is that supposed to mean?'

'Where are we? What are we doing?' Uncle Teddy asks again.

I shake my head and apologise to Ting. Smiling, she gracefully accepts my apology but doesn't seem at all perturbed. I sense, like me, she sees the fear dancing in Dad's eyes. 'Dad, this is not like you, not like you at all. Ting and I are both trying to help, so please stop shouting.'

'Where are we? What are we doing?' Uncle Teddy repeats.

Pausing, I take another deep breath and notice Mum and Simon trying to contain their laughter. However, with cupped hands over sniggering mouths and the gentle rise and fall of heaving shoulders they are making a very poor show of it. I'm not angry, though. In fact, I'm almost on the point of hysterical laughter myself. They do say laughter is the best medicine, after all.

Dad, whose quiff of grey hair looks ever more white today, is clearly agitated, as is Uncle Teddy who, confused, starts to rub his head. I take Uncle Teddy's hand in mine and use my other hand to lift his chin up and turn his face towards mine.

'We're at the hospital Uncle Teddy, remember? To see Salocin, your brother. He's had a stroke, remember?'

'I blady haven't,' Dad shouts out again.

'Has he? Did he? When was that then? I didn't know?'

I try to reassure Uncle Teddy and Ting tries her best to talk to Dad again. 'Mi-er Lemarf, can you pwea wif your wef weg for me?'

Dad's face becomes crimson with anger. 'What the bleedin' hell is that supposed to mean? I don't know what "wiff wag weg" blady means!'

Uncle Teddy is back at Dad's side. 'Whachu you bleedin' doing in bed in the middle of the bleedin' day? Pull yourself to-bleedin'-gether,' he shouts.

I look across at Simon, pleading without words for help, but both he and Mum are now unashamedly in fits of laughter. Wrapping both his hands around his neck, Simon pretends to choke himself. Bizarrely surreal, I feel as though I am in the middle of a *Carry On* movie and I can't help but laugh too.

'Mi-er Lemarf,' the therapist says again, 'I rearwy neet you to wif your wef weg for me.'

Dad looks as though he's about to explode.

'Where are we? What are we doing?' Uncle Teddy repeats.

'Right!' I yell throwing both hands up like a stop sign. 'Everybody just shut the fuck up.'

For the first time since our arrival the room falls eerily quiet. I instruct Mum and Simon to take Uncle Teddy down to the coffee shop and wait for me there. Explaining who I am, I hold my hand out and formerly introduce myself to Ting. I also apologise, again, on behalf of my grumpy dad. Dad does not look amused and folding his arms, he looks away. Ting raises her eyebrows and smiles. I sit on the bed beside Dad and attempt to retrieve one of his folded hands. He sighs heavily but lets me, nonetheless.

I bend down towards his ear. 'Come on Dad,' I whisper.

'Remember, it's not a life, it's an adventure, eh?' Dad turns back towards me, his rheumy eyes locking with mine. The proud exterior of this frightened man fails to hide the apprehension dancing behind those vulnerable eyes. I squeeze his hand and offer a reassuring smile, which he readily accepts and, I'm pleased to say, returns the same.

'Right then Dad, let's get started, shall we? Ting here,' I say, pointing towards the patiently waiting, commendable young woman, 'would like you to lift-your-left-leg please.' Dad jerks his head to look at Ting, his aging brow knitting into a frown. Despite his best efforts not to laugh, an amused grin spreads across his face.

'Well why didn't she just bleedin' say that in the first place?' he replies.

Chapter 8

OLD FRIENDS, NEW FRIENDS

Cassie

It's 10.00 p.m., late. I should go home really and get some sleep but I'm still buzzing from the session with Dezi No-A today. He asked, actually asked Hunter, if he could spare me for a bit of time to work on another one of his tracks. Hunter had to let me help him, of course, because Dezi is a paying customer. And what the customer wants the customer gets. I get the feeling Hunter doesn't like it though, would prefer to be whipping my arse to make teas and coffees and just be the general dogsbody I'm supposed to be. Apparently, he's like that with all the newbies but I think he just likes bossing women around.

'Cas. Cassie?' I look through the heaving crowd towards a waving hand and the voice calling me. The hand grabs me and pulls me towards her. She kisses my cheek and thrusts a vodka and coke in my hand.

'There you go, babe,' Honey says nodding towards the boy next to her. 'Matt bought us these.' She clinks her glass with mine then downs it in one. Matt looks slightly alarmed when Honey asks him for another but he agrees anyway and attempts to push his way through the sea of people back towards the bar.

'Here, you can have mine too,' I say, passing my drink to Honey.

'Why?' she snorts. 'Are you actually turning down a free drink?'

'I just prefer to get my own,' I reply, shrugging my shoulders. Honey looks at me like I'm stupid but snatches my drink from my hand anyway.

It's great sharing a flat with Honey because we both work in the same industry and understand the insane hours we often have to work. We both love the live music scene, too, and share most of the same friends so there's always someone to go out with.

'Aww, poor Matt,' I shout to Honey. 'You should tell him you've got a girlfriend.'

Honey grins and shrugs her shoulders. 'I will … eventually. Gets me a few free drinks though eh? Anyway shhhhhh,' she says, turning towards the stage, 'it looks as though the band are coming on and I've heard good things about this lot.'

I try and look above the mass of sweaty bodies in front of me but I'm not tall like Honey. Through a gap in the crowd, though, I spy four lads coming onto the stage. It looks like a drummer, two guitarists and a singer. There is also a keyboard with no-one standing next to it.

I can't see their faces but the drummer starts drumming and the guitarists start strumming. The singer shouts across the microphone and the crowd start roaring. They've barely begun playing but already the atmosphere is manic.

'Goooooood eeeeevvvening London,' the singer shouts again. 'A-one, two, a-one, two, three, four …' he yells before launching into their first song.

I move my head in time with the music, I like it, I like it a lot. It's a mix of sort of old skool and indie rock. I look up at Honey and smile but she doesn't notice. I can't see what she sees but she lifts both her hands and places them over her mouth. She looks down at me, then back towards the stage before finally resting her eyes on me again. She removes her hands from her mouth and quickly downs the new vodka and coke Matt has just passed her before handing back the empty glass.

'Oh, my god,' she squeals, 'it's only bloody Luke!'

'Where?' I reply turning my head from left to right in confusion. I haven't seen Luke properly now for a couple of years. We sort of lost contact when I went to uni. We tweet the odd message now and again, text each other on our birthdays but I don't really know what he's up to these days. It would be great to see him and catch up.

My beady eyes search the moshing bodies around me, I'm looking for that old leather jacket and shy smile 'Where, where is he?' I repeat, 'I don't see him?'

'The singer,' Honey screams. 'Luke is the fucking singer, of the fucking band!'

I swing my head back towards the stage. 'Really?'

I may be small but I'm strong. I begin thrusting forward to get a better view. Somehow, after lots of pushing and shoving, I manage to get to the front, elbowed in the boob in the process by a pretty looking blonde girl who doesn't say sorry. I lift my hand to rub my aching boob and look at the girl. She glares at me then looks away back towards the stage.

'Luke,' I shout waving my arms at the stage. The blonde girl swings her head round to look at me again. Wow, if looks could kill! Either she has a natural resting bitch face or she just hates me. I shrug my shoulders and shout out Luke's name again. Mid-shout I'm almost knocked off my feet. As I regain my balance I notice the pretty blonde girl, still looking at me, laughing. Stupid cow. I swing round quickly, ready to launch into the person who almost sent me flying only to find it's Honey.

'Sorry babe,' she shouts down to me, 'had to push my way through, lost my balance.' The blonde girl is still watching me. Her perfectly painted red lips are locked in a stupid grin until Honey also starts calling out Luke's name. The blonde girl's eyes flit from my face to Honey's long legs and little skirt. Her smug grin disappears and once again, to quote Grandad, her face morphs into something that looks more like a slapped arse.

The band finish singing their first song and Luke looks down and spots us. He shouts hello to "two of my best friends" and points to Honey and me. Now the blonde girl looks really pissed off. The band is great and Luke is amazing, so confident. Finally, on the last song of the first set, the band start to play something very familiar, something I haven't heard in a long time. I realise it's 'Funky Purple Haze Around the Moon', one of the songs Honey, Luke, and I all played together when we were at college. To my surprise, Luke then calls Honey and me up onto the stage. Honey, never one to miss an opportunity to perform, is gone and up there before I've even had time to think about it. Honey sings here with her band quite a lot so most of the crowd recognise her. Walking a bit like a catwalk model, Honey struts straight up to Luke and plants a huge kiss on his lips, which fills the room with whooping and wolf whistles. Not to mention a death stare from the pretty blonde girl. Nervously, I climb the couple of steps onto the stage and Luke nods his head towards the keyboard.

Safely standing behind the plugged-in piano, I look out at the black mass of heaving bodies and feel my legs buckle at the knees. I don't perform much these days, I much prefer the production stuff, and I've forgotten just how bloody nerve-racking it is. I soon get back into it, though, and once I relax, I really enjoy it. Honey loves it of course, strutting her long, brown legs up and down the stage; she's a natural performer. She kind of reminds me of David Bowie. Her skinny legs are strong and powerful and she has that male-female look Bowie carried off so well. Can't believe he has gone. He wasn't much younger than Grandad is when he passed away but what an amazing musical genius. I swear, the whole campus went into mourning the day we woke up to the news, followed by a week long celebration of all his songs. All the young dudes celebrating the ultimate Dude.

I wince when I drop a few dud notes. I look up from the keyboard to see if any of the other band members have noticed but either they haven't or, if they have, they don't give a shit. Because of the bright lights, it's hard to make out faces in the audience but I spot the pretty blonde girl again still standing at the front. Arms folded, she wears her resting bitch face with pride, her eyes continually following the dynamic singing duo. Honey is dead professional but she doesn't outshine Luke, he's amazing, really has stage presence. He's so much more confident than when we were at college, a proper front man. He sort of reminds me of Alex Turner from The Arctic Monkeys and it's almost impossible to believe this is my shy, best friend from school.

The song draws to a close and Honey drapes her arm around Luke to share his microphone for the final words. I look down at the pretty blonde girl whose perfectly pissy face now looks even more pissy.

Who the hell is she anyway?

Luke tells the audience to bugger off and buy more booze while the band take a fifteen-minute break. One of the guitarists lifts his guitar over his head, carefully placing it on the stand next to him. I walk towards him and he introduces himself to me as Chris. Out of nowhere a hand is thrust between us and I realise it's the drummer. He shakes my hand and tells me his name is Jay. His gorgeous brown eyes match his dark skin and wide smile. He asks me how I know Luke and I explain we've been friends since junior school.

'Ah hah, you're the one that got away then?' he states. I look at him, confused but he simply smiles and asks me if I play in a band too. I shake my head and explain about my job at Hunter Black Productions. His eyes grow huge. 'Shit me, that's amazing. Any chance of getting us some free studio time there? Or better still, a meeting with the man himself?'

'Piss off, Jay,' a voice says behind us. I turn to see the other guitarist. He introduces himself as Marti and with his shock of floppy, blonde hair and blue eyes he is the perfect contrast to Jay. 'Scuse him,' Marti says nodding his head towards Jay, 'he means well but he's always trying to get free exposure and shit for the band.'

I laugh and tell him it's fine, that my best friend Honey, who just sang with them, is always doing the same thing too. 'And my mum,' I add. 'She's a writer and she's always trying to get free publicity for her book.'

'Wow,' Marti replies, arching one of his eyebrows, 'talented family, then?' I laugh and wonder why the hell I mentioned Mum. Marti then looks over at Honey who has cornered Luke and the blonde girl from the audience. It looks as though Luke has introduced them both and in typical Honey fashion, and much to the blonde girl's surprise, Honey throws herself at her, kissing each cheek (followed by a third kiss because she is half Spanish) before wrapping her arms around her in a tight embrace. Confused, the girl flinches, just like Mum did when she first met Honey, and I can't help laughing. Luke, who is rolling his eyes and shaking his head, is also laughing.

'She's fit,' Marti says, keeping his eyes firmly fixed on Honey. 'Does she have a boyfriend?'

I tell him no and his mouth lifts into a hopeful smile. 'But she has a girlfriend,' I add.

Marti's blue eyes narrow with disappointment. 'Really?' he asks.

'Really,' I reply.

'Shit, what a waste,' he continues.

'I'm sure her girlfriend doesn't think so!'

He laughs and shrugs his shoulders. 'Oh well, *que sera, sera*,' he says, which immediately makes me smile and think of Nan singing Doris Day and Grandad trying (but sounding more like a dying animal) to join in. I can't wait to get home and tell Grandad about this. I hope he's okay. Mum said he was when she called me, said he was waiting for some test results but otherwise he was just being a grumpy old bugger, which means he must be okay.

A familiar voice interrupts my thoughts. 'Cas, Cassie?' I turn to see Luke, one of my oldest school friends, looking at me. He looks so different, but somehow the same. More like a man now but he still has the same shy smile, now he's off stage. Luke, like Mum, reminds me of home. I think of Grandad and everything that's happened to me over the last couple of weeks and somehow, seeing Luke makes me feel as though I want to burst into tears again. I throw myself at him and hug him, really tight. I bury my face into his chest and immediately recognise the smell of his old leather jacket. It reminds me of a different time in my life, a bad time, a really dark time but also a more innocent time.

Luke hugs me back but I feel him squirm a little. I pull away again and examine his lovely face. I'm surprised at the rising heat in my cheeks when, for some reason, I choose this moment to remember the one and only time we stepped out of our friend zone and spent the night together. It was lovely, it really was, but it didn't mean anything more to me than that and it didn't change the way I felt about Luke. I've always loved him and always will I think, but only ever as a friend.

Luke puts his hand under my chin and tilts my head up. 'Are you okay Cassie?' he asks. 'You look really … thin?'

I feel my eyes blur and I want to scream. I want to tell Luke, my oldest, bestest friend, that I'm not okay, and that I'll probably never be the same again.

I smile and nod my head. 'I'm fine,' I lie. 'Just a bit tired, a bit overworked.'

'Who's this then?' a rather nasally, impatient voice that I don't recognise interrupts us. I turn and see the pretty blonde girl staring at me.

Coughing, Luke pulls away from me and puts his arm around the girl. 'Okay, … um … Felicity, this is my oldest friend … Cassie,' he says pointing at me. 'Cassie … this is Felicity … my girlfriend.'

'Fiancée,' Felicity corrects him while purposely raking her left hand through her long hair so the stone in the ring on her finger catches the light.

I feel my bottom jaw drop. 'Wow, really?' I ask.

Luke smiles. It's a warm, safe smile but I suddenly feel kind of embarrassed. I've been at work all day and didn't have time to change and I'm cringingly aware that I probably look like a real skank. Especially when compared to the immaculately dressed Felicity. And Honey of course, with her model looks and rock star confidence, I simply fade into the background when I'm with her. And tonight is no exception. Tonight, I feel dull and ugly. What worries me more, though, is that I actually give a shit. Luke is the only real friend I've never been afraid of being myself around, so why am I so bloody bothered now?

'Really,' Felicity replies flatly. 'Don't worry though, we'll make sure you both get an invite to the wedding,' she continues, glancing at Honey and smiling.

'Wedding!' Honey shouts. 'How wonderful.' And for the second time tonight, Honey almost knocks me clean off my feet again as she flings her arms around the happy couple, smothering them in kisses.

But it doesn't feel wonderful, at least, not to me it doesn't. I want to grab Luke and shake him and tell him he's too young to get married. That his band is great and have real potential. And that he looks great and a shed load of other mixed up thoughts crashing around in my head. Sad? Why do I feel sad? I wish I could talk to Luke on my own.

'Oooh, I know,' Honey continues (never one to miss an opportunity), 'you can hire me and my band to play at your wedding. Mates rates and all that.'

'Sod that,' Jay declares as he wanders over, playfully elbowing Luke in the stomach. 'Luke will be singing in his own band on his wedding day. Eh, Luke?'

'He will not!' Felicity declares.

Jay clicks his tongue and raises his eyes. 'I need a piss,' he says and wanders off again.

I look at Luke. 'Wow, marriage?' The word sticks to the roof of my mouth. 'Congratulations, I'm really pleased for you both,' I lie.

Luke hangs his head and smiles his shy smile that so reminds of the twelve-year-old boy that used to fancy me. 'Thanks,' he replies.

'And congratulations to the band.' I add. I start to tell Luke how brilliant I think the band is but Felicity, who is pulling him away from me, insists he needs a drink before the next set. Luke smiles weakly and says he'll see me after the gig before he disappears with Felicity.

I turn around and see Marti grinning at me.

'Bossy cow that Felicity,' he says. 'Don't get me wrong, she's nice enough, just not sure she's right for our Luke. Not really sure she's enough about the music if I'm honest?' He looks at Honey, then back at me, shrugs his shoulders and tells us it was nice to meet us before also disappearing out the back with the others for a quick smoke.

Honey drags me back to a patiently waiting Matt who is holding, what looks like, more drinks for us. As we pass through the thick sea of people, most of them turn and congratulate Honey, telling her what a great performance it was. No-one notices, or says anything to, me.

'Well that was pretty awesome, eh?' Honey says. 'Can you believe Luke? Getting bloody married? I mean MARRIED? Why now, when he's so young and the band are doing so well?' I shrug my shoulders and Honey wrinkles her nose. 'Felicity seems like a babe though, doesn't she?'

'Yeah, I guess so,' I sniff. I'm not sure though. I was buzzing when I turned up here tonight and now I feel, kind of flat. 'They look good together,' I continue, but Honey has looked away, talking to someone else and isn't even listening to me anymore.

'Oh what the hell,' I shout out as I swig back the vodka and coke I've bought myself. It's too late to worry about it now anyway.

Rummaging around in my pockets, I pull out some flyers I said I'd hand out for a demonstration, taking place tomorrow.

March for the right to pubic hair
Neat and tidy, not bald and bare

It's to demonstrate against the idea that women shouldn't have hairy fannies. I'm fine with either, bald or hairy, just not dictated to, not made to feel like we should all have to fit into a certain look. And to tell stupid boys that we can't all look like porn stars, because some of the stupid idiots think it's real. Duh, I'm sorry to tell you boys, they're just bloody movies made for stupid entertainment. I mean, really, how would you like it if we watched *James Bond*, although he is actually a bit old to be fair, or *Jason Bourne* or whatever the hell else stupid action films you all watch, then expected you lot to look like the lead actors do in the buff. To carry guns, drive fast cars and live in a world of perfection where only bad people are ugly. Well, yeah, I guess most of you bloody shallow idiots would love it. But guess what? We don't expect it because it's NOT BLOODY REAL! What's wrong with a little hair anyway? Not to mention the fact, shaving rash is a killer.

I wander around aimlessly, handing out leaflets before the band come back on for their second set.

'Fight for the right for a hairy fanny,' I say.

Honey says she's in and passes a leaflet to Matt and tells him he's in too. Matt reads the leaflet then flinching, quickly scrunches it into his pocket. Some people smile and nod as they take a leaflet, others turn away and ignore me. And then, of course, I hear some of the usual comments behind my back like "fucking lesbo" or "feminist bitch" and as usual, I ignore them.

Chapter 9

STAGE FOUR

Lizzie

Simon unlocks the front door and gently pushes me through it. I stand in the darkened hallway unable to move. All reassurances I gave Mum have all but disappeared. I feel like screaming. Fumbling, Simon snaps on the hallway light and looking away, I shield my eyes from its brightness with both my hands. Only, once they are there, I find I can't pull my hands away. Instead I bury my head deep into them and finally the tears that were threatening to come all evening, fall. My face becomes a hot mess of wet confusion and anger. I knew something was wrong but not even I saw this coming. None of us did.

Thinking of breaking the news to Cassie, Connor, and Maisy, my heart, if it's at all possible, breaks just a little bit more. The nice doctor with the firm voice broke the news just after the text from Michelle advising me, via a number of joyful emoticons, that my book had gone to number one in its listed category. A brief moment of elated joy which surged through my weary body was quickly extinguished by the bad words of the good doctor.

'Stage four, how can it be stage four cancer? Dad is, was, looks too well? Where were all the warning signs?' I ask Simon.

Simon holds me, in the hallway that is too bright, and doesn't say a word. He strokes my hair with his hand and kisses the top of my head. An icy wave of nausea washes over me and I have the sudden urge to vomit. I rush from Simon's grip towards the downstairs loo. My digested lunch from earlier burns my throat as it rises into my mouth. I lift the lid of the toilet just in time.

Simon follows me and is behind me, holding my hair back for me. Once I manage to stop heaving and emptying my stomach of its contents, I sit up and wipe away the dribbles of sick from my mouth with the back of my hand. I start shivering and my head starts to throb. Before I know it, Simon has pushed me upstairs and bundled me into bed, clothes and all.

He wraps the duvet around my trembling body and tells me not to worry. He says I'm in shock and should just try and rest for a while. My eyes feel heavy and the room is warm and dark. I feel myself drifting off to troubled sleep.

I wake with a start at the sound of my phone ringing in the darkness. I reach out and pat the bedside cabinet, searching for the lamp. There's a loud thud as I knock one of the many books off the cabinet. My phone continues to ring angrily, drilling into my throbbing head. I panic and think of Dad. I finally find the lamp switch and snap it on. The light hurts my eyes and my vision is blurred, but fear brings it quickly into focus. I realise my phone is in my bag on the floor beside the bed. I sit up and throw the duvet off; surprised to see I'm still fully clothed. I hold my aching head and reach down into my bag for my phone, which had, for a brief moment, stopped ringing but is now pulsating again. I swipe the screen of my screaming phone while looking for Simon, but his side of the bed is empty?

'Hello,' I say into the phone.

I hear Connor's voice, clearly upset, clearly agitated. 'Mum, you have to come, it's Dad. He's sick, being sick. And he's crying. He's lying on the floor in the hallway and I can't move him. Help me Mum, please.'

Connor sounds noticeably unnerved and as Connor never panics about anything, I know it's serious.

I tell him I'll be there in twenty minutes.

Chapter 10

THE HALLWAY OF HELL

Connor

Well, this is a shit ending to a peng night. Well, at least it started off sweet. Hayley Patterson was at the party and she looked well impressed when I was working the decks. She smiled at me a couple of times. I swear she was gonna talk to me when she sat down next to me but Maximus Anus completely messed that up. He gate-crashed the party with his tosser friends, who all thought it was hilarious to mess about with my decks, wankers. One of them tried to work the turntables, not really knowing what he was doing, while another one put the headphones on and danced round the room like a twat. Max Anus was laughing his stupid fat head off until he spotted me sitting next to Hayley. Then all the knobbing around with my decks stopped and it was like a spotlight from above shone down on me for all the world and Hayley Patterson to see. I knew from Max's idiot fucktard face he was gonna enjoy making me look like a loser.

'Oi, Conman, show us your hairy muff,' he said.

'I don't, I didn't,' I stuttered my reply. 'It was just some dodgy puff.'

'You're a fucking dodgy puff. Why are you sitting next to that loser?' he asked Hayley, shouting it from the top of his fat gob so everyone could hear. 'He only likes girls with hairy clunge. Big, fat, hairy fannies. Are you insulting Hayes, Conman? Are you sitting next to her coz you think she has a hairy gash?'

The whole room erupted into stupid laugher, half of them coz they had to coz it was Max's law and he'd shine the light of embarrassment on you if you didn't, and the other half laughed coz they were born without a brain and thought it was hilarious instead of fucking ridiculous. Hayley was pissed off though; she even managed to put Max Anus down, sort of.

'I'm done with this loser party,' she said to her friends. 'Let's go to the pub where hopefully the boys are more mature and don't think it's funny to sexually objectify girls.' I knew she was talking about Max Anus but I'm not sure he did. He scratched his head like the dumbass he is then ordered his lot to leave and head for the pub, too.

Everyone breathed a sigh of relief when they left.

Robbo threw himself onto the sofa next to me. 'You bloody love that Hayley gal dun cha?' he asked.

Jake then proceeded to plonk himself on the sofa, squeezing himself between me and Robbo. 'Nah, nah, he doesn't, do you Conman?' he replied for me. 'He just likes having a bit of crack with her.'

'Phwoar, what you mean is, he wants her crack.'

'Oh, piss off Robbo,' I replied.

The Rickmeister then joined us by lying across all three of us. 'Shall we go to the pub too?' he asked.

'Oh yeah, let's go to the pub and not get served and look like even bigger losers?' I replied.

'Yeah, he's right,' Robbo agreed. 'Besides I've got to get home, Mum said I have to get up early tomorrow and do some more revision for my final exam.'

'Sod that,' Jake replied. 'I've only got sociology left to do and frankly I don't give a shit. The answers to every question are always evolutionary or revolutionary, anyway.'

'So? Don't you still need to revise?' Robbo asked.

'Nah, coz I've got a fifty-fifty chance of getting it right, it means I can just guess!'

'Or just revise,' I add.

'Nah, I'll be out on a muff hunt with me other mates.'

'Aww, are you going out to play with your imaginary friends again Jake?' the Rickmeister replied.

'Nah, what he really means is he has to go shopping with Mummy,' Robbo added.

'Piss off,' Jake replied.

'Shut the fuck up the lot of ya,' I yelled. 'I'm getting my decks together and I've gotta go, promised my dad.'

I could have stayed a bit longer I suppose but the party was winding down and for some stupid up reason I felt guilty about leaving Dad. I folded my decks away and agreed to share a taxi with Robbo and the Rickmeister and, after ten minutes moaning about what a bunch of pussies we all were, Jake joined us in the taxi too.

And now, here I am, in the hallway from hell. I look down at the mess in front of me though and I realise it's probably good I did come back. Dad is lying in his own puke, which really stinks, and I can't wake him up properly. I nudge him and he murmurs. I feel relieved coz that means he's still alive.

I sit beside him in the stinking, rotten hallway still unsure whether to ring an ambulance or not. Thank god Mum is on her way, she'll know what to do. I laugh to myself coz this thing laying in his own vomit is supposed to be a man, and men are supposed to be strong but he's nowhere near as strong as Mum is. Good job she didn't do this when he left us. He didn't give a shit about any of us when he left, and now the same has been done to him, he can't cope.

He's never really been there for me and Cas, only when it suited him. I suppose he did make an effort to see us once a week but we still never had a room or place in the house he shared with the step-monster. She didn't like us and we weren't welcome, and he went along with it. He swapped us for fast cars and big houses, and things. And now the step-monster has thrown him out without a penny. Now he's struggling like Mum did, and he can't fucking cope.

I think of Grandad, grumpy coz he doesn't want to be in hospital, and laugh. I knew he'd be okay. Grandad has always been there for me, Simon too, I suppose, but Grandad, he's always, always been there for me.

And he always will be coz I know who he really is.

Chapter 11

LOVE HURTS

Lizzie

It's a beautiful June morning and I've been up and awake for hours now. I'm on my third cup of coffee but I can't stomach any food because I feel so nauseous again. Maybe it is a stomach bug? Or the menopause? Maybe both? The possibility of it being something worse doesn't bear thinking about right now. Hopefully my GP will shed some light on it.

Mug in hand I stare out of the window, enjoying the gentle warmth radiating through the window. The day is new; barely a couple of hours old, and the heat from the sun is pleasantly warm with a promise of more to come. I pull my phone from my dressing gown pocket, and using my one free hand, I swipe the screen and search for my book on the internet. I smile. Number one it flashes, blink, blink, blinkity blink, like a brightly lit neon sign. My slight ripple of euphoria is short lived, though, dampened by other, more pressing thoughts. My book is number one but my dad, my rock, is seriously ill. My book is number one but my ex-husband is gently snoring in the room next door. Lying on our sofa because I, much to Simon's annoyance, didn't have the heart to leave the father of my children in the state Simon and I found him in when we drove to his flat last night.

A tiny part of me should have, did maybe, whoop and rejoice at the squalor my ex appeared to be living in, but it was short lived. Even Simon was shocked at the state of both the place itself and Scott. Scott had told Connor he'd only been living in the flat for a few weeks but from what I could gather from his odd lucid moments of speech, interspersed amongst his general incoherent ramblings, it's probably been more like six months. Scott's BMW is parked outside, but other than that he doesn't appear to have much else. I don't think Sharon is letting Scott see their daughter either. Annoyed, because I really didn't want to, I actually felt sorry for the broken man before me.

Simon and I wiped Scott down as best we could, then with Connor's help we bundled him into the car. Reluctantly, Simon agreed we couldn't leave Scott there, that he'd have to come back to our house, just for one night. Simon wasn't happy about it at first, said we should take him to the hospital. I said that judging by the state of his hallway he'd vomited everything up anyway and there wasn't really much a hospital could do that we couldn't. Simon, like the good man he is, conceded in the end. Connor barely said anything the whole time, which isn't unusual for my sixteen-year-old son, who now only speaks to me in 'yes and no' grunts. However, for once, my son's wordless contribution was both disturbing and deafening.

Overwhelmed by the anger that engulfed me on the drive home, I like to think I hid it well. Staring out of the car window, aside from my mood, I was at a loss as to why this night in particular appeared so black. I soon realised it was an absence of lighting. It was true then, the council really did switch off the streetlights late at night. Another cost cutting exercise in the name of austerity. Oh, how the politicians love to bandy that word around. It's amazing what can be swiped from under us in the name of austerity, always affecting the most vulnerable and disempowered members of society. What does it actually mean though? Austerity. As far as I remember, in 2008 there had been an international financial crisis and some of the world's largest banks had been on the brink of collapse. We, the people, bailed them out and ever since, in order to pay for this, public services are continually slashed and benefits cut. But it's worth it, we're told, because we've all been living beyond our means and "we're all in this together." Bollocks.

Why? Why is life so unfair and how can Dad be so ill? He's not old enough to leave us, not yet. He still has some time, though. The nice doctor, with the Alan Rickman voice, said he had a year, maybe two. Oh whoopee-fucking-doo, twenty-four months, if we're lucky! At least the NHS still exists, just! And, thank god, Dad qualifies for some treatment.

Simon, who was driving, placed his hand on my knee. I looked across at him and managed a half smile in response before craning my neck to check on the passengers in the back. Connor, back turned, hood up, was scrunched against the car door with his head leant against the window. A flicker of light emanated from his hand, clearly reading his phone, and a white lead dangled from his ear. I stared at the back of my little-big man who was not so little any more and wondered, with a heavy heart, how on earth was I going to tell him about Dad? My gaze shifted from my son to his drunken father next to him and my anger rose like burning bile in my throat. A pathetic bundle of bollocks with his stinking breath, so well matched to his stinking attitude. Finding himself dealt the same hand he so easily traded the kids and me for all those years ago, and what? He seeks solace in a bottle because he can't cope? He left us with virtually nothing and yet I didn't descend into a cesspit of alcohol and self-pity. Why must he? Why is the spotlight on him? This is supposed to be my time. Why must my moment be overshadowed by death and wankers?

Troubled sleep has woken me early, though, and my anger this morning has dissipated, once again replaced with sadness and shame at my own godawful selfishness. I think of my poorly Dad in hospital, I think of my sleeping ex-husband in my living room, I think of poor Uncle Teddy and his waning once alert mind, I think of Cassie and how thin she looked, I think of my quiet son with his quiet thoughts, I think of Maisy who still hasn't phoned me back and I think of my book being number one. I hear Dad yelling "It's Not A Life, It's An Adventure" and I smile at the accuracy of those words and I think of some poignant words of my life-long companion Mr William Shakespeare.

> *Love all, trust a few, do no wrong to none; be able*
> *for thine enemy rather in power than use; and*
> *keep thy friend under thine own life's key; be*
> *checked for silence, but never taxed for speech.*

Odd noises above and around me tell me the house and its other occupants are beginning to stir. It is the start of another day and life is okay, not necessarily all good but not necessarily all bad, just life and the start of another day.

Cassie

Tummy pains and a crap night's sleep filled with strange dreams have woken me up. I reach into my knickers and press my hand against the clean pad I put there last night. I carefully pull my hand out of the duvet to look at it. I'm upset to see the blood. How many more weeks is this supposed to last? My mouth feels dry and my tummy hurts. I need caffeine and pain killers, but I can't be bothered to move.

My window is open slightly and a breeze outside lifts the curtains. Sun creeps into all the gaps in the curtains and I can hear birds singing. The birds sing differently in the summer than in the winter and it sounds like a nice day. It's 5.00 a.m. and our street is slightly quieter than it will be in a few hours' time but this city never sleeps and London is calling. London is always calling, day or night. Crossing my hands across my tummy I screw myself into a ball. Mum's text said to come home as soon as I was able to, no rush and nothing to worry about, apparently. Just let her know when. If I get my shit together this morning I could be on a train in a couple of hours and home before lunch. But then again, there's a lot going on in the studio at the moment. And even though I've worked god knows how many extra hours, I can't see Hunter letting me go before the weekend.

My phone pings. It's a text from Luke saying it was good to see me and we should catch up over coffee. I smile and think of Luke when he was little at school and fancied me. "Lovely Luke" Mum always called him. He did indeed look lovely at the gig, and what a performer! But why is he engaged, to Felicity? I don't think I like Felicity but then again, I don't think she likes me. And it's not because I'm jealous, like Honey said. It was unfair of her to say what she did, that I don't want Luke but I don't want anyone else to have him either. That was just bloody stupid and I don't regret telling her.

Maybe she's right, though, but I don't think so. Until last night, I'm ashamed to admit I haven't thought about Luke for ages, and although I love him, as a friend, I've never really fancied him. And I still don't, even though he did look pretty amazing last night. I'm just not sure about Felicity for Luke, she seems so different to him. Oh well, what the hell does it matter what I think.

A knock on my door interrupts my thoughts. It's Honey. Her big lips are turned down. 'Do you still hate me?' she asks.

'Honey, I'll never hate you,' I reply. I pat the bed and her face transforms into a huge smile. She strides over and gets in next to me.

'Sorry I was a cow,' she says.

'Sorry I called you a bitch,' I reply.

Smiling, we lay in silence for a moment, staring up at the ceiling.

Eventually Honey breaks the silence again. 'I think she's okay you know. Felicity I mean, I don't think there's anything to worry about with her and Luke.'

I sigh. 'Yeah, you're probably right,' I lie. 'I'm just not sure she really gets Luke and, you know, music?'

'She was there, at the gig supporting the boys, wasn't she?' I nod in agreement knowing full well I can't argue with that. 'Besides, not everyone is as passionate about music as us, you know? Lou isn't, but I still love her. I think?'

'They certainly look good together don't they?'

'Like god yeah,' Honey replies, 'I bloody fancied Felicity myself. For god sake don't tell Loopy Lou I said that, she gets sooooooo bloody jealous.'

Louise, Lou, is Honey's girlfriend but they don't live together. I sense all is not well between them.

'You two okay?' I ask.

Honey shrugs her shoulders but doesn't really reply and I know not to ask anymore. 'Didn't Luke look the bollocks though, bloody brilliant front man?'

I laugh and agree with Honey but I feel weird, really weird. I can't put my finger on why though. I pull my legs up to my aching tummy and suddenly feel sad.

What does it matter anyway? It's not my life and it's not actually any of my bloody business at the end of the day.

So why do I feel so bothered?

Lizzie

I turn to see who has come into the kitchen. I'm surprised to see Scott. I knew it wouldn't be Connor, I've found that either turning off the Wi-Fi or frying bacon beats any amount of shouting to get him out of his bedroom in the mornings, and as Scott was still comatose ten minutes ago, I assumed it was Simon.

'Oh, it's you. Morning.'

Scott puts a nervous hand up to scratch a head I suspect doesn't need scratching. Or maybe it does. Judging by its limp greasiness and the untidy facial hair sprouting from his upper lip and chin, it doesn't look as though he's had a good wash or shave in days. 'Morning,' he replies, coughing to clear his throat.

I feel uneasy and find myself undoing my dressing gown just so I can re-do it up, tighter and more securely. Completely covering and swaddling myself within its grey, faded material.

'Coffee?' I ask.

Scott nods. 'Thanks, coffee would be great.'

Looking at Scott's bloodshot eyes I'm surprised how quickly my anger has once again re-surfaced. I point to a chair and Scott sits down. He pulls the chair instead of lifting it and the scraping noise grates on my already agitated nerves. I wince and turn my back on Scott, busying myself with cups and spoons, anything not to look at him, anything to give me time to find my civil tongue.

I pass Scott a mug of hot, black coffee and nod at the sugar bowl and bottle of milk in front of him. 'Help yourself,' I offer. He thanks me and taking a deep breath I grab my mug and sit opposite him. Once confident, once arrogant, I'm confronted with a face worn out from living. I tell Scott he has to get his shit together. He tells me he can't because he's broken. I tell him it's not that bad, that he'll survive. Scott goes quiet for a moment and I find myself wishing Simon would come down.

'I'm sorry Lizzie,' Scott says.

'For what? Last night?' I wave my hand dismissively.

Scott looks down into his mug of coffee. 'For everything,' he replies. 'I didn't fool you, but I made a fool out of you. Out of us, our marriage, everything.'

This confession, admittance of guilt, renders me speechless. Old, painful memories re-surface and add to my newfound worries. 'Yes, yes you did,' I agree.

'You must be laughing now,' Scott states. 'On the inside anyway, you must think I deserve all this?'

I look at the pathetic man sitting opposite me. The father of my children, who left us for money and all the material things it enables one to buy, and although I have every right to feel smug, I find myself (foolish though it may be) feeling sorry for him.

'Well, you were a bastard,' I reply.

We both laugh and an invisible barrier between us is broken. I am suddenly at ease with my ex-husband in a way I haven't been for years. I watch Scott's shoulders deflate and sense he feels the same. He explains how Sharon kicked him out without a penny and because he was the main carer of their daughter, Harriet, he hasn't worked properly in years. With old contacts lost and lack of experience, not to mention younger, keener candidates snapping at his heels, he describes his struggle to find work.

I tell him I know only too well, thanks to him (to which he winces and cowers as though about to receive a blow to the head), how difficult it is but that it's not an excuse to give in. I tell him it's sad that he can't see his daughter but I remind him that he is lucky because he still has Cassie and Connor. He tells me he doesn't deserve them and I agree.

'But you do have them, nonetheless,' I continue. 'And they're going to need you now, more than ever,' I add.

Scott looks up, confused. I'm surprised, surprised that after all the heartache my ex-husband has put me through over the years, I feel confident enough to show my vulnerability. My voice cracks but I explain as surely and as concisely as I can about Dad's diagnosis. Scott's face drops.

'Shit, I'm so sorry Lizzie. I never knew ...'

'None of us did,' I interrupt him. 'The kids, Cassie, Connor, and Maisy still don't know yet. I'm still ... still trying to figure out how and when ...' I trail off and begin to sob.

Scott scrapes his chair back and stands up. I feel him; smell him in fact, a repugnant mix of alcohol and stale sick, at the back of me. After a moment, I feel my ex-husband's hand on my back. He doesn't say a word but gently pats my back in a way that reminds me of Dad.

I look up when I hear someone else walk into the kitchen. 'Everything all right here?' Simon asks. His voice is friendly enough but it rings with authority. Simon looks at Scott and it's a look that states, without words, "this is my house and if the woman I love is crying because of something you've said, you may just find yourself at the end of my fucking fist."

Scott moves his hand quickly, abruptly away from my back. 'She ... Lizzie has just told me about Salocin,' Scott replies.

Simon nods at Scott. 'Right, yeah, not good. Not good at all.'

An uncomfortable silence floats amongst the sounds of a boiling kettle and metal spoons banging against ceramic mugs. Simon makes himself a coffee and offers Scott and me another refill. I happily accept but Scott declines. Scott coughs to clear his throat and suggests he ought to perhaps be on his way. I'm surprised when Simon orders Scott to sit down and even more surprised when Scott does as he is asked.

Simon explains they have a vacancy at work. He says that Scott can shower here then he needs to go home, put on a suit and get himself to their offices by 11.00 a.m. for an interview. Simon explains that it's a temporary contract and he'll be up against ten other candidates but if he gets his shit together and can convince the two others (as well as himself) conducting the interview that he's the man for the job, it'll help get him back on his feet.

I look at Simon and smile, reassured of just why I love this man. Simon winks at me and smiles back. 'Oh, and no fucking booze, right?' he adds. 'It won't be tolerated.'

Scott looks stunned but nods his head like an excitable school-boy. He pushes his chair away and stands, hand outstretched to shake Simon's.

Simon recoils a little. 'No problem mate but I've seen what that hand was lying in last night and if it's all the same to you, we'll save the hand shaking until later, at least until you've had a shower anyway.'

Scott laughs nervously and pulls his hand back quickly. I can't help laughing too, at least, that is, until we are interrupted by the loud, out of character, ranting of my teenage son.

Connor hovers by the kitchen door, his dark eyes focussed on me. He looks angry, very angry. 'When, Mum?' he asks. His voice is low but loud and full of intent. 'When the hell were you going to tell me, eh?'

I'm completely taken aback and barely have time to comprehend his question before Connor walks deliberately towards me. I stand up, as does Simon, so that we are all now standing. Connor's shoulders, normally quite rounded from carrying the weight of the world on them, are remarkably erect and, standing at almost six feet in height, he is strangely intimidating. I am nervously aware that my boy is becoming a man.

Connor uses his height to corner me. 'When, then?' he demands of me again.

I feel threatened and back away. 'Tell you about what?' I ask.

'Grandad,' Connor shouts. 'I heard you, just now, telling him,' he points to Scott. 'How dare you tell him before me?'

Simon looks as stunned as I feel and I'm surprised to hear Scott's voice interrupt Connor's ranting. 'Connor, don't talk to your Mum like that?'

Connor pivots on one leg, turning towards Scott. He tilts his head sideways, almost robotic in fashion, and wears a frown of amused cynicism that is far too old for his years. Two large steps forward and Connor's gangly frame, a couple of inches taller than Scott's, hovers menacingly above his father.

Connor laughs. 'You? Don't you dare tell me what to do! You walked out on me years ago, and you didn't give a shit.' Simon and I look at each other. I look at Simon who shrugs his shoulders but neither of us appears compelled to intervene. Judging by the venomous intonation of my normally quiet son, these feelings have been bubbling under his calm exterior for some time.

'You left us,' Connor continues, waving his hand in my direction, 'me and Mum and Cassie, for that bitch. The bitch that didn't want us. We were here first, before her, but you didn't care, did you? You were happy to swap us, for what, FOR WHAT?' Connor shouts. Scott looks mortified but we all remain speechless.

Connor pauses for a moment and a deafening quiet descends. He keeps his eyes firmly focussed on Scott before shaking his head and laughing again. 'The funny thing is,' he continues, 'you left us for a big fancy house and flash cars and now look at you, you have nothing. Nothing. Exactly what you left us with.' Connor turns and points an outstretched arm towards me. 'What did she do, when you left us with sod all? She managed, that's what. And she was there for us, me and Cassie, every single fucking day. Not just when it suited her. Like you. You can't dip in and out of my life then expect to tell me what to do. And you know who else was there for me, right from the start? From the very beginning? Grandad was.' Connor throws Simon a sideway glance. 'And Simon, later,' he adds. 'But NEVER YOU!'

Simon walks towards Connor and gently grabs his rigid shoulders. 'Come on son, you need to calm down.'

Connor swings round to look at Simon. 'No Si, what I need is for adults to stop fucking lying to me.'

Connor's eyes begin to fill up and his angry voice is breaking, as is my heart. He turns back to look at me. 'So, when were you gonna tell me, Mum, about Grandad?' I open my mouth to speak but Connor continues before I have a chance to. 'He can't die Mum, I know who he is. I know who he *really* is.'

I'm thrown for a moment. What does Connor mean? I search the dusty crevices of my tired mind and regurgitate memories in a bid to try and understand my distressed son.

I shake my head at Connor as confusion knits together my furrowed brow.

He looks as desperate as I now feel. 'I know who Grandad is, Mum,' Connor urges. 'You know, Salocin Lemalf.'

The penny finally drops and smashes through my chaotic thoughts like a wrecking ball.

'Oh god, no baby. I didn't think you still believed that? Grandad is just, well, Grandad. Salocin Lemalf, mere mortal man.'

Connor shakes his head violently. 'No! No, he's not. He told me who he is. I KNOW WHO HE IS. And ... and ...' Connor trails off using the back of his hand to wipe the tears that now fall so easily. His bottom lip trembles and my bold, bolshie son is once again reduced to the needy child he still is.

'He gave you hope Connor, that's who Nicolas Flamel represents, hope. Not immortality.'

Simon and Scott throw me confused glances and Connor starts to cry. I walk towards him and try to hug him but he shrugs me off. 'No, get off me. Grandad lied to me too, then? He's a bloody liar like the bloody rest of you. Fucking adults, all fucking liars. Leave me the hell alone.' Connor strides out of the kitchen and marches back up the stairs.

I start to follow him but Simon pulls me back. 'Leave him, he's angry and he's frightened. He just needs some time to calm down.'

I feel sick and just want to comfort my boy. I sit down again, deflated. The door-bell rings and Simon heads to answer it. I wonder who the hell it is. Whatever or whoever it is had better be bringing good news, I've had my fill of shit over the last couple of days.

I hear the door open and Simon sounds surprised. I strain to listen to the muffled voices at the front door but am interrupted by the voice of a nervous looking Scott.

'Nicolas Flamel?' he asks.

I shake my head. 'Not now, Scott. Not now.'

He doesn't ask anymore but instead points upwards towards the ceiling. 'Erm, do you think ...? I mean should I at least try and ...? What I mean is, should I go and try and talk ...?' He trails off when I shake my head again. 'No, probably not a good idea,' he agrees.

I grab a clean towel from the tumble dryer and point out the direction of the bathroom as we climb the stairs. 'You can get showered in there,' I say, 'but let me just find you some clothes to change into.' I rummage amongst Simon's drawers and find an old pair of tracksuit bottoms and an old (I'm rather amused to find) Wham T-shirt. I think about giving it to Scott to wear, just for the sheer hell of it, but, worried there may be some sentimental value attached to this hidden treasure, I think better of it and grab a faded plain T-shirt instead. I pass the clothes, along with the towel, to Scott. 'Here, you can borrow these and bring them back another time.'

'Thanks,' Scott replies.

I descend the stairs towards Simon's voice. Clearly whoever was at the door has now moved into the house and is conversing with Simon. I can't quite make out whose voice it is, except to say it's definitely that of a woman. I take each step of the stairs very slowly and wonder if this day, week, can get any worse.

'Surely not?' I say out loud.

'Still talking to yourself then Mum?'

I look up, shocked to see Maisy standing at the bottom of the stairs to greet me. 'My prodigal daughter has returned,' Simon says shaking his head and raising his eyes.

'What? Why?' I stutter.

'Oh cheers,' Maisy snorts.

'No, I mean. I'm just a bit surprised, well a lot surprised actually, but how lovely to see you! Give me a hug.' I fling my arms around my step daughter whether she wants a hug or not, it has been a couple of years since I last saw her after all. 'Why didn't you tell us you were coming?'

Maisy lowers her eyes and shrugs her shoulders. 'Wanted to surprise you.'

'Well, you certainly did that.' I step back from Maisy and look past her in search of Crazee but I don't see him or evidence of him anywhere. 'So, where is he? Where's Crazee?'

Maisy purses her lips. 'He's not coming,' she replies.

'Not coming?' I repeat. 'Why ever not? You mean you've travelled all this way from Australia, by yourself? But, why? Is everything okay?' Simon, who is standing behind Maisy, rolls his eyes and shakes his head.

'We've split up,' Maisy states.

I look from Maisy to Simon, who is now shrugging his shoulders and holding his hands questioningly, back to Maisy again. 'You've split up? But, why?'

'I don't really wanna talk about it. I was just asking Dad if I can crash here for a while, you know, until I get back on my feet?'

'What, oh yes, of course. You can have your old room.'

'Thanks, now if you don't mind I'm gonna crash. I never sleep very well on planes and I'm absolutely done in.'

Despite having my feet firmly fixed on dry land, another familiar wave of sea sickness washes over me. I feel slightly faint and grab the bottom of the stair bannister to steady myself. I swear I can hear laughter, somewhere, and if I didn't know better I'd have said it was Dad.

Chapter 12

NICOLAS FLAMEL, FATHER CHRISTMAS AND THE TOOTH FAIRY

Lizzie

I descend the stairs confused by the shouting and laughter wafting its way from the living room. The prominent voice, at least the one that stands out, is Dad's. And yet, I know he's not here. Simon is at work, Cassie is still in London and Maisy, thank goodness, has got her backside into gear and has taken the bus into town to see if she can get a bit of work at the tattooists she used to work at before she went to Australia.

I can't say I'm displeased. Clearly her break-up with Crazee, whether it was instigated by her or not, has hit her hard. She has barely said a word since she's been back, which on reflection isn't anything particularly out of the ordinary, but she's not herself. And she's put on weight, quite a bit actually, which isn't necessarily a bad thing, at least she looks a damn sight healthier than Cassie does. But it's almost as if she's given up. Mooching around the house in the same pair of grey track suit bottoms and grimy, oversized T-shirt.

'Oi Connor, over here, son.' I hear Dad shout from the living room. 'That's my boy. Good boy. You can do it.'

Walking towards the sound of Dad's voice and I am presented with Connor's back. He is sitting cross legged on the floor, staring up at the flickering images on the TV screen. He is watching video footage of Dad, and other family members, compiled and put together on a CD by Sean, a copy of which was given to each of us all for Christmas, a couple of years ago. My response to the film footage is surprisingly unsettling.

Dad is teaching Connor how to ride his bike without his stabilisers. Connor can't be much older than Ruby's Andrew. Like an agitated snake, his tongue flicks in and out and his little face is racked with concentration as he grips the handlebars. I'm shocked when Dads' face comes into view. I realise now how much he's aged, confronted with the fact he is much sicker than I cared to admit. The Dad I see playing out before me is big and strong. His brown hair is greying slightly but his cheeks are full and his knowing eyes are razor sharp. He laughs as he holds onto the back of Connor's bike seat, who, after several wobbly false starts, once again attempts to ride his bike with two wheels rather than four. Dad, back bent over, runs a little behind Connor before finally letting go of the seat, flinging his arms up in a triumphant wave.

'Whoo hoo. Go on Connor boy. You can do it. You're doing it. That's it. That's my boy!'

After a slightly wobbly ninety-degree turn, Connor, head bent forward, pedals ferociously back towards Dad, grinning with triumphant pride. Cassie comes into view and she, along with Mum (I'm obviously behind the camera) are whooping and cheering Connor on. Painful though it is, I feel compelled to keep watching. My vision blurs as the younger versions of my family play out before me, and I feel both desperately happy, yet desperately sad at the same time.

Part of me is enchanted re-living these sacred, snatched moments of time; part of me can't bear it. I remain where I stand, though, silently hovering as grainy film footage regurgitates memories it would be far easier to suppress. Birthdays, Christmases, family holidays, visiting Sean and Nat after Summer was born, school plays, Cassie playing an angel and a devil, Connor a superhero and a crocodile, Andy laughing along with Simon, Dad and Uncle Teddy, visits to me in hospital, visits to Ruby when Andrew was born, Cassie playing piano, Connor playing guitar, Maisy before she was a goth and afterwards with the notorious tree tattoo, all play out before me in glorious technicolour.

I clutch my throat with my hand in a bid to stop the tightening of my thorax. The film comes to an end and the closing finale is Dad shouting his infamous "It's not a life, it's an adventure" and I swear I feel my heavy heart cracking just a little more. I want to scream but thankfully I have the good sense not to. Hot tears slip down my cheeks, despite my best efforts to suppress them, and it is only when I wipe them away I notice the gentle rise and fall of Connor's shoulders. Head bent forwards, he doesn't make a sound but it's clear that my little-big man is also crying.

I cough to make my presence known but Connor doesn't acknowledge it. His shoulders continue to rise and fall in time with the intense beating of my fractured heart. I walk towards him and hover long enough for him to know I'm there before I reach down and place my hand on his head. Connor looks up, his face red and tear stained before he grabs my legs with both arms. He wraps himself around me, tight, his heaving shoulders shuddering against my imprisoned legs. And then comes the crying. A pitiful, muffled mix of man versus boy sounds fall from his mouth and my broken heart breaks just a little bit more.

I quickly take hold of the situation. I am a mother, I need to be strong, and almost immediately my tears cease. As Connor's grip around my legs lessens, I manage to break free and drop down to his level, pulling him towards me, enveloping my grieving son into the safety of my arms. I tell him everything will be okay as I rock him back and forth and stroke his hair, much like I did when he was a toddler. The gangly bulk of my son reminds me he is sixteen but it makes no odds, he could just as well be four years old right now. Our two bodies, intertwined, continue to rock, back and forth, back and forth. Eventually Connor's shoulders stop shuddering. He pulls away from me and uses the backs of both hands to wipe away his tears.

'He can't go Mum. What am I going to do without Grandad?'

Swallowing hard, I move the hair that has fallen across Connor's eye and shake my head. 'I don't know baby,' I reply. 'I don't know what any of us are going to do without him. We just have to make the most of the time we have left.'

'But, I thought. I really believed …' Connor falters, his bottom lip trembling.

'Believed what, baby?'

'Well, you know. That he was, Nicolas Flamel. Immortal.'

I let out a faint laugh and cup my hand around Connor's wet cheek. 'He had us all believing that at one time or another.'

'You mean you believed it too?'

'For a while, when I was a girl. Uncle Sean and I both believed it.'

Connor shifts uncomfortably, his cheeks burning. 'But, spelled backwards, his name *is* Nicolas Flamel. And Uncle Teddy calls him Nicky, sometimes.'

'It's true, it is, and Uncle Teddy does call his brother, Nicky. But that has more to do with his mother's warped sense of humour than anything mystical.'

Connor frowns. 'What do you mean?'

I laugh and shake my head. 'The trouble with Grandad is, he has a huge heart, an overactive imagination and is, as you know, an avid reader of many books.'

'You mean the ones in his laboratory?'

Connor wears the look of an expectant, excitable little boy and I smile, touched by my son's need to believe in something other than the cold, harsh reality of life. Dad's garage conversion, despite the odd decorative set of test tubes and mortar and pestle, is more bijoux library than laboratory but I'm happy to play along with Connor.

I nod. 'Yes, the one's in his laboratory,' I reply. 'And, although some of his books are very old and very rare, like Grandad,' I add, trying to inject some humour to our sombre conversation, 'they're just books. And Grandad, well, Grandad is just a man.'

Connor looks down and picks at a mark on his jeans. 'I still don't understand?' he mumbles.

I sigh, suddenly exhausted. 'Ask Grandad, he'll explain. But Nicolas Flamel is no more real than Father Christmas or the Tooth Fairy.'

Dad used the idea of his being the great alchemist to spice up his storytelling to both Sean and me when we were children, each of us believing that only we knew of his secret. Something we've both laughed about on many occasions. However, once grown, Nicolas was sent packing, and although Dad continued to be a great storyteller, Nicolas was never again (as far as I was aware) resurrected. However, a couple of years ago I learned, via a rather suspicious Cassie, that the great alchemist had once again been revived. Mr Flamel was summoned from his resting place and offered to Connor as a symbol of hope during a very dark time. I never considered for one moment that Connor still maintained such belief.

'So, he lied to me?' Connor asks. 'Grandad lied to me?'

'Not, lied exactly. He gave you hope. Grandad tried to give you some hope at a very worrying time.'

'Humph,' Connor snorts and rather abruptly stands up, slowly turning away to look elsewhere. Recently accustomed to these strange, stilted movements, I feel slightly uneasy, aware they are in fact a precursor to a sudden outburst.

'Fancy a cuppa?' I ask. I am met with a scowl. Connor takes two strides towards the sofa and, despite being a very warm, very pleasant summer morning, grabs his jacket and proceeds to chuck it around his shoulders.

'I'm going to Jake's,' he states, flicking his hood over his head. 'To get away from all the lying, idiot adults in my life,' he adds.

Hunched over, he heads towards the hallway and leaves with the typical teenage perfunctory slam of the front door.

'Oh, god help me,' I shout to no-one.

Chapter 13

CODE RED

Connor

'Are you sure you wanna do this again?' Jake asks as he holds a lighter under the freshly rolled spliff.

'Just light the bloody dooby and pass it over here,' I reply

'But what if you see a giant muff again?' Robbo asks.

'Just light the bloody thing,' the Rickmeister repeats. 'Conman needs it, he's had some bad news.'

Jake cocks his head to one side and looks at me, his face suddenly serious. 'S'up Conman?' he asks.

'Just light the fucking dooby and I'll tell ya.'

Jake flicks the lighter with his thumb a couple of times until a hissing blue and orange flame jumps up. He waves it under the scrappy looking roll up he is holding between his fingers and sucks hard on the spliff until it glows. He smiles and exhales a puff of smoke before passing it to me. I take the spliff from Jake's hand and put it to my mouth. Inhaling too hard, I splutter and choke as I try to breathe out again. Everyone laughs. I pass it to Robbo, who smokes it like a pro and then passes it to the Rickmeister who, like me, chokes.

My head feels woozy but my tensed-up body starts to relax and I lay down on my back with my hands behind my head. Jake, Robbo, and the Rickmeister do the same.

'So, what's up Conman?' Jake asks again.

I think of Grandad and the lump in my throat stops me replying.

'His grandad's got cancer,' the Rickmeister replies for me.

'Shit, man,' Jake says.

'My nan's got cancer,' Robbo adds.

'Shit, man,' Jake repeats.

'Yeah, she had to have one of her boobs taken off the other week.'

'Shit, man,' Jake says again.

'A vasectomy or somink, I think it's called? And all her hair is falling out coz she's having that chemotherapy shit. God knows why they call it therapy though, nothing therapeutic about flooding your body with all that chemical shit.'

'Sorry Robbo,' I say. 'You should have said. Is she gonna be okay?'

Robbo chews his bottom lip and throws his hands up. 'God knows, I think she is. How about your grandad then, has he gotta start having treatment and shit then?'

'Dunno,' I reply. 'No-one's really told me too much yet but I think it's too late for treatment. Stage four I heard my mum telling my dad.'

'Fuck, man,' everyone says.

I don't think any of us really know what stage four actually means, except the end. The last full stop. Code red. Red alert. The no more chances saloon. The end of the tunnel. The final frontier. The end of the line. The big, fat, fucking END!

Shit, did I just scream that out loud or was it just in my head? I'm not too sure but everyone is suddenly really quiet.

'How do you keep milk from tuning sour?' Robbo suddenly asks.

'What? What the hell are you going on about now Robbo?' Jake replies.

'No, seriously. That was one of the questions in my biology exam, at least I think it was biology, the other day. I couldn't think what the answer was so I just wrote the first thing that came into my head.'

'Which was?' I ask.

'Keep it in the cow.'

'Robbo, you are such a twat,' Jake replies but it's done the trick. Everyone is rolling around on the grass in fits of laughter and for some reason, most likely the effects of the dodgy dooby, I find myself watching a giant cow jumping over the moon. Oh well, beats a hairy fanny I suppose.

'And, and a caesarean section is a place in Rome, right?' Robbo continues. 'And a seizure was a Roman Emperor?'

Jake and the Rickmeister clutch their stomachs as if they are in pain.

'No more Robbo,' Jake says laughing. 'I can't stand it.'

But still Robbo carries on. 'And artificial insemination is when the farmer does it to the bull instead of the cow, right? And varicose means nearby? Shit, I really don't get that. Why do people go to the doctors for having veins too close together?'

I'm laughing really hard and it feels soooo good. Somewhere in the distance I keep seeing a laughing cow, I remember Grandad singing me a nursery rhyme about a cow when I was little, jumping over the moon. But other than that, I feel chilled, chonged and the world and its problems can go fuck itself.

Robbo is still chuntering away though. 'And benign is what you be after you is eight. And a terminal illness is when you get sick at the airport.'

Terminal illness, that's what Grandad has. Robbo's words sting for a second but I'm so chonged I can't help but see the funny side.

'Terminal illness, airport,' I laugh. 'Must remember to tell my grandad that. That'll make him laugh.'

I look up at the church and think how amazing it looks. The bottom half of it is parked in darkness but the roof, the pointy bit, is surrounded by a halo of light from the huge moon sitting just behind it. I still keep seeing a cow but rather than jumping, it is floating around the moon like an air-filled balloon. I'm not religious but I've decided I like churches and I thank god for the spliff taking away my anger.

I look across at Robbo, who is still talking shit, and the Rickmeister and Jake who can't stop laughing, and smile. It's a warm night and I'm lucky to be chilling with good friends. Robbo's ramblings and Jake and the Rickmeister's laughing become muffled. A woozy chongedness washes over me and I think of Grandad. I love that man so fucking much, even though he does tell everyone to "fack orf" when he's pissed off. He can't go. I know people have to die but Grandad can't, not yet. It's too soon. He's always been there for me and it's too early. I still need him.

I think of him singing nursery rhymes to me, terribly out of tune. Of when he taught me to ride my first bike. Of being scrunched up on the sofa on a Saturday night watching *Doctor Who*. Of teaching me how to box, to play guitar and how we made those lotions and potions in his laboratory. And despite what Mum says, I know who Grandad really is. I can't tell this lot, even though they are the best mates anyone could wish for, they wouldn't understand. It would be like telling them I still believe in Father Christmas. But Mum's got it wrong, I know who Grandad is and it doesn't matter that he has stage four cancer coz I know he will tell it to "fack orf".

An unexpected screeching noise breaks my concentration. Jake jumps up, so quick he almost falls over again. 'Fuck, Conman, that's your fucking sister,' he says.

'Maisy?' I reply. What a shock it was to see her back from Oz.

'No! Can't you fucking hear her, it's bloody Cassie.'

Jake looks terrified, which only makes me laugh, but almost cry at the same time. All my friends spend half their time thinking my sister is fit and the other half being completely terrified of her.

'Connnnor! Connor, I know who you're with and what you little shits are up to. Show yourself.'

Jake grabs the ganja stick from Robbo and bends down, tapping it on the floor, carefully trying to put it out. A shadow of darkness falls around us, and from out of nowhere, it seems, Cassie is hovering above Jake.

'Give it to me,' she orders holding out her outstretched hand. 'Now!'

'I didn't know you were coming home?' I say but Cassie is still looking at Jake. Jake looks pissed off and opens his mouth to speak but seems to change his mind and closes it again.

'Now!' Cassie orders again.

Jake sighs heavily. He mumbles something I can't quite make out, except the word fuck, and passes the spliff to Cassie.

I look up through foggy eyes and realise Maisy is also with Cas. Cassie orders Jake to sit down again and she sits down next to him, patting the grass for Maisy to join her.

'Whose is this, then?' Cassie asks holding up the rolled herb.

We all look at each other, eyes darting from left to right.

'It's mine,' Jake says.

'Shit, you're not gonna grass us up are you, Cas?' I ask.

Robbo and the Rickmeister start giggling. 'Grass him up about the grass!' Robbo snorts. At which point we all, even Cas and Maisy, start laughing.

Cassie doesn't laugh for long though and her face becomes serious again. 'You shouldn't do this Connor. Getting stoned is not the answer to life's problems.'

Cassie then pulls out a lighter from her jeans pocket and starts to re-light the stub of the unfinished dooby. She takes a drag and passes it to Maisy. Maisy shakes her head no, which surprises us all.

'Really? You're always the first to want some?'

Maisy shrugs her shoulders and her face morphs into moodiness. 'Well I just don't right now, kay!'

'Kay, okay. You don't have to get arsey.'

Cassie takes another drag then drops the spliff on the floor and proceeds to stub it out by twisting it into the ground. She hauls herself back up and looks at everyone. Robbo and the

Rickmeister are still laughing and Jake has his eye firmly fixed on the mangled dooby.

'Right you lot, don't let me catch you doing this again,' she orders. She looks at me and nods. 'Connor, come on, home. Mum sent us to look for you. She said they, her and Si, have something to tell us all, apparently.' Maisy hauls herself back up behind Cas and Jake keeps looking at the splattered spliff.

'Oh shit,' I mumble. 'I bet it's about Grandad.'

Cassie wrinkles her nose and frowns. She looks just like Mum. 'What about Grandad?'

'I dunno, nothing. It doesn't matter.'

'No Connor, what do you mean? What's wrong with Grandad?'

'He's got cancer,' Robbo replies.

Cassie's mouth falls open and her face drops. She swings round to look at Robbo. 'What? What the fuck ...?' she shouts.

'Oh, fucking great, cheers Robbo.' I reply, 'Thanks a fucking bunch.'

Chapter 14

TAKE MY BREATH AWAY

Lizzie

I float into the doctor's surgery, the remnants of 'Take My Breath Away' still playing in my head. I have just got off the phone to Oliver and am slightly concerned that even the mere sound of his voice can send me into a catatonic state, despite all my current worries. However, I'm also very grateful that the lovely Oliver has, albeit temporarily, transported me away from more pressing concerns.

Oliver wanted to confirm some dates for attendance at book signings and book fairs. I'm more than happy to do the book signings but after my last dire attempt at public speaking, the thought of doing any more now fills me with absolute dread. And what with Dad, and everything else going on at the moment, I can't help but feel slightly overwhelmed. Unfortunately, mostly due to my disturbed mental state and the loss of my ability to speak whilst listening to Oliver, I think I agreed to all the dates suggested. Oh well.

Sighing heavily, I find a seat in the waiting room and my thoughts drift back to Dad. How? How can he be so ill? Telling the kids was, as I knew it would be, heart breaking. Cassie sobbed, Connor just looked angry, again, and Maisy barely said a word.

'Why?' Cassie asked. 'Surely if they're going to do chemo they must think there's a chance for him? He just has to fight it, like Nan. She had cancer but she got better.' I tried, did my best at least, to explain something I don't fully understand myself. I explained that Dad's cancer, lung cancer, was much more advanced and much more aggressive than Mum's breast cancer which, caught early, had given her a much better prognosis than Dad. Then I talked about the fact that death was just a part of the circle of life and I thanked god Cassie broke the awful seriousness of it all by asking what the hell *The Lion King* had to do with it all. I reiterated that Dad had a year; maybe two, and that we should be grateful for that. And I reminded them of poor Ruby losing Andy, gone in an instant in a car crash and not even fifty years old.

I tried to remain calm whilst being the bearer of such bad news, determined to act as an emissary on behalf of my wonderful father who has given so much of himself and his wisdom to me and mine over the years. But what I really wanted to do was scream from the rooftops about the unfairness of it all. To stop the terrible landslide of dread that rises with me every morning and follows me to bed every night. The invisible rock I have always leant on is crumbling and the ground below looks terribly shaky. I'm an adult but I'm also a child who is going to lose her dad, and it's just too difficult to comprehend.

How can I sign books and smile at the people good enough to buy my drivel? How can I give speeches to an audience in awe of me merely because I have written a book? I never really understood, until it happened to me, but being a writer affords one a certain amount of power. As far as I'm concerned, I'm just a person who wrote a book but for some reason, writers are assigned more power than this. It's a privilege I suppose but one that demands caution and responsibility. People want to listen to me, whether they agree with me or not, and I'm not sure I'm strong enough to manage such a responsibility right now. I love being a writer but surely everything should just stop and I should spend what little time I have left with my dad?

Dad's having none of it, of course. "Fack orf," he said, "you'll do no such bleedin' thing. It's not a life, it's an adventure and yours is just beginning, Lizzie Lemalf. Go, enjoy."

Those were the exact words I stole and claimed as my own in response to Cassie, who immediately threatened to chuck in her internship. Despite her protests, we finally agreed that she would come home every weekend, when possible, and Simon and I would help her with the travel costs. Connor, my gorgeous little-big man that once was, just sneered at me. And it hurt far more than it should. Wordless, he shook his head and got up to leave. When I asked him where he was going, I was promptly told to leave him the hell alone.

Connor is taking this hard and I hate to admit it, but I'm pretty sure he blames me, for everything. He reminds me of Cassie and Maisy when they were his age. Thank god they've both grown up a bit, but they still give me grief and cause for concern. Cassie still looks far too thin and Maisy, virtually comatose, spends most of her days slouching around the house, hair scraped back, devoid of make-up, wearing the same baggy T-shirt. And I swear, the minute Crazee is mentioned, she disappears, bam, in a puff of smoke, like a magician's assistant. That's the thing about being a parent, the worry never stops. The worries change over the years, but they never stop.

I look up and see two young girls, probably around the same age as Connor, looking at me and giggling. A woman, sitting next to me, leans in and whispers that I was talking to myself, out loud.

'Unless, maybe you were on the phone?' she says peering across me, her intonation apologetic as though that were a possibility she hadn't thought of.

I shake my head and raise my eyes. 'No, you were right, I was talking to myself. Do it all the time and don't seem to be able to break the habit. Sorry.'

'Me too,' she confesses. 'Supposed to be a mark of genius,' she suggests.

We both have a little chuckle at this but I feel uncomfortable because I notice the two young girls now pointing at me and whispering to one another. I look round, grab a magazine from the seat next to me and hold it in front of my face but this only seems to add to their amusement.

Pretending to read, I sneak a look at the girls above the corner of the magazine. One of the girls, egged on by the other, gets up. She looks as though she is about to walk towards me. I'm both slightly alarmed and intrigued at the same time. I'm also very relieved when a buzzing noise from the digital screen at the front of the waiting room advises me I'm up next to see the doctor. I quickly stand up and place the magazine back on the seat next to me, and that's when I see it. My face, splashed across its glossy front advising the reader to turn to page twenty-four for an in-depth interview with me about my debut novel. My cheeks burn in response and I suddenly feel slightly ridiculous. I realise the girls were pointing at me because they recognised me. They probably only wanted to say hello, or tell me they think my book is shit. It's usually one or the other, but I still can't get used to people recognising me.

I sit down in front of my GP. Wearily handsome, he asks me what the problem is. I explain my continued nausea and constant fatigue. He asks me if I have any problems or if I'm dealing with anything particularly stressful at the moment and I laugh. I explain about Dad, my son, my ex-husband, my daughters and my new writing career and he asks a few more questions and takes my blood pressure. He then asks me about my sex life and I tell him to mind his own business. Unfortunately, he fails to see the humour in my response so I tell him the truth. The truth being I feel far too old and too tired for much in the way of hanky panky these days, and I don't think Simon feels a lot different.

'But you are still having sexual relations?' the doctor asks.

I think back to a couple of months ago and the last drunken fumble Simon and I shared before collapsing into exhaustion as we often do of late. I feel my cheeks glow but I'm convinced that's more to do with the core temperature of my menopausal body than any embarrassment felt. 'Yes, sometimes,' I reply.

'Hmmmmm. Do you use contraception?'

'No glove, no love,' I laugh. This usually never fails to raise a chuckle, but I'm not even awarded a flicker of a smile and the good doctor carries on regardless.

'Any other symptoms?'

I wrinkle my nose in confusion. 'No, not that I'm aware of? Well, I haven't had a period for a couple of months, and I keep having hot flushes, but as I'm fast approaching fifty I've put that down to the start of the menopause?'

'Hmmmmm.'

And another hmmmmm!

My GP passes me a small clear pot and asks me to pop to the toilet and pee in it.

'Okay, but why?'

'If you could just do as I ask Ms Lemalf, I'll have you out of here in no time.' The slight ripples of irritation in his voice tell me it's an order, not a request.

I skulk off to the toilet like a chastised child and return with a pot of yellow liquid. Doctor Brown takes it from me, unscrews the lid and places what looks like a strip of paper in it. He waits for a moment and asks me how the book is going. I like to think I'm modest in my boasting but another "Hmmmmm" rudely interrupts my mumblings.

Doctor Brown once again takes his seat opposite me. 'How old are you now Ms Lemalf?'

'Forty-nine,' I reply. 'Why?'

'Hmmmmm.'

Really? Another hmmmmm!

Doctor Brown takes a deep breath. 'Okay. I have to inform you, you're pregnant.'

I open my mouth and feel my jaw drop where it remains in situ for several seconds. 'What?' I finally manage to utter in disbelief. 'But ... But ... I can't be. I'm too old? I'm going through the menopause?'

'Evidently not. Now, I don't know how far along you are. We'll need to get you booked in with the nurse in the first instance.'

'But ... But ... I'm too old.' I repeat. 'So ... I'm not going through the menopause?'

Doctor Brown shakes his head. 'No,' he replies.

I feel as though I have just been thrown into a vat of ice cold water. Winded and barely able to catch my breath I find it almost impossible to speak, or think, for that matter.

'But I'm too old,' I whisper.

I stand up but Doctor Brown asks me to sit down again. His voice remains very matter of fact but his tone is slightly warmer, slightly kinder than it was a few moments ago. 'I take it this wasn't planned?' I shake my head. 'So, I assume you'd like a termination?'

'What? I don't, I don't know? Maybe? No, I mean, I don't know. I'm not actually sure?'

'Look, this is clearly a bit of a shock. I'll make an appointment for you to see the nurse and any questions you have, you can put to her. Would that be okay Ms Lemalf?'

I think the doctor is still talking to me but I'm not sure. How can I be pregnant? I put my head into my hands and shake my head.

'Ms Lemalf? Lizzie? Are you okay Lizzie? Would you like me to ring someone for you? Someone from home, to collect you?'

I quickly look up. 'No! No, it's fine. I'm fine. I'll be fine.'

'Look, given your age this is what's classed as a geriatric pregnancy, there's a more than average chance you could miscarry anyway.'

Geriatric? Who the bloody hell is he calling geriatric?

If's he's trying to reassure me, I'm finding very little comfort in his words. I open my mouth to reply but change my mind and close it again.

'Are you sure I can't ring someone for you?'

I shake my head again. 'No, I'm fine. I'll be fine.'

But I'm not.

Fuck. It never rains but it pours.

Chapter 15

THE LOVE MONKEY

Connor

I look at Robbo, who clamps his enormous mouth around the enormous burger he has just ordered. Half of its contents plop into the tray he holds underneath it whilst a thick mayonnaise moustache forms above his top lip.

'You eat like a pig,' I say.

'He looks like someone's just wizzed on his face,' the Rickmeister adds.

'He wishes,' Jake laughs.

'Piss off,' Robbo attempts to say through a mouthful of dead cow and lettuce leaves.

'For god sake Robbo, close your bloody mouth will ya. I don't want to see your chewed-up shit,' I say.

This only seems to make Robbo do it more. He tears off lumps of burger with his teeth as his jaw clamps open and shut whilst making a constant "nam-nam" sound.

'Pig,' I repeat.

'What, me?' someone that isn't Jake or the Rickmeister says. I look up and see Hayley Patterson smiling at me. She looks across at Robbo and wrinkles her nose, her cute, lovely, perfect little nose.

'Ugghh,' she says. 'I see what you mean.'

I use my elbow to knock Robbo.

'Ouch,' he replies, rubbing his side. 'Whacha do that for?'

'S'up Hayley?' I ask. Jake and the Rickmeister start sniggering but thankfully Hayley doesn't seem to notice, or if she does she doesn't give a shit.

She sits down next to me and looks at her friend. 'Get me a Frappuccino please babe, I'll be there in a minute, I just need to ask Connor a favour.'

'Only if you do Conman a favour back,' Jake snorts.

Hayley looks at Jake and shoots him a short, sarcastic smile.

'Co-mar!' another voice shouts. I turn and see Ruby and baby Andrew, well he's not really a baby coz he's about three years old now, I think, but he still seems like a baby to us.

Andrew jumps straight on my knee and shows me what he's holding. 'Look Co-mar, I got a new car,' he says.

'Hello Connor,' Ruby says. 'Hello boys,' she says looking at the lads. 'Ooh, and who's this?' she says smiling at Hayley. 'Is this your girlfriend, Connor?'

'No, I'm just Hayley,' Hayley replies.

'Well, it's very nice to meet you, just Hayley, and you should be Connor's girlfriend, he's a lovely boy.' I feel my face burn and know it's the same colour as the ketchup dripping from Robbo's burger. 'Connor, do me a favour will you sweetheart?' Ruby continues. 'Keep an eye on Andrew while I grab him something to eat and me a much-needed coffee?'

It's not really a question because Ruby has already walked off, leaving Andrew sitting on my knee and is now driving his new car across my face.

'Aww, he's so cute,' Haley says.

Not when he's driving his toy car across your cheek, he's not.

Andrew looks at Hayley. 'What's your name?' he asks.

'Her name's Hayley,' I reply.

'Do you love her Co-mar?'

I laugh, as does Hayley and feel myself go even redder when the lads start snorting again. 'No, course I don't, Andrew.'

Andrew turns to look at Hayley. 'Do you love him?' he points to me and asks. Hayley laughs again. 'Coz I can make you love him and I can make you love Hay-wee,' he says turning back to me.

I laugh nervously. 'I don't think you can, Andrew.'

'I can, I can.' Andrew jumps off my knee and folds his hands under his arms and starts making an ooohh ooohh sound. He takes it in turns to point from me to Hayley whilst speaking in a really comical deep voice. 'I can make you love her coz I'm the luuurve monkey,' he says. Hayley continues laughing as the boys throw themselves across the table in hysterics. Which only seems to encourage Andrew more.

'I. Am. The. Luuurve. Monkey,' Andrew states in between his ooohh ooohhs and hands under his armpits dance. 'You will love her and she will love you, coz I am the luuurve monkey. The luuurve monkey.'

'What's going on here, then?'

I look up and see Mum.

'Oh god, it's you, Mum!'

'Nice to see you too Connor,' she replies. 'Hello boys and oh now, who is this?' she asks, looking at Hayley.

'Hi, I'm Hayley. I was just about to ask Connor if he can help me with some revision for my last exam?'

'Ooohh-ooohh-ooohh. I'm the luuurve monkey,' Andrew repeats.

'I'm sure he can,' Mum replies. 'Are you Connor's girlfriend?'

'No, she's not my bloody girlfriend, okay. Will everyone stop bloody asking me that?'

Hayley gets up to leave. She looks pissed about something. 'I'll text ya later, Connor,' she says.

'No, no. It's okay, you don't have to leave, Hayley.'

'See you later,' she repeats.

'Don't leave on my account,' Mum says.

Hayley smiles at Mum and lifts her hand in a half wave. 'It's okay, I was just leaving anyway. Bye.' She turns back to me. 'Catch ya later, Connor.'

And with that she disappears.

'Thanks a bloody lot Mum.'

'Oh great, I've only just got here and already I'm in the wrong?'

'Hello Lizzie, looking good today,' Jake says leeringly.

Mum laughs. 'Thanks Jake, how are you?'

'I'm good, thanks. My mum told me to tell you she's read your book and she loves it.'

Mum opens her mouth to reply but I stop her. 'What *are* you doing here anyway?'

'Meeting Ruby, and Andrew,' Mum replies as Andrew now throws himself at her shouting "Wizzie, Wizzie."

'Oh for god sake, why here? Why not in some little coffee shop instead of this burger place?'

Mum shrugs her shoulders and says something about it being easier for Ruby to bring Andrew here than some fancy coffee shop. Mum knows I come here, though, I'm sure she does it to humiliate me.

'C'mon boys, let's go.'

The boys say goodbye to Mum and I say goodbye to Andrew. I'm glad to get away. I love Mum, but right now everything she says and does annoys the hell out of me. And she's so wrong about Grandad, I know who he really is and I know he's gonna be okay.

'Shit, your mum's a milf,' Jake says.

'Shut the fuck up, Jake.'

'I'd give her one,' he says thrusting his arms and hips backwards and forwards. 'Bet you would too, if she wasn't your mum.'

'You're a sick man, Jake.'

♥

Chapter 16

IT'S NOT A LIFE, IT'S AN ADVENTURE!

Lizzie

I look at the three lovely women sitting before me and wish I could tell them my shocking news. I could of course, if I felt so compelled. Jokes would be made; options would be discussed and reassuring arms would be placed around my worried shoulders. I would be temporarily relieved of my burden, but ultimately what would it change? Each one of these women has their own problems, their own crosses to bear. None of them need the added weight of my problems too. Anyway, the decision, about whether to keep the life growing inside me, is mine and mine alone. Simon's too, maybe?

'So, how is Uncle Teddy?' I ask a weary looking Aunt Marie.

She shakes her head and rolls her tired eyes. 'Worse!' she exclaims. 'I swear he's getting worse. I'm soooo grateful I found that charity group. Someone comes by once a week and gives me a break for a couple of hours.'

'Is it someone from the charity sitting with him now?'

Aunt Marie nods and pats her hair, several inches of grey roots clearly visible against the warm honey colour of the rest of her hair. 'Going to get my roots done after I'm finished here.'

'I'll watch Uncle Teddy while you get your hair done,' I offer.

Aunt Marie waves her hand dismissively. 'I'm fine, Lizzie love. You've got enough on your plate right now. You all have, in one way or another. I'll manage, always have, always will.' Aunt Marie smiles and the tone of her voice suggests this is not up for argument.

I look at Mum, although only a couple of years younger than her sister-in-law, Mum always looked a good deal younger, but not so much of late. Mum's smooth, plump face has aged rapidly in the last couple of weeks. Equally lined with worry and fatigue, both women look worn out.

'You two should have gone to a nice little teashop somewhere, had a proper break,' Ruby says to Mum and Aunt Marie. 'It's just easier for me to bring Andrew here, with the play area and everything. I can, well, you know, relax a little, without raised eyes and stares if he plays up a bit.'

'Not at all,' Aunt Marie replies. 'I'm just glad to be out, in fact, I might just consider bringing Teddy here and putting him in the play area next time I go shopping. I swear it'll be safer.'

'Oh dear,' Mum replies. 'What's he been up to now?'

Aunt Marie sighs, heavily, but still manages to smile nonetheless. 'Are you sure you want to know? It's not pretty?'

We all nod in the affirmative and Aunt Marie describes a shopping trip she and Uncle Teddy took last week.

'I needed a few bits, milk and bread,' she explains. 'I had a food shop on order to be delivered the next day but because Teddy seemed okay, and it was lovely weather, I thought, why not. What can really happen in a thirty-minute trip to the supermarket? Well, I certainly found out what, I'll tell you that for nothing!'

Aunt Marie says that while she was deciding which loaf to buy from the fresh bread section, Uncle Teddy disappeared.

'I knew I'd found him though,' she continues, 'when I heard music drifting across the aisles. It sounded like a piano and appeared to be coming from the Toy Department. Turns out it was Teddy playing a kids piano on display. 'Great Balls of Fire,' by Jerry Lee Lewis, of all songs! I think he thought he was at one of his gigs,' Aunt Marie says, rolling her eyes (Uncle Teddy having played piano in a number of pubs and clubs during his younger years). 'Course, he'd gone by the time I got there,' she continues. 'But not without scaring most of the children first, especially some of the younger ones. At least, that's what a rather amused onlooker said. Poor little things. I have to confess; some of them did look a bit dazed, a bit, shell-shocked. It was all their parents could do to convince them to uncover their ears. Mind you, with their wide-eyed, somewhat, vacant expressions, I'm not sure who looked more surprised, the children or their confused parents?

I do my level best not to laugh but the mental image I have of Uncle Teddy hammering the tiny keys of a kid's piano, singing loud and proud about his 'balls of fire' from the top of his lungs causes me to snort into my coffee. Aunt Marie, who shakes her head again, sighs heavily. She doesn't appear to be in the slightest bit offended, though.

She then goes on to explain how she overheard a customer telling one of the shop assistants that an old man in the clothing area had jumped out of the clothing rack she'd been happily browsing shouting "Pick me! Pick me!"

Maybe it's sheer relief from everything that's happened over the last couple of weeks, or maybe it's the way a perfectly poker-faced Aunt Marie delivers such a story of woe that only adds to its hilarity, but I start to laugh, hard, and it feels really good. The intellectual demise of poor Uncle Teddy is not a laughing matter and yet right now, at this very moment, we can all see the comedy amongst the tragedy of life. We all start to laugh and it's something so base and so instinctive, it doesn't feel anything less than fundamentally right to do so.

Aunt Marie then describes how the shop assistant now helping her look for Uncle Teddy, whom she explained had Alzheimer's, is then approached by another member of the public who thought it important to point out that someone appeared to be trying to make, and set fire to, a stack of Twiglets placed outside a tent, erected for display purposes, in the camping area of the Homeware Department. A supervisor then approaches them, saying she has had reports of an old man running around the store throwing packets of condoms into customer trolleys whilst loudly singing, 'How Deep Is Your Love.'

Mum is now laughing so hard, her face has turned red and she has to wipe the tears falling from her eyes. 'Did you find him?' she asks.

Aunt Marie tuts and rolls her eyes again. 'Eventually,' she replies drolly. 'After getting a call to the customer service desk, where it transpires that an old man had tried to reserve a banana, we finally located him in the toilets.'

'How did you find him there?' I somehow manage to ask through much guffawing.

'It was the general gasps of horror at the trail of blood from one of the food aisles to the toilets that gave it away I think.'

'What!' we all reply in confused unison.

'Well, as it turns out, it wasn't blood, it was tomato ketchup. Which was just as well really!' Aunt Marie adds, the tone of her voice very matter of fact.

'Just as well?' Mum repeats.

Aunt Marie shrugs her shoulders. 'Well, I was just grateful that we'd found him. It could have been worse.'

Aunt Marie's stoic outlook only pushes us all into further fits of laughter and I'm pleased to see she follows suit.

'How can you manage to laugh, and make it sound so funny?' Mum asks Aunt Marie.

Aunt Marie stops laughing and looks thoughtful. 'Because, it is funny, isn't it? Admittedly it wasn't so funny at the time, but afterwards when the dust had settled, I could see the funny side.'

'Wasn't it Mark Twain who said, "Humour is tragedy plus time?"' I add.

'Exactly,' Aunt Marie replies. 'That's what he would want anyway, Teddy I mean; he'd want me to see the funny side. That's how we've always got through the hard times.' Aunt

Marie turns to look at Mum. 'You know what I mean, Ellie? Salocin is just the same?'

Mum nods and a lone tear rolls down her cheek. She places a reassuring hand on top of Aunt Marie's and pats it. 'Absolutely,' Mum states. 'Abso-bloody-lutely. After all, it's not a life ...' Mum pauses.

'...it's an adventure!' Aunt Marie, Ruby, and I finish.

Aunt Marie heads off for her hair appointment and Mum leaves at the same time.

'And then there were two,' Ruby says looking at me.

'No, Mummy!' Andrew interrupts. 'It's free, Mummy. Look!' Andrew points at me. 'Wizzie, one,' he says, 'you is two, Mummy. And I am free!' he declares turning his perfectly pink, plump finger on himself. 'So not two, Mummy, is free!'

Ruby smiles at Andrew and scoops him up in her arms. She lifts up his T-shirt and blows several raspberries on his perfectly round pot belly. Andrew responds with infectious squeals of laughter and mock calls of protest.

'No, Mummy, top it! 'Top it, Mummy!' But of course, when Ruby does desist she is met with cries of 'again, again!'

For a moment, I'm reminded of my own sweet boy. Connor, before he became a "grunt in a hood" as Dad now likes to call him. I mourn the loss of my younger son and those moments of uncomplicated love.

'Make the most of it,' I tell Ruby, 'he'll be all grown up before you know it, then he won't be seen dead with you. Well, unless he wants to borrow some money, or needs a lift. Or food. Food seems to work with teenage boys.'

Ruby responds with a laugh and a shake of her head. 'Never!' she declares. 'My boy will always love me,' she states, blowing a final raspberry across a delighted Andrew's tummy.

'Yep, we'll see.' The delivery of my response is far more acerbic than I intended it to be and causes Ruby to look at me rather quizzically.

Ruby sends Andrew back towards the cushioned ball pool and I grab us another couple of coffees.

'He hates me,' I tell Ruby as I pass her a polystyrene cup of steaming hot coffee. 'Connor, I mean. He blames me for Dad getting ill.'

'I'm sure he doesn't.'

'I'm sure he does.'

'You know, I seem to recall having a similar conversation to this a couple of years ago. About the girls, when they were teenagers. Remember?' I smile a wry smile. I do remember. How could I possibly forget? I've written a whole survival guide for parents approaching that awkward stage with their own teenage daughters.

'And that hasn't turned out so badly, has it?' Ruby continues.

I shrug my shoulders. 'I'm not so sure.'

Ruby looks confused. And, because I've been so engrossed in my own worries and concerns of late it's only now I realise how tired my lovely friend looks.

'What do you mean? The girls aren't giving you any trouble, are they?'

'No, not purposely anyway.' I let out a heavy sigh. 'It's just …'

'Just what?'

I explain my concerns about Cassie's rapid weight loss and the mute lethargy of Maisy.

'Maisy, at least, owes us some kind of explanation about leaving Crazee and Australia.'

'She will, when she's ready,' Ruby replies. 'And Cassie? I suppose you need to keep an eye on her but maybe she's just got shit going on that she doesn't want to burden you with?'

'But I'm her Mum, if she can't tell me, who can she tell?'

Ruby's brow crumples into an amused frown that simply spells out one word, "Really?"

'I seem to remember there are plenty of things I know about you that your parents don't, Lizzie Lemalf.'

Sitting back, I feel my shoulders deflate, conceding that my oldest friend is, once again, correct. I run a tired hand through my equally tired hair and make some remark about the worries of parenthood never really leaving us.

Ruby nods in agreement. 'Yes, thank god I wasn't any older when I fell pregnant with Andrew. I know he's nearly four, but I was forty-six when I fell pregnant, can you imagine getting pregnant now? At our age? Fifty, and pregnant. Doesn't bear thinking about, does it?'

I shudder and instinctively cross my arms across my stomach. 'No, doesn't bear thinking about,' I hear myself repeat.

Ruby looks away, temporarily distracted by a message on her phone. I turn towards Andrew and smile. He is giggling with another little boy as they each take it in turns to throw coloured plastic balls in the air. I haven't told anyone about the pregnancy, not even Simon. This is my body and my choice, and I think I've made my decision. I'm going to get a termination. Only, as my gaze is once again drawn towards Andrew, I realise it's not an easy decision, not black and white.

Andrew, who is perched on the edge of the soft blocks surrounding the ball pool, spots me watching him and waves. 'Watch me Wizzie,' he shouts. After a count of three, egged on by his new friend, Andrew launches himself off the squidgy wall and dives back into the sea of coloured balls. Their tiny giggles of delight invade my thoughts and I find I'm suddenly racked with guilt. I look back at Ruby, in case perchance, she has read my thoughts, but am relieved to see she is still busy with her phone, clearly typing a response to a message. The sleeve of her long-sleeved T-shirt lifts slightly at her wrist to expose a rather large bluish, black bruise.

'What on earth have you done to your wrist?' I ask.

Ruby looks up from her phone. 'Oh this?' she replies holding her arm up and pulling her sleeve down. 'I'm officially getting old?'

'Sorry? What?'

Ruby's cheeks flush a little as she crosses then uncrosses her legs. 'Well, it's like this. I've developed a new skill set just recently.'

'Ri-ght. Which is?'

Ruby coughs to clear her throat. 'Okay, so, it takes real skill to choke on air, fall upstairs and trip over absolutely nothing. And I, I have discovered, appear to have those skills in abundance.'

I laugh, somewhat relieved. 'So you tripped over?'

'Yep, by the stairs. Don't even know how it happened? Anyway, look Lizzie, what was it you were going to ask me? I promised Harvey I'd be home by four o'clock. I'm cooking his favourite tonight. He's so tired when he gets in from work he likes me to have a meal ready for him.'

'Really?' I scoff. 'Since when did you become a domestic goddess? I know exactly what you would have said to Andy if he'd asked you to do that. Piss off and make your own!'

Ruby throws me a half smile. 'I know…' Looking thoughtful she trails off, her face etched with obvious pain. 'I do still miss him you know, terribly at times.'

I reach for my friend's hand and squeeze it, tight. 'I know you do. We all do. Simon still really misses him.'

Ruby nods her head and sniffs. 'They were the best of friends, weren't they? But …' she adds, 'Harvey is a nice distraction. Very different to Andy, bit stiffer. But he's been good to me. And to Andrew. They adore each other actually. Except if Andrew wants to get into bed with me at night, usually if he's ill. Harvey gets really pissy about it. He says Andrew is not a baby and I shouldn't treat him as such. And he's right, I suppose?'

I'm a little taken aback by Ruby's words. 'Sorry, what? Of course he's still only a baby. Well, not a baby, but you know, little. He's still little and for the first years of his life it has only ever been the two of you. Harvey needs to make allowances for that. And besides, every child, no matter what their age, wants their mum when they're ill. Even me!'

'You think?'

'I do.'

'Oh god, now I really do feel like shit,' Ruby says, placing her head in her hands.

'Why?'

Ruby looks up from her hands straight at me. 'It was awful,' she says shaking her head. 'The other night. Andrew wasn't well. Well, to be fair, I think he was just a bit overtired and sniffly, as did Harvey. But, as he's always done when he's not been well, he wanted to sleep with me. Harvey said no. Said he had to learn that I wasn't always at his beck and call. He made me leave Andrew – crying. He cried for two hours. Two hours. And now all I keep thinking is, why? Why did I let Harvey tell me what to do with my child? I still feel awful about it.'

I don't know what I'm more surprised about, that Harvey insisted Ruby do such a thing or that Ruby, of all people, allowed him. I raise my eyes and suggest his views are slightly extreme. 'Verging on Victorian,' I add. I look at Andrew's carefree, smiley face and I can't help feeling vaguely disturbed at the thought of him crying, for two hours. Concerned, I ask Ruby if everything is okay between her and Harvey?

Ruby looks at my anxious face as hers softens. 'Of course it is!' she replies. 'What an absurd question. He's an absolute darling, to both of us. Andrew adores him. We're all still trying to settle into a routine is all? And Harvey has never had children, so, well; it's not easy, is it? Look at you lot, for god sake. Both you and Simon had kids when you met but it still hasn't been easy, has it?'

I roll my eyes and shake my head. 'God no, still isn't, at times.'

'Exactly. So, you know precisely what I'm talking about.'

Unfortunately, I do understand and, what at first sounded quite sinister to my rather suspicious mind suddenly seems perfectly normal, amongst blended families, anyway. And most other families, I suspect.

'Anyway, what is it you wanted to ask me?' Ruby says glancing at her phone again. 'I really do need to get going soon.'

When I explain to Ruby that I'd like her to pop by and keep an eye on my ex-husband while I'm away doing bookish stuff during the summer, my best friend's rebuttal is every bit as spectacular as I'd imagined it would be.

'Are you kidding me? No! Abso-fucking-lutely not. No fucking way.'

In a way, I'm comforted by Ruby's response because, despite the fact she is still obviously, albeit quietly, grieving and still trying to find a comfortable niche with Harvey, it is evident my feisty, foul-mouthed best friend is still very much alive and kicking.

Chapter 17

GOOD FRIENDS AND BAD SECRETS

Cassie

Pulling my phone from my jeans pocket again, I check the time. Luke is late and if he doesn't get here soon he may as well forget it. I really do have to get back to work. I realise now, though, just how much I've been looking forward to seeing him again. It was only meant to be a quick coffee and a catch up but Luke always feels like the older brother I never had. I can always tell him everything and he never judges me. At least, he never used to.

Stretching my neck to see, I look again for Luke amongst the passers-by at the window. An older woman, probably about Mum's age, with long, sleek hair and far too much make-up hovers by my table. She balances a huge handbag in one hand and large white cup and saucer in the other. The place is heaving with people and she's clearly looking for somewhere to sit. She peers over at my now empty cup and gives me a snotty look. I look straight at her and force my lips into a sarcastic smile whilst tapping out a tune on the side of my cup with my metal spoon. The moody woman walks off and a flustered Luke plonks himself opposite me.

'Shit, sorry I'm late,' he says, pulling off his leather jacket and slinging it over the back of the chair. He looks straight at me and frowns. 'Shit, what happened to you Cas?'

'What?' I reply, looking down in confusion.

'That,' Luke continues, pointing at my forehead.

I raise my hand and tentatively touch the egg-shaped lump

on the side of my head. 'Oh yeah, that,' I reply, wincing from the pain of my touch. 'I forgot about that, did it yesterday.'

'How?' Luke asks.

I look down sheepishly. 'Walked into a lamppost.'

'What! How?'

I cough, then snigger. 'We-ll. I was on my way to work and did that thing everybody does.'

Luke grins, raising one eye questioningly. 'What thing?'

I cough again. 'Looking into the window of a parked car, that you think is empty, to check out your reflection. Only it wasn't empty but the window was blacked out so I didn't realise. So, there I was, busy pouting and pulling my hair into place when the bloody window wound down and the driver yelled "BOO!" at me. I jumped so hard I nearly wet my knickers. Didn't see the lamppost as I turned away, hit it head on, I did.'

Luke throws his head back in loud laughter.

'Wasn't funny!' I protest. 'Saw bloody stars, I did.'

Luke shakes his head and can't speak for laughing. I didn't see the funny side yesterday, but I do now, and I laugh along with him. We eventually pull ourselves together and I realise I haven't laughed so much in ages. It feels good.

'I don't know which was worse that day, the bump on my head or the sticky BO.'

Luke wrinkles his forehead. 'Sticky BO? What the hell is sticky BO?'

'Sticky BO,' I reply in a serious voice, 'is when you rush out of the house in the morning and spray your underarms with hairspray instead of deodorant. Only you don't realise until you get to work and it dawns on you, after a couple of hours stuck in a hot recording studio, that everyone is avoiding you and your arms are stuck by your sides!' Once again, Luke roars with laughter, and although it was embarrassing at the time I can't help but join in.

I look at Luke's worn leather jacket slung over the back of his chair, the one he bought during the last year of school and wore all through college where we studied music together. 'How can you wear that bloody thing, when it's so hot out?'

Luke winks at me. 'Because the girls love it.'

'Ooooohh err, listen to you. Bet Felicity doesn't like that?'

Luke shrugs his shoulders. 'It's only a bit of flirting, and besides, it's all part of being the front man of a band. You know that.'

'And a very good band and a very good front-man you are indeed.'

Luke smiles. 'We're not bad, are we?'

Luke offers to buy me another drink and wanders off to get us some. He comes back five minutes later and carefully places another frothy topped, chocolate sprinkled, coffee in front of me and tells me to catch as he throws a packet of sandwiches at me.

'Eat,' he orders. 'You're way too thin, and it doesn't suit you.'

I'm tired, dreamed all night again about giant blue fish. I don't feel particularly hungry but I'm surprised how much I actually enjoy the sandwich when I do start eating. Luke polishes off each half of his sandwich in three easy, man size bites, but I'm not that far behind him.

I don't have long, so I tell Luke everything (well, not everything) at a quick-fire pace.

I tell him about Dad.

Luke raises his eyes. 'Oh how the mighty fall, eh?'

'You should see the state of the place he's living in, nothing like the palace he came from. It's karma, I reckon.'

Luke looks at me and smiles; we both launch into several seconds of harmonising to Culture Club's 'Karma Chameleon.'

'Idiot,' Luke says to me.

'Loser,' I reply.

Then I tell Luke about Connor smoking weed and not knowing whether to tell Mum. Then I tell him about Grandad.

'Shit,' he replies. 'Lung cancer?'

And it still doesn't feel real, even when someone else says it. I feel my eyes fill up so I look down at my cup and fiddle with my spoon. Luke reaches across the table and grabs my hand. He rubs his fingers across mine and I notice how rough his fingertips feel; indented thick skin, forever changed from years of running them across the fat, wiry strings of his guitar.

'Why are you getting married?' I ask.

Luke grins at me and shrugs his shoulders. 'Because ...' He trails off for a minute. His cheeks turn a pinkish colour, quickly spreading across the rest of his face and down his neck. He stumbles over his words and suddenly he is the boy I went to school with, suddenly he is eight years old again. 'Because I love her, I guess?' he eventually manages to reply.

'You guess?'

'Well, no, not I guess, I know. But. Well, I suppose I'd be happy to wait a bit longer but Felicity seems set on sooner. And her dad's loaded, paying for the whole thing. Which is okay, I suppose. But he does want me to go and work for his company, have a proper job. And, you know, keep the music as a hobby.'

'No!' I yell. 'You can't do that, it's not a hobby, it's ... it's ... your life!'

Luke laughs at me. 'Calm down, Cas. Besides, we all have to grow up, eventually.'

I tell Luke that doing something that you love isn't about not growing up, it's about being happy.

'Even if it doesn't pay the bills?' Luke asks.

'But it will, in time. You have to give it time.'

Luke stares at me and I'm slightly surprised by the slight fluttering in my tummy. 'What are you staring at, loser?'

Luke's whole face breaks into a smile. 'You look so different, but at the same time exactly the same.'

'Different? Different how?'

Still grinning, Luke cocks his head to one side to study me. 'Do you know your nose wrinkles up when you frown?'

I touch my nose, the same Roman nose I inherited from Mum. I still hate it, despite my promise to the universe to try and be happy with it. But why does it have to be so bloody big! No cute little button nose, like Felicity, for me.

'You still haven't answered my question. Different how?'

'Plainer, I guess.'

'Oh great. So, I'm a plain Jane, thanks!'

'Nah, nah, nah,' Luke protests. I don't mean that you're plain, just that you've got rid of all that fake crap, lashes and hair extensions. And, well, you look better for it. More natural.'

'Felicity's very pretty.'

Luke looks thoughtful. 'Probably wears too much make-up but, yeah, yeah she is pretty. I done good. Speaking of which, how's Joe? Do you still see him? Did you get back together?'

I shake my head and laugh. 'Nah, despite his declarations of undying love for me when I went to uni, he quickly moved on to someone else. I see him now and again, when I go home, works as a car salesman I think? It's funny though, when I see him because, well … although he's still drop dead gorgeous to look at, I wonder what I actually saw in him. Do you know what I mean?'

Luke stares at me a little too long. 'Not really,' he replies. 'So, has there been anyone else? Anyone at uni?'

I shift uncomfortably in my chair not knowing whether to mention *him* or not. 'There was one boy, Nat, Nathanial Fitzroy,' I reply. I don't tell Luke that Nat was the most popular boy at uni. That, in effect, all I did was swap Joe for Nat and spend the next three years pining after someone who didn't even know I existed. Until that one drunken night earlier this year at a party. That was the night my heart skipped a beat and Nat's whispered promises led me straight to his bed. And for a very short while, less than an hour, I felt like the happiest girl in the world. I felt important and truly believed that all my painful waiting to be noticed by Nat had been worth every minute. And as he thrust himself into me and I arched in response, I honestly thought it was the start of something wonderful. Then he grunted as he came inside me, rolled off, grabbed his phone and started swiping either left or right as photos of various girls who had downloaded pictures of themselves on a dating app flashed up on his phone screen. I laughed, for a minute, thought he was winding me up, but he kept doing it. Then he thanked me for the shag and asked me to leave because he needed to get a good night's kip before his exam in the morning.

'And?' Luke asks.

I shrug my shoulders. 'And nothing really. Didn't work out. How did you propose?' I ask, changing the subject. 'Was it all romantic and shit?'

Luke laughs and shakes his head. 'She actually proposed to me.'

'Really?'

'Don't do that?'

'Do what?'

'Wrinkle up your nose all disapprovingly.'

I put my hand up and touch my nose, with its bump that I still hate. 'I'm not, I wasn't. I actually think that's brilliant. Why can't a woman propose to a man? Good for bloody her! Did you pick the ring then?'

Luke shakes his head again. 'Nope, she picked that too. Pointed it out after we'd been paid quite a bit of cash for a local gig, so I thought, why not? I am a bit ...' Luke trails off.

'You are a bit what?' I ask.

'I'm just a bit surprised how quickly she's arranging the wedding, next May I think it's gonna be but ...' Luke shrugs his shoulders again. 'Then again, why not?'

'Because, because, you're too young. And you need to keep doing your music. You're too talented not to give it a proper shot.'

Luke laughs at me again and reaches across the table to move the hair that has fallen across my eye. 'Let's not lose contact again eh Cas, it's been too long. And I love having you in my life. You mad, crazy girl!'

Luke tucks my hair behind my ear and lightly touches my face as he pulls his hand away. I quickly grab his hand back and place it on my cheek, pressing it hard into my soft flesh. I feel a strange sensation in the pit of my stomach and I imagine telling him everything that's happened to me just recently, but I don't, though. Just like when I was with Mum, I stop myself.

I always believed I could tell Luke anything, but now I realise I can't.

I know I can't tell anyone.

Chapter 18

THAT'S WHAT FRIENDS ARE FOR

Lizzie

After much protest on her part and much persuasion on mine, I managed to convince Ruby to pop by once a day to check up and keep an eye on Scott for me over the next couple of weeks. Her anger towards my ex-husband was somewhat amusing and her loyalty towards me very reassuring.

'What!' she'd exclaimed. 'You want me, after everything that scumbag has put you through, to keep an eye on him? To look out for his welfare? Are you crazy?'

I did my best to calm my best friend down and explain.

'He's still the father of my children, Ruby, and he is still part of their life, and what with Dad's illness and everything. Well, Connor is not taking it at all well. He's really angry. I know Simon has been great with Connor over the years but it's Dad who has been the constant male figure in his life. The last thing Connor and Cassie need to see is their dad having a breakdown, too. Besides, I do actually feel quite sorry for him. He even apologised to me.'

'So he fucking should!' Ruby replied lifting her phone from her bag to check the time again. 'Andrew?' she called for the third time. 'Where are your shoes darling?' Andrew shrugged his shoulders and blissfully continued to throw coloured balls back into the ball pool he'd taken them from. 'How come he can find the tiniest bit of finely chopped onion in his food but he can't find his shoes?' Ruby mumbled.

'So, you'll do it then Ruby? You'll check on Scott for me?'

'Found them,' Ruby replied waving a tiny pair of blue trainers in the air. 'Andrew, come and get your shoes on darling. We need to get home. Harvey is coming home early today.'

'Yay, Har-vey, Har-vey,' Andrew replied, climbing out of the ball pit and running towards Ruby.

Ruby looked at me, her eyes narrowing with suspicion. 'Is this a test? Are you testing me?'

To say I was a little thrown by such a question was somewhat of an understatement. 'Don't be so bloody ridiculous Ruby. It's nothing of the sort. I told you why I want you to check on Scott.'

'Does he know about Lilly? Did you, have you told him?'

'Who is Lilly, Mummy?' Andrew interrupted.

'No-one, darling. Well, she was someone. Someone very special and if she was still here she would have been your big sister.'

Andrew's already big eyes widened in surprise. 'My sis-ter? I have a big sis-ter?'

Ruby looked at me, her expression one of twitchy alarm. 'If she was here, she would have been.'

'Where is she, Mummy?'

'She became very poorly, darling. And …'

'And had to go to heaven,' I added. Ruby having opened a can of worms she obviously hadn't meant to.

Ruby sighed heavily and placed a weary hand on her forehead. Andrew, by then sitting on Ruby's knee whilst she put his shoes on, ceased his wriggling and twisted his head round to look at his mother. His expression was one of sweet concern as he cocked his head to one side and placed his little hand on top of Ruby's head.

'Mummy got an-urrver headache?' he asked.

Ruby looked at Andrew and smiled, pulling his hand away from her head to kiss it. 'Go on,' she said lifting him from her knee, 'go and say goodbye to your friend.' Ruby turned back to me. 'I'm sorry, I understand. I'll do it. It's just, well, you know,

I nearly lost you because of all that shit with Scott. And I don't ever want to risk losing you again.'

Relieved, I smiled at my lovely friend. 'We've talked about that, several times,' I reminded her. 'You know it's all water under the bridge. And besides, I'm not going anywhere. We've been through too much and been friends for too long to ever let anything jeopardise it again.'

'I know,' Ruby smiled. 'I'm only doing this for you though, I still think Scott's a bloody wanker!'

Chapter 19

MIRROR, MIRROR ON THE WALL

Lizzie

Hovering by the stairs, I'm aware time is passing and I need to get dressed. I think everything is sorted, no thanks to the kids. All three of them have remained in their rooms for the entire morning. I can almost forgive Connor, he is a teenager, after all, but why do the girls revert to being teenagers when they're home? Oh well, we have enough booze to sink a battleship, Mum has made fresh coleslaw and a pasta salad and Ruby is bringing dessert. We should have more than enough. Heavy footsteps above my head break my train of thought. A door swings open and I look up. Connor staggers into the hallway. His shock of blonde hair stands on marathon-sleep-induced-end. Bleary eyed, wearing boxer shorts and a T-shirt that has seen better days, he stretches his mouth open to yawn before reaching inside his boxers to scratch his obviously itchy balls. I cough loudly and he turns around, immediately withdrawing his hand from his boxers.

'Bloody hell, Mum,' he exclaims.

'Good afternoon, Connor,' I reply. His unintelligible grunt makes very little sense. Something about my purposely making him jump, I think. Using the same hand that seconds ago was scratching his balls, he now rubs his eyes and mooches off towards the bathroom. I remind him our guests for the barbeque will be arriving shortly.

'Okay,' he replies, wandering back towards the top of the stairs 'Do you need any help getting shit, I mean stuff, sorted?'

'No thank you. It's all done,' I reply, unable to suppress the slight exasperation in my voice.

'Okay, sweet. Oh, and Mum?'

'Yes, Connor?'

'I'm … well … I'm sorry I've been a moody git lately. It's just what with Grandad and stuff …' Connor, unable to finish his sentence, falls silent using one hand to scratch his head, the other to tap the bannister.

'I know, baby,' I reply reassuringly.

'I still love you and shit.'

'I know you do. I love you too.'

Connor smiles. 'Oh, ummm, also, would it be okay if a couple of my friends smoke?'

'Smoke what?'

'Fags!' Connor replies defensively.

I tell him I'm not happy to condone smoking, especially considering Grandad's diagnosis, but if they must, can he please make sure they limit their smoking and to make sure they only do it in the shed. This is followed by a smile and a grunt and a slam of the bathroom door quickly followed by the sound of running water and the loud wailing of something supposed to resemble music, I think.

Climbing the stairs, I'm vaguely aware of the dull ache at the base of my spine and the small marching band in my head. Why did I suggest having a barbeque today? I still need to get my shit sorted for the book signings and fairs fast approaching. My head is all over the place and I'm not sure I'm up to playing the hostess with the mostess. I know, though, deep down, why I'm doing it of course. I'm afraid. Dad is living on borrowed time and somehow, in between paying the bills and the everyday living I want to make the most of the time we have left.

I finish applying my make-up and stare at the reflection in the mirror. I'm repulsed at the haggard face staring back at me. More powder is needed to seal the foundation covering the cracks of my aging face. Picking up an over-large brush I wave it like a wand across my cheeks and nose. Sadly though, this wand is not a magic wand and fails to miraculously transform me. No amount of foundation can hide the crevices becoming more obvious every day. The slightly delicate lines above my lips are the worst. Not immediately noticeable, at least not first thing in the morning, but slap on a bit of lipstick and within a few hours I am left with tiny rivers of blood leading from my mouth to the base of my nose. Threads of colour seeping and creeping along miniscule gaps where they remain stubbornly embedded, no matter how hard I rub them. Then there are the lines around my eyes, of course. Laughter lines, Simon calls them. Haven't laughed much lately, though.

Pulling child-like faces, I use the finger and thumb of each hand to stretch and lift the sagging skin around my eyes. After several seconds, I admit defeat and let go again. Reaching for my reading glasses and leaning into the mirror, I decide to take a closer inspection. It's a bad idea and one that finds me stumbling backwards, horrified at the clarity of my aging skin. Huge pores, the size of craters, sit in clustered groups around my deflated cheeks. So, this is why one's eyesight fails as one gets older, it's nature's way of protecting one from the shock of the mirror. On second inspection though, the crow's feet are not actually that bad. I suppose, one does get used to them, eventually. What is more alarming is the ability of said wrinkles to spread and multiply, just by the simple act of smiling. Oh well, there's an easy solution to that, I simply won't smile any more, and given recent events that shouldn't prove too difficult.

Licking my finger and using it like an eraser, I rub vigorously at the two frown lines above my nose. It does nothing to improve their trench like appearance and I'm pretty sure I'm making my headache worse in the process.

How the hell can I be pregnant? I'm too old! I wouldn't mind, but we barely have sex these days. Too bloody tired. And

I'm too bloody old! How can a woman still get pregnant at my age? It's insane. What the hell was Mother Nature thinking?

Alarmed, I swing round as Simon wanders into the bathroom. Knowing my propensity to talk to myself out loud, often without realising it, I'm not entirely sure Simon hasn't heard me. He hovers behind me but the mirror in front of us merely reflects his bemused smile.

'What are you doing?' he asks.

Reluctantly, I lean into the mirror again, this time using my finger and thumb to pinch the same frown lines. I pinch and hold, pinch and hold for several seconds before ironing the lines back out again. I repeat this procedure several times as Simon looks on.

'It's supposed to help,' I reply.

'With what?'

'With these,' I respond, using my finger to stab at the deep fissures lodged between my eyebrows.

Simon raises his eyes and smirks. 'I didn't realise you were so vain?'

'I'm not! It's just that, well, with all these book signings, people get a little too close for comfort. See too much of me. They'll realise what an old hag I am.'

My efforts to massage, pinch and smooth away the deeply dug trenches above my nose have reaped little reward.

'Oh, sod it!' I declare. 'Sunglasses it is.'

'You're going to wear sunglasses, to do book signings?'

'Why the hell not?'

Simon moves up closer and presses himself into me. 'You do know you are officially mad, right?' He wraps both his arms around me and rests his chin on my shoulder. His reflection smiles at my reflection that bounces off the very same mirror that has been my tormentor for the last couple of minutes. Simon continues to look at me, at us, folding his hands across my tummy. He squeezes, a little too hard. 'And you do know I love you, mad or not?'

I smile back at Simon's reflection but it's a forced smile. I criss-cross my arms to hold onto his. His skin feels clammy and he smells of fresh sweat after his run. I try to swallow the lump forming in my throat as tears swell at the back of my eyes. I look down so Simon doesn't see me.

How many more tears can I cry, for fuck's sake?

I use all my strength to fight them back.

'I know you're worried about your dad, but, you know I'm here for you. Right?' He squeezes me affectionately, but it's all too much. I'm conscious of my stomach and its content and I can't stand Simon next to me. I pull away.

'I love you too,' I reply.

There's briskness in my voice, though, and Simon looks hurt. 'Why do you keep doing that?'

'Doing what?'

'Pulling away from me all the time?'

'I don't, I'm not. I just need to finish getting ready. Everyone will be here in a minute and I've still got loads to do.'

Simon raises his eyes and shakes his head. 'Okay, Lizzie. Have it your way.' His tone is one of annoyed resignation. He watches me as I slip past him and into the bedroom.

'Sorry, I just feel a little nauseous again.'

'And that's normal, is it? To keep feeling sick all the time? What exactly did the doc say to you Lizzie? You still haven't really told me?'

That I'm pregnant for god sake! Old and pregnant. And you did it to me. Is that what you want to know? Could you handle it if I told you!

I know he cares but Simon's tone is almost condescending. He talks to me like a father talks to a petulant child. Unintentionally though, it makes me think of Dad and once again tears threaten to disrupt my fake calm exterior.

I wave one hand dismissively, using the other to open the door of the wardrobe. 'Oh I don't bloody know. He said something about trying HRT,' I lie. 'I've made another appointment to go back and see him next week.'

'Yeah, well. I may just come to that appointment. See if they can't sort something out,' Simon mumbles in response.

'No.' I protest. 'It's fine. I'm fine.'

The slight lift in my voice is enough to alert Simon that something is wrong. He looks at me, his eyes narrowing in suspicion.

'You're far too busy,' I continue. 'I'll sort it.'

Simon's eyes bore into me. He doesn't say a word but the expression he wears tells me I've been rumbled. Every line, every frown, every twitch of his face tells me he knows something is wrong.

'I will!' I exclaim. 'I'll sort it.' I laugh nervously and decide distraction is my best tactic. I hate lying to him but I can't bear telling him the truth. Not yet, anyway. I look away from his suspicious eyes and begin shunting clothes hangers back and forth in search of something to wear.

'What the bloody hell am I going to wear?' I mumble. I hope and pray if I stay there long enough Simon will just piss off. I hear movement and the sound of clothes being discarded and when I turn around Simon is sitting on the edge of the bed wearing just his boxers. His legs are still very dark and hairy but his slight chest hair, once the same colour, is now greying. He looks good for a man close to fifty years old, though.

'Shouldn't you get showered?' I ask.

Simon mumbles something I don't catch and hangs his head in his hands. He rubs his face, hard, then looks up and smiles. It's a forced smile and he looks as worn out as I feel. He voices his concerns about Maisy and explains that his reasons for not addressing her elopement from Australia are not because he had his head in the sand, as I accused him of the other day, it was simply that he believed she was having a moment. A blip. That after a week or two away from Crazee, Maisy would be back on the next plane out to Oz.

'Have you heard from him? Crazee, I mean?' Simon asks. 'Has he tried to contact you?'

I shake my head. 'No. You?'

'No,' Simon replies. 'I have tried his number a couple of times but it just rings then cuts off.' We both agree we need to speak to Maisy. 'And Cassie too,' Simon adds. 'You're right, she has lost a lot of weight.'

I feel both alarmed and relieved at the same time.

'I've been thinking about it though. Cassie is a lot like you. Can't eat when she's distressed.' Simon pauses for a moment to let his eyes wander up and down my half-dressed body. 'If I'm honest, aside from looking a little gaunt in the face, I'm surprised you haven't lost more weight?'

'Thanks a lot!'

That's because I have put on weight, baby weight! Oh god. I must stop thinking that. It's not a baby. Not yet.

'No,' Simon says holding his hand up like a stop sign. 'I mean that in a good way. I'm pleased. I worry when you start losing weight because I know it means you're stressed. Unlike me,' he says standing up, slapping his slightly rotund belly like a drum, 'who is the complete opposite and puts it on just as easily as you lose it.'

I laugh. 'And what a fine belly it is. Andy would be proud.'

Simon raises an eyebrow and smirks. 'He would, wouldn't he? Anyway, getting back to Cassie, maybe she's struggling with the job? She hadn't even finished uni before she started working there. And now with your dad and everything ...' Simon trails off, as if mentioning Dad too often is a mortal sin.

Wandering over to the bed I sit down next to him, taking his hand in mine. 'Thanks,' I say. He smiles, leaning in to kiss the top of my head. We agree we need to speak to both the girls, but not today. Then, much to my relief, Simon heads back into the bathroom and turns on the shower. Listening intently, I hear the water splash against the bath. The dispersed interruption of the flow signifies Simon is safely ensconced in his watery cocoon, and I breathe a sigh of relief.

Still sitting on the edge of the bed, I hold my head in my hands trying to work out what exactly it is I feel. Angry? Scared? Weepy, about everything. I still can't believe I'm pregnant. How? How the fuck can I be pregnant, at my age?

The nurse was nice enough, when I went to see her, a couple of days after my GP visit. At least twenty years younger than me, she was sympathetic, I suppose. But very matter of fact. She explained I had *options* but also pointed out there was every possibility I could miscarry, given my age.

Geriatric my arse!

'Maybe you should consider discussing this with your partner?' she'd suggested when I'd confessed I hadn't.

And maybe you should piss off.

My blood pressure was taken, I pissed in another pot and the nice nurse with the cold hands examined my tummy. Then papers were shuffled and notes were tapped onto a tired old keyboard to update the computer screen displaying my patient details, in toxic green of all colours. After which, the nice nurse stopped, and gave me her full and undivided attention. We talked options.

'Would you like to continue with the pregnancy?' the nurse asked.

'Not an option,' I replied.

And so we talked termination, except, I noticed, every time I mentioned the word abortion she kept referring to the procedure as a termination. To terminate or to abort, I couldn't decide which terminology was worse. To terminate, in my mind, means to end and abort means to abandon. For some ridiculous reason, because it doesn't change a bloody thing, I decided that to end, or to terminate, was better than to abandon, or abort. So, like the nurse I no longer talked of abortion, but of termination. I was advised that there are two options open to me.

One is a medical termination, which involves taking medicines to end the pregnancy; the other is a surgical termination which involves a minor operation that can be carried out while I am awake or sedated. As the gestation of my pregnancy is less than ten weeks (I am approximately six weeks) the nurse and I agree that a medical termination is the best option for me.

'It'll just be like having a heavy period,' the nurse informed me. Her tone was reassuring but I found little comfort in her words.

An appointment was made for me to attend the hospital next week. It was explained that I would pop a pill on the first day then return on the following day to have two different pills shoved up inside me. Or, as the nice nurse phrased it, placed inside my vagina. The first pill, on the first day, I was informed, which may cause some nausea or vomiting and some slight bleeding, works by blocking the hormone progesterone. Without progesterone, the lining of the uterus breaks down and the pregnancy cannot continue. On the second day, the second lot of medication is placed inside me, which will make my womb contract, causing cramping and bleeding, similar to a miscarriage.

Looking down, I cup and hold my stretch-mark scarred stomach with both hands. I swear I feel a slight flutter. Is it movement from the life forming inside me? Surely not? I know it's too early, therefore not possible so it must be wind. Yes, that would explain it; trapped wind is what it is. Biting my bottom lip, I try and fight the tears building behind my eyes, but they come anyway. They are surprisingly hot as they scurry down my face. I quickly wipe them away, knowing full well they are now ruining my carefully applied mask. Why? Why does it feel as though everything is falling apart?

Six very short weeks ago, life was good. Simon and I celebrated my three-book publishing deal with drunken sex,

Maisy was in Australia, Cassie looked well, and Dad? Six weeks ago, Dad wasn't dying and I wasn't pregnant. The success of my book marches on, though, and I wonder at the bitter-sweetness of life. It's not the end of the world, not really, but why does it feel like it is. My thoughts are interrupted by the hapless whining Simon calls singing, coming from the shower. Something from the eighties, I think, possibly Rick Astley's 'Never Gonna Give You Up'? It's hard to tell. He sounds happy, though. I listen for a minute and laugh, until his happiness annoys me.

I'm filled with a sudden rage because I realise I want to stand in the shower and sing without a care. I don't want to worry about our children or think about my dying dad and I don't want to think about ridding myself of the life growing inside me. Why? Why does it feel like it's all sitting on my shoulders? I know Simon would support whatever decision I make, but ultimately, like most women, I'll be left with the consequences. An abortion, termination, call it what you will, it's me that must live with the guilt. Simon can merely shrug his shoulders. One step removed, ultimately, it's my decision, not his. I know I don't want a baby. But it's still me that has to make that decision. It's me that must go through the forced physical discharge.

Massaging my tear stained cheeks with the palms of both hands, I pace the bedroom like a restless dog waiting for its owner to return. Romeow, who has been sleeping in the middle of our bed with his tail tucked under him, seems to sense my anxiety and lifts his lazy head. He looks at me and lets out a gentle meow. Sitting down next to him, I stroke him. He purrs loudly in response.

I remember the day Dad and I went to collect Romeow as a kitten. The sheer look of surprise on the faces of Cassie and Connor when we brought him home was priceless. Like the rest of us, though, Romeow has aged, but I like to think he's had a good life. As if reading my thoughts, Romeow nudges my hand. I stroke him in response and find it mildly comforting as I remember my children, small and giggly, wondering if I can do it all again, if keeping the baby growing inside me is an option. For the briefest of moments, I seriously consider going through with my pregnancy. I smile as I remember Cassie and Connor as babies, and then it hits me again, hard, like it has many times this week. I'm forty-nine years old, for fuck's sake. I can't, I really can't do the sleepless nights and nappies again. I'd be a pensioner by the time the baby was Connor's age.

I stand up again, much to Romeow's disapproval, suddenly stronger and determined. Why do I have to be so emotional anyway? It's just a procedure, and one many women go through. There's barely anything there at the moment anyway. The nurse as good as told me so.

'It's just cells,' she said. 'At this early stage, the pregnancy is not really a baby. Not at the moment.'

I imagine cells inside me, dividing and multiplying to create new life, whilst the cells inside Dad divide and multiply to destroy life.

I feel nauseous again, my head thumping. I'm so tired. I feel as though I could sleep for days and yet when I try to, at night, my ever-whirring mind won't let me. Walking back towards the bed again, I curl up into a ball next to Romeow. I bury my head into the duvet and sob uncontrollably.

I don't want to be an adult.

I want to be a child again. Where life is black and white.

I hate all the colours in between.

Now I'll definitely have to do my make-up again.

Chapter 20

FUNNY OLD LADIES

Connor

The handle to the shed door slowly turns. Thank god I locked it. 'Who is it?' I shout. Muffled giggling drifts under the door and I wonder if it's Cas, only it doesn't sound like Cas. Maisy, maybe?

'Can we come in?' a familiar voice asks.

'Shit, It's my bloody nan!' I exclaim. 'Robbo, put that dooby out NOW!' Robbo looks at me, grinning, as smoke escapes from the corner of his mouth. The Rickmeister grabs the spliff from Robbo's hand, takes another quick drag then stubs it out, placing it in the sacred tin. I grab the deodorant can out of my bag and spray the shed to within an inch of its life, manically wafting my hands around like some demented ballerina. Everyone starts coughing and I realise I've sprayed way too much deodorant. Jake unlocks the door and we all fall out of the shed, desperate for some fresh air.

We are greeted by my smiling nan and Aunt Marie. 'Hello boys,' Nan says. 'Ooh, smells very nice in there,' she continues as she sticks her head inside the shed. To my surprise, Nan asks us for a smoke.

'But, you don't smoke?' I reply.

'Aunt Marie used to,' Nan says.'

'When?'

'About forty years ago.'

'What? And she just happens to fancy a smoke now, forty years later?'

Nan explains that Aunt Marie is a little stressed right now. 'As am I, so I'll have one, too.'

'Did you used to smoke as well, when you were younger?'

Nan shakes her head. 'Nope, but I know I could do with one right now.'

We all follow Nan and Aunt Marie back into the shed. I explain that we only have baccy and Rizlas so they'll have to wait a minute while we roll them one.

'Or they could have a drag of the one we've already made,' Jake suggests, tapping the sacred tin.

Panicking, I look at his huge grinning face. 'No. Jake.' I reply through gritted teeth, 'we'll make them a new one.'

'Oh, don't roll a new one just for us,' Nan replies, 'we're not fussy.'

Before I know it, Jake has lifted the spliff from the tin, lit it and passed it to Nan and Aunt Marie.

Aunt Marie takes a drag then pulls a strange face. 'Tastes different to how I remember,' she says, expertly blowing smoke from her mouth as if it was something she did all the time.

Aunt Marie passes the dooby to Nan who drags heavily on it and then starts to choke. I pass her my can of fizzy shit, which she greedily drinks then, to my surprise, I watch as Nan takes another huge drag. Jake, Robbo, the Rickmeister, and I all look at one another. We each wear the same look of horror as we watch the spliff get smaller and smaller. I tell Nan that I think I can hear someone calling her and somehow, we manage to push the two very high, very giggly, old ladies out the door.

'Shit man,' Robbo says, 'your nan rocks.'

I can't help thinking there may be hell to pay for this later but that doesn't stop me laughing my arse off.

Chapter 21
LIFE

Lizzie

Andrew and I lead the way and Ruby follows close behind. I can't believe they're leaving already. This is not turning out to be the nice little get together I had hoped for.

'I don't want to go home, Wizzie,' Andrew says, looking up at me. I look down and smile; his big brown eyes are wide and questioning.

I hear Connor and his friends, sniggering again, as they crash into the kitchen in search of more food. Covert, they think, muttered declarations of needing to leave at four-twenty followed by guttural bursts of stifled laughter.

'Am I missing something?' Ruby asks. I swing round to look at my lovely friend and realise how tired she looks. 'What's with all the references to four-bloody-twenty?'

Pointing to Andrew, I sigh and roll my eyes. 'I'll explain another time,' I whisper.

There's more crashing behind us and I'm just about to shout out to Connor and his friends when Mum and Aunt Marie stumble into the hallway. Their tired, haggard faces have morphed into girlish giggling ones.

'Your Aunt Marie needs the loo. And I do too!' Mum declares. 'She's had too much Prosecco.'

'More like too much shed,' Aunt Marie replies drolly.

Ruby looks at me, grinning. 'Are they, stoned?' she whispers.

I raise my eyes and shake my head. 'I'll kill Connor,' I reply. 'I told him his friends could use the shed to smoke in.'

'Ah be Jaysus and so they are,' Aunt Marie replies. For some reason her accent has changed to an Irish one and she looks equally as surprised by this as we all are, which only leads to more giggled outbursts. 'I always smoked when I was a young woman,' she continues. 'Don't remember it feeling this good though.'

And with that, Mum pushes Aunt Marie up the stairs. Ruby and I watch in awe at the struggled ascent of the two cackling hyenas, who may as well be attempting Everest, given how long it actually takes them to reach their summit. Ruby and I look at one another and we, too, burst into laughter. We briefly reminisce about the time Ruby took me to Amsterdam just after Scott left the kids and me. We talked about how we avoided men, got drunk and smoked pot. And of how, slowly but surely, with Ruby's help, I found my way back to the land of the living.

I suggest that perhaps a trip to Amsterdam is something we should repeat. Ruby laughs again and it's good to see her happy. She hasn't really been herself since Andy died. Harvey seemed to help for a while but lately she seems withdrawn again.

I weave my fingers through Andrew's silky soft hair and tell Ruby to make the most of him. 'Enjoy him while he's still young, it passes too quickly.' Andrew reaches up and pats down his ruffled hair with a spread-eagled hand of fat fingers before flashing me a gorgeous smile. 'Do you really have to go?' I ask again. Ruby's smile fades and she looks away, rummaging in her bag for her keys. 'After all, surely what's done is done? It was an accident after all and rushing home now won't get it sorted any quicker?' Ruby looks up at me again, her expression one of pained uncertainty. 'It's, well, sort of funny. In a way, isn't it?' I continue.

Ruby shakes her head and her bouncy brown curls dance in response. I smile but she doesn't smile back, if anything she looks pissed at me and I find a nervous laugh escaping from the corner of my mouth.

'It's not funny Lizzie. It's going to cost a fortune to put this right.'

'Well, a new hob and a new laptop,' I declare. 'It's not exactly a fortune and it's not like you can't afford it?'

'I'm sorry Mummy,' Andrew apologises again.

Ruby's face immediately crumples in concern and she falls to her knees to comfort Andrew. 'It doesn't matter baby,' she says stroking the fat cheek of her son. 'You must remember not to switch things on, though, without checking with Mummy first, okay?'

'O-kay Mummy.'

'Good boy,' Ruby says as she gets to her feet again. She looks at me and forces the corners of her mouth to lift into a smile, but she doesn't mean it.

I know it's annoying but it's just a bloody accident as far as I can see. One of those things. And Harvey is as much to blame as Andrew. Yes, I agree Andrew shouldn't have played with and twisted the knobs of the halogen hob in their kitchen but by the same token, Harvey shouldn't have placed his laptop on it. It's a huge kitchen for god sake, why place his laptop there? If nothing else, it's funny. Andy would have seen the funny side of it and so would Ruby, once upon a time. And unlike Harvey, Andy wouldn't have even phoned Ruby. He would have turned up here as planned, and told us all what happened. And he would have laughed and so would we. All of us would have laughed about it because, at the end of the day, it's not that big a deal, it's not the end of the world.

I smile back at my friend and wonder where the gregarious, easy-going woman I have known for most of my life has disappeared? I know Ruby grieved for a long time after Andy died, even I still grieve for him, but she doesn't seem the same of late. I thought Harvey would be good for her, bring the light back into her eyes. And he did, for a while. But lately she seems anxious and distant. I ask her if everything is all right and she just shrugs her shoulders and says the insurance money paid out to her after Andy's death isn't going as far as she hoped, which, even given Ruby's expensive taste and generosity, I am a little surprised about.

The splintered sound of breaking glass catches my attention, quickly followed by a collective chorus of deep voiced 'whoas' rising and filling the air. I realise something has been accidently, or deliberately, smashed. Trying to ignore it, I turn back to my friend, deciding now is not the best moment to question her. Instead I place my hand on Ruby's shoulder and squeeze it. 'Andy would be so proud of you both, you know?'

Ruby places her hand on mine and pats it gratefully. A sharp pain travelling deep into my groin takes me by surprise and causes me to gasp. The short, sharp shot of agony gives way to a dull ache that sees me grasping my stomach and Ruby's face contorting into crumpled lines of worry.

'Lizzie! What on earth is the matter?'

I wave my hand dismissively. 'It's nothing, indigestion I think!'

I'm touched by her concern but once again my attention is drawn to other goings on around the house. More boyish, rambling guffaws of 'four-twenty' emanate from the garden and raised, angry voices drift from the kitchen. Ruby and I look at one other, listening intently.

'The girls,' we both say in unison.

'You haven't seen them both in a while, how do you think they both look?'

'Honest answer?' Ruby replies. I nod my head. 'Well, like shit actually.' I laugh. The focus, thankfully, safely shifted from me. 'I mean, she was always slim but Cassie is skin and bone since I last saw her. And Maisy? Well, she just looks like she doesn't give a shit, about anything, especially herself.'

I nod, somehow comforted that my best friend's observations match mine. That I am not going slightly mad (although, granted, it would be a short trip) and that there is – must be – more to Cassie's weight loss than simple diet and more to Maisy's melancholy than her separation from Crazee.

Once again Cassie's voice interrupts our conversation. Shrill, she reminds me of the tormented blackbird who frequents our garden, when a prowling Romeow is scaring him off. Maisy shouts back in response to Cassie's raised voice and I am immediately transported back to the angst-ridden years of my teenage daughters.

'You are not the boss of me, Maisy!' Cassie declares.

I roll my eyes and sigh heavily.

Did I? Did I really reminisce about those erratic and volatile days with my daughters? Did I actually believe I missed them, missed their noise, their mess, and their sulky, surly indifference?

Dad walks into the hallway and, seeing Ruby and I stood still like statues, also pauses to listen. Farting noises and guttural guffawing comes from one direction and a spat of high pitched, choice words from another. Dad grins and points upwards saying he is nipping to the loo.

'Good luck with that,' Ruby replies.

Dad frowns. I explain that Mum and Aunt Marie are already up there. 'They snuck off down the shed earlier for a smoke with the boys and now they seem to be, how shall I put it, very high on life.'

Dad's serious face morphs into a huge grinning one. He chuckles to himself as he ascends the stairs, bidding goodbye to Ruby. 'Say hello to Harvey for me,' he says.

'I will. Thanks, Salocin.' Ruby replies, laughing. It's good to see her relaxed, like the Ruby I know. It doesn't last, though. Ruby's phone buzzes. It's a text, I think, and I watch as the black letters on her white screen slowly but surely drain the colour from her face.

Cassie

What a mess! What a complete bloody mess. The bag lady from Australia has only been home a couple of weeks and, for some reason, she's slipped right back into the role of older, bossy sister. Only by a pissing year, and she thinks she can tell me what to do and how to think! How did we even start talking about abortion anyway? She's winding me up so much I can't even remember now.

'I'm just saying, Cas, from the minute of conception the foetus is a human being. That means abortion is murder and murder is illegal.'

Murder? Murder! I'll murder her in a minute! 'Actually *Maiz*, the pregnancy of a woman is not considered to be a foetus until the twelfth week of the pregnancy; it's just a bunch of dividing cells. Even then, it's not considered human because it can't live outside the uterus on its own.'

Maisy folds her arms and looks at me. She screws her face up in the same way she does when Romeow does a whiffy dump in his cat litter tray, always when it's just been cleaned out. 'Humph, whatever, Cas. If you think it's *that* easy, that black and white.'

'I do, it is. Besides, it's mostly always the woman left with the responsibility–'

'It is her responsibility!' Maisy interrupts. 'If a woman is stupid enough to get pregnant, then she should take responsibility for it.'

'Oh yeah, like your mum you mean.'

With a face that now looks like a slapped arse, Maisy scowls at me. 'Nice one Cas,' she sneers. 'Actually, my mum did want to abort me, it was Dad who persuaded her not to. Dad was the one that said he'd look after me.' Maisy's slapped arse face morphs into a triumphant grin.

What the hell is that look for? What does she think that proves? She thinks she's won this argument, because, what, she has a good Dad? 'Yeah, well he's the bloody exception, not the rule. Look at my useless dickhead of a father. As good as left Mum to it. Moved on, had another kid and didn't give a shit about us!'

'Yeah, but she, Lizzie, Mum did. She took her responsibilities and brought you and Connor up.'

'Only because she had no other choice! She couldn't just piss off, pick and choose when she saw us, she was left with us and just had to get on with it. But what if you do have a choice? What if you, the woman, are going to be the only carer or the only one that gives a shit and you decide you just can't do it, that you can't afford it or, or you're just not ready?'

Mum walks into the kitchen. She doesn't look at all well. Her face is pale and she's clutching her stomach. 'Now, now, now, what's all this noise about? What are both my lovely girls arguing about?'

'You okay, Mum?'

Mum winces and pulls out a chair to sit down. 'I'm just tired love. Got a lot going on. Deadlines to meet. I shouldn't have arranged this today, should have waited until the end of the summer when we all go down to Sean and Nat's in Cornwall.'

Mum cups her belly and makes a groaning noise. She asks Maisy and I if either of us has a hot water bottle. 'Time of the month,' Mum mouths in a whispery voice. Maisy volunteers to get hers for Mum and I'm glad it gives us an opportunity to stop the ridiculous argument. What does Maisy know anyway, how can she be *so* judgemental?

Mum asks me if she thinks Ruby was acting strange, different to normal. I said she seemed quiet, not as bubbly and loud as usual. More like she was when Andy first passed away. I still find it hard to believe Andy has gone, even though it's been quite a few years now. I liked Andy, more than Harvey. Harvey is better looking than Andy but Andy was funnier, more laid back. I suppose it's not great that Harvey's laptop melted on the hob that Andrew switched on before they left home, but if that had been Andy, he would have laughed his socks off.

Or should that be cock? Laugh your cock off? Oh, god knows. Whatev's.

Maisy wanders back into the kitchen carrying a purple, fluffy-covered hot water bottle. Filling it from the newly boiled kettle, she looks at me, chewing her bottom lip. She opens her mouth to speak but is interrupted by Uncle Teddy, who wanders into the kitchen and asks Mum if she knows what time the train to Kings Cross is leaving. An embarrassed Aunt Marie, who sadly is no longer laughing, rushes in behind him. She rolls her eyes and says the word "sorry" way too many times. Aunt Marie insists on taking Uncle Teddy home and Mum insists I call a taxi for them.

I help Aunt Marie guide Uncle Teddy into the back of the taxi and am quite surprised to find she smells of weed when I kiss her goodbye. When I step back into the kitchen I'm also surprised to hear Mum talking more abortion shit with Maisy, or maybe Mum started it by asking what was going on between us two?

'I'm just saying it's not always that straightforward, Maisy. Sometimes women are raped. Or during their pregnancy some women discover that the baby has a life-threatening illness, or–'

Maisy folds her arms across her chest again and purses her lips. 'I suppose there are *some* exceptional circumstances,' she interrupts. 'But if a woman chooses to terminate just because she doesn't think she can manage it or because she doesn't have enough money ...'

I feel the heat inside me rising like the stinging nettle rash that covered my body when Chelsea Divine pushed me into a bush of them when we were six years old, an accident she said, lying cow. 'Oh okay, so what's a girl supposed to do then? Have the baby, apply for benefits to get the financial help she needs, only then to be labelled a scrounger, a drain on society?' I suggest.

'Oh, just shut the hell up, Cas, what the hell do you know about it?'

'And just what makes *you* the expert, you judgemental cow?'

'Girls, please!' Mum interrupts. I look at Mum and her pale face has now turned grey, she really doesn't look good but I'm too angry to care.

'Every woman has every right to choose what she does with her own body,' I scream. 'It's a free bloody country, after all.'

'Actually, it's not,' Maisy spits back at me, 'we're governed by corrupt politicians, bankers and pharmaceutical companies who are slowly eroding away our moral freedoms!' She lowers her voice. 'Least ... that's what Crazee reckons,' she adds.

'Exactly!' I reply, although scratching my head, confused, I can't help frowning. Surely, if she can see that, she can see it's more important than ever for women to maintain control over their own bodies? I shake my head. 'This doesn't make sense, not coming from you, Maisy?'

Maisy unfolds her arms and lets them swing by her sides. Her dark eyes bore into me as her face becomes redder and redder and her voice, although low, is threatening. 'Don't judge what you don't know,' she says.

Now it's my turn to fold my arms across my chest. 'Humph ... you might wanna follow your own advice there, *Maizzzz*!'

'Bet I know more about it than you do.'

I raise my eyebrows, 'Bet you don't.'

'Girls ... please!' Mum pleads.

Maisy walks up to me and puts her face so close to mine I can smell the garlic on her breath from the bread she was stuffing her face with earlier. Fat cow.

'Bloody do!' she yells.

'Bloody don't!' I scream back, until we are both screaming so loud it sounds like the ear-piercing feedback from badly set up speakers at a music gig. We continue screaming for what feels like forever until, quite by accident, the one thing I've been hiding from everyone gushes forward from my mouth, only to collide with Maisy's own dirty little secret.

'What?' I reply, unable to hide the disbelief in my voice. 'You're pregnant?'

'What?' Maisy says at the same time. 'You had an abortion?'

'Arrrggh,' Mum screams. 'Help me to the bathroom girls,' she says trying to heave herself to her feet.

Confused and concerned I look at Mum clutching her belly as she tries to drag herself up, before I once again look at the shell-shocked face of Maisy. The same shell-shocked face I know is the mirror image of mine.

'Oh god, too late,' Mum says.

Maisy and I look at Mum and I am, if I'm honest, a little repulsed to see blood running down her leg.

'Ugh!' Maisy declares before slapping her mouth shut with both hands.

Feeling slightly embarrassed but protective at the same time, I quickly grab a handful of kitchen towel and shove it into Mum's hands. 'Oh shit, don't worry Mum, looks like you've been caught out and just had a bit of an accident. Here,' I offer her my arm to lean on, 'c'mon, I'll help you upstairs.'

Slightly mortified, Mum scrunches the kitchen roll into a ball and quickly stuffs it up her skirt in between her legs. I look again at Maisy and am annoyed to see she still has her hands over her mouth. Stupid cow. 'Thanks, love,' Mum says weakly. 'Not an accident though, you'll have to get Simon, I think I'm losing the baby.'

'What!?' Maisy and I gasp.

'I think I'm having a miscarriage' Mum says.

Chapter 22

EVERYBODY MUST GET STONED

Connor

Jake looks gutted. As if he's never going to see me again.

'Blimey, Jake, it's only for the summer. I'll be back before we start college.'

'I know man, but it's shit. I thought we, all of us, were gonna have the summer to get chonged, do a few festivals. I mean, what about Reading? I just bought a tent and ...' Jake makes a cheeky clicking sound and winks at me, '... I spoke to the main man about some stash. Gonna cost me a bit, like, but he said it'll be good shit.'

'What man?' Robbo asks.

'He's my dealer innit.'

'What, a drug dealer?'

'Piss off, Jake,' the Rickmeister says.

'What, a real-life drug dealer?'

I roll my eyes and the Rickmeister starts laughing.

'You piss off, Rickmeister. S'right Robbo, I got this dealer who said he'd get me a shipment of puff, for the festival. But as you bunch of losers ain't coming no more, I'll have to cancel it now.'

'You're so full of shit, Jake,' the Rickmeister says.

'Who's not coming?' Robbo asks.

'You're just jealous coz you don't have a dealer, Rickmeister.'

'Righto, Jake.'

'Who's not coming?' Robbo repeats.

Jake nods his head at me and the Rickmeister. 'These two knobheads,' he replies. 'Rickmeister is going to Spain with

Mummy and Conman is going to Cornwall, for six fucking weeks!'

'Yeah, well, if you bunch of idiots hadn't kept going on about four-twenty when you came round the other day I might still be going to Reading. Instead, I'm being packed off to the country like some naughty bloody school boy.'

Thinking about it still pisses me off. I should have known Mum would work it out. That phone of hers never leaves her hand now she's a writer. "I'm just checking my book rating," she says, or "I'm just reading my reviews" or "Ooh, I have another follower" or "Did you know that ..." whenever she's doing some research. How was I supposed to know she was researching four-bloody-twenty!

I did feel pretty sorry for her when she called me into her bedroom to talk. Her eyes were red, like she'd been crying and she looked really, ill, I suppose. Her skin was pale, see-through almost, with bluish-green veins around her eyes I'd never noticed before. She looked old, which I suppose at forty-nine, she is. Which makes knowing she was pregnant, grim. She doesn't know I know, but with Cassie and Maisy around it doesn't take long to find stuff out. As long as I keep my hood up, my earphones in and nod my head up and down everybody thinks I'm listening to music, which I am, most of the time, but not always.

'That morning I found you,' Mum had said, waving her phone at me, 'outside at 6.00 a.m., it was 21 April.'

'And?' I gulped hard, knew I'd been found out. 'What about it?' I continued, shrugging my shoulders.

Mum tapped her fingers on the diary sat next to her. Her bloody phone and her bloody diary are the only bloody things she cares about these days. 'Don't make out you don't know what I'm talking about, Connor.' I shrugged my shoulders again. 'It was 21 April, the day after the 20 April, 4.20? The day after the night you snuck out.'

I opened my mouth to protest. Deny, deny, deny, that's what

Grandad always advises me to do if I ever found myself in trouble. And judging by the tone of Mum's voice, I was in a shit load of it.

'Don't!' she said. Her voice was low but menacing and I wondered how she did it. How Mum could speak so quietly but still manage to frighten the hell out of me. She looked at me, carefully studying my face until I had to look away. I stared at the carpet, then at my feet. I decided I needed to clean my trainers or ask Mum for a new pair, but not yet!

Mum coughed but I didn't look up. 'So, I think it was 4.20 and the first time you and your friends tried weed!'

'Was bloody not!'

'Don't swear at me Connor. You may be one of the Facebook, tweeting, mobile phone, social media obsessed generation but what you forget is, we oldies have access to it all, too. All I have to do is tap into my phone and hey presto, what comes up? Anything and everything there is to know about 4.20.'

Swiping the screen of her phone with her glasses sat half way down her nose, just below the bump, she started reading, like she was at one of her bloody book festivals:

'And, I quote. "The number 4.20 has become a popular code for marijuana."' I sniggered then quickly tried to cover it up with a cough. '"There are more myths surrounding April 20, or, as it's written numerically, 4.20, than there are facts. The facts are it was a group of five friends from Northern California back in 1971 who met after school, at 4.20 p.m., to smoke pot. The group began using the term 4.20, as did friends and acquaintances. The term spread and became synonymous with smoking pot."'

At that point, I slapped my hand across my mouth for fear of laughing.

'"Cannabis smokers tend to spot the 4.20 sign everywhere,"' Mum continued, '"including building numbers, prices, even clocks in the film *Pulp Fiction*."' At this point Mum looked up from her phone. 'Well, I never knew that,' she said. 'I'll have to watch that film again. John Travolta was very good in it, and Samuel L Jackson. I like Samuel L Jackson. What was that film he did? So awful it was actually funny?'

Still stifling my laughter I shook my head. 'Dunno?' I replied.

'Oh, you do,' Mum replied, clicking her fingers. *Snakes on a Plane*!' she shouted and I jumped. 'Something about getting the mother fuckin' snakes off the plane,' Mum attempted to say in her best American accent before bursting into fits of laughter.

She's losing it, I thought to myself.

'Anyway, I digress,' Mum continued, looking down at her phone again. 'Ooh, this is interesting. Bet you didn't know this?' she grinned. 'Here are some of the things *not* true about 4.20: "4.20 is not the number of active chemical compounds in marijuana, it's 315. 4.20 *is* Adolf Hitler's birthday, but that's not where the tradition comes from. 4.20 is what you get if you multiply 12 by 35, the numbers from the title of the Bob Dylan song 'Rainy Day Women no. 12 & 35' that does contain lyrics suggesting everyone should get stoned, but that is not why 4.20 became the pothead's favourite number."'

'Well, well, well,' Mum said once again, looking up from her phone and removing her glasses. 'I never knew that. I love Bob Dylan. It's amazing what you can find on the internet. Isn't it Connor?'

I shrugged my shoulders for a third time and, looking down, drew a circle in the carpet with my foot.

Mum went on to tell me that my friends and I had been sussed and because she couldn't trust me she was sending me to Cornwall for the summer to stay with Uncle Sean, Nat and Summer. When I protested, she explained she had no other choice, as she would be away a lot, travelling up and down the country doing book stuff. She also pointed out that Simon would be working away a bit, and that Nan now had Grandad to look after.

'What about Cassie or Maisy?' I asked.

'You know Cassie lives in London during the week and Maisy? Well, Maisy can barely take care of herself right now!'

I called Mum a cow and told her all she cared about was her bloody writing and her bloody phone. I said I wanted to stay with Grandad, before he died, so she grounded me. And now here I am, my last night with the boys before I disappear to Cornwall.

'What about Maisy?' Jake asks. 'She's back from Oz, can't she keep an eye on you?'

I shake my head. 'Nah, she's pregnant and Mum says she can barely look after herself.'

'Shit!' Jake replies.

'Really?' the Rickmeister asks.

I wonder whether I should tell them about Cas, whether they'd judge her? But without realising it, I've said it. The words just fall out of my mouth and they all look at me. My three best friends look straight at me and for the first time ever I don't know what they're thinking.

The Rickmeister looks away and starts pulling up chunks of grass. Robbo frowns but Jake holds my stare. 'Shit, man, an abortion. Cassie had an abortion? Is she okay?'

I shake my head and the Rickmeister throws the green blades of grass he's collected high into the air. They scatter then fall and cover us like green confetti. 'Dunno?' I reply spitting a bit of grass from my mouth. 'Think so. Don't think she knows I know though.'

'Well, it's not a problem, is it?' Robbo joins in. 'It's her body, it's up to her what she does.'

'Some people say its murder,' the Rickmeister replies.

'Well, it's not,' I reply defensively. 'Not really. Is it?'

I tell them about some of the girls I know Cas is following on Twitter who have openly admitted having an abortion, and I tell them about some of the comments people have made like:

Fuck off Bitch

Baby murderer

Who wants 2 of u, ugly bitch

I hope u burn in hell

Bitch, I hope you die of cancer

You are evil

'Yeah, and I bet those people eat meat.' Confused, we all turn to look at Robbo.

'What the hell has that got to do with abortion, Robbo?' I ask.

'Thousands of cows are slaughtered every day,' he explains. 'In a really shitty way too. Go on the net and look at what some of those sick bastards do to those poor cows before they die. Genocide, my mum calls it, but no-one says a fucking word, do they? Then a girl, who'll probably get left with the baby anyway, has an abortion and everyone calls her a murderer. There's something really messed up about that. Why is an unborn human life worth more than a living cow one?'

I look at Robbo, shocked.

'Well, you eat burgers,' the Rickmeister points out.

'Did,' Robbo corrects him. 'Mum's gonna go vegetarian, and I think I'm gonna try too.'

Normally, at this point, I'd expect one of us to take the piss, but none of us do. We all remain quiet and lost in thought.

It's Robbo who breaks the silence again. 'I bought a onesie, for Reading.'

Jake looks at Robbo like he's just let one rip. 'You've bought what?'

'Yeah, it's pretty peng.'

'What the hell,' the Rickmeister snorts as orange Tango runs out of his nose.

Robbo shrugs his shoulders. 'Yeah, I thought it'd be, well, like, practical. And I can keep it on for the whole weekend.'

'Have you got shit for brains?' Jake asks.

Robbo looks offended. 'No!'

'Well, I'm telling you now. You ain't going to no festival with me wearing a bloody onesie!' Jake rolls his eyes and turns to me. 'Can't you stay with your dad?' he says pointing to Robbo, who is now rolling around on the ground with the Rickmeister. 'You're not seriously going to leave me with him all summer, are you?'

I think of Dad and his pokey horrible flat and I think of Dad, the man I barely know. I know he'd probably let me do whatever the hell I want, that I'd see Jake and go to Reading and smoke pot. But I can't stand it. Somehow, I can't stand the thought of staying with my dad.

Chapter 23

CONFESSION

Lizzie

Simon pats the empty space beside him on the bed. I look away and sigh. 'Yep, be there in a minute,' I smile as I continue massaging moisturiser into my hands, elbows and neck. He's given me time to recuperate and now he wants to talk. I disappear back into the bathroom and quickly change my sanitary towel. It's only been a couple of days so I'm not surprised to find I'm still bleeding. For reasons that don't quite make sense, I feel vulnerable and exposed wearing just my baggy T-shirt. I wander back into the bedroom and grab some pyjama bottoms, slipping them on under my T-shirt and over the huge knickers holding my pad in place.

'How are you feeling?' Simon asks as I crawl into bed next to him, laying my head on his chest. He wraps his arm around me and I'm comforted by his familiar smell. Fresh from the shower a bouquet of soap and deodorant fills my nose.

'Pregnant eh? When were you going to tell me?'

I shrug my shoulders, happy I can't see his face or his reaction. 'I thought it was the menopause,' I reply, to which we both laugh.

'Were you going to tell me?' I give another shrug and imagine Simon's eyebrows knitting together as they quite often do when he's annoyed.

Silence falls between us for a few moments and I'm aware of the familiar sounds of nightfall unfolding outside our open bedroom window. The clarity of nocturnal noises in our small town during the summer is remarkable. At times, it sounds

more like a jungle than the Fens. The blood curdling screams
of foxes, the rasping croaks of natterjack toads, not to mention
the incessant singing of reed and sedge warblers, all providing a
constant background noise that every now and then is interrupted
by the hum of a passing car.

'How's Scott getting on?' I ask.

'Don't do that,' Simon replies.

'Do what?'

'You know what, change the subject.'

I hear a car door slam up the road and the gentle beat of
Simon's heartbeat against my ear. 'I'm not,' I protest, 'I'm
genuinely interested. He is my ex-husband after all.'

Simon sighs heavily and my head, still resting on his chest,
rises and falls accordingly. 'He's fine, struggled with the system
we have for a few days, but now he's got the hang of it there's
no stopping him.'

'And drinking? Is he drinking?'

'Not as far as I'm aware.'

'That's good then,' I reply just as my ears pick up the familiar
"who-o-o, who-o-o" sound of an owl in the distance.

Despite my reluctance to speak I'm glad I had a miscarriage.
I'm too old to be having more children and thankfully the
decision has been taken out of my hands. Instead, we now have
Maisy's baby to look forward to, as grandparents, as it should
be, in the natural order of things. Although that, in itself, is a
worry. God only knows what's going on there. I mean, why
in God's name hasn't she told Crazee? Unless, she has and he
wasn't happy about it?

I lift my head off Simon's chest and look at him. 'I was
planning an abortion.'

Simon chews his bottom lip and nods his head. 'Okay,' he
replies, 'but you could have told me.'

I ask him how he would have felt if I had had an abortion

and he says he would have supported any decision I made. This annoys me and I tell him that's a cop out.

'So, if I'd wanted to keep the baby?'

Simon arches his left eyebrow. 'We'd have managed, somehow.'

'Really? You'd have been okay with it?'

'I didn't say that.'

'So, you wouldn't?'

Simon lets out another sigh. 'Truth? No. I've given it some thought and well, frankly, doing it all again, the nappies, the sleepless nights, I'm not sure I could. I mean, I would have, I guess, if you had really wanted to but to be honest, babe, I like the idea of all the kids flying the nest and it just being the two of us.'

'Humph, except Connor hasn't left home yet, Cassie will be here most weekends and Maisy? Well, I don't know what the hell is going on there. Have you managed to talk to her? Are we going to have a baby in the house anyway?'

Despite her refusal to speak about what happened back in Australia, Simon explains that he did manage to get Maisy to open up after she'd admitted to being pregnant. Apparently, she's been homesick for some time and as far as Simon can tell, Crazee has no idea about the baby.

I lay my head back on Simon's chest. 'So, what's her plan then?' I ask, closing my eyes in dread. As much as I like the idea of being a grandparent, I don't particularly relish the sound of a screaming baby filling the house on a full-time basis. I need the quiet to write.

'She'll stay with us, I suppose, until she gets back on her feet. You don't mind, do you?'

I open my eyes again and instantly feel bad for feeling bad. 'Of course she can stay, she can stay as long as she needs to.'

Simon leans forward and kisses the top of my head. 'Thanks babe,' he replies.

Once more silence reigns between us, and as hedgehogs snort and snuffle, owls hoot, foxes scream, and car doors slam, my thoughts turn to Cassie.

'How's Cassie?' Simon asks, as if reading my mind.

'Ye-ah, okay, I think? I knew there was a reason she'd lost weight. Told you, didn't I? A mother knows when something is wrong.'

'Do you think she regrets it, the abortion I mean? Do you think she regrets having it and that's why she didn't tell you?'

'No, I know Cassie, and I don't think she does regret it but …' I trail off.

'But what?'

I shrug my shoulders again. 'Oh, I don't know, I guess I just feel a little hurt that she didn't think she could talk to me about it.'

'Perhaps she didn't want to? Perhaps it was something she wanted to do by herself, without the influence of anyone else? So it was her decision and hers alone?'

'Humph, maybe,' I reply.

Maybe. Except I don't actually believe that.

'Did she say who the father was?'

I shake my head. 'Na-ah, won't give me a name, she just said it was some boy from uni. Said she quite liked him but he had no real interest in her, except on that night, of course.'

Simon asks me if Cassie had considered the morning after pill, which Cassie assures me she did, and would have purchased had she known there was a problem. She said they used a condom and it must have split and the boy in question had failed to tell her, or had been too drunk to remember.

'Oh well, at least she was sensible, acted fast and did what was right for her.'

'You think?' You're not judging her then, you know, because Maisy chose to keep her baby?'

With surprise in his voice Simon laughs. 'No, what on earth

makes you say that? Of course I'm not judging her. She made a decision, on her own and I'm proud of her, as you should be.'

I look up at Simon and smile. 'Thanks babe.'

I rest my head again and, my eyelids suddenly heavy, I realise just how exhausted I feel.

Closing my weary eyes, I feel myself drifting off to sleep.

Chapter 24

FISHY DREAMS

Cassie

I am surrounded by blue fish. Thousands of them swimming around me. I do everything to swat them away but still they keep coming. They seem to want to hurt me and I don't understand why. I always thought fish were friendly. Not sharks, I know sharks are dangerous but these fish look like normal fish and I always thought normal fish were okay? These fish are not nice, though. I just know it. They swim up to me and hit me. Butt me with their huge heads and whip me with their scaly tails. They move really quickly, too. Twisting and turning, they dart in and out of my twisted body and no sooner have I swatted one away, another ten have surrounded me. I lash out at them, time after time, manically waving my arms but still they come. Hovering for the briefest of moments to stare at me with their huge, black eyes. Soulless eyes. Deep wells of black without a trace of kindness in them.

They smell, too. Not of fish but of puff. A pungent, skunk like smell fills my nostrils and makes me feel sick. I can also smell lemons and limes and burnt popcorn and every now and then, strong, expensive whiskey. The water surrounding me changes to a grey smoke but still the fish keep coming, hitting me, slapping me, and surrounding me. I wave my hands violently above my head and thrash my legs below me.

One of the fish starts to grow before my eyes. Inflates like an oversized party balloon. He swims up to me and presses his ever-growing body against mine. The bigger he gets, the harder he presses and the heavier he feels. He pushes me down and I feel his wet rubbery, blubbery lips on my skin. The oversized blue fish has me trapped. His hugeness weighs me down, and the harder I try to push him off the more he pushes against me. I try to scream but no sound leaves my mouth. I lift my hands, now screwed up into fists, to pound his scaly skin. This seems to excite him as he wriggles and squirms above me. He wraps his huge tail around the top of my head and slaps me, hard across the face. I try to scream again but still no sound leaves my mouth.

Then the big blue fish, with his botoxed lips, tries to kiss me. His salty, rubbery mouth presses hard against mine. I can taste whiskey on my tongue and the stinking smell of rotting vegetables rises up my nose. Imprisoned by his weight, I turn my head away but the big, blue fish yanks it back. He pulls my hair with his huge tail, still wrapped around my head. His lips are back on mine, slobbering, sucking and gurgling.

I start to cry but no one can hear me. I'm frightened, really scared. I want to go home. I want Mum. But no one is here. No one can help me. The big, blue fish presses harder and harder against me until I feel a terrible burning down below. I scream out in absolute agony … but nobody hears me.

'Babe? Cassie? Cas, wake up hun.'

I wake up, soaked in sweat and petrified. It takes a few seconds to realise where I am. I look up and see Honey's concerned face looking at mine.

'You okay, babe?' she asks. Struggling to focus, I ask what time it is. 'It's early but I heard you shouting. Thought you were being attacked!'

I realise I've been dreaming and I'm so relieved. 'I was,' I reply. 'By the big, blue bloody fish again. Only this time, one of them grew. Massive it was. And it started to attack me.'

Honey shakes her head and laughs. 'You and your bloody, blue fish.'

'I know, right. It's weird eh?'

'No, it's just you. You're weird.'

'Thanks! I'm in good company then.'

'Well, if you're sure you are okay I'm gonna go back to bed, babe. I'm gigging tonight and it's gonna be a late one.'

It's ridiculous because I know I'm safe. But I don't want Honey to leave me. I know it wasn't real. I know it was just a dream. But it felt real. And I don't understand where the big, blue fish are coming from? Maybe it's a psychological thing. Maybe blue fish symbolise something for people that have done bad things? Maybe that's what it is, I'm being punished. God knows. All I do know is, I slept badly, again, and it felt real to me.

I look at Honey. Even without a scrap of make-up she still looks so pretty. She yawns. She does look tired. 'Okay hun,' I reply. 'Sorry I woke you.'

Honey shakes her head and yawns again. 'Not a prob babe. You going back to your mum's again for the weekend?'

I nod my head. 'Yep, sure am.'

'Okay.' Honey puts her hand to her mouth and tries to stifle another yawn. 'I don't think I'll be up when you leave but I hope your grandpop is okay.'

I smile. 'Thanks, hun. That means a lot to me.'

Honey gets up to leave and gives me a little wave as she heads for the door. 'Honey,' I call, as she's half way out the door. She looks back, still yawning. 'Have you, me, I mean us, have we ever been to a pub, club, someone's house with blue fish?'

Honey yawns and laughs at the same time. 'No!' she replies but she frowns, her forehead wrinkling like she's thinking about it. After several seconds, she shakes her head. 'No,' she repeats. 'Definitely not. It's just you. You're a bloody loon.'

I laugh too because I think she may be right. I think I am going slightly mad.

Chapter 25

STRANGER THAN FICTION

Connor

Looking out of the window I watch as fields of greens and yellows, and browns and purples rush by in a blur. I press my head against the window in some stupid hope it might give me some relief from the hot, sticky air filling the carriage. It doesn't, the sun has made the glass hot. What is it with the weather, anyway? It's rained, for three bloody whole days at home and now, when I'm stuffed on a bloody train that I don't even want to be on, it's one of the hottest days of the year, ever. It's like a sauna. I feel like I can't breathe. I can even feel sweat trickling down my armpits. Maybe I should give in and take off my hoody.

I stand up, which seems to startle the woman sitting opposite me, who puts down the magazine she is reading and peers over her glasses. She's old, probably about Mum's age, and watches me as I flick my hood off and yank down the zip of my hoody. She smiles, sort of, and looks kind of relieved. I screw my hoody into a ball and stick it behind my head like a pillow as I sit back down again.

The woman waves her magazine in front of her face like a fan. 'Gosh, it is hot on here, isn't it?' she says.

'What? Erm ... yeah. I s'pose it is,' I reply looking away.

Oh god, please don't start talking to me. I just wanna listen to my music and get through the last couple of hours in this oven until I get to Perranporth.

Grabbing my headphones, I make a point of flashing them in front of the woman. I even pull the wire out of the socket in my phone only to put it back in again. I DO NOT want to talk. My phone starts to flash and vibrate in my hand and I can see it's a text from Jake.

Hey Conman. Are you there yet? Check out the inside pocket of your rucksack, me and the lads have left you a little pressie.

I lift my rucksack, that until now has been tucked away on the floor between my legs, and bang it down on the table between us. The woman opposite peers over her magazine again then quickly goes back to reading it when I stare back at her. I unzip my bag and reach down into the inside pocket. I feel something soft and squidgy between my fingers and pull it out before giving it a second thought. I'm chuffed to bits to find it's an enormous, big, fat, rolled-up dooby. I smile for exactly 0.2 seconds until I remember that the thing I am holding between my finger and thumb, is illegal. I freeze when I hear the booming voice of the ticket checker man behind me.

'Tic-kets please,' he says. 'Why, thanking you,' he continues saying to whoever it is he is talking to.

I have my back to him but I can tell he is close. I panic. Look from left to right and then at the woman in front of me before letting go of the spliff. I drop it as if it were on fire and burning my fingers. My brain has gone to mush and I don't think to watch where it goes coz all I have in my head is visions of being arrested. I see myself, handcuffed to my seat, head hung in shame as I am escorted off the train by one of the many policemen waiting for me at the next station.

The ticket man is now next to me. 'Tickets please, young man,' he says staring down at me.

I look up. He looks drunk as he sways from side to side with the motion of the train. I stand up and for some stupid reason I run one hand through my hair using the other one to reach inside my jeans pocket for my ticket. I lose my balance and almost fall into the ticket inspector man as I pass my ticket to him. He brings the ticket up close to his face, looking at it intently, clipping it with his hole punch thingy (that always reminds of the train guard in *The Polar Express* film) before passing it back to me.

Sitting down again, I breathe a sigh of relief. My mouth feels dry and my tongue sticks to the roof of my mouth. I reach into my rucksack again and pull out a half empty bottle of bright blue liquid, supposed to give me energy (so the label says). Screwing off the lid, I down the whole lot in two noisy glugs before wiping my mouth with the back of my hand and stuffing the empty bottle back in my bag. Sitting back, I suddenly remember the spliff and am filled with panic. Frantically patting but finding the seat next to me empty, I bend down to look under it before looking across the narrow passageway, quickly turning my head from left to right. The rolled-up dooby is nowhere to be seen, though. Sitting up again, I feel part relieved, part pissed off, only to find the woman sitting opposite me is looking straight at me with a great, big, stupid grin plastered across her face. She leans forwards and nods in the direction of my rucksack, now stuffed at my side. I look down and spot something white sticking out beneath it.

'Yours, I believe?' she asks, raising her eyebrows. I cough and nod my head. 'Well, I must confess to having no idea what it is, and nor do I wish to. But I do suggest you put it away and keep it away.' She winks at me and I nod my head again, quickly stuffing the dooby back into the inside pocket of my bag which I then shove back on the floor safely between my legs.

Looking up again, I find the woman still staring at me, smiling. She has dark hair and bright blue eyes. I don't know her but she somehow seems familiar. The train speeds towards a level crossing, and as I look out of the window I spot a line of cars waiting patiently either side of its closed gates. We clatter past and the woman opposite tells me her name just as the train blows its horn so I don't quite catch what she says. Did she say Jo? Flo? Bo? I'm too embarrassed to ask her to repeat it. She offers me one of her sandwiches. I smile back at her, cough again and tell her my name is Connor. I say no to the sandwich but happily take the chocolate bar she offers instead. She's nice, kind of reminds me of Mum, which makes me feel shit for a minute coz I know, deep down, I keep blaming her for everything. Perhaps that's the real reason she's sending me to stay with Uncle Sean, because she's pissed off with me?

Jo, Flo or Bo asks me if I can stand up and open the window, as she isn't tall enough to reach which, as she didn't rat on me, I'm more than happy to do. We talk quite a lot and I'm surprised when she pulls out a copy of Mum's book from her bag. I tell her that the writer of the book is my mum, then nearly have a massive internal fit when I realise what I've done. I have just told the woman who may or may not know what I lost from my bag, and then found again, who my mum is. And given that Mum now uses every single social media platform known to man, woman and child, it is only a matter of time, minutes probably, seconds in fact, before Mum finds out. The woman, thankfully, seems oblivious to my worries and just keeps talking. She says she is a writer too and is on the train today to get some inspiration.

'I'm in disguise though,' she whispers, raising her hand to pat her hair.

I ask her what she writes and she tells me that she's written loads of books for children and more recently, thrillers for adults. I ask her to tell me some of the names of the books she's written but she responds like a politician by ignoring my question and asking me if I read.

I shrug my shoulders. 'Sometimes,' I reply. 'I used to read more when I was little.'

I explain about Grandad and his laboratory, which is really a library, full of all kinds of books, old and new and how he used to read to me and Cassie, and later Maisy, when we were little. The woman's eyes twinkle. She laughs and seems interested in everything I say. So, for some reason, I find myself telling this stranger on the train about how Grandad told me he was Nicolas Flamel and how, just recently, he was diagnosed with cancer. She tells me she is sorry about Grandad's cancer but she says he sounds like a wonderful man and that I'm lucky to have such a great person in my life. She tells me to enjoy the time I have left. Then she recites a quote by Ralph Waldo Emerson, which makes me smile and once again reminds me of Mum.

"It is the secret of the world that all things subsist and do not die, but retire a little from sight and afterwards return again."

Before I know it, the train journey is nearly at an end and I can't quite believe I've spent most of it talking to a complete stranger, and an old woman at that. As the train starts to slow down, the woman starts to gather her things together and I'm surprised to see the ticket inspector man back again. I don't ask why, but apparently he is there to help her off the train. She doesn't look like she needs help, but what do I know? Before she goes, she reaches inside her huge handbag and pulls out a book and a pen. She begins scribbling ferociously inside the book, before looking up at me. Smiling, she passes me the book face down. She says I remind her, in a way, of the main character in her book. I suddenly feel my cheeks burn like they do when I talk to Hayley Patterson. I realise she's just given me a signed copy of one of her books and I feel slightly embarrassed and decide not to read what she's written until she's gone.

I cough to clear my throat. 'Thanks,' I say.

She winks at me for the second time that day. 'You're very welcome,' she replies. 'You'll find another familiar character in there. too,' she adds. 'Good luck, Connor. I think you're a lovely young man. Why don't you write about your feelings, about your Grandad, you never know, it may make a good book someday?' And with that the stranger, who could be called Jo, Flo or Bo and is also a writer, like Mum, leaves with the ticket collector man.

I flip the book over and look at the front cover.

'Oh. My. God. Really…?' I yell.

And it's all I can do to stop myself falling off my seat, even the though the train is now stationary.

Chapter 26

A WRITER'S LIFE

Lizzie

After diving out of the shower I was sat in front of my computer. Strong, black coffee in hand my plan, to write. I have a deadline looming and after all the recent upheaval, I'm behind. My phone buzzed and I was tempted not to answer it but it was Mum, and of course I was concerned it may something serious, something to do with Dad.

'Mum?' I replied.

'Lizzie? Is that you Lizzie?'

'Yes Mum.'

'I can't see you,' Mum said.

'How would you see me if you phoned me?'

'I thought I'd done that face thingy whatsit, where you can see each other. Oh well, never mind. Anyway, what are you up to today?'

'I'm working.'

'Working?'

'Yes Mum, writing,' I replied.

'Oh good, so you're in all day? Dad and I will pop round for a natter then just after lunch, if that's okay?'

Glad that Mum couldn't see me; I put my head in my hands. When I say I'm writing it means I'm working so why is it that people fail to see that? The occupational hazard of a writer, unfortunately. Not that I mind, in this instance. I'm more than happy to down tools, for Dad.

Oh well, it was still reasonably early; I reasoned. I still had the morning to get some work done. Except, a quick exploration of the kitchen cupboards revealed we were out of milk and sugar and when I investigated further, I realised, much like the old nursery rhyme, the cupboards were bare. A plan formed in my head. A quick dash to the supermarket followed by a couple of hours writing, followed by an afternoon spent with my parents. Totally achievable. Sadly, though, the gods of chaos had other plans for me.

To begin with, I hadn't planned on the help, I use the word loosely, of my rather weepy step-daughter who, when strolling the supermarket aisles, looked nothing short of shell-shocked when observing sleep deprived parents pushing the prams of screaming infants. Maisy's expression was one of utter mortification as she stared, positively perplexed, at toddlers in the throes of the terrible twos, insistent on hurling themselves across the floor, screaming and shouting, "I want, I want" from the top of their developing lungs.

'Oh. My. God!' Maisy declared. 'I can't do this. I've made a huge mistake. I'm just like my mum. I should have had an abortion, like Cassie.'

After finding a seat at the front of the store for my hyperventilating daughter to rest, I asked her to explain what she meant.

Maisy said that she had been in contact with her biological mother. They exchanged several emails and when it transpired that Maisy's mother was flying out to Australia to holiday with her third husband, mother and daughter agreed to meet. My information about Maisy's mother via Simon is sparse, to say the least. I knew that not long after she and Simon had met, Maisy's mother became pregnant with Maisy and after persuading her against an abortion, Simon proposed and they were married several months before Maisy was born. Eighteen months later, Maisy's mother left. Her contact with Maisy across the years has been minimal. Every now and again, when she remembered, birthday cards would be sent, some bearing gifts of money, others not.

'We met for drinks,' Maisy said. 'She was so beautiful. To look at, that is. She's a barrister, on her third marriage and you can tell by her clothes and shoes she's loaded.' I asked Maisy if her mother had had any more children and Maisy shook her head. 'Na-ah. She fell pregnant once more after leaving Dad and me but had an abortion. She eventually opted for sterilisation. Said she didn't have a maternal bone in her body and wasn't cut out for motherhood. Having me had been a mistake but she said she's glad it worked out for me with Dad meeting you.'

'Wow, I suppose you have to appreciate her honesty,' I replied. 'Being a parent is difficult, and never ending. And let's be honest, yes, she walked out of your life, which isn't right, but she's no different to a lot of fathers who abandon their children. Look at Scott for god sake. Are you going to see each other again?'

Maisy shrugged her shoulders before bursting into tears. 'What's the point?' she wailed. I wrapped my arms around my daughter, cradling her like an infant. I thought back to her argument with Cassie at the time of my miscarriage, and suddenly understood Maisy's venomous reaction to Cassie's pro-choice comments about abortion. 'She said we could stay in contact, as "friends"' Maisy hissed.

Lifting her head from my shoulders and wiping the hair from her face, I told her to think about it. 'At least she didn't completely dismiss the idea of being in your life.'

Looking up at me, her long lashes blinking away more tears, Maisy smiled. 'Thanks, Lizzie,' she said.

Pulling a clean tissue from my bag, I wiped my daughter's black, mascara stained cheeks and told her that having and bringing up another daughter had been my absolute pleasure. Even through all the difficult teenage years. However, as is often the story of my life of late, my intimate mother-daughter moment was cut short by Ruby's rather desperate phone call begging me to meet her at the hospital.

At that point, I abandoned all hope of writing, today, or ever again in fact.

Chapter 27

IT'S A DOG'S LIFE

Connor

I sniff the air. The sun is out but a cold breeze wraps itself around my neck. I shiver, zipping my hoody up as high as it will go. My nostrils flare, filling with the smell of damp sand as salty seawater, drifting off the sea, stings my eyes. It's a familiar smell, one of family and holidays. Flicking my hood up I pull the rolled-up sleeves of my hoody back down to cover my white, skinny arms that, now dotted with goose bumps, make me look like a plucked chicken. Deciding not to bother with the weather-worn bench that smells suspiciously like the lamppost Freddy likes to cock his leg up against at home when I walk him with Grandad, I cop a squat on the sand. The dry, powdery bit, so my arse doesn't get wet.

Squinting, I look up, covering my eyes with my hand. The sun is already quite high and warms my face. It's going to be a nice day, I think. It's just waaaaay too early. I should still be in bed, sleeping. Not up with the fat, crooked nose seagulls squawking above my head. I'm disappointed with Uncle Sean, thought he'd be way more chilled than he is. Out of him and Mum, he's always been the more laid back out of the two. Bohemian, Mum says. So I didn't bloody expect to be up every day "earning my keep". It's supposed to be the summer holidays!

He's punishing me, I reckon, or he phoned Mum and she told him to punish me, for nearly losing the chickens. It's not my fault though. I don't remember Nat telling me to keep the dog on his lead when I brought him back from his walk. Maybe she did and I just forgot. I had smoked a bit of the dooby the boys sneaked in my bag. So maybe it is my fault but why would anyone keep a rescue dog that hates chickens? And it had to be a pug, didn't it! I've never seen such an angry little ball of fur. He's nothing like Freddy, Nan and Grandad's dog. The only thing I'm ever in fear of Freddy doing is licking me to death. And why? Why, in this whole entire world did they let Summer choose the dog's name, Sir Lancelot. I mean, like, really? Do they have any idea how ridiculous it sounds shouting for a pug called Sir Lance-a-fucking-lot? Barks-a-lot is more like it. And yeah, okay, granted, I was stoned, a bit, when we got back from our little walk. But it was my first day here and me and Barks-a-lot were still getting used to each other. How the hell was I supposed to know he'd run after the chickens as soon as we got through the gate.

I didn't even know chickens could fly, not that high anyway. What a waste of time. A whole hour spent trying to grab Sir Lancelot, who yaps-a-lot and loves to terrorise chickens. Round and round I ran. Must have looked like a right knob. I didn't know chickens could shit that much either. Ruined my bloody trainers they did. It didn't help that Uncle Sean's neighbour saw me and did sod all to help either. "Best bit of live entertainment I've seen in years", he told Uncle Sean. Ha, bloody ha. Now every time he sees me, he breaks out into huge fits of laughter and calls me Rocky. God knows what that's all about? Thank god Nat and Summer came home when they did, at least they managed to catch the chickens. Quite quickly too, if I remember rightly.

Uncle Sean said it's not a punishment though, says that the summer is a busy season for them. A time that him and Nat must try and make enough money to see them through the winter. So, if I'm going to stay, I must help out. Which is fair enough, I suppose, but why do I have to get up at 6.00 a.m. every day, including Sunday? It's bollocks is what it is. My stomach gurgles and I regret not having the poached eggs and toast Nat offered me. Even though it was brown bread.

Bored, I lean over and scoop up a handful of powdery sand in my fist, watching, fascinated, as it slips away through the gaps in my fingers. Things could be worse I suppose. I could be stuck at home, watching Grandad get sicker and Maisy get fatter. Wiping the chalky crap from the sand onto my jeans, I look up. The two fit girls I spotted running up the beach ten minutes ago are still there and are now doing some sort of exercise routine involving them standing back to back, passing something between them. I swipe my phone from my jacket pocket and snap the girls in action before sending the pics onto the boys and asking them what they think of my sea view. I imagine Jake, sleeping until midday then spending the rest of the day and night, joint in hand, headphones on, listening to his music full blast and slowly getting chonged. 'Anything to drown out the arguing between my mum and dad,' he said.

The pics disappear into the twilight zone and my phone pings. It's a text from Dad telling me Mum has invited him to spend the weekend with all of us at the end of August. What the hell? Why? Why is Mum so nice to him when he was such a dick to us? He says he's not sure if he should accept and what do I think? What does he want me to say? Yay, it's great you're getting your shit together and just coz you want me now, need me coz no one else does, you want me to want you back. Have the father and son relationship you chose to ignore for the last god knows how many years, until what? You choose to piss off again?

I read a poem once, at school I think it was, something about your parents fucking you up. And it's true; I think a lot of parents really do fuck their children up. Not intentionally maybe, but they do, nonetheless. Especially my generation, there's a whole bunch of us just completely messed up by divorce and shit. I've decided I'm never getting married and I'm definitely never having kids.

'Why the sad face? It could be worse.' I look round and see a girl, about my age, looking directly at me, smiling. 'You could be in a wheelchair, like me,' she says, tapping the sides of the chair she is sat in. 'You'd have a reason for a face like that if you were stuck in one of these all day, believe me.'

Taken aback, I laugh nervously. Running my hand across the top of my head, I cough to clear my throat, which doesn't really need clearing and wonder why we do that, why we cough when we're nervous? I'll ask Grandad. I bet he knows. He knows everything. I open my mouth to speak but I'm not sure what to say. I look at the face in front of me and realise how pretty the girl in the wheelchair is, how smooth her brown skin is, not an angry zit in sight.

'Look, I know I'm a spas but it's not contagious, honestly. You *can* talk to me. Or I can piss off if you prefer?'

'What? I didn't say you were,' I protest. 'I just–'

'It's okay,' the girl continues, still smiling, 'I was only saying what you thought. What most people think of the poor girl in the wheelchair.'

'No, that's not actually true!'

The girl's eyes narrow in suspicion. 'Really? That's what most people think when they meet me.'

'Yeah, well, I wasn't. I was actually thinking …' I trail off as my cheeks start to burn.

The girl frowns in a way that reminds me of Grandad. Everything reminds me of Grandad lately. 'Well?' she continues, 'What *were* you thinking then?'

I cough again. 'That you have nice skin,' I reply.

The girl looks confused. She raises her hand to her cheek and holds it there. 'Thanks,' she replies, 'no one has ever said that to me before.'

I tell her my name is Connor and she introduces herself as Alesha. She points to the two girls exercising and explains that used to be what she was like until the drunk driver of a car hit her two years ago. She says the first year was the worst and she spent most of it wishing she were dead but that gradually, she's getting used to it. 'I'm slowly coming to terms with the fact that I'll be in a wheelchair for the rest of my life. And don't get me wrong, it's shit, but it's not necessarily the end of the world.'

Funny and friendly, Alesha is so easy to talk to. Nothing like the girls at school. We continue chatting and I find myself telling her about Grandad and Maisy and, well, just about everything really.

'So, you're stuck here for six weeks then?' she smiles, her soft eyes flickering mischievously. I smile back and nod my head. I'm not sure why, but my tummy flips in the same way it does when I see Hayley Patterson.

I hear a familiar voice at the back of my head. 'Hi Alesha, how's it going?'

'Oh, hi Sean. I'm not too bad thanks, how are you? And Nat and Summer?'

'We're not too bad thanks, love. I see you've met Rocky,' Uncle Sean says, reaching across to ruffle my hair. 'My nephew?'

'Your nephew!'

'He sure is. A chip off the old block I reckon, just not quite so good looking,' he laughs. 'Give us a nod if you fancy a swim later, and careful not to let your wheelchair roll off this ramp, you don't want to get stuck in the sand again like the other day.'

'I've got my phone this time,' Alesha replies, pulling a mobile from the side of her chair and holding it up as proof.

Uncle Sean nods and sticks his thumb up. 'C'mon then Rocky, time to get some work done.'

'Why, do you keep calling him Rocky?'

Uncle Sean's face cracks into a huge smile. He looks directly at me and raises his eyebrows questioningly.

'Do you want to tell her, or shall I?' he asks.

Chapter 28

UNEXPECTED VISITORS

Lizzie

Back from the hospital and still talking to Sean on the phone, I usher Mum and Dad through the front door. Somewhat embarrassed but unable to stop myself from laughing, I thank Sean, promising not to mention what he's told me to Connor. 'I'm dealing with it, so you don't need to,' he assures me. I thank him once more and tell him we send our love and are looking forward to seeing them all at the end of August.

'Whachu bleedin' laughing at?' Dad asks as I put the phone down.

Both Mum and Dad listen intently as I relay my conversation with my brother back to them. Half way through, Dad starts to choke. Panicking, I jump up, smacking him across the back. Dad points to a glass of water that Mum lifts from the side table and I snatch it from her hand. Holding the glass to his mouth with a shaking hand, he tips the glass towards his dry lips, taking several sips before placing the glass back down next to him. Relieved I sit down again.

'You okay, Dad? You scared the bloody life out of me.'

Dad chuckles and shakes his head. 'You've made my week Lizzie, my gal. I don't remember the last time I laughed so bleedin' much. Rocky, you say? Brilliant. Just brilliant.'

'Aww, poor Connor,' Mum interrupts.

'My arse!' Dad replies. 'Little bugger was probably up to no bleedin' good.'

'Just taking the dog for a walk, wasn't he? Angry little thing by all accounts, loves Summer though, apparently.'

'Hates chickens though, eh,' Dad replies, filling the room with yet more guttural guffawing.

Visions of Connor chasing chickens fill my mind. I imagine the wild-eyed squawking of panic induced hens attempting some sort of great escape and Connor, gangly, flaying arms, flying in this direction and that, caught somewhere in between trying, and no doubt failing miserably, to capture the tiny perpetrator of such carnage whilst somehow sabotaging the chickens fight for freedom.

Dad's howling fills the house. With tears streaming down his face, he laughs so hard he actually has to hold onto his stomach. It's highly infectious, though, and I can't help but join in, even at the expense of my own son. Once I start I find I can't stop, at times barely able to catch my breath. Mum joins in and we all just look at one another, crumpled, ugly faces of pure unadulterated laughter, bereft of speech. It gets to the point where I no longer know if I'm laughing at Connor or laughing at my parents laughing at Connor.

Eventually, the laughter subsides and Dad uses his hands to wipe the tears from his face. Good tears. The kind of tears I like. The kind of tears we all like. It's good to see him laugh. Good to see him in such high spirits. He hasn't shown it, but Mum said he's been a bit low of late. I stare at him, my father, my dad, for slightly too long. But this is the face I want to remember. The one marked by laughter, not etched in pain. Dad catches me staring at him, smiles and winks. I smile back then quickly look away to see Maisy wander in.

Solemn and pasty-faced, she looks across at Mum and Dad and raises her hand. 'Hey,' she says.

'How you doing, gal?' Dad asks.

Maisy instinctively lays a hand on the developing bump she felt so compelled to hide these past weeks and shrugs. 'Dunno,' she replies. 'Okay I suppose.'

'It will be all right you know, Maisy,' Mum suggests. 'Things have a way of working out.'

'Course they do,' Dad booms. 'It'll all come out in the wash.'

Looking slightly quizzical but clearly eager to change the subject, Maisy asks what the joke is. 'I could hear you laughing, upstairs,' she says. Dad explains and although she tries her damnedest not to, reminding me of her surly, adolescent self, the corners of Maisy's mouth lift into a smile.

Dad lets out another little snort and shakes his head. 'Rocky,' he says. 'Bladdy brilliant. Bladdy brilliant!'

Turning to me, Maisy then enquires after Andrew.

'Andrew?' Mum interrupts. 'What, Ruby's little Andrew? What's happened to him?'

I explain about the panicked phone call I received from Ruby earlier this morning from the hospital. 'He tripped and fell down the stairs, apparently.'

Mum slaps her hand across her mouth. 'Oh my goodness, is he all right?'

I nod in the affirmative. 'Bit shook up but lucky to escape with just a broken leg, methinks. They've put a temporary cast on for now, to help relieve the pain, then they're planning on taking him to theatre later today, knock him out, then re-set the bones in the leg.'

Mum lets out an audible gasp, as does Maisy. 'Oh poor, poor little thing,' Mum says. 'Maybe I should go to the hospital, to help?'

I shake my head and smile at my mother's built in prerequisite to constantly help those in need. 'She's fine, Mum. Besides, Harvey is with her.' Not that this thought fills me with much confidence.

'But can you imagine how Ruby must be feeling? I mean, she already lost one child, then Andy.' Mum looks towards Dad. Suddenly tearful, she looks away and pretends to search for something in her handbag. 'I can't imagine what that must have been like for her,' she whispers.

'He'll be all right, Ellie,' Dad interrupts. 'You know what littluns are like at that age, bones so soft they almost bounce. Not like us old gits, bit of strong wind and we snap.'

Mum winces but it brings a smile back to her face. We all laugh and agree how quickly kids bounce back. This has opened the floodgates, though. Going into great detail, Mum feels compelled to explain to Maisy about the time, as children, I flew over the handlebars of my new bike and broke my nose and Sean fell out of a tree and broke his arm. A slightly bemused Maisy looks to me for an escape route, everyone knows this could take hours. I grin and shrug my shoulders while Dad rolls his eyes and reaches for a newspaper. Seizing the opportunity to make us all a nice cuppa, I manage, much to Maisy's horrified face, to sneak out and put the kettle on, taking my troubled thoughts with me.

I replay my conversation with Ruby and shudder.

'I was in the kitchen,' she said, 'when I heard this god-awful crashing sound. When I ran into the hallway, Andrew was in a heap at the bottom of the stairs. I looked up to call Harvey but he was already there, standing at the top of the stairs, staring. I screamed at him to call an ambulance. Which to be fair, he did straight away, but it was awful. All I could think about was Lilly. She wasn't much older, was she? And all I could think was, not again, please god, not again.'

Ruby went onto to explain that Harvey had been upstairs helping Andrew get dressed while she had been downstairs making breakfast. 'I called out to them both to come down and eat, and the next thing I knew, Andrew was in a heap at the bottom of the stairs. Harvey said Andrew tripped on something and before he realised it, before he could do anything about it, Andrew was rolling down the stairs.'

At this point Ruby had asked me what I thought of Harvey, what I *really* thought of him. Slightly suspicious, I asked why.

'Do you suspect foul play?' I asked, almost disbelieving I had asked such a question.

Ruby responded with a resolute shaking of her head. 'God, no! I'm just, not sure, if he's the one for me. Not sure I rushed into this relationship. Do you like him, Lizzie?'

'He's okay,' I had replied, shrugging my shoulders as her eyes met mine in elegiac but unspecific appeal. 'He's not Andy but he was always going to be a hard act for anyone to follow.'

I didn't confess the nagging doubt at the back of my mind, because that's all it is. I have nothing substantial to back it up with. Harvey is polite, successful, good-looking and clearly adored by Andrew. What isn't to like about the man? Mum, always a good judge of character, is positively mesmerised by his charming smile. It's true Harvey and I clash a little. He, I feel, resents my closeness to Ruby, my presence always ostensibly met with a permanently combative frown. Truth be told, the stick up his arse and his need to keep Ruby close do make me slightly uncomfortable. But what do I know? And really, at the end of the day, what does it matter what I think? Ruby has had enough shit for one lifetime. More than enough loss for anyone to bear. First Lilly as a child to meningitis, and then Andy, of course, instantly killed when the driver of a car hit his. I can't believe it has only been four years. Sometimes it feels much longer, at others, like yesterday. I make a resolute decision to try harder with Harvey, if only for the sake of my dearest friend.

A knock at the door distracts me from my thoughts and looking down I realise I've been stirring the same cup of tea for the last five minutes.

'Where's that bleedin' tea?' Dad shouts through. 'Gawd and Bennett, man could die of thirst around here.'

I laugh. 'Be with you in a minute, Dad,' I shout back.

I head towards the front door, my head filled with a myriad

of thoughts about my strange, rather eventful day. As I approach the door there is another second, more urgent knock. I wonder who it is and if, indeed, with flying chickens, friends in need and a weepy daughter, my day can get any stranger. I open the door, a little taken aback, realising it can.

'Crazee!' I declare. Still wearing the same unruly mop of brown hair, his skin kissed by the Australian sun, he looks well enough. However, he also looks tired and very travel weary.

'G'day Lizzie. How are ya?'

I tell him I'm fine and invite Crazee in. He steps through the front door, dragging a rather large suitcase with him.

Looking around nervously as if he's never seen the house before, which he has, on a handful of occasions, he asks if Maisy is here? I nod and shout for Maisy to come through.

'Still waiting for that bleedin' tea,' Dad shouts back.

Crazee and I both laugh nervously and I offer him a cup, too.

'Thanks, Lizzie, I'd love one.'

Maisy steps into the hallway and the two of them just stare at one another. For some reason the music to the film *The Good, The Bad and the Ugly* starts to play in my head, reminding me of the spaghetti westerns Dad still loves to watch.

'Where'd ya go Mais?' Crazee asks. 'You know you can't just go off like that, it's not right?'

Maisy bites her bottom lip and rubs a hand across her belly. Crazee follows Maisy's hand, his weary, concerned expression now one of disbelief.

'Is that,' Crazee lifts a hand to point. 'I mean, are you …' Crazee trails off and Maisy, who still says nothing, merely nods her head.

'Whose is it?' Crazee asks.

I wince and watch as the countenance on Maisy's face changes from hurt to pure bloody-minded anger. Fixing Crazee with a bug-eyed resolute glare, arms swinging with military precision, left, right, left, right, Maisy marches towards Crazee. She reaches him within three, large, easy strides. Crazee doesn't see it coming and frankly, neither do I, but in less than a nanosecond Maisy has raised an anger-fuelled fist and smashes it straight into Crazee's face. Completely taken aback, clutching the side of his face, Crazee staggers sideways, falling over his own feet, ending up in a heap on the floor.

'Wanker!' Maisy shouts.

Almost foaming at the mouth like a rabid dog, I pull Maisy away (mostly for his own safety) from Crazee's curled up, crumpled body, at which point Mum and Dad rush through to see what the noise is all about.

'Whose baby do you think it is, you fuckwit idiot?' Maisy shouts. Thankfully for Crazee, I still have Maisy restrained.

Dad looks at me, then across to Crazee, then to Maisy before looking back towards me again.

'Fack me,' he says laughing, 'it's not a life, it's an adventure!'

Chapter 29

"HELL IS EMPTY AND ALL THE DEVILS ARE HERE"

Cassie

I look at my reflection in the mirror. Using my hand to flatten down what's left of my hair, I have the sudden urge to cry. Again.

I look like a boy.

I move away from the mirror and walk towards the window, pressing my nose against the glass. The sea view is immediately framed in the misty haze of my hot breath. I lift the latch to the window and push it, hard. After several hard taps, the window opens, squeaking like a creaky door from a horror movie. The smell of the sea comes rushing in and carries me off on a wave of childhood holidays. Most of which were spent here, in Perranporth. This is where Uncle Sean taught me to surf, where Connor and I, and later Summer, went on hunts with Grandad, searching for lost pirate treasure around Dollar Cove, and where, of course, Maisy met Crazee. Using my hand to shield my eyes I look up. A tangerine sun sits in a bright blue sky that melts into the sapphire ocean below, glistening like diamonds every time the sun catches the rolling waves playing percussion to the squawking seagulls overhead.

Dropping my hand, the past drifts away again and the present comes crashing back. I look at the window. The frame is old, the paint peeling but it's somehow fitting. Uncle Sean and Nat's old farmhouse is, and always has been, as far as I can remember, permanently run down. But somehow it suits it. Sort of shabby chic, or as Mum says, rustic. At least they've finally made most of the other bedrooms fit for human consumption, or whatever the word is. Apparently there is a bit of leak in the room Mum and Si are sharing, though. I'm bunking down with Summer, which is okay. She's pretty sound as far as younger cousins go and her rescue pug is quite sweet too, I suppose. Barks a lot though.

A gentle tap, tap, tapping noise on the wooden floor of the bedroom interrupts my thoughts, and when I look over my shoulder I see Freddy, Nan and Grandad's dog, slowly walking towards me. His mouth hangs open, exposing a fat, pink tongue and his curved tail wags a friendly hello. Old now, like Grandad, he looks hot and bothered. I move away from the window and sit on Summer's bed, patting the empty space next to me for Freddy to join me. Panting, he just looks at me, with big sorrowful eyes, like I'm some sort of an idiot, which I am, of course, because I remember he has arthritis and can't jump or climb any more, like he used to. Poor old thing. He's probably waiting for Uncle Sean to carry him downstairs. I stroke his head and he happily lets me, before lying down on the floor beside my feet.

Bored, I touch the back of my head again, reminded of the hair no longer there. I feel … agitated. I need a fag. I reach across for my bag at the end of the bed and rummage around inside for my baccy and Rizlas.

'You … shouldn't … smoke. Could get … cancer. Like Grandad.'

I look up and see Summer, standing in the doorway. Bent forward holding onto both knees, she is clearly out of breath. Choosing to ignore her irritating comment, I continue sprinkling brown tobacco into the tiny piece of white paper balancing on my knee, before rolling it up and sealing it with a quick lick of my tongue. 'Have you been running?' I ask. Summer nods her head up and down. 'Why?'

'In case,' she replies, shrugging her shoulders.

'In case what?'

'In case there's an evil presence behind me. Me and Lance do it all the time.'

'Lance?' I reply. Summer's face suddenly burns red. Almost as red as Grandad's roses in his garden. 'Who's Lance?' I ask. She smiles and looks down at her feet. 'Is he your boyfriend?'

Giggling, Summer puts her head in her hands. 'Yes,' she mumbles before opening her cupped hands to reveal a now even redder face. 'His real name is Lancelot but everyone just calls him Lance. But pleeease don't tell Mum and Dad,' she whispers.

I look at Summer and smile. I feel sad. I wish I were eleven years old again. I swear life was much simpler then. 'Is that why you called your dog Sir Lancelot?'

Summer looks over her shoulder towards the bedroom door, which is slightly ajar, and listens for a few seconds. Satisfied no one is there she then swings back to look at me, nodding, her finger pressed to her mouth. 'Shhhh …' she hisses. 'Promise?'

I promise Summer I won't say a word to Uncle Sean and Nat and once again, this time for Summer instead of Freddy, I pat the empty space on the bed beside me. Arms outstretched to steady her; Summer carefully steps over a now snoozing Freddy and sits beside me.

'I was gonna call him Ten Miles,' she says. 'Sir Lancelot, I mean. I was gonna call him Ten Miles so, you know, I could say I walked ten miles every day. But then, well, you know …'

Summer trails off and laughing, I nudge her. 'I know,' I reply playfully.

She nudges me back and asks me if I have a boyfriend. 'Nope,' I say.

'Why?'

'Don't want one.'

'Is it coz your hair's too short?'

I put my hand up to touch my hair, again. 'You think it's too short?'

'No. I like it. Even though I heard Connor say you look like a boy.'

'Oh did he, now?'

Summer's face morphs into panic. 'Don't tell him I told you.'

'Little shit,' I mumble before lifting my arms above my head and throwing myself across the full length of Summer's bed.

Summer looks down at me, alarmed. 'What, me?'

'No, you idiot. Connor.' Relief spreads across her face. She lies down next to me, her head close to mine. 'Cool room,' I say eyeing up all her artwork and posters that seem to fill every square inch of every wall. 'Are all the drawings yours?'

'Yep.'

'They're brilliant. You should be an artist.'

'Meh. I'd rather be like you. I wanna be just like you, Cassie … when I grow up.'

I can't help snorting. 'Believe me, you don't,' I reply, arching my back slightly to reach into my jeans pocket and pull out my green plastic lighter. It makes a hissing sound every time I press the silver button before eventually bursting into a bright orange flame. I wave it under my newly rolled fag, now hanging from my mouth, as it sways hypnotically from side to side, until my roll-up crackles and catches light. I suck hard and enjoy the rush of nicotine to my head. Summer asks me for a drag and I tell her to get lost. 'Do as I say. Not as I do. Okay?'

She sighs and says okay then asks me if I believe in heaven. I don't reply for a minute and, except for the sounds drifting in through the open window, the room is bathed in silence. I blow smoke rings from the corner of my mouth and wonder what to say. I know Summer is thinking about Grandad. 'I don't know,' I finally reply, as wobbly rings of smoke float up into the air and Summer stabs at them with her finger as if to burst them like bubbles, like she used to do with Grandad when she was little.

'I think there probably is one. Heaven, I mean. At least … I hope there is.' I'm not sure she's convinced though, and if I'm honest, neither am I.

I do believe in hell, though.

Chapter 30

MR BLUE SKY

Lizzie

Using my hand to shield my eyes from the sun, I look up. Cloudless and empty, save for a few stray seagulls, squawking and gracefully gliding along the brackish breeze, the cerulean sky provides the perfect backdrop for our family gathering. The anticipation of another glorious day hangs like a promise and I'm eternally grateful, especially today. Intermittent laughter disturbs my thoughts and I look down again. My eye is drawn towards the end of the garden where Dad sits. Having already been up for several hours, he is perched on a chair in the shade. Cassie and Connor sit either side of him, bleary-eyed and yawning.

Cassie seems a bit better of late but is still a little distant. She hasn't talked much about her abortion, or my miscarriage, for that matter, and doesn't seem inclined to, despite some gentle probing on my part. I can only assume she doesn't want to, so I don't push it. I'm not entirely convinced about her new haircut, either. It's extremely short. I barely recognised her. Connor too, for that matter. How can he have changed so much in the last six weeks? Several inches taller with sun kissed skin and broad shoulders, the skinny boy with overly large feet is now becoming a man.

More ripples of laughter carry through the air. Mindful, I watch my father and children, intently. In between the quiet rustling of butterfly wings and the gentle drone of large bumblebees, several of which hover precariously atop the magnificent purple flowers of the Buddleia davidii at my side, I catch snippets of their conversation. I hear the word "Rocky" mentioned, to which Cassie throws her head back in delightful laughter whereas, forlorn, Connor merely hangs his in shame, shaking it from left to right.

Absorbed, I continue to watch them, reminded of another summer. Still in situ, the garden, although less established, looks much the same but we are all much younger. Cassie is a chattering eight-year old and Connor, who is three, wears a wild shock of blonde hair. Dad has a mass of thick, dark, curly hair albeit sprinkled with flecks of grey, and I'm much thinner, gaunter looking. Scott has just left us and I'm struggling, really struggling. Dad is telling the kids not to worry, that it will all be alright. He has a new portable CD player and as the silver disc he balances on his finger, catches the sunlight, Dad loads the player. A song starts to play, Bob Marley's 'Three Little Birds'. Dad tells the kids that that's what they are, three little birds, and as long as they have each other, everything will always be all right.

Drifting back to the present, I realise the song isn't just playing in my head, Cassie is playing it on her phone. Cassie stands up and starts to dance and the three of them wail, Dad quite literally, along with Bob and his Wailers. My vision blurs and a lump forms in my throat. Another one of Mr Marley's songs springs to mind, 'No Woman, No Cry'. I realise today, of all days, is one that I must use to take a very deep swim in the river, the one known only as De Nile. If I remain in denial I can believe that Dad actually doesn't look too bad. I can believe that he hasn't lost a lot of weight and the thinning of his wispy, silver hair is a mark of old age and not failed chemotherapy. And, if I choose not to listen, I can believe that the prognosis given by the consultant at the hospital was actually six to twelve years, not six to twelve months.

Feeling a heavy hand on my shoulder, I jump. Quickly wiping my eyes, I turn to see Sean standing behind me. Despite a healthy suntan and sandy coloured hair to match, like me, Sean has aged with the worry of Dad. Only he looks rugged and I just look like an old hag.

'Alright sis?' Sean says, his eyes firmly fixed on the inhabitants at the bottom of the garden. His pained look of concern reflects mine. 'He doesn't look good, does he? The chemo's not working, is it?'

I struggle to find my voice, so shake my head instead. 'What are we going to do without him?' I eventually manage to whisper.

Looking down, Sean kicks at a bare patch in the grass. 'Bloody dog,' he mumbles. When he looks up again I notice his eyes are watery. Sean shakes his head. 'I dunno sis,' he replies, 'but he's a strong old bugger and he's not done yet.'

The sound of yet more laughter forces me to look away. Dad is doing his best to copy some fandangled dance movements Cassie is showing him, while Connor shakes his head and rolls his eyes in mock embarrassment.

'Silly old fool,' Sean laughs.

Although I laugh too, I feel my throat constrict. 'Thanks for looking after Connor,' I say, changing the subject.

Sean waves his hand dismissively. 'Don't mention it. He's been great.'

'And the smoking weed, pot, drugs thing?'

Taking a deep breath, Sean sighs. 'I didn't lie, Liz. Told him that smoking pot from time to time recreationally was, in my book at least, okay. It's the other shit that can ruin your life.'

Sean goes on to explain that rather than preach to Connor, he believed it was better to show than tell. And, as Sean helps out on a voluntary basis at drugs rehabilitation centre and Nat works with the homeless, some of whom have ended up on the streets because of drugs, Connor saw first-hand why it was better never to touch the stuff in the first place.

'He was shocked, I think. But that was the idea, I suppose. He made great friends with a lad called Ben, only in his mid-twenties. Frequent and prolonged misuse of drugs has caused some lasting damage, including mental illness caused by drug-induced psychosis. Long story short, if he forgets his meds he can flip, appearing quite normal one minute, then convinced he is some sort of futuristic terminator the next.'

I feel my forehead wrinkle in confusion. 'Huh?'

Sean shrugs his shoulders. 'Too many computer games, or sci-fi movies maybe. I don't think anyone knows why or where that reoccurring thought comes from, but he becomes very agitated and is convinced everyone is out to get him. Wears a gun, here,' Simon says tapping his shoulder, 'to kill the enemy.'

'Sorry, what?' I reply, my voice an octave higher.

'It's cardboard sis. The gun on Ben's shoulder is made of cardboard.' I can't help but let out a small sigh of relief. 'It sounds funny,' Sean continues, 'but it's actually quite tragic to witness.' I nod my head and agree it must be very distressing for all concerned. 'Then there's Pru, of course, good friends with Nat, she lost her daughter a couple of years back to a dodgy E. She was only fifteen.'

'Oh my god, how awful,' I gasp, clamping my hands across my mouth. 'What did Connor think?'

'Let's just say that in this instance, showing, not telling, definitely did the trick. Don't be fooled though, Lizzie. There's plenty of prescription shit out there acting as a gateway to other, more sinister drugs.' Sadly I agree and nod in the affirmative. 'Anyway, how's you? How's the writing going?'

'Yeah, okay, I think. My debut's selling well but what with Dad and everything I do find myself getting a bit distracted, you know, from the actual writing. Talking of which, that reminds me, did Connor mention anything to you about a woman he met on the train? A writer?'

Sean looks thoughtful. 'Not that I remember. Why?'

'Connor said she was reading my book and she gave him a signed copy of hers. But now he says he's lost the book and I'm not sure I believe him. I wonder if it was someone winding him up. Or if maybe he's just winding me up.'

Sean cocks his head to one side and frowns. 'Who was she supposed to be then?'

I can't help but laugh. 'I'll let him tell you. Or better yet, he can show you, and me, if the book turns up. Which no doubt it will, magically, because like most things with Connor, he never looks any further than his nose. In fact, it wouldn't surprise me if it was still in his bag.'

Looking rather bemused, Sean grins back at me. 'Okay …' he says, lifting his eyebrows. 'I can't say I've seen any stray books lying around but I'll keep an eye out and if I find one I'll be sure to let you know.'

'Thanks. And thanks again for looking after him. You sure he's been no trouble?'

'He's been brilliant. Worked really hard. Makes a great surfing instructor. And I've loved having him here. He's like the son I'll never have.'

'You and Nat definitely not having any more then?'

'Nat had a hysterectomy last year, so we can't. It's just the three of us.'

'Really? I never knew. You never said?'

Sean shrugs his shoulders. 'What's to say. Nat was having a few problems but there was no need to worry anyone else. We managed, between us.'

The same feelings of rejection I felt after discovering Cassie's abortion wash over me. Wounded, I wonder why those closest to me feel the need to protect me from their problems. I let it slip that I suffered a miscarriage. Sean looks genuinely surprised then breaks into a smile and I can't help but laugh when he mimics me. 'Really. I never knew. You never said.'

Sean cracks a joke about Simon being a dirty old man just as Maisy, cradling her bump with both hands, appears at the back door, quickly followed by Crazee, who stands behind her massaging her shoulders and kissing her cheek. Sean asks me if I'm sorry about the miscarriage and I shake my head.

'No. Not at all … I'm not even sure I'm prepared for grandparenthood,' I reply nodding at the two lovebirds giggling at the door. 'But being a parent again, at fifty, doesn't bare thinking about.'

'Why did Maisy come back from Oz?' Sean asks, putting his hand up in response to Crazee's waving hand.

I sigh and roll my eyes. 'I'm not entirely sure, if I'm honest. From what I can gather, the pregnancy wasn't planned and Maisy had this mad idea that once the baby was born she wouldn't want it and would take off like her own mother did. She believed that if she left Crazee, she wouldn't be tempted to leave the baby.'

Sean raises his eyes wearing a look of mild surprise. 'There's nowt as queer as folk, or so the saying goes, eh?'

I laugh and nod my agreement then, alerted by a high-pitched squealing, I look again towards the door. Crazee has taken Maisy by the hand and is spinning her around in a way that reminds me of Dad, who is often prone to grabbing Mum by the hand and give her a quick twirl.

With one arm folded across his chest, the other stroking the stubble on his chin, Sean watches Crazee and Maisy, and laughs. 'Reminds me of Dad,' he says.

'That's just what I was thinking,' I reply.

Connor

Alesha's Dad pulls away and we both see him off with a wave. I look at Alesha sitting in her chair and wonder if I've made a mistake asking her to come.

'Are … um … are you sure about this?'

Alesha smiles. 'What?'

I cough and swing my arm, pointing towards the door. 'This, here, today, with my family. It's just that …'

Alesha's smile vanishes. She looks away from me and reaches down the side of her wheelchair, pulling out her phone. Swiping the screen, she uses her finger to scroll down before tapping the screen and holding the phone to her ear. She says nothing but smiles sarcastically.

Confused, I hold my hands out questioningly. 'Um … what … err … are you doing?'

'Don't worry. I get it,' Alesha replies.

I scratch my head. I can tell she's annoyed, her voice has the same tone as Cas and Maisy's do when they're irritated with me. 'Umm … get … what exactly?'

'Me,' Alesha snaps. 'You asked me to come, out of kindness. Probably didn't think I'd come but now, now I have turned up, you realise you're stuck with me. The disabled girl.'

I'm shocked, confused and hurt all at the same time. 'What? No! That's not what I meant at all.'

'Don't worry. Like I said, I get it. It happens a lot. My dad won't have got far. I'll get him to pick me up.'

Angry, I take a deep breath. 'That's. Not. What. I. Meant,' I state. 'But if you wanna go, fine!'

Alesha pulls her phone away from her ear and taps the screen. 'I don't wanna go. It just sounded like …'

Alesha breaks off and we both remain silent. My anger disappears and I feel awkward, as if I've just been told off, and I do what I always do when I've been told off. I look down at my feet and kick non-existent stones.

I cough, again, and decide to break the silence. 'I'm just worried, about you meeting my family. They're all a bit, well, mad.'

Alesha frowns but her lips turn up into a beautiful smile. 'What do you mean?'

I sigh heavily. 'Okay, where to start! My sister Cas, Cassie, tends to say whatever's on her mind, without thinking about it. She has a mouth like a magician's hat, my grandad says.' Alesha looks puzzled. 'You never know what's going to come out of it.' Alesha laughs. 'She blurts things out and gets sayings wrong, half the time I'm not sure if she does it on purpose or if it's because her brain is rushing ahead of her mouth. Then there's Maisy, my step-sister, she used to be an Emo freak, black hair, black lipstick, black clothes, black eyes, make-up, I mean, not the kind you get in a fight, and well, black everything really! Not anymore though. But she's still as scary, in a way. And she's pregnant! And she has a crazy Australian boyfriend called, Crazee!'

Alesha shrugs her shoulders. 'So far, so good.'

'Then there's my nan, she's lovely, yeah, just lovely. But my grandad,' I can't help but smile, 'comes across as a grumpy old git, but he's not. It's all an act. He's actually really great. Swears a bit though, especially the F word but because he's a cockney, you know, from London, it always sounds like "fack orf" instead of, well, you know, eff off.' I feel embarrassed; find I don't want to swear in front of Alesha. 'Then there's his brother, Uncle Teddy, also a cockney, and well, he's funny too and sometimes I laugh but I know I shouldn't coz he's got Alzheimer's. So, it's sad coz he's losing his marbles.'

I pause for a minute and realise how strange life is, how cruel. Grandad's body is dying and Uncle Teddy's brain is dying. Wouldn't it be great if they could put Grandad's brain into Uncle Teddy's body, then we could keep them both?

'Connor. Connor, are you, okay?'

I look up and notice Alesha staring at me. She looks concerned. 'Yeah, sorry. Drifted off there for a sec. Where was I?'

'You got up to your Uncle Teddy?'

'Oh yeah, that's right. So, then yeah, there's his wife, Aunt Marie, also lovely, like my nan. Then there's my mum!' I groan and roll my eyes. 'She really is mad, talks to herself, a lot. But then again, she is a writer! Then there's Simple Simon who–'

Alesha snorts. 'Simple who?' she asks.

'Simple Simon, a name given to him by Cassie. He's our step-dad, although in a way I suppose he's not officially, coz him and Mum have never actually married but they've been together like, forever. They met a couple of years after my dad left us, who, incidentally, is also coming today.' I roll my eyes again. 'My mum thought it would be a good idea!'

'Oh, that's nice. Your mum and dad get on then, despite splitting up?'

I cough and nearly choke. 'No!' I declare. 'My dad re-married, some rich bitch, who didn't like us and didn't really want me and Cas. Dad seemed happy to go along with it, too. Then they had a baby, a girl called Harriet, my half-sister. You should have seen the stuff they bought her, the places they took her to on holiday. And don't even get me started on her bedroom, fit for a princess, it was. And what did me and Cas get? Sod all, nothing, that's what. They even worked it out so Dad stayed at home to look after Harriet, and Sharon, the step-monster worked, that way they wouldn't have to pay Mum any maintenance for me and Cas. Even though their house was like a mansion, with maids and shit and mega expensive cars on the drive.'

Alesha's forehead wrinkles into a frown. 'Oh, okay. So why is your dad coming, today?'

I tell her about how the step-monster left Dad, with nothing. And how that now he has nothing he suddenly wants us.

'Well, it's good that he's trying, isn't it?'

I shrug my shoulders, look down and kick some more non-existent stones again. 'Dunno,' I mumble. 'Maybe. We'll see what happens when someone new comes along eh? Anyway, I think of Simon more as my dad, he's the one that's always been there for me, and Cas and Maisy. So even if I call Dad, Dad, in my head, Simon is my dad.'

I look back up to find Alesha smiling at me. 'You know what?' she says.

I shake my head. 'No, what?'

'They sound amazing. I can't wait to meet them all.'

Cassie

Guitar in hand, Luke accepts a beer from Simon and heads over to sit with Grandad and Uncle Teddy. Thankfully, Uncle Teddy doesn't seem too bad today. Grandad is in good spirits too, although he looks frail. It's obvious, although, no one is saying so, the chemo isn't working. Luke spots me staring at them and raises his beer bottle. Grandad also sees me looking and raises a hand showing three fingers, meaning me, Connor and him, the Three Little Birds. I swallow hard and use all my strength to fight back the tears I feel forming behind my eyes. I really must stop crying. Somehow, I force my mouth into a smile and wave back.

I replay my conversation with Grandad this morning, when Connor and I sat with him on our own, at the end of Uncle Sean's garden, like we used to when we were little. I told Grandad I was scared, that I didn't want him to die. I was shocked when Connor told me to shut the fuck up, that Grandad wasn't dying and to stop talking like that. Grandad told Connor to calm down and made him apologise to me, which he did, then we both started crying.

Grandad held both our hands and I got the one with the small missing finger. He tells everyone, including Mum and Uncle Sean, that he lost it in an accident when he worked at the shoe factory but I know it's not true. I've seen old photos of Grandad, of when him and Nan still lived in London, before they moved to Great Tossen and before he started working in the shoe factory. And, if you look very carefully, a few of the photos show the missing finger. When I asked Mum about it she said she doesn't believe it was an accident at the factory either, but as it was obvious Grandad was never going to tell us, it was best just to let sleeping dogs lie. Still don't know to this day what the hell she was going on about and why she brought dogs into the conversation.

Still holding Grandad's hand, he started to hum the tune to Bob Marley's 'Three Little Birds' and asked me to play it on my phone. After we sang and danced around a bit, Grandad said he wasn't going anywhere, not really. He said death wasn't the end and that if we looked hard enough and listened long enough, we'd always find him, somehow. He said he'd always be there to guide us.

'When you think of me, I want you to think; he is not dead. He is just away. I'll be in my laboratory, reading, or at the bottom of the garden tending my roses, or dancing, with Nan. Not dead. Just ... away.'

'Not dead, just away,' I repeated. I vowed to try and tell myself that, when the time comes, but I'm not convinced I'll manage it, because he will be gone.

Grandad explained that the words were part of a poem by a writer called James With-a-comb Riley, at least, I think that's what he said? Then Grandad read some more of the poem out loud.

> *I cannot say, and will not say*
> *that he is dead. He is just away.*
> *With a cheery smile, and a wave of the hand,*
> *he has wandered into an unknown land*
> *and left us dreaming how very fair*
> *it needs must be, since he lingers there.*
> *And you, oh, you, who the wildest yearn*
> *for an old-time step, and the glad return,*
> *think of him faring on, as dear*
> *in the love of there as the love of here.*

Think of him still as the same. I say,
he is not dead, he is just away.

I love the words, have pinned them to the top of my Facebook page. I love that Grandad knows so much … about everything.

Lost in thought, I feel a pair of hands on my shoulders and turning around I see it's Mum. She looks, tired. 'Love the new haircut,' she says, touching my head. 'Short hair suits you.'

'Really? Thanks,' I reply. 'I'm not so sure. Did it on a bit of whim. Just woke up the other morning and decided I wanted to look, different.'

'Well I love it,' Mum replies. 'And isn't it great that Luke could make it,' she says looking over my shoulder.

Smiling, I nod. 'Yeah, it is. I'm pleased he did.'

'Such a lovely boy. I always thought you two would end up together.'

I roll my eyes and tut. 'How many more times, Mum? We're just friends, always have been and *hopefully* always will be. I could never fancy Luke though. It'd be like fancying, well, like fancying my brother or something! Besides, he's engaged.'

'Really!' Mum exclaims. 'What, to be married?'

'Yep. People generally tend to get engaged to marry. Except you and Si of course. Why haven't you two ever got married?'

'He's far too young to be getting married,' Mum replies, totally ignoring my question. 'Is she nice?'

'Who?'

'Luke's girlfriend, is she nice?'

I shrug my shoulders. 'She's okay. Pretty. And her dad's loaded.'

Half smiling, Mum frowns. 'And what about you, love? Anyone on the scene?' I shake my head and tell her I'm far too busy to think about having a relationship. I don't tell her that I've had my heart broken and that thanks to him, the bastard that got me pregnant, I'll probably never trust anyone again.

'Are you okay, Cas?'

'Yeah, why?'

Mum says she's still worried about me and asks me if I want to talk about the abortion. I shake my head. 'No Mum, I'm fine.'

'It's just, you never really talked much about it,' Mum says reaching out and placing her hand on my shoulder.

I shrug her hand off by bending down and pretending to wipe something off my trainer. 'What's to talk about? I made a decision and I don't regret it.'

'I wish you'd told me?'

'Why?'

'Well. Because I hoped you'd always feel like you could. And it's such a big decision, I suppose I thought you would want to talk to me about it.'

'Look Mum, it's simple. The bloke that got me pregnant didn't know he had and wasn't interested in me anyway. Least, not after he got what he wanted. And I knew if I'd have gone through with the pregnancy, I'd never be able to give the baby up. And well ...'

Trailing off, I run my hand through my non-existent hair. 'Well, what?' Mum asks.

Chewing my bottom lip, I look down. 'Cassie, please look at me?'

I lift my head again and sheepishly my eyes meet Mum's. Before I know it, my words tumble from my mouth. 'I just don't wanna end up like you. Stuck. Binging up a kid on my own and waiting till I'm old before my life begins.'

I see the flicker of pain in Mum's eyes but as usual she tries to mask it with humour. 'Thanks,' she says laughing, 'but less of the old, eh?'

'I'm sorry, Mum, but you know what I mean, don't you?'

Folding her arms across her chest, she nods her head and blinks a lot. I can see I've upset her, and I hate myself for not thinking about my words before I let them fall out of my fat gob. When will I ever bloody learn?

Mum coughs. 'So, this is what divorce does to kids then, eh? We've done a great job haven't we, me and your dad? Really fucked you up?' she says still laughing, sort of.

Stepping forward I grab Mum's face with my hands and pull her towards me. Standing on tiptoes I plonk a huge kiss on the top of her forehead.

'Oh god, Mum, I'm sorry. But don't everyone's parents fuck them up, one way or another!'

Lizzie

Just for a moment I stop playing hostess and observe all that is unfolding around me. For I know this is it. This is one of those wonderful moments. A snapshot in time when everything comes together and it's important to be mindful of it. Everyone I care for is here. The sun is shining and the sky is blue. Dad, after a brief nap, appears well and happy and even Uncle Teddy is on great form, almost lucid, despite his ever-advancing Alzheimer's. I thank god, the universe, and any one at all, for allowing this brief interlude, these few hours, where everyone is together and life is very simple. It is a safe place where the cares and worries of life don't disappear exactly, but fade into the background.

A loquacious cackle rises into the air and breaks into my thoughts. Balancing her lit cigarette between her perfectly painted, red fingernails, Ruby throws her head back. Loud and gregarious, something has clearly tickled Ruby's fancy and it's great to see her much more like her former self. Harvey couldn't be more attentive either. Strange though it is, Ruby said she and Harvey have been getting along much better since Andrew's fall. 'He's been wonderful. An absolute darling,' she said. And as Andrew is now out of his cast, and there is no permanent damage, I'm pleased to say any nagging doubts I had about

Harvey have all but disappeared. Even though he is a bit of a stuffed shirt at times. He is good for Ruby and it shows in her face. Maybe it has taken him a while to settle in, and being around my madcap family isn't particularly easy, but Harvey is attentive and graceful with everyone alike, especially my rather awestruck mother, who is quite taken, much to Dad's amusement, with the rather handsome Harvey. Or at least, she was, until Michelle and Oliver turned up. That moment will forever remain in my collection of amusing memories.

Thanks to the rich tapestry of life, beauty, it could be argued, is diverse, dependent on all manner of similarities and differences, including colour, shape and size, but ultimately remains in the eye of the beholder. And yet one man, one enigmatic individual, transgresses all those boundaries. One man named Oliver leaves everyone he meets transfixed, or else a nonsensical jabbering wreck, whenever they find themselves in his presence. And, of course, my family and friends proved to be no exception.

I led Oliver and Michelle into the garden and did my level best to avert my gaze from the said individual as, once again, my own private orchestra accompanied me, as usual, playing 'Take My Breath Away'. The chattering maelstrom that was, descended into deathly silence as all eyes fell upon Oliver. One by one, like a domino effect, gobsmacked jaws fell open, where they remained in situ for several uncomfortable minutes. Oliver, as usual, unfazed by this common response to his unearthly presence, kindly shook hands with everyone before pulling up a chair next to Luke. He pointed to Luke's guitar and asked him if he minded; is there no end to this man's talents? Luke, clearly unable of forming coherent speech, shook his head and passed Oliver his guitar. Checking it was tuned, Oliver cocked his head to one side and listened as he strummed the frets and adjusted the tuning pegs accordingly. Everyone stood and stared, still like statues, in awe of the beautiful stranger, except Mum, who up until that point had been flirting, quite outrageously, with Harvey. However, when Oliver arrived, I couldn't see her for dust. She literally abandoned poor Harvey, mid-conversation. I hadn't seen her move so fast in years, despite a supposedly dodgy hip. Harvey, I have to say, though, looked relieved, or was it resentment that flickered across his face as his biggest fan, at least, up until that moment, traitorously deserted him for the beautiful Oliver.

Oliver began to play and as sweet music emanated from the plucked strings of Luke's old guitar, flabbergasted individuals stood and listened. His choice of music was, rather surprisingly, 'Fur Elise' by Beethoven, which, of course, we all knew very well, Cassie having played many angst ridden versions of it on the piano at home. Especially during her teenage years. Mesmerised, my stunned family and friends relaxed a little as Oliver's playing gradually drew to a close and, thankfully, a semblance of wary normality resumed.

'Fuck me!' Sean exclaimed. 'You'd turn gay for that, wouldn't you?' he asked Simon, who was standing next to him.

Simon didn't reply and instead turned to me. 'You never said he was *that* good looking.'

Ignoring Simon, I turned again to look at Michelle. Laced with lashings of liqueur, freshly plucked mint leaves from Nat's herb garden and fat, bobbing, home-grown strawberries, I passed her a glass of Nat's homemade summer punch. We clinked glasses and I asked her once again, as I have on so many other occasions, 'where the hell did you find him, Oliver, I mean?'

Tapping the side of her nose, she grinned. 'Wouldn't you like to know?'

Thankfully, my family's bewildered curiosity with Oliver appears to wax and wane and at the moment the spotlight is on Dad who, in his element, is surrounded by a posse of fascinated listeners as both he and Uncle Teddy reflect on their younger years; a very different time and one almost unrecognisable to the younger members of his audience.

Chapter 31

SALOCIN LEMALF

Salocin

'So, shall we begin? I'd like to start at the beginning. Well actually that's a given, I suppose. What is debatable is where the beginning is. For most that would be the day of their birth, a particularly cold night in my case, 13 December 1945. The midwife was called and arrived by bicycle. Brushing snow off her shoulders and carrying her bag of tricks, she happily accepted a cup of rosie lee before attending to my rather unremarkable birth and arrival into the world.

Salocin Lemalf, I was reliably informed, entered the world kicking and screaming. Second son and last child to Wilfred (Wilf to his friends) and Martha Lemalf. Martha, an avid reader with ideas above her station, wanted to call her second son Nicolas, but Wilf was damned if any son of his would be burdened with such, and I quote, "a pansy, poofter, shirt-lifter of a name". As a joke, Martha simply turned the letters of the name Nicolas around and convinced her ignorant husband the name Salocin was synonymous with that of a great ancient warrior. Wilf accepted this story and hence I was christened, much to my mother's eternal amusement, Salocin Lemalf, aka famous alchemist, Nicolas Flamel.

Any show of affection by my parents towards me was rare, towards each other, rarer still. Their fights were loud and physical, but that wasn't unusual where I came from. Family life in the overcrowded East End of London was lived at close quarters. As kids, my friends and I ran freely in and out of each other's homes, including extended family. Aunts, uncles, cousins and grandparents all lived within a stone's throw of each other. The backstreets, with no cars, were perfectly safe and used as our playgrounds, as were the many bombsites with their 'Danger, Keep Out' signs, which were slightly less safe, but much more alluring.

Times were tough. Folk were still reeling from a World War following a previous one that had promised to be a "war to end all wars". Most of the men from the area worked the docks. Employment was high but wages were low, especially for the unskilled casual labourer, which was the category my father fell into. The more skilled jobs had relatively high pay and regular hours but those jobs were ferociously guarded, their skills kept in the family, passed from father to son. Wilf, virtually illiterate, had been afforded no such opportunity. Dragged up, motherless and responsible for five brothers and sisters, the stories I heard about the brutality of his father, my grandfather (whom I never met), made the hidings I got seem like a walk in the park.

Wilf managed as he had always done, diligently working both sides of the law. A charming chameleon, he was as capable of a good, honest day's work as he was of thieving. When an honest day's work did present itself, usually unloading a boat, it would mean anything from a twelve to eighteen-hour day of unremitting manual labour. It wasn't unusual for my father to start work at five in the morning and finish between eight and ten o'clock at night. But when the honest work had its dry spells, Wilf would always do what he had to do.

Gang warfare and organised crime were rife and sometimes, somewhere amongst it all, Wilf played a part. We never knew what he did exactly, but it often involved some interesting and sometimes less desirable individuals visiting our house, much to my mother's disgust. As far back as I can remember, the ability to fluctuate between the honest and the dishonest had been imperative to my father's survival, and often meant the difference between having food on the table or going hungry.

Even in his later years, when work became more reliable and Teddy and I had left home, the fear of being destitute never left my father and old habits die hard.

Intelligent and well read, Martha, my mother, never forgave Wilf for deceiving her. When she met Wilf, she had been completely won over by his charm, thought she had found her Mr Darcy but instead found herself embroiled with a cruel Heathcliff. Hard and proud, she despised Wilf's dishonest earnings; ironically though she never had trouble spending them. Martha was determined my brother, Teddy, and I would not follow in our father's footsteps and would eventually elevate her to her rightful position in life.

This was my start in life but my real existence never genuinely began until I met Elle, or as we all prefer to say, Ellie.'

I look at my beautiful wife and still see the person I fell in love with all those years ago. The girl with the long, blonde hair, wearing a mini-skirt, even though it was mid-November and there was snow on the ground, one of the coldest winters since records began. Elle laughs in response and waves her hand dismissively, but I reach for it and she lets me pull her close. For a few brief seconds it's just the two of us, like it was all those years ago, and everyone else disappears. 'You were my real beginning, Elle, you do know that, right?' I whisper. Tearful, Elle throws her arms around me and kisses me softly on the lips.

'Get a room,' Sean shouts.

'Aww, they're so cute,' Cassie says.

'You are an old fool,' Elle whispers in reply, 'but you're my old fool.' We are the giggly teenagers we once were with nothing more than a deep love for one another and a gritty determination to make it, together, despite the odds. I breath in the familiar smell of the woman I've always loved and feel an overwhelming sense of sadness. My time is running out but I'm not ready to leave this mortal coil just yet. My children and grandchildren will be fine; I know that. I'll be missed, for a while, but I also know they are strong, and life without me will carry on regardless. But the thought of leaving Elle is – unbearable.

Now older and wiser, I realise I'm certain of far less than I ever was during my younger years. Life was much more black and white then. But now, as I enter my twilight days, I'm grateful. Grateful that I've had the time and inclination to see all the many colours in between. Even darkness taught me a thing or two. However, I'm also steadfastly certain of one thing, my love for the same woman I've spent more than fifty years of my life with. Good times or bad, no matter what, Elle, is always there, and always has been.

My constant. My life. My wife. My soulmate.

I'm almost embarrassed to see my parents locked in such a passionate embrace and I'm suddenly reminded of the many times Dad waltzed Mum around the kitchen during my youth, often to Love Affair's 'Everlasting Love' or The Beatles' 'Love Me Do'. Looking around I catch Summer who, although not quite a teenager but already showing the signs of such, wrinkles her nose in disgust. Connor simply rolls his eyes but Cassie and Maisy remain riveted.

'Aww, that's so cute,' Cassie declares.

'Get a room,' Sean shouts.

'Fack orf,' Dad replies laughing.

Ruby, who is sat with Nat, turns and smiles at me. Tilting her head to one side, her forehead wrinkling into an affectionate frown, she mouths the words 'so sweet.' She also nods her head towards Oliver's direction. 'Ding dong,' she says, grinning, fanning her face with her hand. I laugh and, raising my eyebrows, nod my head in agreement. She looks relaxed and much happier than the last time I saw her. Andrew is a lot chirpier, too, now his leg is out of its cast. It's amazing how quickly children bounce back. Harvey, who is watching Ruby, follows her gaze and when our eyes meet, I'm pleased to say, he returns my smile with a rather dazzling one of his own.

As the laughter subsides there are calls for Dad to tell us more and he is only too happy to oblige.

'Always did like the sound of my own voice,' he says. 'It's the only one that ever made any sense.'

He asks for a few minutes respite and stands up to accept the cold bottle of beer Sean passes him. Putting the bottle to his mouth, Dad tips his head back and drinks greedily from it, like a hungry baby that hasn't been fed for hours, his Adam's apple bobbing intermittently between large, thirsty gulps. Draining the brown bottle of at least half its content, Dad then wipes his mouth with the back of his hand and burps, loudly, much to Connor's amusement, before once again taking his seat, like a king before his loyal subjects.

'Philistine,' I think I hear someone mutter behind me. Surprised, I look around but other than Mum, who is shaking her head and sighing, no one else appears to be taking any notice of Dad. I am slightly taken aback though when I hear Sir Lancelot, or as Connor now refers to him, Sir Barks-a-lot, fiercely protective of Summer, yelp rather loudly. Summer hurries towards him. His head is down and I can't help but feel sorry for the poor little ball of fluff who appears to be whimpering and cautiously edging away from Harvey, and a rather stunned looking Andrew.

'What did you do to him?' Summer demands, glaring at Harvey as she bends down and scoops Sir Lancelot into her arms. 'Shush … there, there,' she says, rocking him in her arms like a baby as he excitably licks her face in response.

Harvey holds his hands up and explains that he merely pulled Sir Lancelot away as the dog was trying to bite Andrew. I look at Andrew who, robbed of speech, seems to be on the verge of tears, and Ruby who looks every bit as confused as the rest of us.

'You're a liar,' Summer hisses. 'He doesn't bite. Only barks. At people he doesn't like.'

Sean intervenes and Summer, who is still holding Sir Lancelot, stomps off towards the other end of the garden. Harvey's calm expression hints at something else, supressed annoyance, maybe? He continues to reiterate how he only meant to scare the dog away. 'I thought he'd bitten him,' Harvey says nodding towards Andrew.

Sean assures Harvey that the rescue pug's bark is much worse than his bite. Harvey raises his eyebrows but before he has time to reply, Sean puts his hand up and laughs. 'I'm joking! He does bark … a lot. But I promise he doesn't bite.'

A grey shadow falls across the garden and I feel a prickling sensation across my neck. Using my hand to massage the back of my head I look up and notice a couple of dark rain clouds drifting towards us.

No! Please, not rain. Not today.

Sean calls Summer back from the other end of the garden and Harvey apologises profusely. Summer simply nods. Resolutely angry she refuses to meet Harvey's sorry eyes, unlike Sir Lancelot who, still wrapped in Summer's arms, is openly growling and snarling at him. Ruby, who is now consoling Andrew, looks at me again.

'What happened?' I mouth, but Ruby merely holds her hands up and shrugs her shoulders.

'Bloody mad, that dog,' Connor says, behind me. 'Always barking at me for no good reason.' I laugh, finding myself strangely comforted by Connor's words.

Quiet resumes and thanks to a slight westerly breeze, the dark clouds that only moments ago threatened rain have thankfully moved on. With said grievances dealt with, everyone drifts back towards Dad to hear more stories about his colourful past. He is also joined by a rather tired looking Freddy. Somewhat disgruntled by all the previous commotion, Freddy has emerged from the shade to resume his rightful place, namely his chin and front paws resting on Dad's feet. Although not in the best of health himself, with arthritic back legs, Freddy never leaves Dad's side of late. Mum said she thinks he senses Dad is not well and feels duty bound to protect his master. Maybe? Or maybe he just thinks of Dad like him, as a trusty old companion, both in their twilight years.

Dad begins talking again but is rudely interrupted by Sir Lancelot, who has now turned his attention to a rather bemused looking Freddy. In between yaps and barks, snarls and growls, Sir Lancelot makes quick lunging movements towards Freddy, only to dart back in fear every time Freddy twitches an ear or lifts his head. Half frowning, half smiling, Summer, hands on hips, strides up to the young pup and once again scoops him into her arms.

'That's enough now, Sir Lancelot,' she insists, whereupon he immediately desists, again licking her face with enthusiastic affection. I look at my niece, amazed how grown up she is becoming. The dreadlocks, like Sean's, have gone and are now replaced with long, blonde, silky hair. A perfect combination of both parents, Summer has her mother's full lips and her father's dark eyes. The girl is becoming a woman and again I wonder where the time has gone. 'Sorry about that Grandad, you can carry on now,' she says.

Dad talks about his formative years, when London was swinging and the place to be. Times were changing and the naïve hope of a better world for all hung heavy with the heady scent of possibility.

'Started married life in a tiny two room flat, we did. Nothing more than love and an old paraffin heater to keep us warm at night, eh Ellie?' Dad says winking at Mum.

'None of the gadgets like this lot have today, eh?' Dad continues.

Smiling, Connor looks at Alesha and rolls his eyes.

'Computers didn't exist,' Dad continues, 'and we couldn't afford a TV, or a phone or a washing machine.'

'Sounds like student digs,' Cassie adds drolly.

Connor frowns. 'What did you do?' he asks, 'you know, for fun and stuff?'

'What, besides working all the hours god bleedin' sent, you mean? To keep a roof over our heads. Especially once madam there,' he nods at me, 'was on her way. Not too bleedin' much, that's what!' Dad snorts.

'We went dancing,' Mum says. 'Do you remember the dance halls?' Mum asks Aunt Marie, who smiles warmly. 'I loved getting dressed up to go dancing. We took a couple of trips down to Brighton too. Remember, Salocin? On your scooter?'

Dad smiles. 'And you in your miniskirts, too. Even in the middle of winter. You must have been bleedin' freezin', now I look back on it.'

'I was!' Mum replies. 'Surprised I didn't die of hypothermia.'

Aunt Marie shivers. 'We didn't even have the good sense to wear tights, either. Miniskirts and nylons, on a scooter. What were we thinking?'

'Always was a bit of a sucker for stockings and suspenders, eh Teddy?' Dad adds.

'Great for fixing the fan-belt on a motor, too,' Uncle Teddy replies.

'Weren't you a Mod?' Connor asks.

Uncle Teddy snorts. 'He was. And the only Mod I knew who spent most of his time with Rockers. Mortal enemies, the Mods and Rockers, yet Salocin was always welcome in both groups.'

Dad laughs. 'Never hurts to be friends with the enemy, eh Ted?' he says winking. Mum and Aunt Marie look at one another and, suddenly sombre, Uncle Teddy nods his head in agreement. They are talking about a life that I, and everyone else, are only allowed censored access to.

'We did get a TV eventually,' Mum adds thoughtfully.

'Yeah, a portable black and white with a dodgy aerial,' Dad replies.

'And we did have a radio and that old record player your aunt gave us,' Mum continues.

'Music, books and love, what more does a man need to sustain him in life?' Dad declares.

Dad looks across at Mum and smiles. 'Do you remember those nights up on the roof, Ellie? Just you, me, and the tranny?'

Connor, mid-sip, coughs and, face reddening, almost chokes on the drink now spewing from his mouth like a fountain. Cassie reaches round and smacks him, a little too hard, across the back. 'Tranny?' he eventually manages to ask. 'You and Nan were friends with a tranny?'

After much guffawing and several confused faces later, Dad explains that the tranny was, in fact, their transistor radio. 'Always tuned in to the pirate stations, too, so we could listen to the good stuff. The Beatles, The Rolling Stones, The Who–'

'Pirates?' Cassie interrupts. 'You listened to pirates?'

This statement is met with yet more laughter and Dad, pausing to explain, shakes his head and sighs heavily. 'Gawd and Bennett girl, if you had a brain you'd be dangerous.'

Dad reminisces about the summer before my birth. 'Like an oven in the flat, it was. I'd get home from work. You'd make a spot of supper, eh Ellie? And we'd take the *tranny*,' Dad says purposely looking at Connor, 'up on the roof.'

Biting her bottom lip, Mum smiles and nods her head, but I notice the sadness in her eyes. 'And there we'd sit, amongst our neighbours' washing blowing on the line.'

Mum rolls her eyes. 'So romantic,' she quips but Dad's eyes dance mischievously in response.

'We'd hug for a while,' he continues. 'And watch as the Waterloo sun set, The Kinks reminding us, even if we were avoiding the landlady again, we were actually in paradise.'

This appears to be one memory too much for Mum who

makes some excuse about refilling the punch bowl and leaves, while Dad continues his colourful soliloquy. He talks about the time he started working at the scrap metal yard just down the road from Smithfield Meat Market, for the infamous Georgie Wakefield. Businessman and owner of several yards dotted around London, he was more gangster than scrap metal merchant and, I'm pretty convinced, had something to do with Dad's missing finger.

'Just nineteen years old I was when I went to work for Georgie,' Dad says.

'Yeah, and still wet behind the ears and green as a bleedin' cucumber,' Uncle Teddy adds.

I laugh as Cassie's eyebrows knit together in obvious confusion. I read her lips, silently mouthing the words 'wet behind the ears?' as Dad's shoulders rise and fall in time with his cheeky chuckling. 'Not by the time I bleedin' left!' he replies. To which Mum, who is once again flirting with Harvey (as she is too dumbstruck around Oliver), looks up rather abruptly and throws Dad one of her, I don't swear very often but "shut the fuck up" looks. He catches it, winks and smiles.

Dad talks of his old boss and his sidekick, Mickey. Seemingly somewhat larger than life, I'm not entirely sure Dad hasn't made them up, or at least added a liberal sprinkling of embellishment for the sake of a good story. A tall man of medium build, Georgie's slightly greying, slightly receding dark hair was always worn as a comb over, partly because he considered himself suave, but mostly out of vanity to hide his bald spot.

'Liked a smoke, too, Dunhill if I remember.'

'And posh motors,' Uncle Teddy adds. Aunt Marie who hasn't taken her eyes off Uncle Teddy this whole time, looks on affectionately. She sniffs and smiles and I feel a lump form in my throat. For a man who now spends most of his waking days forgetful and very confused, Uncle Teddy is surprisingly lucid and alert today, if only for brief moments.

'S'right Ted,' Dad replies, 'Jags were his favourite. And his clothes were just as swanky.'

For some reason, Connor finds this word highly amusing.

'He also wore the finest, hand-made Italian shoes and a large diamond ring on his right-hand ring finger,' Dad continues. 'He had this way of looking at you, too. Strange looking eyes, sort of bulbous. Always reminded me of the eyes of the colossal squid. Except for his slightly droopy eyelids, about the only thing about him that was, though. When it came to business he was sharp as the Saville Row suits he wore. Had a distinctive way of talking, too, particularly noticeable when he spoke to his sidekick, Mickey.'

'Do it, Grandad. Do your impression of him,' Connor asks enthusiastically.

Dad explains how Georgie always said Mickey's name slowly, pronouncing the two distinct syllables but using a different, much higher tone on the second. 'Like this; "Mick, eeee! Mick, eeee! Who's the new boy then Mick, eeee?" Dad says in his best cockney, barrow boy accent, which is met with yet more raucous laughter.

Dad, with his captive audience, is in his element and it is blatantly obvious, at least to me it is, despite spending the best part of his life away from the city of his birth and formative years, London still has a great hold on my father. And there are most definitely skeletons dancing in his closet.

Dad also talks of a mythical London. Growing up, his head had been filled with stories of a city aligned with fire and plague, wars and executions, as well as creatures of mythology. Aunts and uncles relayed stories about minotaurs within its labyrinths of brick, and nymphs alluded to along the banks of the River Thames. They also talked of the Angel of the Thames and one of his aunts swore; 'to her bleedin' dying day,' Dad said, she had actually seen her for herself, during the war. She also warned Dad and Uncle Teddy about the ravens guarding the Tower of

London, a tradition maintained for hundreds of years, whereby the wings of these sacred black birds are clipped to keep them there, guarding the historic building; 'the consensus being the day they leave will surely mean Arma-bleedin'-geddon.'

'Arm-a-what?' Cassie asks.

Connor slaps his head with his hand and sighs heavily. 'It means the end of the world. Loser.'

Dad also describes the sights and sounds of Smithfield Meat Market. His words painting pictures of barrows filled with huge animal carcasses, making rattling sounds as the porters pulled them down cobblestoned avenues, and blood stained, white-coated men, shouldering mammoth pieces of meat, shouting across one another. He talks too of the roar of the salesmen, standing on tables, making it their business to be heard; "Ha-a-andsome bit of beef, who's the buyer? 'Ere, this way. Nice leg of lamb, best in the market. Ye-o-o! Ye-o-o. 'Ere you are guv'nor, come along, come along. Splendid bit 'o' pork belly, you won't see betta. Glass of nice peppermint to stave orf the chills?"

'Salesmen, pedlars of food and hawkers of hot toddies would all bawl together until the place was a right bleedin' hullabaloo,' Dad said.

He pauses for a moment, his eyes glazing over, clearly lost in thought. He sighs, heavily, and then speaks again. 'London,' Dad says, 'is a city preoccupied with light and darkness, where both angels and demons continually strive for dominance within it. Like life,' he adds.

Grabbing my notebook, I hurriedly scribble down his words. Then, looking up, I'm suddenly aware, despite all the sounds associated with being outside, how quiet it is. You could, as the saying goes, hear a pin drop, so eager are Dad's listeners to hear more of his fabled tales. I realise now, although my track record for public speaking to date is crap, my ability to spin a good yarn comes from my father, albeit in the written form. The only person looking suitably disinterested is Harvey. He wears a look of sheer befuddlement and I can't work out if it's boredom or arrogance, rather than the good spirited amusement of everyone else. It also appears that I'm not the only one to notice.

Michelle is at my side, nudging me. 'What's wrong with him?' she whispers, nodding in Harvey's direction.

'He clearly isn't enjoying the ramblings of an old East Ender,' I reply.

'I think your dad is lovely,' Michelle continues. 'I could listen to him for hours. There's a story here you know, Lizzie.' And with that she winks at me and wanders off in search of some more of Nat's summer punch.

Connor

Shit. Did I just see that right? Did Harvey purposely knock that cigarette out of Ruby's mouth? I look around me to see if anyone else has noticed, but no one has. Ruby stands up and, pulling her top down, runs her hand across her belly. Harvey is saying something to her and she looks upset. He's smiling though so god knows what that's all about? Alesha taps me on the shoulder and asks me if I mind getting her another drink. 'It's so hot today,' she says waving her hand in front of her face. Her beautiful face.

'Shit. Sure. Sorry,' I reply, jumping up. 'I didn't notice you'd finished.'

Alesha laughs. 'It's okay Connor, it's not like I'm dying of thirst or anything.'

I laugh, nervously, not sure if she's joking or not.

'Connor,' a familiar voice booms behind me. 'Have you nicked my baccy?'

'No! Anyway, I thought you'd given up smoking?'

'I have, did. Anyway, what the f–'

'Cas.' I interrupt. 'I haven't introduced you yet, but this is Alesha.'

Cassie looks behind me, surprised. I don't think she realised

Alesha was there. 'Oh, hello,' Cassie says. 'Are you Connor's girlfriend? You're really pretty, love your hair.'

'Yeah, that's a point, why the hell did you cut your hair so short?' I ask.

Cassie shrugs. 'I set fire to it.'

'What?'

'Yeah, I set fire to it the other night when I was out with Honey. Don't tell Mum, though,' Cassie whispers from the corner of her mouth, 'you know what she's like.' Cassie rolls her eyes. 'She'll only worry.'

'So ... what happened?'

'Well,' Cassie sighs, 'there was a group of us sitting at a table in a pub that had a lit candle in the middle. I'm not sure how but somehow I leant over and my hair brushed the candle and caught fire.'

'Shit! What did you do?'

'Spent the next ten minutes trying to pat it out while the rest of the pub rolled around laughing at me. It was dead embarrassing. A guy with dreadlocks came over and told me not to worry, said he'd been having a bad hair day for the last thirty years. Which only made everyone laugh more. Anyway, despite washing it at least fifty times, I couldn't get the burning smell out. So, I had it cut. Wish I hadn't now, looking at Alesha's.'

'I think your hair looks lovely,' Alesha replies, 'wish I was brave enough to cut mine that short.'

Cassie smiles and touches the back of her head with her hand. 'Thanks,' she says. Then, looking at Alesha's empty glass, Cassie's smile vanishes. 'Oh, for god-bloody-sake Connor, look! Poor Alesha hasn't even got a drink. Follow me, Alesha,' she says offering her hand. 'I'll show you where the drinks are.' When Alesha doesn't get up, Cassie looks confused until, coughing, I nod at Alesha's chair. Eyes suddenly wide, Cassie lets out a small gasp. 'Wow, you're in a wheelchair!'

'That's right,' Alesha replies.

'Were you born in one?'

I feel the heat rising in my face and it's not from the midday sun.

Alesha laughs and shakes her head. 'No. I was already quite a big baby, don't think there was enough room in my mum's stomach for a wheelchair too!'

Cassie screws up her face in confusion. Cringing, I close my eyes and hang my head. 'See what I mean?' I say turning to Alesha.

Alesha simply smiles. 'It's great to meet you though, Cassie. Connor's told me so much about you. Why don't we let him get the drinks and I'll tell you all about ...'

Alesha is suddenly interrupted by the loud wailing of my stupid sister. Starting off slowly, her screaming becomes louder and higher pitched like the siren sounds in old war films. Manically waving her hands above her head like an idiot, she literally takes off, running down the garden, screeching like a monkey. Frowning, Alesha looks at me. Sighing, I roll my eyes. 'It's a ...'

'WASP!' Cassie screams.

'Oh!' Alesha replies, her whole face breaking into a lovely smile.

'WASP!' Cassie screams again. Her fear is infectious and sees Summer, Andrew, Aunt Marie and even Mum, to a certain degree, taking part in what looks like some sort of ritualistic arm waving and screaming ceremony as they run, duck, and jump away from the angry wasp. Both Uncle Sean and Si look slightly amused at the unfolding commotion, casually wafting the annoyed wasp away when it heads in their direction before resuming their conversation.

'Stand still!' Harvey shouts. 'Stand still and there's less chance of getting stung.'

I disagree, and much like Si and Uncle Sean, Alesha and I prefer to waft, as do Oliver and Michelle, whereas Cassie,

Mum, Nan, Aunt Marie, Summer, Andrew, Ruby and, rather surprisingly, Luke, seem to prefer screaming. Uncle Teddy just looks confused and Grandad is the only one who doesn't seem to give a damn either way. He is laughing so hard I swear he's going to fall off his chair, and he actually does when the wasp lands on Harvey's face and stings him. For, despite Harvey's stern reassurance that keeping still is the best policy, the wasp stings him anyway. Grandad's roar of laughter is so loud I'm pretty convinced the whole of Perranporth can hear him.

'Told ya,' I say, turning towards Alesha.

Cassie

Grandad, who still has blood on his chin, is singing as loud as his now wispy voice will let him. Uncle Teddy is beside him. Shoulders erect, he looks just like his younger brother, only his white hair is much thicker. He seems much bigger than Grandad now, too. Even though Grandad always used to be slightly rounder. It's easy to see the obvious pride Uncle Teddy has for Grandad by the way he smiles at him, which makes it even more difficult to believe what just happened. Everything was going so well up until then. And now, just to add insult to injury, Flippity, a.k.a. Felicity, has also turned up.

'You don't mind, do you?' Luke asked, 'only Felicity's here to see the gig me and the boys are doing up the road tomorrow night. We've booked a room at a B&B and I told her to drop by if she got here early enough.'

'Of course, I don't mind,' I smiled.

I love that your girlfriend, who saves her resting bitch face just for me, has come to ruin my afternoon.

Grandad, who only an hour ago was still talking about London, now looks tired and exhausted and I don't know whether to laugh or cry. I love his stories of *his* London, old London. But that will all stop soon, when he leaves us, and it's not fair. Life is not fair. You got it so wrong Grandad. Life is not an adventure. Most of the time it's just pure bloody shit. I look away and notice Simon staring at me. Tilting his head to one side, he points at me, and miming the words, asks me if I'm okay. I nod my head but swallow hard to fight back the tears that once again threaten to fall. I mustn't cry. I promised Grandad I wouldn't. Simon sticks his thumb up and smiling, I do the same, before quickly looking down, pretending to read my phone.

When it's safe to look up again, I glance across at Dad, who is standing next to Ruby, both of them singing. Everyone is singing, in fact, except, it seems, Harvey. Arms crossed, standing on the other side of Ruby, he looks confused. He is quite posh. Maybe he doesn't know the words. At least Dad doesn't look as nervous as he did, after Grandad's grilling. I did actually find myself feeling quite sorry for him when he turned up.

'Well fack me,' Grandad said, 'look what the cat dragged in. Confirmation, if ever a man wanted it, this really must be my last bleedin' supper.'

Turning to see who he was looking at, I was surprised to see it was Dad. I put my hand up to say hi and he nervously lifted his in response before walking towards Grandad. Red faced, Dad coughed and thanked Grandad for inviting him.

'Don't thank me. I didn't bleedin' invite ya!' Grandad replied.

Nan suddenly appeared and stood at Dad's side. 'Don't take any notice of him, Scott,' she said placing her hand on his shoulder leading him away towards the drinks table. 'It's lovely to see you and you're more than welcome.'

'No he's bleedin' not!' Grandad shouted after their retreating backs to which Nan stuck her hand in the air and waved. 'And if you ever facking let these kids down again I'll come back and haunt you, forever. You 'ear me.'

Connor and I looked at each other, chewing our lips like

we did when we were little after being told off for laughing at something that wasn't funny.

'Take no notice of him, Scott. He's just a grumpy old git,' Nan said rather loudly.

'I heard that,' Grandad replied.

'You were meant to,' Nan continued.

'I can leave …' I heard Dad mumble, '… if me being here is a problem, I can leave.' Nan shook her head and I was almost as surprised as Harvey seemed to be when Ruby joined Nan and also placed a reassuring arm around Dad's other shoulder.

Mum looked at Grandad and fake frowned. 'What?' Grandad replied to her stern stare, which quickly melted into laughter when she looked at Simon and Uncle Sean who were also grinning.

Smiling, Grandad caught me looking at him and winked. I returned his smile but like Grandad, I didn't see it coming. An angry fist from nowhere smashed straight into his face with such force he completely lost his balance and fell backwards off his chair. And like an idiot, both hands locked across my mouth, I felt too shocked to move. Couldn't understand why the hell I started to shake so much?

Uncle Sean and Nat immediately rushed towards Uncle Teddy. Standing straight backed with glazed eyes; his arms kept swinging around and around. Stupid, I know, but with his white hair and white T-shirt he kind of reminded me of the huge wind turbines I often spy, dotted amongst the landscape, from the window of the trains home from London.

Thrashing his arms and yelling stuff that made no sense at all, Uncle Sean and Nat tried to calm Uncle Teddy down. Grandad, still on the floor at this point, rubbed his head with one hand and his mouth with the other which, when he pulled it away, was covered in blood. I suddenly felt icy cold. And, not for the first time this year, I also felt helpless. Uncle Sean managed to grab and hold down Uncle Teddy's waving arms but he was still violently jabbering away, none of it making any sense. He seemed angry and confused and I felt as sorry for him as I did Grandad. Aunt Marie rushed forward and tried to calm him down but sadly, really sadly, Uncle Teddy didn't recognise her either. Spitting and shouting, Uncle Teddy loosened his grip from Uncle Sean and began swinging his arms again, throwing punches left and right. I heard someone calling me and when I look round, I realised it was Grandad.

'Cassie. Oi Cas, give us a hand gal,' he said, one hand balancing on his knee, the other outstretched towards me. Rooted to the spot, I just stared at him and his blood stained mouth. I kept willing my wobbly legs to move but it was like my brain wouldn't let them. I wanted to move, and I tried, but I couldn't. 'Cassie,' Grandad repeated. 'Look at me gal.' I tried. I really did, but my legs wouldn't move.

'For god sake, Cas,' I heard behind me. 'What the hell is wrong with you?' I watched as Maisy charged past me towards Grandad. She offered to help him up, but I heard Grandad say something about letting me do it.

Grandad's voice, soft and warm, asked me again to help him. I looked again at his bloody chin and suddenly wondered what the hell I was doing just standing there. Why wasn't I helping my grandad? I tried once more to step forward and this time, when I told my legs to move, they did. I offered Grandad my arm and he gave me his in return as I gently pulled him to his feet.

'Sing to him, Salocin,' Aunt Marie begged. 'For god sake just sing to him.'

Wearing his serious face, Grandad looked at me. 'You know I'm here for you, Cassie, if you ever need to talk?' Confused, I laughed, telling him of course I knew that. Then, regaining his composure and much to my surprise and everyone else's, Grandad started singing, as badly as ever, the words to 'Maybe It's Because I'm A Londoner'. And just like that, like a switch turning on, or off, Uncle Teddy stopped his ranting and concentrated on listening. In less than sixty seconds Uncle Teddy was 'back in the room' telling Grandad how much he loves that song.

'Tough old days but good old days, eh Salocin?' he says, as if nothing has happened. Grandad nods but seems too nervous to stop singing.

'You okay?' Maisy whispers in my ear.

'Yeah, why?' I reply.

'What the hell was all that, just then, with Salocin?'

I shrug my shoulders. I barely know myself. 'Dunno. Think I was just a bit, shocked. It happened so quick and what with all the blood and stuff.'

Maisy arches one of her eyebrows. 'Really?' she asks. 'Kay, have it your way,' she continues before wandering back over to Crazee.

Holding one hand to his chest and the other one out like a welcome hug, Uncle Teddy joins Grandad, singing loud and proud, from the top of his lungs. Before I know it, Luke has joined them with his guitar and suddenly everyone, including Alesha, who has wheeled herself over, is happily singing along to the wartime song about London town. Except poor old Aunt Marie, that is. She is slumped in a chair rocking back and forth with her head in her hands. Mum and Nat join her and every now and then she looks up from her hands, shaking. Nan joins them and I hear her ask Aunt Marie how long he's been this bad. Aunt Marie admits it's been a while.

'Salocin knew' she says, 'but I made him promise not to tell anyone.'

She also explains how, quite by chance, they discovered Grandad's singing of old childhood songs sometimes helps Uncle Teddy, especially when he gets confused. I also hear Nat and Mum suggest that Aunt Marie ought to now give some serious consideration to putting Uncle Teddy in a care home, for her own safety, if nothing else.

Aunt Marie buries her head in her hands again and cries. I sing with all my heart and look across at Maisy, who is also watching Aunt Marie. Crazee, standing behind Maisy, cradles her growing baby bump, which makes me feel – weird.

Aunt Marie stops her rocking and turns to Nan. 'He's been a bastard to live with sometimes, you know.' Aunt Marie never swears so I can hear the tiny inward gasps from everyone around her. 'And I'm not talking about the Alzheimer's, either,' she continues. 'I mean in our younger years, he wasn't always easy to live with, and when we discovered we'd never have children, well, it broke my heart, it did. And his, I think. Although, he never said. But, despite it all, we took a vow, like you and Salocin, for better or for worse and that's what we did, what I've tried to do …'

Her voice begins to crack and Aunt Marie is unable to finish her sentence. Nan assures her she's done as much and beyond any husband could hope for. Then, grabbing both Nan's hands and holding them in hers, Aunt Marie looks straight at Nan.

'Oh god. How are we gonna live without them, Ellie? How are we gonna live without our boys?'

Part Two

Chapter 32

INCEY WINCEY SPIDER

Cassie

I gaze out of the window as I finish talking to Dad on my phone. The common across the way, so green and lush during the summer, is now covered with a carpet of red, orange and brown leaves. The black branches of naked trees bend in the wind and the sky is dull and grey. I tell Dad to take care and maybe try and talk to Mum if he's genuinely worried about Ruby. I always thought Arsy, Harvey, whatever his bloody name is, seemed okay. Not as easy going as Andy, not as friendly I suppose, but nice enough. Quite good looking, too, in an old man sort of way. There's a little part of me, though, deep down, that can't help wondering if Dad wants to believe there are problems between Ruby and Harvey in the hope he can start dating Mum's best friend. And there's only one reason I think this, Ruby is abso-bloody-lutely loaded.

Dad ends his call like he always does, telling me he loves me, and I reply in the same way: 'Ditto, Dad. Have a good weekend.' I can't bring myself to say the actual words because I'm still not sure this is going to last. That he won't meet someone new and go back to not giving a shit about me. I don't think I could bear that again so, emotionally, I'm holding back, but secretly I'm chuffed to bits.

I tuck my phone back in my jeans pocket and feel something tickle my other hand that is leant on the fridge. I turn and scream, continually, as I see a huge spider run up the fridge door. Gigantic body and eight massively long legs; it runs in that familiar way spiders do, almost lopsided, scuttling at lightning speed, up the fridge and onto the ceiling. I watch as it sprints across the ceiling and I swear it's looking back at me. A black mass of creepy crawliness, now hanging above my head. Staring at me. Taunting me.

Despite the loud music, I'm still screaming like an idiot and everyone comes rushing into the kitchen.

'Spider,' I shriek, jabbing the air with my finger, pointing towards the ceiling. 'Huge, bloody spider!'

Useless (real name Eustace), Luke and Honey all laugh at me whilst Flippity (and her resting bitch face), arms folded, merely tuts and rolls her eyes. I knew she didn't like me. I've tried, I really have, but she just doesn't like me and that look just confirmed it, despite what Luke says.

Looking up, half cowering, I'm pleased to see Chris is also wearing the same look of sheer terror as me. 'It is pretty big,' he mumbles, clearly as petrified of our eight-legged guest as I am. At least I'm not the only one.

Luke drags a chair across the kitchen floor and pushes Chris out of the way. With a pint glass in one hand and a magazine in the other, Luke captures the spider which, clearly pissed off, raises its front legs, tapping repeatedly at the walls of its glass prison. Luke waves the magazine covered glass and angry spider in front of my face, and laughs when I tell him to piss off. Honey opens the window and Luke sets the spider free.

Normality resumes and everyone wanders back into our tiny living room, which is filled with smoke and smelling like a weed den. Honey, wafting the air with her hand, wanders over to the window and opens it. Felicity follows her. Despite being uncomfortably hot, I shiver as I imagine the huge spider that just went out the kitchen window coming back through the living room window. I'm about to shout to Honey to close the window when I see Felicity look across at me with the same "I hate Cassie" look in her eyes, and decide not to bother. So what if the spider gets back in. And just why the hell does Flippity dislike me so much? Cow.

Useless, along with Luke, corner me and we chat about college and old times and Luke and I promise to try and catch one of the gigs Useless and his band have booked for next week.

'Only please don't call me Useless if you do come,' Eustace says, his Polish accent still as strong as ever. 'We've been told to expect a couple of guys from some of the "big" record labels and the last thing I want them to hear is people calling me Useless.'

Luke and I laugh. Useless is most definitely NOT useless when it comes to music. In fact, he's one of the best guitarists I've ever known. It's just a name that started at college and stuck. 'Of course,' I reply, 'totally understand. Eustace it is then, Useless.'

Useless laughs and puts his arm around me. 'Oh Cazzie, you haven't changed a bit,' he says, squeezing my shoulder.

Seemingly impressed, Useless says I've done good to work with such a well-known and well-respected record producer. I nod. I don't have the heart to tell him my boss is a wanker.

Luke and Useless wander back towards the kitchen in search of more beer and I weave myself between our other friends. I reach Honey and Felicity just in time to hear Flippity say she's tried but she just doesn't click with me. That makes two of us then. 'She's such a drama queen, too,' Felicity adds. 'Look at that crap with the spider just then.'

Honey looks up and sees me. She smiles, whereas Felicity, who turns to see who Honey is smiling at, looks flushed. Honey stretches out one of her long arms and pulls me to her. She wraps herself around me and kisses the top of my head. 'She takes some getting used to, I'll give you that but Cas is, well, just Cas!' Honey declares.

I feel another arm fold around my back and as I look up I realise its Luke. He asks how his three favourite girls are and pulls us all into a group hug. I smile at Flippity and I'd like to say she smiled back but I doubt lifting the corners of your mouth for a mere split-second counts as a smile, does it?

Am I really a drama queen?

Chapter 33

EFFERVESCENT WHISPER

Lizzie

Pulling up outside Ruby's house, I call her number for the third time and once again it rings and goes to voicemail. I know we're both useless at getting back to one another's messages, but it's been weeks now since I last heard from my best friend. Jumping out of the car I head up the drive. Her car is on the drive and I'm surprised to see the curtains drawn so early. I knock and wait. And wait. I stand back from the door and swear I see movement behind the curtains. I knock again, harder, and this time I hear footsteps. The front opens and a red-faced Ruby meets me.

'Hey, you!' I exclaim stepping forward to go in and more than a little perturbed when Ruby pushes the door forward to stop me. 'Oh. I've err ... been trying to get hold of you for ages,' I continue.

'Oh, don't come in,' Ruby replies, 'I'm a bloody mess. Got a terrible cold.'

She certainly sounds nasally. 'Really?' Ruby nods her head. 'You've got a bad cold and you're too ill to pick up your phone?'

The corners of Ruby's mouth turn up into a smile. 'Sorry,' she replies. 'It's shitty, more like the bloody flu actually. I just don't have the energy to do anything.'

I ask her if there's anything I can do to help but Ruby assures me Harvey has everything in hand. A mass of dark hair pops up against Ruby's leg and I'm met by a bright eyed but sombre looking Andrew. 'Wizzie,' he exclaims. I bend down to say hello. 'Mummy's not well again,' he says.

'No. I can see that darling. You and Harvey must look after her until she's better. Okay?'

Andrew sticks out his bottom lip. 'We are,' he sighs.

Reaching into my bag I pull out my emergency chocolate bar and pass it to Andrew. He squeezes through the half-closed door, grabs it from my hand and hugs me. 'Thank you, Wizzie,' he says.

Standing up again I tell Ruby that I am going to see Scott. 'He has a new flat, apparently.' Whispering, I ask her if she'd like me to take Andrew with me to give her a rest but she declines. 'He's been a bit sniffy today, too' Ruby replies. 'Wouldn't want you catching this cold.' Andrew, who is looking up at Ruby, sniffs the air and looks every bit as confused as I feel. I hover for a minute, half expecting Ruby to ask after Dad or Maisy but when it becomes apparent she's not going to, I wish her a swift recovery and she agrees to meet me for coffee when she is well again.

I turn away and the door closes swiftly behind me. A slight wind rustles my hair and autumnal leaves lift from the ground, thrown skywards into swirling patterns of red, gold and brown. I shiver, ever so slightly, and wonder if what I think I hear is the quiet, effervescent whisper of something significant or simply the rustling of the branches in the surrounding trees.

Chapter 34
BROKEN

Cassie

Luke jumps up on the kitchen worktop and watches me make coffee for us both. He smiles at me and I'm surprised at the slight fluttering in my tummy.

Must be nerves.

'Soooo,' he says, 'what's so important it couldn't wait until tomorrow night?'

I smile back at his dimpled grin. 'Because you know what it's like when the rest of the band are here, and Felicity, it's almost impossible to talk to you on your own.'

Luke raises his eyes and laughs. 'Yeah, true. Honey will be the worst, though. Demanding to be centre of attention as it's her birthday.'

I roll my eyes and laugh. 'Will she ever!'

'Have you bought her a cake?'

'Not yet. I was thinking of making one.'

'Really?'

'Don't sound so surprised!' I reply, flicking his leg with a tea towel. 'Yeah, and now I've thought about it, I can't be arsed, so I'll buy one tomorrow, after work.'

Luke swings his legs and taps his fingers against the washing machine, like a drum. Like a true musician, he has perfect rhythm and I wonder if, like me, music is always playing in his head. I pass him a mug of hot coffee; 'shaken not stirred,' we both say at the same time, and he follows me into the living room that tomorrow will be filled with balloons and streamers and lots of drunk and stoned friends to celebrate Honey's twenty-second birthday.

God, I hope it doesn't get as messy as her twenty-first.

I throw myself into our battered old sofa and Luke sits next to me. Suddenly serious, he asks me how Grandad is. I shrug my shoulders and tell him the truth. 'He's very thin. The chemo hasn't worked but Mum said he's been a bit more stable recently.' I don't tell Luke I'm hoping and praying the cannabis oil Uncle Sean got for Grandad is working, reversing the effects of the cancer and that maybe, just maybe, Grandad may get better. Uncle Sean says he thinks it's too late, that we found out about the cancer too late but he does know people who've had cancer, not as advanced as Grandad's, and it's worked. Taking cannabis oil has made them better.

'Talking of thin,' Luke says nodding at me, 'doesn't suit you Cas.'

'Thanks!'

'Sorry but it's the truth. I'm worried about you. You haven't got one of those stupid eating disorders, have you?'

I sigh heavily and roll my eyes. I know Luke means well but why does no one ever listen to me. I explain again about working long hours in the studio and forgetting to eat. 'And I am worried about my Grandad, I add, 'and like my mum, when I worry, it goes straight to my stomach and I can't eat.' I don't tell him I lost my appetite months ago and the real reason I can't eat is because I'm filled up with guilt.

'It's a good job I brought this with me, then,' he replies, pulling out a huge slab of chocolate. 'Now, eat,' he orders.

I put my hand to my head and salute him. 'Yes sir,' I reply.

Luke throws a cushion at me. 'Idiot,' he laughs. 'So, come on then, why did you lure me here, all alone? If it was to have mad, passionate sex I'm afraid to say I'm taken.'

Taking a big slurp of my coffee, I sigh. Why did I agree to do this? 'We-ll,' I say, placing my mug on the manky, stained coffee table and ripping open the wrapper of the huge chocolate bar. 'The truth is,' I continue, greedily breaking off a couple of chunks and putting them into my mouth as an explosion of chocolate melts on my tongue.

'Bloody hell, Cas, you look like you're having an orgasm rather than eating chocolate.'

'Mmmm ... I forgot how good chocolate tastes.'

Luke mumbles something about some people being easily pleased, then asks me again what it is I wanted.

'Okay. The truth is Jay phoned me *again*. Won't stop bugging me in fact. And asked me to–'

'Oh for fuck's sake Cas,' Luke interrupts, slamming his mug down. He slams it so hard, coffee sloshes onto the table adding yet more stains. 'Not this shit again.'

I jump and feel my tummy twist into knots as I watch Luke's lovely smiley face turn into a big, fat frowning one. I've never seen him look so pissy before. But it's no big deal. I've dealt with people much angrier, like the time, not long after starting uni, when a whole group of us went to the offy late one night. There were shutters on some of the drinks shelves, pulled three quarters of the way down. Some of the boys started lifting the shutters, grabbing some booze then pulling them back down. I was one of the last to get a drink so I just copied everyone else. That's when the shopkeeper called me a little bitch, told the boy in front of me to "control your woman, man." I was stunned, for a few seconds. Never been talked to like that by anyone. I soon put him right though, told him I wasn't anyone's woman and the only bitch in the shop was him. I also told him I'd make it my life's work to tell anyone who would listen, what an arrogant pig he was and to never, *ever* shop there. I then dumped the drink I'd picked up on the counter, and walked out as the whole shop erupted into loud cheering and applause. No one knew I was so frightened my legs had turned to jelly and I thought I was going to shit myself. But that was much worse than Luke getting arsy.

So why the hell do I feel like bursting into tears, again? I swear to god I'm losing it.

'But … but it sounds like an amazing opportunity,' I reply, trying to keep the wobble out of my voice.

'Yeah, coz that's how Jay has sold it to you. It's all right for him, his parents are loaded, so it's no biggy for him if he shells out for the flight and accommodation and it all goes tits up.'

'What do the others think?'

Luke runs his hand through his hair. 'I dunno,' he sighs, 'I think they wanna go but they're worried about the money too, like me.'

'But if you said you'd do it, they would, too?'

Luke shrugs his shoulders. 'Probably. There's no guarantee it'll help us, though. It's just a sort of mini-tour of a few states in America and most of that will be guest slots on radio stations.'

'But they've shown an interest in the band, and you already have a bit of a following with some of their listeners?'

'Yeah.'

'And it includes some live gigs?' Luke nods his head. 'So, sod the money and take a chance! My mum has to do loads of her own book promotion, even though she has an agent and publisher. It's what you have to do if you want to get on, Luke.'

'It's not that simple.'

'Why? It's not as if you're an old married man with kids and stuff.'

'Felicity doesn't want me to.'

'Forget Felicity. Your music is way more important and–'

'Yeah well that's the trouble with you Cas, you always put yourself before others. You're so messed up about your parents' divorce; you won't let anyone near you. You don't have a clue what loving someone means, what you're willing to do for them. And sometimes that means a bit of sacrifice.'

I'm so shocked by Luke's outburst that for once, I'm speechless. I feel my mouth open to speak but no words follow, so it just hangs there, opening and closing, like a trapped fish in a bowl.

'Besides,' Luke continues, 'Felicity's dad wants me to start working full-time for him, and even though it'll be long hours, I'll still have the weekends and shit loads of money to put back into the band.'

'If Felicity lets you,' I mumble.

'What the hell do you know about it, Cassie,' Luke says standing up.

I hear a key in the lock of the front door and Luke and I both look towards it. The door crashes open and a red-faced Honey walks in. Ignoring Luke, she strides straight up to me, her screwed up face hovering above mine.

'You fucking bitch,' she yells.

Flinching, I feel something hot between my legs. Ashamed, I realise its pee, not much, but I've actually pissed my pants. 'What?' I reply nervously inching my way further down the sofa.

Honey bends forward and brings her face closer to mine. She's so close I can feel her hot, angry breath on my cheeks. 'I've just had Hunter Black on the phone,' she replies, sarcasm dripping from her voice. I close my eyes and feel my heart sink. 'He said he's been trying to get hold of me, for ages, for months, in fact. Been asking you to tell me to get in touch with him. He was shocked when I told him we were flatmates coz apparently you told him you don't see me very often.' Luke looks at me, and frowns. I feel my cheeks burn and my throat tighten. 'Why, Cassie? Why didn't you tell me? You're supposed to be my best fucking friend. Surely you know what working with someone like him could do for my singing career?'

'I ... I ...'

'You. You. WHAT?' Honey shouts.

Hot tears sting my eyes. My mouth dries up and I find it almost impossible to swallow. 'I just think you deserve better than him,' I finally manage to whisper.

Honey straightens up and smirks at me in a way that would give Cruella Deville a run for her money. 'Better than the best in the industry!'

Actually, he's not the best, it's the people that work for him who do all the work and he takes all the credit for it.

'Fuck you. You selfish bitch. You know what?' Honey continues, tapping her hands on her bony hips. 'I found this flat, you've got a week to pack up your shit then I want you out.'

'But … But … you can't do that! Please don't, Honey, you don't understand.'

'Too right I don't understand. And I *can* do it. I mean it, you've got a week. And in the meantime, keep out of my sight.' Honey turns to Luke. He wears a look of huge disappointment. 'Luke, take me for a coffee will you, before I smash her smug face in.'

They both leave. Our flat is deathly quiet. My two best friends in the whole world hate me and there's nothing I can do about it. I pull my knees up to my chin and hug them tight. My tears are so hot they sting my already burning cheeks. Rocking back and forth I sob uncontrollably.

I want to die. I actually want to die.

Chapter 35
SORRY

Lizzie

I sip my coffee and politely look around the freshly painted room.

'It's nice, Scott,' I remark. 'Much better than your last–'

'Dump?' Scott interrupts.

'Well, I wasn't going to say that but, yes, I suppose it was a dump.'

Scott smiles, and I immediately see Connor. 'Connor prefers it here, I think? Although, he still doesn't come over much.'

'It's just his age,' I reply. 'He's never at home much these days either, always out with his friends. Or when he does grace us with his presence, he's usually ensconced in his bedroom, laptop in one hand, phone in the other.'

Scott looks down and picks his fingernails. 'Nah, it's not just that,' he says, shaking his head. 'The kids, and rightfully so, don't really trust me.'

I raise my eyes and look directly at my ex-husband. 'It's self-preservation, Scott. You put us, them, through a lot. And you were always letting them down.'

Sitting forward, Scott clasps both hands together and hangs his head. His thick hair is greying much quicker than Simon's.

Stress, maybe? Serves him right.

'I'm sorry, Lizzie.'

'For what?'

'For everything.'

'Oh shit, not this again. I know! You're forgiven. Just don't let the kids down again or I'll come after you, with a carving knife, cut off your balls, fry them and feed them to the cat.' Scott raises his eyes and lets out a nervous laugh. 'You'll get there, with the kids I mean, in time,' I add reassuringly. 'You've just got to keep working at it. Show them they can trust you.'

Scott nods his head and asks me how the writing is going. I tell him it's great. 'When I can get some peace and quiet that is. Having Maisy and Crazee living with us doesn't exactly make for a quiet life.'

Scott coughs and runs a finger around the collar of his T-shirt. 'You, could always come here?' he offers. 'During the day when I'm at work? If you want some quiet time?'

Raising my eyes, I laugh. Scott, whose face is now turning an interesting crimson colour, waves his hand in the air dismissively.

'Forget I said that. Bad idea.'

'No. It's a great idea,' I reply. 'It's just …'

'Just, what?'

I lift my hand to move my fringe out of my eyes. 'I don't know. I suppose I just never imagined a day when you and I would, well, get on.'

We both laugh and I ask him if he's seen much of Ruby lately.

'No. She used to pop round the old flat a couple of times a week with Andrew, lovely kid. So easy going. Can see so much of Andy in him.'

I nod and smile affectionately. 'What do you think of Harvey?'

'Funny, I was just going to ask you the same thing. I never see a lot of him, if I'm honest. I got the impression he didn't much like me talking to Ruby when we were all in Cornwall.'

'Really?'

'Yeah, didn't warn me off exactly, just made it clear he didn't like my presence. And I know a lot has happened, that Ruby still misses Andy, least that's what she told me last time she came round, but …'

Scott trails off and sighs. 'What?' I reply.

He scratches the back of his head the same way Connor

does. 'I dunno, she seems so sad, I suppose. You know, like the spark has died.' I can't help but agree with my ex-husband's observations and find myself nodding my head accordingly. 'What do you think of Harvey, then?' he continues.

'I don't know really. He seems nice enough. A bit square sometimes but otherwise very charming. And Andrew seems to have taken to him, but ...'

'But what?'

'Can't put my finger on it. Maybe it's just that he's so different to Andy.' I tell Scott about my visit to Ruby. 'It just seemed so strange her not letting me in? So out of character.'

'How was Andrew, did he seem okay?'

'I suppose so. Looked a bit down in the dumps like little ones do sometimes but nothing more than that. Soon cheered up when I gave him a bar of chocolate.'

A moment of silence hangs between us and I'm annoyed at the cynicism rising within me. It's all very well that my ex-husband appears concerned about the welfare of my best friend, but in my opinion a leopard never changes it's spots, or so the saying goes. It's true Scott is not the same man he was five years ago, or twenty years ago for that matter and I can see he's really trying with Cassie and Connor, but for as many years as I can remember, Scott has only ever had one true love, money. And Ruby, of course, is loaded, more so since Andy died. And, as distasteful as it is and as ashamed as I am for considering it, I can't help but wonder if my ex-husband's interest in my best friend is for ulterior motives.

'I'm sure they're fine,' I eventually reply. 'Besides, I think we'd soon know it if Ruby wasn't okay, feisty as fuck when something pisses her off.'

Scott smirks and raises his left eye. 'Too right, she certainly gave me what for when she first visited. Said you'd put her up to it but if it was up to her she'd happily watch me burn in the fires of hell for all the shit I'd put you and the kids through.'

'That's what friends are for,' I reply laughing. Scott offers me another cuppa but I decline. 'Need to get back to the madhouse,' I say rolling my eyes.

'Well, don't forget my offer,' Scott says, his face reddening a little again. 'You can always use the flat for your writing. It's the least I can do after everything you and Simon have done for me. I'll get you a key cut if you like?'

Leaning forward I look at Scott. He flinches a little and frowns in a way that reminds me of Cassie. 'Who are you and where has the real Scott, selfish bastard extraordinaire, gone?'

Scott lets out a small laugh from the corner of his mouth and looks down. Eventually looking up again, his face is suddenly serious. He reminds me of the Scott I first met and fell in love with many years ago and for the briefest of moments I feel a tiny flutter in my tummy.

'You were the best thing that ever happened to me Lizzie, and I let you go,' he says.

My thorax tightens and for a few seconds, words fail me. We're so close I can feel Scott's breath on my cheek.

Oh no! He's not going to try and kiss me, is he!

'Too right,' I quickly reply. It does the trick and once again laughter fills the awkward silence hanging between us.

Scott closes the door behind me and I walk away wearing a small but triumphant grin.

That'll do Lizzie. That'll do.

♥

Chapter 36

DESCENT

Cassie

Looking at my phone, I check the address again. Hunter is doing this on purpose; to show me he's mad at me. Making me travel half way across London to pick up a package that could just as easily be sent by courier. Wouldn't be surprised if I no longer have a job when I get back to the studio. That'll be the perfect end to a shit week. Nowhere to live and no job. Not homeless though, of course. I can always go home to Mum and Simon, and Maisy and Crazee and Connor. I wonder if Maisy and Crazee are going to go back to Oz? God, don't think I could live with a screaming baby.

Maybe, if I just give Honey a couple more days to calm down, she'll give me the chance to talk to her. God knows what I'd say though. Where would I even begin? At least she wasn't awake when I left the flat this morning. Don't think I could have handled her screaming at me again.

I look up at the building in front of me and see the number I'm looking for, 66E. It's a beautiful old Georgian house with stark white walls surrounded by black metal railings. The immaculately painted green door with the huge gold knocker opens and a girl steps out with a broom in her hand. She starts sweeping away discarded cigarette butts. I'm sure I don't know her but she seems familiar. She looks up as a rickety old rickshaw containing two men, laughing, passes by. One of the men, wearing a bright pink shirt with a tiny dog tucked under his arm, shouts in her direction.

'Coooo eeeee! Amy darling,' he says. 'Come round for drinks

later?' Resting on her broom, the girl, Amy, looks up, smiles and waves back as the two men in the rickshaw disappear around the corner out of sight. As her eyes follow the rickshaw she spots me and stares for a few seconds then, taking her broom with her, she heads back towards the green door and disappears back inside.

I cross the road and stand in front of the huge polished door. The paint is so glossy I can see my own reflection in it. I spot the keypad to the left of me and press the buzzer beneath it. After a few seconds, a crackling sound followed by a droning, unwelcoming voice asks me for my name. I lean into the buzzer and tell them. There's another, louder buzzing noise and the voice behind the speaker tells me to push the door. I step into a huge, bright hallway with a black and white tiled floor that meets a wide sweeping staircase. It reminds me of some of the old black and white movies Mum and Nan like to watch sometimes. The ones with glamorous ladies with porcelain skin and perfectly arched eyebrows, wearing long, floaty dresses, who always seem to drift down the stairs smoking French cigarettes in long, black holders.

'Cassie?' a voice asks. I turn and see the girl who had been sweeping up outside, Amy. 'You've come to collect a package, for Hunter?' she says.

Nodding, I smile and she asks me to follow her. As we climb the stairs I look up, tingling bits of glass swing ever so slightly from the huge, expensive looking chandelier hanging from the high ceiling. We walk quite slowly because she's wearing heels, although god only knows why because she's already tall. She looks like a model in her tight black skirt and beautiful white blouse. Completely different to me in my jeans and T-shirt. Stopping at the first set of double doors at the top of the stairs, Amy pushes them open. Straight backed and confident, she strides in and I follow, only, as soon as I do, I realise I need to leave again, immediately. Amy points to a comfy sofa and tells me to sit and wait for her. I follow her finger and sit like I'm told but my head is swimming and I feel like I'm drowning in a sea of blue fish. The blue wallpapered walls are covered in the fish from my dreams and like a gun going off in my head something has snapped. Everything comes flooding back to me, like a bad, bad dream.

Chapter 37

USE IT OR LOSE IT

Connor

I get out of the car nervously looking around. The last thing I need is someone like Maximus Anus seeing me (I'm glad I'm done with school and won't have to see much of his twatish face any more) going into the library, of all places. I mean … I get that Mum worked here for years and now she's a writer she still likes to visit, as an author and a customer, but libraries are done, in my opinion. If you want to read a book, all you need to do is tap your phone.

'Connor. Will you stop looking at your phone and help me, please?' Mum, who is wearing her moody face again, passes me a box of books. I shove my phone back into my jeans pocket and take the box she's holding. At least I can hide behind it.

'Hi Connor,' a voice says behind me. I swing around, peeking from the side of the box and die right there and then, of embarrassment.

'Oh, hi Hayley,' I reply.

She asks me what I'm doing and I reluctantly explain I was forced into helping Mum set up her display for her author reading.

Looking up, Hayley frowns. 'I thought all the libraries had closed.'

'They soon will be,' Mum interrupts, 'if the government has anything to do with it. Use it or lose it.'

'I don't really like reading,' Hayley replies.

Mum rolls her eyes. 'God help us,' she mumbles; asking me to please follow her as we are already running late.

I smile at Hayley and keep trying to stop myself imagining her naked. I ask her how things are going at college with her beauty course.

'Brilliant,' she replies. 'I'm the best in our class, even started my own blog about beauty. I already have well over a thousand followers on Twitter. You should follow me, too,' she suggests.

I smile weakly. 'Erm ... not sure I'm really into my beauty stuff.'

'Oh it's not just beauty advice, I give fashion advice for boys, too,' she says, running her eyes up and down my body so that for the briefest of moments I feel my knob start to go hard. 'And you could certainly do with some help,' she adds, as my semi boner shrinks like a balloon losing its air.

Hayley says goodbye and I can't help watching her arse wiggle in her tighter than tight jeans. I suddenly think of Alesha. How hard must it be for her watching other girls our age strutting their stuff, knowing she never can.

As I walk through the library doors, I'm greeted by another, older wiggling arse, Tabitha, nosy neighbour and Mum's hairdresser. 'Thank you. I'll take those,' she says lifting the box of books from my arms and marching towards the table Mum is setting up on. 'Your mum doesn't have a clue about displays.'

Nah, only twenty odd years in the library service.

Mum watches Tabitha striding towards her and looks at me with a "help me" look. I hold my hands up and shrug. Everyone knows there's no stopping Tabitha when she gets an idea about something. And she loves being our neighbour and Mum's hairdresser, tells all her clients all the time. 'I'm very good friends with the famous writer, Lizzie Lemalf, you know,' she says. They must be bored shitless with that news by now.

'Connor!' a voice says behind me. 'How the devil are you?' I turn to see Raj, Mum's gay friend who she used to work with here. 'You're looking good man innit.'

'Thanks Raj,' I reply, high fiving him. 'You too. How's it going?'

'Yeah, good man. Not as good as your mum though, eh?' he says nodding towards the table Tabitha has now taken control of. 'We're all so proud of her. You must be, too?'

'I suppose,' I reply, shrugging my shoulders. I haven't really given much thought about Mum being a writer. Mum is still just Mum to me. It's not like our lives have changed that much. We still live in the same house and the car she drives is just a newer version of her old Beetle. I suppose she doesn't worry about money like she used to, especially when Dad left us, before she met Simon, and she travels quite a bit sometimes. She always has her bloody head in her bloody phone or laptop, too, but other than that, Mum is just, well, Mum.

Raj explains they are short staffed today, and as Mum appears to have plenty of help setting up he asks me if I'd like to help him out with some of the library customers who are here for the computer course. I don't really want to but before I've had time to reply, Raj has linked arms with me and is shouting to Mum that he is going to borrow her handsome son for half an hour.

There's a real mix of people doing the computer course, some old, some young, some girls, and boys, no older than me, with babies in prams. Some, judging by their greasy hair and dodgy smelling clothes, clearly don't have a lot and some people look ill. Raj says some of the people are lonely and like being around other people for company, he also says quite a lot of them are looking for work and as everything is done online these days and quite a few of the customers can't afford laptops or computers, they rely heavily on the library.

Ashamed, I realise not everyone is as lucky as me. We're not rich, in any way, shape or form but we're not struggling like these people. Libraries are not just for books, and the government is so wrong to close them down. What will happen to the people like this? Then again, I don't think the government really gives a shit.

I actually have a really peng time, especially with some of the oldies, they remind me of Nan and Grandad, and find myself agreeing to help out as a volunteer on the computer course once a week. Raj thanks me for my help and we wander back to where Mum is just wrapping up. The turnout is really good and loads of people are laughing at the extract she is reading from her book. I've never properly seen Mum in action before and she seems really happy and relaxed, and it's nice, especially after what happened to her a few years back and now what with Grandad and everything, well, it's just nice to see her smile. She finishes speaking, to a large round of applause and people rushing forwards to get their copy of her book signed. Mum looks up, spots me, smiles and mouths "thank you." I'm surprised, really surprised, when a lump catches in my throat. Nodding and smiling, I look down, kicking one foot with the other, pretending to rub a mark off my trainer. I think about what a moody git I've been lately.

I laugh when I look up again and hear Tabitha telling some of the ladies leaving that she's Mum's hairdresser. Handing out her business cards she shoots me a sarcastic look and marches straight towards another group of people getting their coats on.

Really Tabitha? Is this Mum's event or yours?

Mum said she's alright but I'm not sure I like Tabitha that much, even though she is our next-door neighbour.

My phone buzzes and I'm disappointed to see it's a group chat from the boys, I was hoping it was Alesha. Think I have to accept that I like her more than she likes me. Feeling a heavy hand on my shoulder I swing around to see Raj again.

'We're so, so proud of her innit,' Raj says for the second time today, his eyes all teary. Raj loves Mum coz she helped him when he was trying to come out of the closet, or got stuck in it, or something. I follow Raj's gaze now resting with admiration on

Mum. I suppose I don't always admit it but, yeah, I am proud of Mum and just for a few seconds I stupidly find myself wishing I was ten years old again and could run straight up to her and give her a great, big, bear hug.

Chapter 38

GOING UNDERGROUND

Cassie

Some people don't like the underground, say it makes them feel claustrophobic, which during the rush hours of frantic mornings and work wearied evenings is understandable, I suppose. Squashed people from all walks of life forced together like caged animals. A bit like the poor cows with their huge terrified eyes in the videos about factory farming that Maisy made me watch recently. I know that look, understand that fear, although mine is for a different reason, but nonetheless, fear it is.

It's not rush hour now though; it's late morning. There's plenty of room to move and I don't have to stand next to some pervert with BO whose wandering hands "accidently" touch me. I have a seat and there are plenty of empty ones for anyone who needs one.

The carriage rocks gently from side to side and on this train, full of strangers, I feel strangely comforted, weirdly safe. My phone vibrates again and when I look at the screen I see it's Hunter, again. My tummy flips and the hate and fear crawl up and lodge in my throat again. I stab at his name with my finger.

Go fuck yourself, Hunter.

I tap out a text telling him I've been ill, chucking up everywhere, which is true, and that I'll try and get back into work later or tomorrow because right now I'm going home, back to the flat. Amy will back me up if he calls the club because it was her designer shoes I threw up on.

I tuck my phone back in my pocket, along with Hunter's package, and look up. A woman opposite me smiles. A white blanket is draped across her shoulder and clearly covers the baby she is holding. She starts wriggling, using her free hand to adjust her top, hidden behind the white blanket. It's clear from her movements she's trying to free her boob to feed her baby. She looks a bit embarrassed but smiles at me again and again I smile back. I think of Maisy and her ever growing bump and wonder if she'll breastfeed? Then I wonder how I can think about normal things when I feel as though I'm going to explode from the inside out.

I notice a man a couple of seats down from the breastfeeding woman glance in her direction. Each look is followed by a shake of his head as stubby fingers stroke his carefully groomed beard that I'm pretty convinced he thinks is designer, but just makes him look like a twat.

'Excuse me,' he shouts, leaning forward to look at the woman and her baby. 'Yes! You, the one with her tit hanging out! Can you put it away please?'

There are a few inward gasps as I, and a few others look around at each other in disbelief. Maybe she's used to this kind of abuse, though, because the woman feeding her baby doesn't look anywhere near as upset as I feel on her behalf. She simply states that she needs to feed her baby and looks away from the man. He isn't finished though. His piggy eyes knit together to form a frown and he starts again. Going on about how her exposing herself offends him, how he's had a bad week at work and he doesn't want to be subjected to such indecent behaviour. Feeling helpless, I look around the carriage. It's as though I'm back with the fish from my dreams again, as all around me, mouths open and close. People desperate to say something but scared to at the same time. And I'm no better. As angry as I am, I'm shocked to find myself paralysed by fear.

The offensive man carries on verbally laying into the woman and her baby and when a few brave people, women mostly, dare to speak up for her, he turns his nasty tongue on them. I start shaking and feel sick again. The shaking starts at my feet and works its way up my frozen body, slowly but surely, until one of my legs starts to jump up and down. I cover my knee with my hand to stop it but it doesn't help as my leg continues to jerk up and down, up and down, until I disappear from everything and everyone around me. I can hear a song playing in my head, 'Going Underground' by The Jam, good song. One of Grandad's favourites. I wish Grandad was here now, he'd put that idiot right. Grandad always puts things right. Always makes me feel better. But he can't now, because he's dying. Oh god, Grandad is dying and everything is a mess and I can't tell anyone.

'You're just a sexist pig,' I scream.

I suddenly realise I'm standing up, both fists clenched, and the woman with the baby is staring at me. She looks concerned and pats the seat next to her. I realise the sexist pig now has his back turned and two men, one tall, dark skinned man, the other, smaller but stocky, a bit like a body builder, are sitting either side of the woman. There is a seat gap each side of her, polite space to feed her baby, but it's like they have formed an invisible, protective barrier around her. I'm grateful. Grateful and relieved. Partly that the woman is okay but mostly because it shows that there are good men around.

The woman pats the seat next to her again and nods at me to take it. Which I do. She looks at me. Her eyes are soft and you just know there isn't a bad bone in this woman's body. Taking my hand, she asks me if I'm okay.

I laugh. 'Shouldn't I be the one asking you that?' I reply. She responds with a smile and, although I try to stop them, fat, hot tears run down my face.

♥

Chapter 39

"GUILT SPILLS ITSELF IN FEARING TO BE SPILT"

Cassie

I wake with a start. The curtains are closed and the room is dark. Is it day or night? I can't remember. My bed feels warm and safe. I draw my legs up and curl into a tight ball. I feel ill. Really ill. There's nothing wrong with me, I know that, but I feel ill all the same. With knees pressed close to my chest, I hug my legs with both arms. The foetal position, that's what it's called – I think. I wonder why we do that? Curl up into a protective ball when things are bad. I wonder why the foetal position is so comforting? Takes us back to a safe place I suppose. Away from all the drama, all the crap. I close my eyes as a wave of sickness washes over me. I didn't even give the life that started inside me the chance to find out about the foetal position. A couple of pills and a couple of days later and all traces of new life were gone. Because I am a bad, bad, stupid person, at least, that's what some people think.

I've watched in amazement as Maisy's tummy has swelled. I've also seen how she looks at me. She thinks I'm selfish. She hasn't said as much but I know that's what she's thinking. She doesn't understand how I could have an abortion. But she shouldn't judge me. It's different for her. She's got Crazee. And even if I did have someone that loved me like Crazee loves her, I'm still not sure I wouldn't have gone through with it. I wasn't and I'm still not ready for that kind of commitment. Me and a baby? I can barely look after myself. Anyway, people shouldn't judge me. No one should judge anyone. Maisy wouldn't judge me if she knew what really happened. But that shouldn't make any bloody difference. It was my decision, my body, my choice. No one, no woman, no man, no religion, no one has the fucking right to judge me. I should have taken more care though. Should have been more vigilant. If I'd been more careful it never would have happened in the first place. I deserve everything I got, I suppose.

I release my legs and pull my arms up from under the duvet. Screwed into balls to make fists, I hit my head, repeatedly. 'Fuck off! Fuck off! Fuck off!' I shout. I want my thoughts to just fuck the hell off. I don't want to accept what I've known all along. Why didn't I deal with it at the time? I must have known? Surely, I must have known? I just chose to bury it rather than deal with it. And if I think that, then that's what everyone else will think. How can I tell anyone? They'll think I'm a liar. A bitch who cried wolf. And they'll question why I never said anything before, at the time when it happened. People might say I'm doing it for attention or worse still, for money? I'm fucked. I've been fucked and I'm fucked and I can't tell a soul because no one will believe me. Except Mum, maybe. But how can I tell her with everything else going on? With Grandad and Maisy and her book stuff. I can't. I can't do that to her.

I'm thirsty. Really thirsty. I need to get up. I try and lift my head off the pillow but it feels too heavy, so I put it back down. I try and swallow but my tongue sticks to the roof of my mouth. I'm so thirsty. Should get up. But I can't. I feel too ill.

Someone is laughing. I panic and turn my head to try and listen. Who is it? My heart beats and my head swims. I try and lift my head again but it's still too heavy. I listen, relieved. The laughing is coming from the TV, I think. That's right, I put the TV on. I'm not watching it, though. Not really listening to it either. I just put it on for company, so I wasn't alone. I need to concentrate. Listen to the voices on the telly so I don't have to listen to the voices in my head. Me, my head, and I are not a nice place to be right now. I know what this is. I'm depressed and too afraid to face the truth. I want to tell someone but there isn't anyone, not really.

I think of Honey, or Dad, maybe I can tell Dad? My heart sinks. Honey hates me and Dad is, well, Dad. They wouldn't believe me anyway, especially Honey. There would be too many questions and Dad would probably persuade me to go to the police. I can't go to the police because I'd probably, no I'd definitely, lose my job. Oh god, how can I ever go back to work?

I throw my duvet over my head and scream to an empty flat. I don't want to think. I don't want to tell. Or make decisions. I've managed for all this time. I'll just carry on as normal. But wait. What if this has happened before, to someone else? Or happens to someone else. Shit. I do have to tell someone. But who? Who the hell can I tell? What about all the drama there will be, all the pain it will cause, especially for Mum and Grandad. The two people I want to tell. The two people who will believe me, no matter how much it gets twisted. No matter how much I'll be made to look like a liar. Because I will be. So, no! I can't tell. I have to get over it and move on. Hope and pray I was the first and the last. I'll put it down to bad luck and stupidity. It could have been worse. It could have been much worse.

'Arrrrrgggghh.' Why am I talking like it was all my fault? Like the prick on the train. The man. The stupid man acting like a pig because that woman wouldn't do as she was told. 'Arrrrrgggghh! I hate men!!! What gives them the right? What gives them the FUCKING RIGHT?'

My anger scares me but it disappears as quickly as it came and now I'm frightened again. Frightened and confused. My thoughts are interrupted by a low buzzing noise. I turn my head towards the direction of what sounds like a trapped bee and realise it's my phone buzzing. I stare, fascinated, as my phone, set to vibrate, dances on my bedside cabinet. Someone is ringing me but I don't want to answer it. I wait for my phone to stop dancing then pick it up. I swipe the screen and its bright light almost blinds me. I squint and wait a few seconds for my eyes to adjust. As the blurred words come into focus the glaring luminescent screen of my phone tells me I have six missed calls from Hunter. Relieved it's nothing to do with Grandad I put my phone back down again. Hunter can wait.

Burying my head in my pillow I start crying. It's just a few tears at first. But the more I think about everything the more the tears come. I shouldn't, because I have good friends and a brilliant family, but I feel so utterly and desperately alone. Maybe if Grandad wasn't so sick I could tell someone. Tell Mum. Mum would know what to do. She'd have all the answers. She'd make it all better. But how? How can I tell her when Grandad is so poorly? Wiping my hot, wet face with the back of my hand, my sobbing becomes so loud and so tortured it drowns out everything else around me. Every noise, every thought is washed away by my wailing. I don't hear the front door open. I don't hear the loud voices that fill the living room. The voices, of men, loud and threatening and demanding.

'Get the alcohol out. Where's the fucking party?'

I don't hear them though. I don't hear them until it's too late that is, and one of them is in the room. I don't hear my bedroom door open. I don't hear him enter the room and I don't even realise when he's hovering above my bed. Because I'm crying. Crying so loud it drowns out everything, which is exactly what I want.

I feel a hand on my head and freeze.

'Cas. Cassie. Can you hear me Cas? What's wrong?'

Holding my breath, I slowly pull my duvet down. My room is dark but I'd recognise that leather jacket anywhere.

'Luke? Is that you?' My voice is now so quiet that not even I recognise it.

'Shit, Cassie. You look like, well, like shit. What the hell is wrong?'

I look at Luke's face and for the first time today I feel safe. It takes all my strength but I manage to pull myself up to a sitting position. Luke sits down on the bed opposite me and takes my hand into his. I use the back of my other hand to wipe the tears that still fall as Luke snaps on the bedside lamp next to me. He stares at my tear stained face and frowns. I look bad, I know I do. Part of me feels ashamed to let Luke see me looking so bad, part of me feels relieved to see a friend. Luke smiles at me and lifts his hand to my cheek to move my hair away from my eyes. I hear laughing in the living room and my eyes shift towards the door. Luke follows my questioning eyes.

'It's the lads,' he says. 'And Felicity.'

But my brain does not compute. 'But … how did you get in?'

'Honey,' Luke replies. 'She was at our gig. Remember? She gave me the keys to get in because we all agreed to come back here, for Honey's birthday. Remember? She said, after what happened with you two yesterday, she thought you were going to be out?'

I cringe and shrug my shoulders. 'Didn't feel well,' I reply.

'No, I can see that. Do, you want us to leave? If you're not feeling well?'

I shake my head and force myself to smile. 'No. It's fine. Honey would never forgive me, again. Where is she, anyway?'

Luke twists his mouth to the side. 'Look, I don't know what the hell is going on with you two and frankly I don't wanna get involved. And I'm sorry about yesterday,' Luke adds, looking down, 'I shouldn't have talked to you like that. I know you meant well and …'

My mind starts racing and alarmed, I sit bolt upright. I'm not bothered about Luke's apology right now. 'Luke,' I interrupt, 'where is she? Where is Honey?'

Luke frowns. 'She's gone to some members club, with your boss. She said she thought it would be a good idea to mingle for an hour or so. You know, to help her career. Anyway, she gave me her keys and told us all to make ourselves at home until she gets back. I wasn't sure if you were here or not. I did knock.'

'Oh my god, no!' I gasp, kicking off my duvet. 'We, she can't go there. We have to get her. We have to get Honey!' I yell.

Luke grabs me by the arms and shakes me gently. 'Why? What is it Cas?' he asks.

His voice is warm and safe. It's the voice of a friend.

'I've been raped Luke. That's what's wrong. I've been raped and I haven't told anyone. Until now. Until you.'

Chapter 40

UNDER PRESSURE

Connor

I can feel the anger rising inside me.

'Shit, she's in a wheelchair!' Jake snorts.

'And?'

'You've got the hots for her.'

'Piss off, Jake.'

'Oh my god, you have. You actually fancy a spas. No wonder you didn't wanna tell us about her when you got back after the summer.'

'Don't fucking say that. She's not a spas.'

'Well, what is she then, a flid? She's in a wheelchair so she must be.'

'Now, now girls, stop arguing,' the Rickmeister interrupts.

Anger continues to swell inside me like air fills a balloon. Starting at the pit of my stomach, it travels through my pumping veins like boiling water. I stare at Jake and he leers back. I clench and unclench my fists and open my eyes as wide as I can in order to stop the tears I can feel forming at the back of them.

Jake raises his voice slightly, as if he were talking to a baby. 'Aw … is the little Conman gonna cry!' he says.

I do feel like crying. Everything feels like shit. Maisy's pregnant and emotional all the time. And we've got Crazee living with us now too. Dad keeps trying to be a dad and expects me to be happy about it. But how can I be happy? He didn't want to know me for most of my life and now he's lost everything and everyone, he expects me to spend time with him. Coz he suddenly feels shit for being a shit dad. He's seen the light, the error of his ways. Yeah right! What happens when he meets someone new and she doesn't want us, like Sharon? Knobhead. And Cassie? What the fuck. Raped. How am I supposed to feel about that? Coz the only thing I feel is terrible, terrible anger. A rage like I've never known before. I don't care that the bloke is some rich, famous somebody, I want to kill him. I can't tell anyone, though, because no one is listening. Mum's so wrapped up in her writing and Maisy's baby and Grandad, she doesn't even know I exist. Neither does Simple Simon, come to think of it. The only two people who really care, who really give a shit about me, are Nan and Grandad. And Grandad is dying.

'My old man calls me a flid,' Robbo says, 'not a very nice word. Not really.'

'That's coz you are,' Jake replies. There's real spite in his voice and I wonder where the hell my best friend has gone. Why he is behaving like an absolute tosser.

'Why don't you just shut the fuck up, Jake.'

'Why don't you fucking make me, Conman.'

'He says it's because I'm a lazy, useless, motherfucker, just like my lazy bitch of a mother,' Robbo continues. Shocked, we all look at Robbo then at one another. I always knew Robbo's dad was a bit of wanker but I've never heard him say anything like this before. Everything goes deathly quiet, until Robbo speaks again.

'I suppose I am a bit thick really. Not clever like you lot, am I? Perhaps my dad really did drop me on my head when I was a baby?' He laughs but nobody else does.

There's something really worrying about Robbo's confession and we can all feel it, even Jake has stopped being a twat. We all join in telling Robbo what a great bruv he is. How funny he is and how it's always him that makes everyone laugh. I also remind him what a great guitarist he's becoming and hopefully, if I continue helping him with his maths and English, he'll get the grades needed and will be able to stay on the music technology course at college with me.

Robbo shrugs his shoulders. 'Not much point now, my dad burned it.'

Jake and the Rickmeister's gasps are almost as loud as mine. 'He burned what? Your guitar?'

Robbo nods. 'Yep, when I got home from college the other day, he'd stacked it on top of a bonfire he'd started in the garden, along with Mum's clothes, some of my baby photographs. Shit like that.'

I lay my hand on Robbo's shoulder. 'Shit man. I'm so sorry, I never knew.'

Robbo shrugs his shoulders again. 'S'kay, not many people do. He's an alky. Just wish Mum would leave him, but she won't, too scared – I think? So, I stick around and take all his shit coz if he's giving it to me it means he's not knocking her around.'

'Fuck me, Robbo, I thought the shit going on at my house was bad enough but it doesn't seem that bad compared to you.' We all turn and look at Jake. 'Oh, what the hell, I was told not to say anything but sod it. My mum and dad are splitting up. Turns out, my mum has been having an affair with some bloke in the army or something. For two years. Two fucking years!'

We all tell Jake how sorry we are, especially when he says his mum doesn't want him living with her. 'Her new bloke doesn't like kids, apparently.'

'I know that feeling,' I reply.

'I thought your dad was better with you now?'

'He is. Doesn't mean I can forget what a complete and utter wanker he was while I was growing up, though, when I needed him.'

Jake laughs then sits down and gets out his baccy pouch and starts to roll a ciggy. 'Our parents' generation have got a lot to answer for,' he says. 'They've really fucked us up.'

I nod my head in agreement and sit down next to him. 'Yeah, Cassie and I both said we reckon we'll never have kids.'

Jake lights his freshly made fag and passes it to me and I decide now is as good as time as any to tell them about Cassie. She FaceTimed me the other night, asked me to go and get Maisy, then go somewhere private and for us both to call her back.

I tell them what Cas told us and my three best friends all look as stunned as Maisy and I did. They each open and close their mouths, as if to speak, but nothing is actually said. It's Jake who finally breaks the weird silence. 'Shit man, that's, well, that's fucking shit. Well out of fucking order.' I nod my head and use the sleeve of my hoody to wipe away the tears I'm ashamed of. Patting my shoulder, Jake pulls me into a hug, as do the other two. 'And it was her boss, you say?' Jake continues, 'that famous record producer bloke?'

'Yeah, apparently,' I reply. 'He's the one who got her pregnant.'

'Fuck,' everyone says again.

'What's Cassie gonna do?' Robbo asks.

I shrug my shoulders. 'Dunno? Think she's gonna tell the police, but it happened months ago so I think she's scared no one will believe her. And she loves her job so she's upset that she'll probably lose it. She hasn't told my mum or Si yet though. Or my nan and grandad. Just me and Maisy.

'Why?' Robbo asks.

'She wants to wait until after Christmas coz what with my grandad being sick and this probably being his last Chris ...' I trail off, suddenly unable to talk. My shoulders start to heave up and down and I feel like a huge weight has been lifted off them. Tears run from my eyes and snot from my nose. My boys gather around me and hug me and pat my back. I make them all swear down not to say a word to anyone and they promise they won't.

'My uncle knows some dodgy people,' Jake suggests. 'You

know, some real nut cases. The sort that would happily beat someone up in return for money. Even famous people, I reckon.'

I look at Jake and laugh. 'I'll bear it in mind,' I reply and it's just what we needed to break the crap atmosphere. We all laugh then look at the Rickmeister and ask him, while we're all at it, if he has anything he wants to share? Deadly serious he tells us all he is gay. My jaw drops, as does Jake's and Robbo's. I'm shocked to the core but not coz I'm gay-ist but coz he is always going on about plunging the clunge. It's only when the Rickmeister starts pissing himself laughing that we realise it's a wind up.

'Yous should see your fucking faces,' he says bending over, clutching his stomach and laughing like something possessed.

It does the trick though and well and truly clears the air.

After several minutes of hysterical laughter Jake looks at me. 'Sorry I called your girlfriend a flid.'

'She's not my girlfriend.' She'd never fancy a loser like me.

'Well, whatever, she's not a flid and neither are you Robbo.' Jake throws his arms around Robbo and holds him for approximately 0.2 seconds, as do I, as does the Rickmeister.

Robbo wipes his eyes with the backs of his hands and coughs to clear his throat.

'Thanks boys,' he says.

Chapter 41
BETRAYAL

Cassie

I stuff the rest of my clothes in my bag and look around my room. I love my bedroom. It's not particularly big, can't afford much in London but with my multi-coloured fairy lights scattered everywhere and my scented candles, I've made it mine, made it home. I love my wall collage the most. One wall, completely filled with piccies of all the crazy people I love, including Grandad who sits, with a rather grumpy look on his face, at the centre of my colourful display. Then there's my vinyl collection, stacked neatly beside my turntable, you can't seriously say you're into music unless you have vinyl. It's the law. And then of course, taking pride of place is my Nord, my beloved bright red keyboard. Not quite a baby grand piano but I love playing it anyway. I'm pretty convinced it's saved me at times. Music can do that. Music is part of the soul; at least that's what Grandad says.

The pictures on my wall start moving and my head starts spinning. I feel wobbly and flop down onto my bed, pulling my knees up tight to my chest. The idea of rolling up into a ball and not moving for a couple of years seems like a good one. I wish I could just pull the switch for a while. Turn myself off and recharge my batteries. Now, staring at the ceiling, I realise I'm even too tired to react to the spider running across it. Or maybe, after everything I've gone through, I realise spiders are not the scary ones in life, it's people that scare the shit out of me.

The spider scuttles to one of the corners of the ceiling and I find myself wondering, again, if going back to Mum and Si's on sick leave is the right thing to do. I also wonder if I've ever swallowed any spiders in my sleep? Connor said it's a well-known fact that people swallow at least four spiders in their lifetime while sleeping. The thought makes me shudder, as does the thought of spending another night here. I need to go home. My real home. The place I feel loved and most of all, safe. I need time to think about what to do.

I'm still not convinced it's worth going to the police. What would I say: "Err excuse me, I'd like to report a rape, by that famous millionaire music producer. No, I don't have any evidence, yes it happened months ago and yes I've continued to work for him since the attack. Why did I continue to work for him, you ask? Honest answer, I don't know why. Because I was scared. Because I somehow thought it was my fault and that maybe I gave him the wrong impression."

Yeah right, like anyone is ever going to believe that.

At the end of the day, it's my word against Hunter's. I don't blame Honey for not reporting him, either. She's scared. I get that. She wants to be a singer and if she calls out one of the music industry's biggest and most powerful individuals, no one will go near her, ever. And besides, thankfully, nothing much actually happened to Honey. Clearly Hunter spiked her drink, like he did mine, which is why she was passed out on the back seat of his car. But thanks to Luke's quick thinking when he intercepted Hunter's car as he pulled up outside his house, Honey didn't have to go through what I did.

I'm not sure Hunter believed Luke when he said Honey's mum was seriously ill in hospital, but waving in front of his face the package Hunter asked me to collect for him seemed to seal the deal. I wonder what was in that package? Don't give a shit, if I'm honest. Luke said Hunter seemed agitated, but thankfully he seemed to accept what Luke said, namely that I had sent Luke over to deliver the package and to find Honey to let her know about her Mum because I was too ill to do it. Thank god

I threw up in front of Amy on the morning I went to make that collection for Hunter.

My phone buzzes. It's Honey. 'Cassie babe, that you? Where are you?'

'I'm still at the flat, just finished packing my bag.'

'Well get your arse down the pub now! Luke and the boys are here and we're all celebrating because they've decided to go and do that tour in America after all. Isn't that great?'

I smile, even though Honey can't see me, but I can't make my voice do the same. 'Yeah, that's great, Honey. Really good news.'

'You okay babe? You don't sound so good?' I assure Honey I am and she asks me what time my train is leaving. When I tell her soon, she insists I must catch the later one and I must go to the pub first.

'Is, erm, Felicity there?' I ask.

Honey pauses. 'She is but Jay reckons Luke is going to finish with her. He's telling her tonight, apparently.'

'Really? Why?' I ask, feeling a tiny jolt in my heart.

'Dunno,' Honey simply replies.

Why does this news please me? A tiny spasm of hope immediately forces me to sit up. I've never been injected with adrenaline before but if I had I suspect this is what it would feel like. I feel alert and alive. Banging like a bass drum, I swear I can hear every beat of my heart between my ears. Every loud throb reminds me of the time we visited an anechoic chamber when I was at uni. Then it hits me. Oh my god. Oh my actual god. I think I love Luke. After all these years, I've slowly been falling for him, and, if he's ending his relationship with Flippity then maybe, just maybe, he feels the same way about me? Or am I jumping to conclusions?

Standing up too quickly, my head spins. I sort of feel drunk, sort of happy. At least that is until I look in the mirror. 'No!' I shout. I put Honey on loudspeaker and wave my mascara wand across my eyelashes before puffing the back of my hair up with both hands. It immediately falls flat again.

'Fuckity fuck,' I yell, 'I look a bloody mess.'

'You never look a mess babe,' Honey replies. 'Besides, it's not as if you have anyone to impress. It's only us lot.'

'No, I know that,' I lie, 'but it would be nice, if for once in my life, I didn't turn up looking like an effing bag lady.'

Honey laughs and suggests red lipstick. 'It always helps brighten me up when I feel crap,' she says.

I dig out the brightest, reddest lipstick I can find and run it over my lips. 'Oh no! It's washed me out more than I already was. Now I look like a bloody vampire!'

Honey laughs. 'See, you sort of made a joke there. I told you you'd soon be back to normal again.'

I smile at Honey's words then swear some more as I try pulling my boots on. I'm so used to wearing trainers my feet are wondering what the hell is happening to them. 'Cas,' Honey says, her voice suddenly serious, 'I really am sorry you know, for calling you a bitch.'

I stop what I'm doing and look at my phone. 'I know,' I reply. 'I'm sorry too. I, I should have told you, before.'

'The thing is,' Honey continues, 'Hunter has been in touch, and well, he's invited me to go to his actual studio and ...' Honey trails off.

A sharp wave of dread, cold and icy, scuttles down my spine. 'And, what?' I reply. Silence. 'What, Honey?' I repeat.

Honey coughs. 'Well, I was thinking if I took someone with me, and I was careful and I didn't go anywhere else with him then, well, maybe I should go to the studio?'

I can't quite believe my ears. Surely she didn't just say that? Stunned, I sit down again.

'Cas, babe, what do you think, tell me the truth?'

The truth? You don't want the fucking truth or you wouldn't

dream of doing this. Why does this betrayal feel worse than Hunter's?

'Cas? You still there?'

I struggle to find my voice. 'Yeah, whatever's best for you Honey,' I finally manage to whisper. I don't mean it but what's the point in telling the truth? I'm completely and utterly devastated. I feel like I've done a belly flop in water and I'm so winded I can barely breathe. It's so incredibly clear that what happened to me isn't important to Honey. And it's weird because her words hurt almost as much as Hunter's assault.

I walk to the bus stop, and thankfully I only have to wait a few minutes before a bus arrives. I drag my case on and find a window seat. I look up at the sky that is inky blue, filled with bright twinkly stars to match the gold and silver ones sitting on top of Christmas trees displayed in nearly every shop window I pass. Pressing my hot cheek against the cold window, I wonder about life and people. Life seemed so much easier when I was younger, when things were black and white and there were no colours in between. Dad was an arsehole for leaving us. Mum should have tried harder to keep him. Chelsea Divine had the perfect life and Joe was just the most perfect boy in all the world, alongside Alex from the Artic Monkeys, of course. And Nan and Grandad, and later Simon and Maisy were always there and loved us. I didn't need to know any more than that. It's only as I've started to grow up, noticed all the colours in between, I realise how complicated life is.

I understand Honey's ambition, her drive to get on and I suppose what she says makes some sort of twisted sense but it also belittles everything that happened to me. I didn't see it before but Honey is made of different stuff to me. My mind wanders and I find myself thinking about that lecture we had at uni that started a mass debate about the Hollywood casting couch. I suppose it could be argued that most of those women, starlets I think they called them, gave their consent to be shagged by rich, powerful movie producers, but surely it must have been reluctant consent? I'm sure, given a choice, they would have preferred not to?

Blowing my hot breath on the cold window and thinking of Luke, the one who has always been there for me, through the good and the bad, I draw a heart with my finger. The bus pulls nearer to my stop and I can see the pub in the distance. Someone is walking out the door and I realise it's Luke, immediately followed by Felicity. As the bus pulls nearer still, my cold hands become hot and sweaty and my mouth suddenly dry. Luke turns to look at Flippity. Standing very close to one another, talking, Luke runs a hand through Felicity's hair and she reaches up to touch his cheek. My head swims and my heart drops. Stupid Honey. Stupid, stupid Honey.

Chugging, the bus begins to slow down, pulling up alongside my stop. Swaying, I stand up and am now virtually opposite Luke and Felicity. Without realising it I'm holding my breath, staring at the beautiful couple and to my horror, they kiss.

I sit down again, hot tears welling up, forming fat tears that run down my cheeks. A man, wearing only one earphone, taps me on the shoulder and makes me jump. He nods at the seat next to me. I move my suitcase and he sits down. He nods again, puts his dangling earphone back in his ear and looks away from my tear stained face. He doesn't care that I'm upset. No one does, not really.

I turn towards the window again. Felicity and Luke are no longer kissing but Felicity is looking up at Luke in a way that screams she is a girl in love. What kind of stupid idiot am I? How can I ever compete with someone like her? I'm a loser and Hunter sensed it, and that's why he did what he did. The bus pulls away and my phone buzzes. It's a text from Honey asking where I am. My vision is so bleary from crying I can barely read my screen but somehow I manage to tap out a reply. I tell Honey I've changed my mind, I'm going straight home. I press send and turn my phone off. Looking up again, I notice hundreds of blinking Christmas lights winking at me, but I don't see all their beautiful colours. Suddenly I'm colour blind.

My heart is smashed to pieces and all I see now is darkness.

Chapter 42

HOME

Cassie

I'm home. Everyone is here, including Nan and Grandad, and life feels normal. The Christmas tree is up and looks beautiful. Mum and Maisy decorated it this year, Connor couldn't be arsed. I wish they'd waited for me, though. I loved decorating the tree when we were little. Mum would put Christmas music on, then when we had finished, me, Mum and Connor would all sit down to a Christmas movie (The Polar Express was my favourite, still is!) with hot chocolate and marshmallows to drink and we would all pick a chocolate each off the tree. Why can't I go back to then? When life was less complicated and Grandad was big and strong.

As well as the blinking Christmas tree, flickering light from the TV dances off the walls. Some ballroom programme where celebrities (I wonder if Mum qualifies as a celebrity?) learn to dance is on but I'm not really watching it. Instead, I'm watching my family.

Grandad is lying across one of the sofas with a blanket over his legs and, as usual, Freddy is close by, on the floor, his head resting on his front paws, snoring. Grandad looks thinner than when I last saw him but he still has the same saggy, grumpy face I love. Nan, who is sat at the end of the same sofa, reminds me of someone watching Wimbledon as she constantly looks from the TV screen then to Grandad and back again. Grandad pats her hand from time to time, nods towards the telly and smiles. They've been in each other's lives for so long now I wonder what they're both thinking, knowing one of them isn't going to be around for much longer. I bite my lip and pull my phone out. Glancing down I pretend to look at something until I'm certain I won't cry. When I look up again I notice Mum, who looks almost as tired as Nan, is still sat at the table, frowning at her screen, again. Three screens actually, her phone, iPad and laptop. Probably checking her book's stats or talking to her Facebook writer friends. She actually has way more friends than me, which is dead embarrassing. Maisy, who is on the other sofa next to Si lets out a snort. Squinting at her phone screen she uses one hand to text and the other to rub her huge belly. Si looks at Maisy, grins and shakes his head. Si looks older lately. Maybe it's because his hair is greying or maybe, just like everyone else, he is knackered.

'Ouch! Not so hard,' Maisy yelps.

'Sorry babe,' Crazee replies. Sat on the floor next to her legs, Crazee is giving Maisy a foot massage.

Romeow, who is stretched out on the back of the sofa, above Maisy and Si, slowly opens his eyes and lifts his head, as does a startled looking Freddy. With his ears twitching, Freddy looks first at Romeow, and then Maisy. However, clearly satisfied there is nothing to worry about, he once again lowers his head and closes his eyes. Romeow, on the other hand, stares at Maisy with an expression of complete grumpiness that sort of reminds me of Grandad. He looks as if he's trying to work out if Maisy is going to yell out again. Satisfied she isn't, he yawns, stretches his two front paws, then like Freddy, also lowers his head and closes his eyes again. I catch Crazee and Maisy looking at each other. They smile and I wonder if I'll ever feel as happy as they both look right now.

A smell of aftershave wafts into the room, quickly followed by Connor. He looks good, considering he's my brother. I can't believe how tall he is now. Where did my little brother go? 'Ooh, look at you,' I say as he tells Mum he is going out. 'Looking very *On Fleek.*'

Connor sighs and rolls his eyes. 'Don't Cas,' he says, 'JSYK, that word is soooo peak.'

Maisy laughs and Grandad looks over, his jowly face wrinkling in confusion. 'Yeah Cas, that's so not sound anymore,' Maisy adds. 'I think you'll find the term is, *On Point*,' she replies with a smug grin.

Grandad, who is still watching and listening to the conversation, folds his arms. Connor looks at Maisy and snorts. 'SMH,' he says. (Surely it would be easier for him to actually "shake his head" than use the acronym?) 'FYI, the word you're looking for is Snatched.'

'Snatched?' Grandad declares, 'who's snatched what?'

I ask Connor where he's going and I hear Nan tell Grandad to stop being nosy and watch the dancing.

Connor looks from me towards Mum and nods his head. 'PAW,' he mumbles from the corner of his mouth. It takes me a few seconds to work that one out, Parents Are Watching. Only she isn't, with her glasses half way down her nose, still engrossed in whatever it is she's doing, I don't think Mum even realises Connor is still here.

'Snatched paws,' Grandad declares, 'what the fu–'

'Salocin!' Nan interrupts.

Connor holds up the peace sign to me. 'Going to a party,' he says. 'Supposed to be well lit. Wanna come?'

Frowning, Grandad looks at Nan who shrugs her shoulders. 'Don't ask me,' she says. 'A good party in our day meant the lights turned down.'

Half laughing, Mum suddenly looks up at Nan and Grandad. She is listening after all and I can't help laughing, too.

'Well?' Connor continues. I shake my head. 'Nah,' I reply. Stay here in the warm or spend the night with a bunch of sixteen and seventeen year olds, it's a no brainer for me. 'I'm okay. But, thanks for asking though.'

Connor makes another peace sign and tells Mum he won't be

back too late. 'Okay,' Mum replies. 'And no getting "Lit" at your Lit party,' she adds. Connor's face drops. He looks both shocked and pissed off at the same time while Grandad continues to look as confused as ever. Maisy glances at me then we both burst out laughing. Nothing much gets past Mum. Well, not that much.

I love my mad family and realise how much I've missed everyone. I'm home. Thank god, I'm home. And safe.

Lizzie

Connor, with a somewhat disgruntled face, heads out the door. High pitched, clamorous, squawking permeates the room, as Cassie, Maisy and Crazee remain locked in languid laughter. Mum and Dad, seemingly oblivious to the noisy furore, appear to be braced in confused conversation about what getting lit at a lit party actually entails. Simon, wearing a somewhat amused grin, wanders over and offers to get me a glass of wine. I nod and, with slight pleading in his voice, he also asks if I'll please put my work away for the evening. Closing my laptop, I agree.

As Simon wanders off to the kitchen in search of wine, I reach around with my hand and rub my aching neck. Mum looks weary but not too bad and on the whole, Dad, well Dad is still here, and I'm grateful for that. Cassie troubles me, though. It's good to see her laughing, doesn't do enough of it in my opinion. And yet, there is always, even when she is happy, an air of vulnerability about her. I watch her reading her phone, and laugh, the expression on her face changing just as vividly, just as quickly, as traffic lights, green for happiness, amber for confusion, red for rage, at least that's what I imagine and whatever she appears to be reading is prompting said responses in very quick succession. I sigh inwardly and find myself longing for those past, angst filled teenage years when, although bloody frustrating at times, I did at least have some idea about how my daughter was feeling. Mostly, I'll admit, due to her very loud, very verbose ramblings. At least then, her raised voice or the slamming of her bedroom door indicated there was something wrong, even if it was often ridiculously minor. But now? Now I just don't know. There's a distance between us and I'm not sure if it's natural or if I am the cause of it. Whatever it is, I wish she'd open up to me.

Carrying several bottles of wine in one hand and clinking a number of glasses in the other, Simon asks who'd like wine. Everyone raises his or her hand except a rather reluctant Maisy. 'It's not fair,' she says folding her arms above her round belly. 'I'm telling you now,' she says to no one in particular, 'when this baby is out I'm getting pissed, for one night at least.' Everyone laughs and I'm pleased that at least one of my daughters appears settled. Especially now she is reunited with Crazee.

A loud knock at the front door makes me jump. Crazee gets up and offers to answer it. When he comes back into the room he is followed by a rather serious looking man and woman. 'Lizzie Lemalf?' the man asks.

I feel my brow knit together into a frown. 'Ye-es?' I reply.

The serious looking man, about my age, pulls out a police badge and flashes it at me. 'DCI Wilmot and this is DCI Bainbridge,' he says pointing to the woman standing behind him. With steely blue eyes and short, red hair, she is at least twenty years younger than her colleague. Go girl, I think, rather bizarrely, before becoming completely engulfed in panic. 'Oh my god, what's wrong?' I gasp. 'Is it my son? Has something happened? He only left the house ten minutes ago.'

Looking somewhat bemused DCI Wilmot shakes his head. 'No, no,' he replies reassuringly. 'Nothing like that. We'd just like to ask you a few questions about someone. Can we err–,' he looks around the room, '–talk somewhere a little more, private?'

'Of course,' I reply as I head towards the door. 'We can talk in the kitchen. Simon, can you come with me please?'

Cassie

Watching as Mum, Simon and the two detectives leave the room; I look back at my phone and re-read the article again. Particularly the paragraph about how the slime bag creep that raped the girl after spiking her drink and after making her believe she'd consented to sex, insisted she drink the cup of coffee he made for her. Looking up I let out a tiny gasp. Rocking back and forth and groaning, Maisy eventually hauls herself off the sofa and waddles over towards me. It's only when she sits down beside me and takes my hand I realise I'm shaking. Violently. 'They know,' I hiss from the corner of my mouth, 'the police know.'

'But, how?' she replies, rubbing my back. 'I thought you didn't report it?'

'Report what?' Grandad interrupts. For an old man who says he's deaf, he hears an awful lot when it suits him.

I look at Maisy and see my fear in her eyes. 'I didn't,' I reply. 'Then it can't be.'

'What else would the police be here for?'

Maisy shrugs her shoulders and Grandad asks again what it is I'm talking about. I bend forward and put my head into my hands. The whole horrible night comes flooding back to me. At least, the parts I can remember do. I hand Maisy my phone and tell her to read the paragraph I've highlighted. Finally, I've joined the dots to something that has been bugging me for ages.

I remember that day Hunter asked me to go to his office before going back in the studio. It was after I'd had lunch with Honey, she came to reception to give me my phone back because I'd left it in her bag. I remember standing outside his office and I remember the muffled conversation I overheard Hunter having with his fat friend. Something about "putting it in their coffee in the morning." I'm pretty convinced he was talking about the morning after pill. He crushed it up and put it in my coffee.

That's why it tasted weird. No wonder he said I had to drink it all before I left. It all makes sense now. Only I didn't drink it. I felt sick, really sick, and tipped it in that huge plant pot containing a huge money tree in his bedroom, when Hunter wasn't looking. He said he'd worn a condom but he lied and his back-up plan didn't work, that's why I fell pregnant. He drugged me, fucked me and made me believe I'd consented and he was wearing protection.

I lift my head from my hands and look up. Nan is now also beside me. She places her hand gently on my trembling knee and pats it. 'What is it Cassie? What's wrong darling?' she asks.

Mum and Si come back into the room and Mum is saying something about Amber, the girl who used to go to the library when Mum worked there. The one who was always causing trouble and getting banned but Mum took under her wing and said was a victim of her surroundings and circumstance; abused by the very people who should have loved and cared for her, let down by a system supposed to protect her from those abusers. Fat lot of good that did Mum though, of course! Feels like a bit of a blur now but I'm pretty sure, if I remember rightly, Amber ended up going into a women's refuge, then into some sort of witness protection, in exchange for giving evidence against her boyfriend, who turned out to be a violent, thieving pimp, of course. I don't think Mum has seen her since but she did get a letter from Amber saying she'd been given a new name, had given birth to the baby she was pregnant with at the time, and was just trying to get on with her life. Recently though, she supposedly went to one of the book fairs Mum spoke at earlier this year. Queued to see her, with her little girl, but Mum was sick and Amber didn't get to see Mum after all. And now, apparently, Amber and her little girl have gone missing, and because of her past, friends are concerned for her safety so the police are following up all leads.

Mum, who looks concerned, suddenly stops talking and

stares at me as if it's the first time she's seen me in ages. She looks at Maisy, then Nan, then back to me. 'What is it, Cassie?' she asks rushing forward. 'What on earth is the matter?'

I know now that the visit from the police is nothing to do with me but it's too late. I'm a complete mess. I shake my head and look away but Maisy grabs me by the chin and makes me look at her.

'Tell them, Cassie. You need to tell them. If you don't, I will.'

Chapter 43

HELPLESSNESS

Lizzie

I wake with a start, my heart hammering loudly against my chest. I am shivering but soaked in sweat. I lift my phone from the bedside cabinet to check the time. It's the same time as always, 1.01 a.m. I look across at Simon. Eyes closed, his lower jaw has relaxed so that his mouth, rather unattractively, hangs open. I watch the gentle rise and fall of his chest and envy him. He looks peaceful. Calm. Resisting the urge to punch him, I turn away again, staring up at the ceiling, into the desolate black hole of nothingness.

1.01 a.m., always the same time and always awoken by the same dream. Cassie is six years old, her front teeth are missing. We're at the park and she's laughing in that wonderful way children do, carefree, self-absorbed and incredibly infectious. She runs from one thing to the next, I honestly don't know where she gets her energy from and I'm almost at a loss to keep up. Almost. First, it's the swings, then the seesaw, then the slide, carefully climbing the steps, and then it's the roundabout.

'Faster, Mummy, faster,' Cassie squeals.

I push, with all my energy, with all my heart and soul, faster and faster, round and round. Giggling, Cassie throws back her head and lifts her arms in wild abandonment.

'Faster, Mummy, faster!'

So, I push some more, faster and faster, round and round until I can barely see her. Cassie has become a blur. A mass of colour. Blonde hair melting into a red jacket disappearing into a black skirt.

She screams. 'Help me, Mummy, help me!'

I panic and reach out to stop the moving roundabout but it turns at such speed that to try would be tantamount to suicide, much like attempting to stop a high-speed train by diving in front of it. And yet I am desperate. Desperate to save my baby.

'Help me, Mummy, help me!'

My body twitches and convulses as the synapsis in my brain converts electrical and chemical signals into physical ones. My maternal instinct is firing on all cylinders, mind and body on red alert. I lunge at the high-speed roundabout, desperate to pull my baby to safety, but to my horror it speeds up and throws me hurtling through the air. Racked with pain I see the distorted image of the roundabout below me, picking up pace, accelerating harder and harder, faster and faster. As I begin my descent, the roundabout disappears. I smash to the floor and hear the snapping of bones.

Silence reigns and Cassie has gone.

Chapter 44

REMORSE

Lizzie

I watch my daughter in amazement as she almost inhales the breakfast I've cooked for her. I understand and know only too well what this is. Like me, Cassie is unable to eat when stressed or upset and, also like me, when that stress is removed, her appetite returns with a vengeance. Swallowing hard, I resist the urge to cry, realising it was the fear of telling rather than the assault itself that has been troubling her these past months.

When did I become so unapproachable?

Simon walks into the kitchen, quickly followed by Connor. No doubt led by his nose, Connor asks if there is any more of what Cassie is eating. Nodding, I ask him to give me five minutes, as Simon gives my shoulder a reassuring squeeze followed by a gentle kiss on the cheek. 'You okay?' he asks. 'What time did you get up?'

Forcing the corners of my lips upwards, I smile. 'About five-ish. Couldn't sleep. And yes, I'm fine.'

Of course, I'm not okay! My daughter has been raped. RAPED! And while you slept soundly last night, I didn't sleep a wink, instead visited by demons of the worst kind; guilt, anger, shame and fear. Each one of them having their wicked way with me, dismantling all rational thought, destroying me, destroying my belief system, and eventually confirming everything I'd suspected about both myself and the dark world we live in.

My daughter has been raped. Saying the words again, quietly under my breath, I count them on my hand, like a child.

My. Daughter. Has. Been. Raped.

Five words. Five small words making up one small sentence. Four of those words are fine. But the fifth word? The fifth word will never be okay. The fifth word is vile and disgusting. The fifth word denotes forced physical violence, pain, and suffering. The fifth word represents the violation of one human being against another. In this instance, it happens to be my daughter.

'Had stuff to do,' I continue, very matter of fact. 'Book reviews to check, my blog to update.'

Because unlike YOU, I couldn't sleep.

Dropping his hand, Simon puts his arm around me and pulls me close. His hand skims across my jutting hipbones and we both realise I've lost weight. Like Cassie, the burden of my worries has supressed my appetite and the comprehension of such brings with it another violent rush of guilt.

'Damn, that smells good,' Connor says.

I knew it. Knew when I went to meet Cassie in London, all those months ago, something was wrong. Even after she told me about the abortion, I knew there was more to it.

Why didn't you act on it then? Why didn't you insist she tell you what was wrong? I'll tell you why. Too busy wrapped in yourself. Wrapped up in your own little world of being some big shot fucking writer. And you let Simon talk you out of it, convince you that you were worrying for nothing. As usual. Stupid Lizzie, always worrying for no good reason. FUCK!

I slap both hands across my mouth, one after the other, unsure if I've had this conversation out loud for the entirety of the household to hear or just myself.

'You okay? Simon asks, now refilling the kettle at the sink.

'Splashed myself with hot oil,' I lie, pointing to the pan sizzling on the hob. After rubbing at a non-existent burn for several minutes, I let my arms fall to my sides and breath out, slowly. Ashamed, I know my anger towards Simon is misplaced, but why didn't he listen to me. Why didn't I listen to me?

Flicking the switch on the kettle, Simon flings cupboard

doors open, reaching for a selection of mugs. 'I don't know how, but we'll sort this,' he whispers in my ear. 'I promise you that.'

Fixed smile in place, I nod and listen as the water in the kettle boils. The bacon sizzles, the water boils and somewhere behind me, Cassie, Connor and Simon share a joke. Life goes on. I tell myself it could have been worse. The rape of my daughter could have been worse. Cassie said she doesn't remember much, because of the alcohol and the drugs. I smile to myself; Cassie wouldn't tell me if she did. Even if she remembered every single sordid second. She wouldn't tell me because she wants to protect me. Like I should have protected her.

Bending over I clutch my stomach, as sordid pictures of what may or may not have happened to my daughter disturb my thoughts. And, not for the first time, I am again filled with a controlled but extreme rage rising from the pit of my stomach, burning like acid in my throat. Grabbing a large plate from the side, I heap man size portions of sausage, egg, bacon and beans onto it and place it in front of my ravenous looking son.

'Thanks, Mum,' Connor says.

'Yeah, thanks, Mum,' Cassie repeats. 'That was well delish. Belly feels like it has lead in it now.'

I smile. 'It's good to see you have an appetite again.'

'Yeah, well, as messed up as it sounds, I feel better now that everything is out in the open.'

Nodding, I swallow the lump in my throat. 'Talking of which, what we talked about last night, are you sure you want to–'

'I'm positive, Mum,' Cassie interrupts me. 'I want to wait until after Christmas to decide what I'm going to do. This could be Grandad's last Christmas,' Connor, mid mouthful, looks at Cassie, 'and I want us all to enjoy it.'

I nod, steadying myself on one of the kitchen chairs, noticing how worn the chair looks, the chips in the woodwork and how grubby the seat cushions are. I really should invest in some new chairs, and a new table. We've had this set for years, now.

Gripping the back of the chair like my life depended on it, I listen to the normality around me, and watch, fascinated, as my knuckles turn white. I'm tired and my head hurts and I don't know who I am any more. I don't know what the hell to do to ease my pain and that of all those I love so very dearly. There's only one person who can make this better, Dad. I want my dad. Dad always fixes everything.

I. Want. My. Dad.

Chapter 45

CHOOSE LIFE

Lizzie

I spot Helen. She has her back turned to me but I recognise her short, bleached hair, slightly spiky on top. Shoulders erect, she appears to be focussed on the huge glass window of the coffee shop we agreed to meet at. I suddenly wonder what I am actually doing here, what I hope to achieve. Wearing jeans, trainers and a bolero style jacket that doesn't look warm enough for this drizzly morning, Helen looks different out of uniform, less imposing.

I'm almost within touching distance when Helen turns and looks at me. She smiles and immediately puts me at ease. I return her smile and thank her for agreeing to meet me and am both surprised and pleased when she steps forward to hug me. I reciprocate and after a few seconds she pulls away and her eyes wander towards the top of my head.

'How have you been?' she asks. Raising my hand to my head, I tell her I've been good, all things considered. 'So I see,' she replies, pulling out a rather dog-eared, battered looking copy of my first novel from her shoulder bag. 'I'd love you to sign it for me?' Feeling flattered but somewhat embarrassed at the same time, I let out a rather insipid laugh and let my hand drop to my now hot cheek. I ask her if she's heard about the disappearance of Amber and her little girl and Helen nods. 'I have,' she confesses. 'It's not my case but I did have a quick look into it and they still haven't been found.'

'Do you think—'

'I'm not at liberty to tell you anything about it I'm afraid,

Lizzie,' Helen interrupts. I tell her I understand but ask if she could please let me know, discreetly, if they do turn up. Helen agrees and we enter the glass-fronted door of the coffee shop. Helen wanders off in search of a table while I order a couple of cappuccinos. The waitress behind the glass counter asks me if I want anything else with my coffees and her disposition is nauseatingly sanguine. I look at the delicious array of pastries and muffins but notwithstanding their redolence, decide against it. The caffeine will give me a kick, although a second look does find me looking longingly at the lemon drizzle cake. I impulsively order two squares, despite a sea of waves blowing up a storm in my stomach, and pay Nicole, the waitress; at least that's what her name badge pinned to her rather flat chest says.

I place the tray onto the table Helen has secured for us and sit opposite her. 'I don't like lemons,' Helen says looking at the two squares of lemon cake. I apologise and offer to buy her something else but she shakes her head. 'I don't have a lot of time, if I'm honest. If you could just—'

'Yes, of course,' I interrupt. I fill her in quickly with as much detail about Cassie as possible, including the fact that Honey; her best friend is now working with her perpetrator. Slowly but surely, Helen's features settle into a far more serious look and one I'm pretty convinced mirrors mine.

Helen shakes her head. 'She'll be ripped apart. If Cassie agrees to give evidence against Black, in court, they'll rip her to pieces. I've seen it, time and time again. A lot of the problem is there are no forensics—'

'What do you mean by no forensics?' I interrupt.

'You know, semen in the victim collected at a full examination or the bedding, that kind of thing.' I shiver at the thought. 'And even then, there's very little chance of a conviction. Rape cases are notoriously difficult to prove as it's one person's word against the other. Usually the perpetrator would be arrested, he would deny the offence, the victim would then be interviewed and the CPS usually make the decision for no further action. It's not right, of course, but when I see the trauma some of these poor victims are put through in court, if it makes it to court, I've often thought, well, you know, if it were me, well …'

Helen trails off and takes a sip of her coffee. 'If it were you, what?' I ask. Helen refrains from looking at me and takes another sip of coffee. 'What if there was other evidence? You know, photos or film footage?' I ask.

Helen replaces her cup back on its saucer and looks at me. 'Why do you ask? Is there such evidence?'

I shake my head. 'I don't think so, but, well, if there were, could it be used?'

Helen's eyes narrow. 'Yes, film footage could be used as evidence but then again–'

'Then again, what?' I exclaim. Helen raises her eyebrows to my raised voice and takes a quick scan of the room to see if anyone is listening. No one is, though; everyone appears far too busy to notice the elevated voice of an anguished mother. Even those who are sat alone appear deeply immersed in their mobile phones. I lower my voice. 'Sorry, it's just that what with it being my daughter and everything …'

'If you want to continue with this conversation, Lizzie, I need you to remain calm.'

I nod my head. 'Please, continue.'

'Okay. Well, there would need to be clear pointers to show that she didn't consent, either that she was passed out or visibly upset. But …'

I try to stay calm, dry eyed and articulate. Somehow, I have to dissociate myself from the fact that we are talking about my daughter. 'But what, Helen? I need you to be honest with me.'

'Again, I've seen such evidence twisted in court, used against the victim and made to look as if she did consent. Add to that, in your daughter's case, the fact she went straight back to work for the very man who raped her and well, you see where this is going?'

'But ... but ... she was in shock,' I declare. 'She couldn't even remember all the details until just recently. It was after a night out with Black and some of his cronies. She woke up the next morning in bed with him. He made some disgusting remark about her liking it rough and leading a married man astray but she couldn't remember and ...'

Helen holds her hand up to me like a stop sign. 'The way victims behave after a sexual assault is grossly misunderstood, both by the public and the legal system.' Her voice is warm and reassuring but her words are cold and stab at my heart like an ice pick. 'If survivors ignore the trauma caused to them they don't have to become victims. Women are socialised not to be angry with or confront men and that instinct to appease others results in self-blame and self-hate. Did I lead him on? Did I deserve it? Am I overreacting? Anger tells us we've been violated and it takes women a long time to get to that emotion. Most women don't disclose information they can't make sense of. Instead they tend to deny and minimize it to themselves. The way victims actually behave in the real world is often too unsettling for most. It makes people feel safer to believe that most rapists are strangers and "real" victims are the ones who resist their attackers and immediately call the police.'

I hang my head in resignation.

'Throw in the fact that he's rich and Cassie is in debt.' Confused, I look up again. 'I take it Cassie went to university?' I nod my head. 'So, she's at least thirty-grand in debt, then?'

I rub my face with my hands as the cold reality of Cassie's situation sinks in. 'So, what you're saying is, Cassie has been fucked and there is fuck all we can do?'

My eyes lock with Helen's, warm mocha in colour, fringed by long lashes, they provide the perfect contrast to her cropped blonde hair. She returns my look with plaintive, unspecific appeal. 'You're dealing with a very rich, very powerful man and a crap criminal justice system for rape. You work it out.'

I sit back and close my eyes. 'Auctoritas non veritas facit legem,' I mumble. When I open my eyes again, Helen's brow is locked in a quizzical frown. 'Thomas Hobbes,' I explain, it means "authority, not truth, makes law."

Helen laughs but the sound that leaves her mouth is one of discord and cynicism rather than amusement. 'If it were me,' she continues, 'and I'll completely deny saying this if you ever repeat it, I'd be inclined to seek my own justice.'

'So you're telling me to–'

'I'm not telling you to do anything,' Helen interrupts, 'but I have daughters, one the same age as Cassie, and I've been in this job far too long. I joined the force to make a difference but huh,' she snorts, 'I soon got that knocked out of me. I'm seriously thinking about leaving.'

'What will you do instead?'

Helen's eyes light up and a rather throaty nervous laugh replaces her previous contemptuous one. 'A writer,' she replies. 'I've written four novels and I'm currently working on my fifth, at least that way some of my victims get the justice they deserve.'

I laugh to myself and can't help but wonder if this is the real reason Helen agreed to help me, because she wanted me to help her in return. I half-heartedly attempt to eat one of the lemon drizzle cakes as yet untouched by either of us, but as soon as I take a bite I realise I don't have the stomach for it. I look at Helen, and although I don't feel much like doing so, I smile. 'It's one way of exacting revenge, I suppose. And they do say the pen is mightier than the sword.' I don't believe that, of course. *What a load of bollocks*. But it makes Helen smile.

Overwhelmed and exhausted, I suddenly realise this is all wrong. Whoever wrote this chapter of my life got it spectacularly wrong. The editor should have sent it back for a rewrite. This is supposed to be the happy part, where the kids, all grown, have flown the nest and are happy, Simon isn't exhausted, despite the business being a success, and Mum and Dad are fit and well, still enjoying retirement. And me? I'm a successful writer. Finally basking in my own glory. Except that's not true, is it. Well, the writer bit is but I can't enjoy it because the rest of my life is a mess.

Who was it who said, "choose life"? Irvine Welsh? Danny Boyle? Ewan McGregor?

'Technically all three, I suppose,' Helen replies. I look up from my empty coffee cup and realise I've spoken out loud again. 'And Wham, I think? Didn't they wear Choose Life T-shirts?'

For a few colourful seconds I am immediately transported back in time. It's the 1980's and Ruby and I are watching Top of the Pops as George Michael and Andrew Ridgeley, all bronzed skin and white teeth, jitterbug on stage to 'Wake Me Up Before You Go Go'. I remember lots of hand clapping with Pepsi and Shirley, and bright white, oversized T-shirts screaming at everyone to 'Choose Life'. I remember a different life and a different woman. Not even a woman, a girl in fact, with her whole life ahead of her. Where did she go, the girl with kaleidoscope eyes. Where is she?

Helen leans forward and gently pats my hand. 'Listen,' she says, her face suddenly serious. 'Don't let the bastards grind you down.' And with that she wishes me good luck and stands up.

I suddenly realise our conversation is now at an end. I take Helen's personal email address and promise to put her in touch with a few people I know in the writing industry, after all it's the least I can do and, somewhat deflated, I thank her for her time and honesty.

We agree to keep our meeting and the contents of our conversation to ourselves.

Chapter 46

OUR CHOICES SEAL OUR FATE

Lizzie

It's a cold morning but it's also bright and crisp. There's no sign of snow but a thick layer of frost casts an effervescent glow on everything it touches. In contrast, a low winter sun provides a pale, golden backdrop with just enough heat to thaw the exquisitely formed icicles hanging from the black branches of bare trees. Dad's head bobs rhythmically from side to side and as I take another quick look to make sure his blanket hasn't slipped, I'm filled with the same concerns as a mother pushing her infant child in a pram.

'You okay Dad?' I ask.

Dad, whose voice is barely more than a whisper of late, raises his hand and sticks his thumb up. We stop at one of several discreetly placed benches alongside the riverbank. Newly painted during the summer, the bright orange paint is already peeling. I position Dad's wheelchair next to the bench, kick the brake on and take a pew beside him. Without words, we both sit for a moment, observing both the harshness and beauty of midwinter.

'*In the bleak midwinter Frosty wind made moan, Earth stood hard as iron, Water like a stone; Snow had fallen, Snow on snow, Snow on snow, In the bleak midwinter, Long ago.*'

I smile. 'Christina Rossetti?' I ask. Dad nods just as a raft of rather noisy ducks swim past and a robin, his proud breast radiantly red against the stark winter background, perches on the barren branch of the tree directly opposite us.

'How we doing then, gal?' Dad asks.

Swallowing hard and resisting the urge to cry, I shake my head. 'Okay, I guess.'

Dad reaches forward and pats my knee with his gloved hand. 'She'll be okay, you know? Cassie will be okay. She's strong, like her mother. And her grandmother.' Half smiling, I look away as my eyes fill up. 'Has she decided what she's going to do?'

Rubbing it with my hand, I pretend to be fascinated by the black mark in the middle of my green welly. 'Says she doesn't want to think about it until the new year.'

'Probably a good idea,' Dad replies.

Looking up again, I see the frail face of the strong man in a failing body and bite my lip. I so want to hold it together, to not make my burdens his, but as a parent myself I realise it's a futile quest. Placing my head in my hands I lean forward and sob uncontrollably. I feel Dad's hand on my back, rubbing it reassuringly. After several minutes, rocking back and forth, I find myself looking up again. A man in running gear is jogging towards us. Wiping my face with the back of my hand and placing the other on my jittery knee in a bid to stop it trembling, the jogger glances fleetingly in my direction before looking away again, his hot breath forming intermittent little puffs of smoke as it hits the cold air. Dad, whose hand is still rubbing my back, remains supportively silent and the robin, still perched on the tree opposite, begins calling, in its unmistakable, distinct way.

'Do you know the robin was declared Britain's National Bird on 15 December 1960 and, often mistaken for nightingales, sings at night, usually under artificial light?' Dad says. I shake my head. I didn't know and there's a million and one other trivial bits of information I don't know and will never know once Dad has gone.

Dad asks me to get out the flask of hot coffee he insisted I make. I pour us each a small cup and I'm grateful for the feeling of warmth it brings as the hot liquid runs down my throat. Dad asks me if I've seen Ruby recently, and what I think of Harvey.

'Haven't seen her for a while,' I confess, 'she had a bad cold last time we spoke. As for Harvey, he's okay, I suppose,' I reply, swinging my legs on the bench like a ten-year-old.

'I'm not so sure,' Dad sniffs. 'The word arrogant springs to mind. Reckon he thought I was some sort of uneducated barrow boy when they visited us at Sean and Nat's in Cornwall. That's why I played on it a bit.'

'Really? I didn't think arrogant, more anal.' Dad laughs and almost chokes on his coffee. Passing me his cup to hold, he pulls off his glove to reach inside his pocket for a hankie, wiping away remnants of spilled coffee from his mouth. I gaze at the hand with the missing finger, holding my stare for several seconds too long before passing Dad's cup back to him. 'Are you ever going to tell me?' I ask.

Dad follows my gaze. 'You know the drill by now, Lizzie,' he replies. 'It was an industrial accident.'

'But you and I both know that's not true,' I protest.

Dad's gaze rests upon our red-breasted visitor. Sighing, I let it drop. Experience has taught me no amount of crying, shouting, pleading or otherwise will get Dad to say any more on the subject. Whatever the *real* reason for his missing finger, Dad is taking it to the grave with him.

'I prefer the blackbird,' Dad says.

'Sorry, what, Dad?' Dad nods towards the robin that is cocking his head to one side, flitting from one branch to the next before finally taking flight. 'You've offended him,' I say.

Dad laughs and begins singing, as badly as ever, The Beatles' 'Blackbird'. I happily join in caring very little for the slightly bemused looks of passers-by. 'Do you know blackbirds like to sing after rain,' Dad adds as our singing comes to a painful end. 'And you know it takes both the rain and the sun to make a rainbow? So, don't lose your true colours Lizzie, just because of a bit of rain.'

Forcing a smile, I nod. Dad is, of course, talking about

Cassie. He asks me if we're packed and ready for our trip to Cornwall, partly for Connor to see Alesha again, partly to help Sean and Nat out as their trusted camper van has finally given up the ghost and is headed for the great scrap heap in the sky. 'We certainly are,' I reply. 'Simon has ordered a seven-seater people carrier and –'

'But there's only six of you?' Dad interrupts.

'Seven if you include Sir Barks-a-Lot,' I add.

'Oh, I s'pose,' Dad mumbles. 'And the girls?'

'Are staying here with Crazee, and Mum with you, of course. The plan being we travel back Christmas Eve and all spend Christmas day together.'

'I have a favour to ask,' Dad says. 'I want you to stay here, with me, and let your Mum take your place.'

Confused, I shake my head. 'Why? She'll never agree to that. Never in a million years.'

Dad grips my arm and I'm surprised by his strength. 'I mean it and I want you to arrange it.' The brevity of his smile and flash in his eyes tell me everything I need to know. He means business.

'But, why?' I ask again.

'Because she's tired, needs a rest from running around after me, and,' he adds gravely 'she needs to see that life without me will be okay.'

Speechless, I nod. How can I not agree? 'Okay,' I finally whisper. 'She'll hate me for suggesting it, though.'

Dad's smile lights up his whole face. 'Good gal,' he says, 'be good for me to spend some quality time with you, too.'

Nodding, I return his smile but I'm concerned. I ask him what the plan is if he takes a turn for the worst. Dad waves his hand dismissively, declaring: 'I ain't going nowhere. Plenty of life in the old dog yet.' I sigh, inwardly; deciding Mum is probably the best person to ask about Dad's palliative care.

Once again, quiet reigns and we watch as the wonder of winter unfolds around us. Wild swans, most likely whoopers from Iceland or the Bewick's swans from Siberia, glide along the black river, as orange flanked redwings covet hedgerows and wild holly bushes, while woodpigeons feed on the black berries of trailing ivy. Dogs bark, birds sing and trees rustle. I also hear a tap, tap, tapping sound; it's at least a month too early but I swear it's the drumming of a woodpecker. Standing up, I walk towards the mossy bank and stare at the silent river. Tiny flecks of sun dance on its dark, winding, surface much like a strip of black, glossy ribbon, billowing in the wind. The black river turns my mind to black thoughts. How does one deal with a rapist? And a very rich, very famous one at that?

'There's more than one way to skin a rat,' Dad says, interrupting my thoughts.

'Reading my mind again, were you?' I reply, turning away from the river and back towards Dad.

'We're all connected, Lizzie,' Dad states, 'but then again, I think you know that.'

'I've thought about it a lot, you know, Dad, and it doesn't matter what Cassie decides to do; he has and will get away with it. He's one of life's untouchables, "the haves" versus "the have nots."'

Dad reaches inside his coat and pulls out his wallet. Opening it, he passes me what looks like a business card but save for a scribbled name I can't quite make out, and a mobile telephone number written in black ink, the rest of the card is blank. Dad's expression is at once sombre and serious. 'If I've already snuffed it and things look like they are going tits up, ring this number. You tell em you're Salocin's girl.'

I open my mouth to speak but Dad stops me. 'Don't ask questions and don't ring it unless it's absolutely necessary, but whatever happens, that cunt ain't getting away with it. I promise you that. But in return you must promise me something, Lizzie?'

'Which is what?' I reply, raising my eyes in question.

'I believe every single one of us, given the right circumstances, is capable of great good and great bad. Think of it like a line, and either we choose to cross it or not. Sometimes we may cross that line and if we don't stray too far into the darkness we can find our way back. However, there are always those that cross that line, descending so far into the darkness, it is virtually impossible for them to make their way back to the light. Don't forget that darkness is a force absent of love, just like black is the absence of colour. The more love you can feel, the more colour added, the more light is achieved. And ultimately, in the end, our choices seal our fate.'

Chapter 47

IT'S CHRISTMAS!

Lizzie

With so much raucous hilarity in the background I can barely hear Simon talk. He has me on loudspeaker and says they are making good time. The roads are reasonably good, given it's Christmas Eve. They plan to make one more loo stop, then should be home within the next three hours. Mum asks again if Dad is okay. To the untrained ear, she sounds relaxed but I know different. I notice the tiny ripples that lift her voice indicating her restless anxiety.

'He is fine Mum,' I reply. 'We've just been having a right laugh together, a real trip down memory lane.'

'Can I speak to him? Put him on the phone, Lizzie, will you love.'

I explain Dad is tired and has gone for a nap.

'Oh?' she replies. She sounds disappointed.

'He just wanted to rest before everyone got here. He's okay Mum, honest.'

Her voice is breezy. 'Okay then love,' she continues. But I can tell she's not.

Simon asks how the girls are and I reassure him they are also fine.

'They were both ensconced on the sofa back at ours when I last spoke to them. Watching a film, *It's A Wonderful Life*, I think?'

'And Crazee?' Simon asks.

'Down the pub I think?'

'Down the pub?' Simon repeats.

'Maisy insisted apparently. Told him to make the most of it before the baby comes.'

Simon laughs. 'She's not wrong there! Didn't she want to go with him?'

'Simon, she can't drink alcohol and is as round as a barrel. Would you want to squeeze yourself into the local on Christmas Eve?'

Simon laughs again, as does Mum. I tell Simon to hang up and concentrate on his driving. He agrees that's not a bad idea and somewhere between the hullabaloo taking place at the back of both him and Mum he tells me he loves me. 'Ditto,' I reply.

'Did I tell you about the time I was pregnant with Lizzie ...' I hear Mum say just as Simon disconnects us. I roll my eyes and laugh. I can't help feeling a tiny bit sorry for Simon as I imagine Mum bending his ear with her incessant detailed chattering about my complicated birth.

Wandering into Mum and Dad's dining room, now a makeshift bedroom for Dad, I quickly check in on him. Curled up on the bed with his back to me, I listen. His breathing is quite heavy but confident this is nothing out of the ordinary, I gently pull the door to and wander back into the kitchen. Opening the fridge door, I check the turkey, again, using my finger to prod the carefully wrapped bird. Satisfied it is okay, I then lift lids to various pots and containers holding ready prepared vegetables for the feast tomorrow. We all know Dad is living on borrowed time, and I can't bear it. That's why it's so important that everything must be just right. Not that Dad will eat much. I hate the way this terrible disease has ravished his once strong body.

Sadness engulfs me with frightening immediacy and my buoyant mood drops. A thick fog of darkness bears down heavy about my person and I can barely carry the weight of it. What with Dad and Cassie. Then there is Uncle Teddy and Maisy...

Closing my eyes, I take several deep breaths.

You can do this. You can do this, Lizzie.

Repeatedly clenching and unclenching my hands into fists, I open my eyes again. Bar the hum of the fridge and the gentle rise and fall of Dad's breathing, played out across the baby monitor, the house is bathed in silence. My eyes rest on the sherry bottle Mum has left on the side before flitting towards the kettle. A small glass of sherry would be nice. Reaching up into the cupboard for a glass I quickly pull back when my neck prickles like a small electric shock. I change my mind and decide a cup of tea and a nice film is the order of the day. With a flick of its switch I leave the kettle heating up and wander back into the living room where the large dining table now sits decorated with various candles, centrepieces and Christmas crackers in readiness for tomorrow.

Curling up on the sofa, I pick up the remote control and turn the TV on. A well-spoken, young Jenny Agutter confronts me and I at once have the urge to cry. It's a film from my youth, *The Railway Children*, a firm favourite of mine. Dad's too. Why? Why does life do that? Prod and poke you when you're at your most vulnerable.

Watching the flickering screen, I am once again a child and I feel heart-wrenchingly happy.

Cassie

I sigh heavily. 'Stop it, Maisy.'

'Stop what?'

I turn and look at her, red faced and round, constantly fidgeting because she can't get comfortable. 'Stop looking at me like you don't know what to say. Like … like I'm gonna bloody break or something.'

'I'm sorry. It's just, well … you look so sad. And what with Luke and Salocin and the ra …'

'Rape. Just say it Maisy, rape. Small word, easy to say and easy to get away with too, apparently.'

Maisy flinches like I've just smacked her in the face and I actually feel sorry for her. She looks away from me and pretends to examine her fingernails. 'I just wish I could do something, to make you feel better,' she mumbles from the corner of her mouth.

'I'm okay. Well, no, actually I'm not, but I will be.' I shrug my shoulders. 'It could have been worse, I suppose.'

Maisy looks up at me again and bites her bottom lip. 'Do, do you wanna talk about it?' I shake my head and Maisy looks relieved. 'I know!' she yells. 'We could have him murdered.'

'Who?' I reply grinning.

'Your boss of course. We could take a hit out on him, like in the movies.'

'Yeah, right!'

'No seriously. What about Useless? Doesn't he have some Polish gangster friends or something?'

Throwing my head back, I laugh. We both laugh, but I'm not laughing on the inside. On the inside, late at night, where the blue fish still turn my dreams into nightmares, my thoughts really do turn to murder.

'Can I …' Maisy begins but clearly changes her mind and trails off.

'Can you, what?'

Maisy shrugs one shoulder and twists her mouth. 'Nah, don't worry about it, it's nothing.'

'For god sake Maisy, whatever it is just say it, will you.'

Maisy shifts and changes position again. She looks at me and reaches up with her hand to scratch the side of her neck. 'Well I just wondered, just wanted to ask …' she pauses again.

I'm getting annoyed now but try not to show it in my voice. 'Yessss?'

Maisy coughs. 'Well, I just wondered. What I'm asking, what I mean is,' she sighs heavily. 'Would you have kept the baby … if it hadn't been rape? If it had been a mistake?'

I think back to our argument in the summer and what with the news that Maisy herself was pregnant and Mum suffering a miscarriage, we've never really discussed our difference of opinion since. I get it; she still doesn't really understand my decision.

Shaking my head, I feel annoyed. 'No, Maisy, if it had just been a mistake I still would have had an abortion because it was my choice to. I know you don't get it, and I'm not asking you to. But I am asking you to accept it.'

Maisy looks thoughtful for a minute and chews on her fingernails. 'Okay,' she eventually replies. 'Soooo, you're saying, your body, your choice?'

I nod my head. 'Yep, that and a few other things like I'm not ready to be a parent and, although it can't be helped sometimes, I don't want to start out as a single parent. If I ever do become a mum, I want a partner to do it with me. And right now, I don't have any money, or a secure job.'

Maisy wrinkles her nose. 'What about adoption?'

I laugh; I've had this argument with others before. 'You know what? Some people suggest that having an abortion can cause trauma and guilt for the rest of a woman's life. But what do they think carrying a baby for nine months does to you? Feeling it grow, feeling it kick, then giving birth and giving it away? How on earth can that not be traumatic? Add to that the baby finding out later in life it was given away and you've got two people's trauma.'

Maisy, very quiet, wraps both her hands around her baby bump. 'Kay,' she eventually replies. 'I don't understand, still, but I do accept and respect your views.'

She laughs and I ask her what's funny. 'I was just thinking back to when we were younger, when you were a drama queen and me, with my black hair and Goth make-up, not to mention all my piercings.'

'God, yeah. And what about the time you got your leg tattoo!'

Rolling her eyes, Maisy laughs again. 'The fuss that caused, eh? Was the first time I'd ever really seen my dad lose it. Was also when I met Crazee too, of course.'

'Hmmm,' I reply smiling. 'I remember it well.' It was only a few years ago really, but life seemed a lot less complicated then.'

'Ooohh,' Maisy yells, cupping her ginormous bump with both hands.

'What? What is it?'

'Arrrggh, ooohh.'

'For god sake Maisy, what? What the hell is it? Is it the baby?'

Maisy swings her legs off the sofa and holds one hand out like a stop sign, using her other hand to cradle her bump. Her face is red like she's holding her breath. 'Nope, that's better,' she eventually replies. 'Bit of a twinge.'

'What, like those Branston Picks things you had the other day?'

Maisy laughs. 'It's Braxton Hicks, you bloody idiot.'

I wave my hand dismissively. 'Oh, what the hell ever. You know what I bloody mean?'

'Yeah, I'm pretty sure that's what it is, nothing to worry about.'

Now it's my turn to feel relieved. 'So, it's not the baby coming or anything?'

Maisy shrugs her shoulders. 'Bloody hope not? I have still three weeks to go!'

Lizzie

Oh my god. I don't know what to do. Dad is really struggling to breathe and there's blood, everywhere. I rub his back and in between raspy, gasps of air he coughs and brings with it yet more blood. I reach for my phone and notice two missed calls from Cassie. I swipe the screen and call Dad's palliative care team. The number is engaged. I try another number but that just seems to ring and ring – forever. I terminate the call and do my best to help Dad but he continually struggles to breathe. I swipe the screen on my phone again and this time I'm not taking any chances. I press 999. In my panicked voice, I ask for an ambulance, immediately. The operator on the end of the phone sounds calm, bored almost, and asks me for information that doesn't feel relevant when the person sitting next to me is choking on his own blood. I stress the urgency of the situation and after several minutes of questions, that feel insurmountably too long, the operator with the normal voice assures me an ambulance is on its way. She advises me to stay on the line but an irritating buzzing noise that only I can hear advises me I have another caller. I pull my phone away from my ear and squint at the screen. I've missed the call again and see it's from Cassie.

I manage to prop Dad up and do everything the operator advises me to do until the ambulance arrives. Blood runs down his chin and onto the beloved Queen T-shirt that Connor bought him for Christmas last year. He looks like a helpless toddler who has managed to get his dinner everywhere but his mouth. There's blood over me too and the smell of it fills my nose, reminding me of the drinking water I would sometimes sip from an old, rusty tap whilst playing, as a child, in the garden during the long, hot summers of years ago.

Rubbing Dad's back, I try and reassure him everything will be okay. I'm not convinced it will be, though. If truth be known, although this is not the first time Dad has coughed up blood, it is by far the worst occurrence. Looking at his face and rheumy eyes, I can't stand to see the pain etched into them. He opens his mouth as if to speak, but the only sound to leave his lips is a wheezy gurgling. Clearly suffering, he clutches his chest with his hand and screws up his face. I tell him not to speak. Tell him whatever he has to say can wait. He has to save his energy. I try to stay calm but my head is spinning. What the hell can I do to make him feel better? I feel so utterly helpless.

The operator on the phone is still with me. She repeats again several things I can do to help Dad and asks me how he is doing. I pull my phone away from my ear and look at it like a bad smell.

How is he doing? How is he fucking doing? There's blood everywhere and he can't fucking breathe! Now forgive me if I'm wrong, Mrs-Calm-Speaking-Operator-Person, but I was always under the impression that if you can't breathe, you die.

The realisation of this causes me to take a sharp intake of breath. Panic crawls up my throat leaving me feeling both icy cold and burning hot at the same time. As Dad continues to clutch his chest my phone buzzes again. I gently wipe his chin with the now blood-stained towel I managed to grab and look at the screen of my phone. It's Cassie, again. I ask the operator if she can kindly hold while I take the call from my daughter.

'Mum? Mum? Is that you? Oh, thank god you've answered, why didn't you answer?' Cassie's voice is an octave too high, like it always is whenever she gets excited or panics. 'It's Maisy, Mum,' she continues. 'I think the baby is coming.'

'What? What do mean, coming?'

'Duh, what do you think I mean? The baby is coming! She's having contraptions and everything.'

'Do you mean contractions?'

'Yeah, them too. And her waters have cracked.'

'What? Her waters have broken? Already?'

'That's what I just said didn't I!'

'But ... But ... she still has three weeks to go?'

I look across at Dad. He makes another unpleasant gurgling noise but looks a little calmer and my thoughts are interrupted by the sweetest sound. The sound of sirens up the street.

'You have to come home, Mum,' Cassie continues. 'We'll swap. I'll stay with Grandad and you take Maisy to the hospital.'

'Where's Crazee?' I ask.

'God knows? We've tried him on the phone like a million times but he's not picking up. Maisy's fuming.'

'Cassie, I can't. Grandad is very poorly. An ambulance is on its way and …'

'What!' Cassie replies. 'You didn't say? Why didn't you ring me and tell me?'

Keeping my voice as calm as possible I explain to Cassie how it has only just happened. How completely shocked and surprised I was. Still am. Cassie puts me on loud speaker and Maisy tells me there's about ten minutes between her contractions. I tell them both to stay calm and the best thing to do is for Cassie to drive Maisy to the hospital in my old, yellow Beetle. Cassie sounds horrified but I tell the girls they have little choice in the matter. Whether they like it or not, this baby is coming and I can't be with them. Not at the moment anyway.

Ripples of blue light flash through the window and a heavy hammering on the door interrupts our conversation. Heart pounding but relieved I sprint out of Dad's bedroom and head for the front door. Still hanging on the phone, I remind Maisy to grab her baby bag. I tell Cassie to drive quickly but carefully and reassure them both that I'll meet them in the maternity ward once Dad is settled.

Cassie

Oh, my god, this can't be happening. Why? Why did the baby choose to come now? I look at Maisy. Her face is red and she's holding onto the back of one of the kitchen chairs.

'Right. The thing is, not to panic,' I declare. This seems to make Maisy laugh.

'The only one panicking is you,' she replies.

'I'm not! Oh hell, what do we need to take with us?' I find Mum's car keys in the kitchen drawer then, for some unknown reason, I begin opening other drawers and cupboards.

'Cas, what the …?' Maisy pauses and, still holding onto the chair, bends forwards. 'Arrrggh!' she yells. 'Here comes another one. Fuuuuccckk meeeeeee!'

I freeze, not really knowing what to do. Her shouting melts into groaning as she slowly rises back up again. Her red face now even redder.

'Where the hell is Crazee?'

I realise my mouth is still hanging open so I close it and shrug my shoulders. 'Dunno.' I suddenly have a great idea. 'I know! I'll quickly nip to some of the pubs, see if I can find him?'

Maisy shakes her head. 'Not enough time, Cas, Mum's right, this baby IS coming and I need to get to hospital.'

I nod my head up and down in agreement and grab what little we need and start to walk Maisy to the car. It's only four o'clock but the light is already fading. It's cold, too, so cold I can see my breath when I talk and there is a thin layer of ice across the windscreen of Mum's rusting yellow Beetle. *Why the hell doesn't she sell this rust bucket for god bloody sake?*

Maisy and I both agree it's probably best for her to sit in the back of the car, more room to spread out if she needs it, but just as I open the car door for her, she has another contraction. Holding onto the door for support, Maisy bends forwards again. I rub her back and she pants fast, like Freddy, Nan and Grandad's dog does when he's been on a long walk.

Maisy stands upright again and sort of laughs. 'Wow, I swear they're getting more painful.'

She looks worried and I can't help feeling the same. Please god, don't let her have this baby before we get to hospital, I wouldn't know what the hell to do if she did. I decide that I, at least, have to stay calm. I help her into the back of the car, quickly but gently. I reach forward for the seat belt and tug at it until I have enough of the belt to go around Maisy's fat belly. I click the belt in and Maisy looks at me and grabs my arm.

'Thanks, Cas,' she says.

I smile back and shrug my shoulders. 'It's fine,' I reply. 'After all, it's not a life, it's an adventure, eh?' Only, no sooner have the words left my mouth have they reminded me of Grandad. My throat tightens and I feel the tears forming at the back of my eyes.

'He'll be okay, Cassie. I know he's really ill but he's strong too, yeah?' I nod my head in agreement and sniff back the hot tears hovering above my eyelids.

Please god, let Grandad be okay and please god Maisy don't have your baby yet.

Lizzie

Thankfully the paramedics have let me ride in the ambulance with Dad while they drive him to the hospital. This, however, is not a good sign. I sit and watch as they connect various medical equipment about Dad's person.

A machine that looks worthy of a place aboard the Starship Enterprise makes all fashion of strange noises. Its small monitor displays a confusing array of different coloured lines, each one observing the various organs within my father's withering body. The only line I recognise, the one that forces my eyes to flit in its direction every couple of seconds with irritating ease, is the green line connected to my father's heart. As long as that line continues to rise and fall, I know Dad is safe. I plead, silently, with whoever can hear me, not to let Dad go yet, not like this.

One of the paramedics looks at me. She has a round, friendly face. 'You okay?' she asks.

'A bit worried,' I reply, wringing my hands in dumb show.

She smiles and tells me her name is Bernie. 'I've spoken to the hospital,' she continues. 'They have all your dad's details so they'll make him as comfortable as possible on arrival. Is it just you with your dad or do you have anyone else you can call?'

I explain that everyone else is travelling back from Cornwall and that my daughter is driving my step-daughter to the hospital at this very moment because she appears to have gone into labour.

Bernie raises her eyes. 'Wow. It never rains … and all that.' Half laughing, I agree. 'Look,' Bernie continues, glancing at Dad then back towards me, 'how far away are your family?'

I frown. 'I'm not sure, less than an hour I think. Why?'

'I think you should contact them and tell them to hurry.'

Cassie

I know it's Christmas Eve and people are travelling home from work or last-minute shopping but the roads seem far too busy to me.

'I need a siren,' I shout to Maisy in the back. 'A fucking siren and flashing lights so every idiot on the road will just let me bloody pass.'

'You're doing fine, Cas …' Maisy starts to say but stops talking as another contraction comes. I look at her through the rear-view mirror and her face is all screwed up with pain. I wait for the contraction to pass and ask Maisy if she's heard anything back from Crazee. Maisy looks down at her phone then looks back up and rolls her eyes. 'Not a bloody thing,' she replies. 'He better bloody get to the hospital before the baby comes, or I'll bloody kill him!' She looks worried again. 'Cas, you will stay with me, right? If that idiot doesn't turn up, you'll help me with the birth, won't you?'

I feel sick with fear. I hadn't even considered this. And what about Grandad? Mum said he was really poorly. I hadn't really given it any thought but I was hoping I could just drop Maisy off and then go and see Grandad. I feel annoyed. Crazee should be here with Maisy, not me. It's not my job. I didn't sign up for this.

'Cas? Cassie? You won't leave me on my own, right?'

I look again at Maisy's scared face through my rear-view

mirror. 'Of course I'll stay with you, you silly cow, right till you have the baby if I have to. But I'm sure I won't need to. I'm sure Crazee will see his phone and with a bit of luck, he'll be at the hospital when we get there.'

Maisy looks relieved, at least one of us is. Her phone starts ringing. 'Is it him? Is it Crazee?' I ask raising my eyes. Maisy looks down at her phone and shakes her head. 'No,' she replies. My heart sinks and my fear rises again. 'It's Dad' she says. 'Dad's calling me.'

Lizzie

The ambulance pulls into the hospital and Dad seems comfortable. His voice is faint but it's still there, nonetheless. I've just got off the phone to Simon and as luck would have it, they're stuck in traffic. I explained to Simon, and all the others as I was on loudspeaker, the situation with Dad and Maisy. Mum didn't say a word but her silence spoke volumes. Highly contagious, Mum's silence quickly spread, weaving its way amongst everyone else. And, what at first had been, when Simon responded to my call, the delightful background noise of festive merriment, quickly became sombre silence.

Several gasps and nonsensical mumblings eventually broke the glut of silence. Sean was the first to speak. He asked me truthfully if I thought Dad would make it. Sighing and running my hand through my hair, I was glad none of them could see my anguished face. I didn't want to tell them the truth. I imagined them all in the car before my phone call, before my bombshell smashed to pieces their jolly pre-Christmas Day reverie. Sean winding Connor up; Connor, in turn, winding Summer up; Nat refereeing, Mum bending Simon's ear about nothing and everything and all of them, despite tiredness, despite other problems, determined to make this the best Christmas possible. I knew Dad didn't have long; Bernie as good as said so and I owed it to them all, especially Mum and Connor, to tell the truth.

'No,' I eventually replied. 'He really isn't in a good way Sean and, if you can, you need to get here as quickly as possible.' I immediately heard Mum gasp, followed by a terrible wailing noise I recognised as Connor.

'No! No, no, no, no, no,' I heard him repeat over and over again. I imagined his face, crumpled up from shock, two fists held to the top of his head, rocking backwards and forwards in disbelief.

I could hear Sean trying to comfort him and Simon reassuring everyone he would make it, if it was the last thing he did, he would get them there.

'I knew it,' Mum said. 'I knew I shouldn't have left him. Why Lizzie? Why? Why did I let you talk me into leaving him?' Her voice, small and faint to begin with, grew with each word, until it was an agonising shrill. 'Now I may not even get to say goodbye,' she continued. And, if it was at all possible, my heart broke a little bit more. Simon told me not to worry and get back to Dad. He reminded me he loved me then ended the call before I had chance to say anything else. And, just like that, before I could tell my baby boy not to cry, before I could explain to Mum how sorry I was, they were gone again.

Cassie

For god bloody sake we've stopped again. I look at the huge, worn out backside of the waiting bus and I want to scream my head off at it and all its passengers. I want to wind down my window, this car is so bloody old it's never heard of electric windows and tell them all to get out of the bloody way. Instead I watch, as tired looking people form an orderly queue and slowly, painfully slowly, board the chugging beast in front of me. I tap my fingers on the car steering wheel like a drum and quickly glance at Maisy again through the rear-view mirror. Both her hands are wound round her belly and she looks like she's clutching a huge beach ball. She catches me looking at her and smiles, only it looks forced. Her mouth moves up at the corners but the rest of her face stays exactly where it is.

I imagine us not making it to the hospital, which forces the butterflies in my tummy to start flying again. I turn away from Maisy's false smile and look out of my window for some distraction. I can see the main high street in the distance to my right. Fake Christmas trees, some traditional, some not, some black or white, some gold or silver, all dripping with multi-coloured balls of treasure, fill the shop windows and bright, twinkly lights blink off and on as they snake their way around displays of things they want us to buy. All of it is just stuff, though. Stuff we already have and don't really need and yet, we still keep buying it.

I think of Dad and wonder why people get so caught up in stuff. I wonder why he thought a fifty thousand pound car or five hundred thousand pound house was worth more than me and Connor. And I also wonder why he had to lose everything to realise what's really important? He's doing his best, of course, to make it up to me and Connor but I don't trust him. A cheetah never changes its dots, or whatever the saying is. What happens if he decides, when he can afford it all again, that stuff is better than me and Connor. Will we be thrown away again, like all the wrapping paper on Christmas morning? What a waste of paper.

'Arrrggh. I'm having another one.' I look in my mirror and see Maisy's face all twisted up again. 'Are we ever…' she stops speaking as her lips form into a whistle and she starts blowing short little breaths, quickly, in and out. As I watch her I realise I'm doing it too. After a few minutes, she stops panting and continues speaking. 'Oh, my god, the contractions are getting worse, and closer together. Are we ever gonna get to the fucking hospital?'

Looking up ahead I'm relieved to see the bus pulling away. 'Yep, I'll get you there, sis,' I reply, filling my voice with far more confidence than I actually have. 'Just hang on a bit longer.' Please, please, don't have that bloody baby yet.

I see an opportunity to overtake the desperately slow-moving bus. I slam my foot down hard and crunch the car into third gear. Virtually rocking back and forth in my seat and willing the car to go faster, it starts to pick up speed and for the first time this evening I feel like we're getting somewhere. I indicate and pull out, giving the steering wheel a high five in triumphant hope. 'Go on girl, you can do it,' I shout.

The road looks pretty clear up ahead. I decide to ignore the flashing lights of the speed cameras that blind me for a few seconds and drive like the Formula One racing driver I have now suddenly become. The fines for speeding won't stand because this will be classed as distinguished circumstances, or whatever it's called. Excitement replaces my fear because, now she's going, Mum's old Beetle doesn't want to stop. I drive carefully but fast and I ain't stopping for anyone. More flashing lights go off and I imagine all the fines I'm building up. Plopping through the letterbox in a few days' time, and I don't give a shit.

Maisy screams out, 'please Cassie, please!' But I'm in the zone now and I tell her not to worry, that thanks to my expert driving we will definitely, without a doubt, make it to the hospital. I approach another bend and with my hands gripped tight to the steering wheel, my arms cross quickly, first to the left then back to the right. The car corners brilliantly and I swear, just for a minute, I feel the car lift off the ground. Sod the music industry, maybe I've found my new calling in life. Maybe I could become a stunt woman. I'm speed hungry now and lost in the thrill of the ride until I hear Maisy's voice calling me back.

'Please Cassie, stop,' she yells. The reflection of her concerned face bounces off my rear-view mirror and I'm confused. Why is she telling me to stop? Shit, did she actually give birth in the last thirty seconds and I missed it? As my concentration comes crashing back down to earth again I realise, in between Maisy's pleas to stop, the bright flashing lights of the speed cameras are still flashing, only they're not white, they are blue. And Maisy isn't shouting 'please, stop.' What she's actually saying is 'police, stop!'

Lizzie

Dad has been put in a private room and I can't fault the hospital staff. More or less, they had everything ready upon his arrival and thanks to their care and attention he is now breathing better and is in much less pain. His eyes are closed – he doesn't look like a dying man. He just looks peaceful and asleep. I'm assured he is dying, though. This is actually it and, thanks to me, Mum may not get the chance to say goodbye to the man who has been by her side, through the good times and the bad, for over fifty years.

I hang my head, and despite my desperate attempt to stop them, my tears fall anyway. When I eventually lift my head again, I take a deep breath and sniff and am relieved to see Dad still has his eyes closed so I take the opportunity to wipe away my tears with the backs of both hands. Composed again, my eyes flit around our charmless surroundings. Aside from the limp blue curtains hanging from the window, framing an inky black sky between them, the room is functional and sterile. Thankfully though, it is remarkably quiet. And, although I can hear Dad's shallow breathing, it is the gentle rise and fall of his chest that catches my attention. I stare at the crisp white sheet, now slightly blood stained, that covers him, and watch the rise and fall, rise and fall, willing, praying, imploring it to continue long enough for Mum and the others to get here and say goodbye.

I think of Mum and Dad and my favourite photo of them hanging in their hallway. Dad, skinny but strong and wiry, dark curls slicked into place by Brylcreem, Mum, long blonde hair, mini-skirt and boots and of course the signature black eyeliner and false lashes of the 60's. I smile, still in awe of my parents' relationship. Especially given their difficult and humble beginnings.

Their own parents, my grandparents, were born of a time where everyday people were still reeling from the abhorrent legacy of the Great War, the "war to end all wars" apparently. Entering a world of turmoil and loss, and still, long after the last bloody battle had been fought, struggling to make sense of a war that didn't make any at all, my grandparents and their loved ones then found themselves thrown amongst the horror meted out to them during yet another war, World War II. It was akin to a tale of two cities, the one being those who remained here, like both my grandmothers, bombed out of their homes, losing loved ones along the way, the other being the experiences of my grandfathers, both POWs, both survivors and both witness to, and exposed to, unbelievable torture and cruelty. These damaged people did their best to put their wartime experiences aside. Tried to forget that in one way or another, they had had to fight for whatever they could, be it extra food, a place to shelter, their life. Tried to forget the place where loss became an everyday occurrence and stories of atrocities meted out between fellow human beings were so great, it was actually easier to bury their heads with regards to such matters than discuss them. But it affected them all greatly and although such experiences can sometimes bring out the best in people, it most definitely brings out the worst in others. And sadly, it appeared to erode what little humanity my grandparents had left.

Struggling with loss, with grief, with nightmares, and living through years of austerity took their toll on my grandparents. Only too aware that what they had could be cruelly snatched from them in less time than it took to blink, they became hardened to life. Their existence became one of perpetual mourning, wrapped in a great cloak of fear. Even time, the supposed great healer, failed to soften their petrified hearts. It was as if they had wandered into the darkness and failed to make their way back to the light, even though they were afforded the opportunity to do so on many occasions.

Living meant survival to my grandparents, they were therefore firmly of the belief that if you made your bed, you had to lay in it, no matter how uncomfortable it proved to be. Desperate to hold on to whatever they had managed to accumulate in life and always in fear of losing it again, they did little to help my parents. Handouts, in any form, were frowned upon. So far as my grandparents were concerned, they had fed and clothed their children, put a roof over their heads, and sent them to school. Once they came of age, the rest, they believed, was up to them. Self-reliance was the key to survival.

So, barely out of their teens, married and pregnant with me, my parents were pretty much left to it. And, despite all the odds, they made it. Like two turtledoves working together to care for and incubate their brood, my forward-thinking parents used their experiences, their mistakes and their struggles to love and support us. And, despite whatever hardships were thrown at them, my parents were the antithesis of their parents. Soulmates, I suppose.

'I'm so sorry, Mum,' I say out loud.

'She'll be okay,' Dad whispers without opening his eyes. 'They don't make 'em like her any more.'

I laugh, pleased Dad can still hear me but desperate for him to sit up and tell me this is all a big mistake, that he is feeling much better now and is ready to go home so we can all celebrate Christmas tomorrow. I look at the fading light immersed within the decaying body of my once strong father, and am consumed with a grief so great I can hardly bear it. He's leaving me. The one man who has remained a constant in my life is actually going to leave me, forever.

Lifting Dad's limp, bony hand, I hold it in mine, staring at his long fingers, now devoid of any flesh that once fattened them out, instead covered by a thin layer of sallow, almost transparent skin. Using my finger, I trace a line along his fingers and follow the bluey, green veins that spread across his hand like road markings on a map. Once again, my eye is drawn to the missing little finger and I can't help but smile.

Despite his secrets, I cannot imagine my life without this man. I swallow hard as hot tears burn the back of my eyes. Death is not new to me and is probably the only certainty in our limited lives. But I'm not ready to lose my dad, not yet. This is the man who has nurtured and cradled me, who provided for and protected me. The man who sang terrible tone-deaf songs to me, who took me on wild and wondrous made-up places from his imagination and who told my loser boyfriends to "fack orf." This is the man who gave me away to another man, who, as it turned out, only wanted me for better, not for worse. So, discarded and afraid, this same man, my father, took me right back, along with both my children, sheltering us all from the fall-out of divorce, helping me back to the path of sanity. I don't want a life that doesn't include him. How will I ever cope? I know there are other men in my life, good men, like Simon and Sean and just lately, even my ex-husband has proved himself worthy of my respect and the love of our children. But none of these men are my dad. None of these other men have known me as long as this man has, nor loved me so unconditionally.

Cassie

The blue lights from the police car parked in front of me blink continually. I twist my neck to look back at Maisy and ask her if she's all right. She nods her head but holds her belly and starts groaning again. Panic creeps across my head and makes my face feel hot and my armpits slimy and damp. I turn away from

Maisy and back towards the windscreen and am hit head on by another blast of blue light that almost blinds me. I put my hand up to shield my eyes and strain to look for something, someone, some movement from the parked police car but there's none. Bloody idiot. What on earth is he doing?

Maisy's groans grow louder and I can hear her panting again. I lean across the steering wheel and feel for the car keys still hanging from the ignition. I grip the ignition key hard between my forefinger and thumb and seriously contemplate turning it back on and driving off again. Looking up, I notice the door on the driver's side of the police car open, finally, and a tall man in uniform slowly step out. I watch as he walks *slowly* towards me. He walks so slowly, it's actually painful to watch, and my eye begins to twitch.

'Yeah, that's right, you just take your bloody time,' I yell from my yellow cocoon.

I think about jumping out to face him, but knowing how quickly I can go from plain talking to a thousand mile an hour nonsensical ranting, I decide it could cost us more time if I do. At least when the policeman looks in the car he'll see Maisy laid up in agony with her baby bump. And then, hopefully, when he realises what's happening, I can drive straight off again to the hospital. Looking down at my hands, I notice my knuckles have turned white from gripping the steering wheel so tight. I look up again and I still can't believe the slow walking policeman hasn't reached the car yet. I watch and I watch and I watch and after what feels like forever, the slow, slow walking policeman reaches my window.

He bends down, his face level with mine, and looks at me. The window is down because I wound it down ten hours ago when he first got out of the car. He's old, about the same age as Mum and Si, and his forehead is crumpled from frowning.

'Now then, young lady,' he starts to say.

'My sister,' I interrupt, 'she's having a baby, right now. And I have to go to the hospital, right now. You have to let me go or I swear she's going to have it, in this car, right now. And. And …'

'Hey now. Calm down a minute,' the frowning policeman replies, and for the first time tonight I'm really pleased to hear Maisy yell out in pain again. The policeman pulls out a torch from somewhere and shines it into the back of the car. When it falls on Maisy's face of pain the frowning policeman flinches. Instead of frowning he now looks gobsmacked. 'Right then,' the policeman says, coughing. 'Right then,' he repeats, 'what's your name?'

I don't know if he's asking me or Maisy but frankly I don't give a shit! 'I'm Cassie, she's Maisy.' I'm interrupted by more groaning from the back seat, only this time it sounds more urgent. 'And if you don't mind I really need to get her to fucking hospital,' I continue.

'Right O', no need for swearing young lady, but yes, yes. I think you may be right. Follow me. I'll give you an escort.'

And with that the shocked policeman, who is no longer frowning, runs back to his car and signals me to follow him and his blazing, blue lights.

Simon

The mood in the car has dropped dramatically, despite mine and Natasha's best efforts to lift it. For once in her life, Ellie doesn't say a word. I steal another look at her and am moved by the pitiful little woman, staring straight ahead, eyes glazed over, lost, no doubt, in thoughts of her dying husband.

I reach out and pat her shoulder and she turns to look at me. 'I'll get you there Ellie, I promise I'll get you there. In time. In time to say …' I pause and Ellie nods her head and forces the corners of her lips to lift into a smile. She manages to maintain this pose quite successfully for several seconds then looks away again taking her smile with her.

I change the subject and try once again to lift the mood. 'Can't believe the baby is coming eh? Can you imagine, Cassie driving Maisy? Right couple of drama queens together!' This causes a ripple of giggles, mostly from Nat and Summer.

'Is she having a boy or a girl, Uncle Si?'

'I don't know, Summer. Maisy and Crazee wanted to wait and see, so we won't know until the baby is born.'

'Why isn't Crazee driving Maisy to the hospital?'

Again, this causes a few sniggers of laughter. 'Good question. I think he's down the pub.'

'Soooooooo … he'll be in trouble then?' This proves to be the relief that great storm clouds bring to the relentless heat of a stifling summer. The car fills up with laughter once more, not unlike it was a short while ago, before the frantic phone calls.

Ellie turns to me frowning, her lips small and rounded as if sucking on lemons. 'I should say,' she replies to Summer's question. 'Wouldn't want to be Crazee when they do get hold of him eh?'

I match Ellie's frown with mine. 'Can you imagine?' I reply, shaking my head. And then, like a great wave of relief, as if surfacing for air after being under water for too long, we both let out a great guffaw of much needed laughter. It's deep and guttural and infectious. The whole car fills up with the stuff as mental images of Crazee, head hung in shame, eyes downcast, being chastised, first by Cassie, then by Maisy, fly between us all. We laugh and laugh and laugh, until we cry. And then, as if it were completely natural, tears of laughter give way to tears of sadness once again. Except mine. Fuck all this new man, new age shit, I am a man and I will not cry. I refuse to, even though I feel as if I'm drowning inside, worried about Maisy, worried about Lizzie and sad, really sad, that I may not get to say goodbye to the cockney, swearing, pain in the arse, larger than life, extraordinary man that I have had the privilege to know and come to love.

I feel a piercing pain shoot up my arm and turn to see Ellie's hand curled around my arm in a vice like grip. Her eyes are damp and her face is racked with fear.

Her voice, slightly broken, is quiet but strong. 'Get me back, Simon,' she says, 'get me back to my Salocin, before it's too late.'

Lizzie

Cassie is on the phone and somewhere between her rushed ranting, with mention of flashing blue lights and police escorts, I understand they have made it safely to the hospital.

'How's Grandad?' Cassie asks after pausing for breath. I close my eyes in a bid to find the right words, finding it impossible to lie.

I swallow hard and cough. 'He's not good sweetheart, not good at all.' I hear a sharp intake of breath then all goes quiet. Seconds pass, although it feels like minutes, and Cassie doesn't make a sound. I look across at Dad, who is now drifting in and out of consciousness, and am filled with a terrible sense of panic.

'I want … I want … to see him, Mum. I'm coming up there. I'll leave Maisy for ten minutes and come and say goodbye.'

I don't have time to respond, though, because Maisy beats me to it with her screaming. It may be on the end of the phone but I can hear very well and I'm alarmed. Something is wrong. I ask Cassie if anyone is with them.

'Someone was but they've gone again. She said she'd be back in five minutes but that was nearly twenty minutes ago.'

Dad stirs and starts to ramble incoherently. Something about birds and Bob. He keeps saying the name Bob. In between Dad's nonsensical ramblings I hear Maisy scream again. It's a disturbing sound, almost primal, and immediately causes the hairs on the back of my neck to stand on end. I ask Cassie if she can put Maisy on the phone to speak to me but when offered the phone Cassie advises me that Maisy simply shakes her head whilst continuing to pant.

'Okay, listen to me Cassie. It sounds like this baby is in a hurry and, I don't want you to panic, because it's probably all fine, but there could be complications –'

'Complications? What do you mean complications?' Cassie interrupts followed by more panic-stricken wailing from Maisy. 'Oh shit, what did you say that for? Now she's bloody crying! Arrrggh, this isn't even my job. Crazee should be here! Not me!'

I quickly find my former authoritarian librarian's voice. 'Cassie! Stop it, this instant. Your sister needs you.'

Silence follows. Followed by more screaming from Maisy, followed by an apology from Cassie. I tell her to find someone, quickly, and not to accept any crap from them. I tell her she must explain that it's an emergency.

Cassie's voice is calm but I can sense the panic in it. 'Okay. Okay. But ...' she pauses again as if too frightened to ask but then does anyway. 'What about Grandad?'

I wander back towards Dad's bed. Except for the nonsensical musings falling from his chattering mouth, his eyes remain closed and he lies perfectly still. 'I don't know Cassie,' I reply. 'I really don't know. Whatever happens, happens, I suppose. All I know is Maisy needs you right now and I'm pretty sure Grandad is fine with that.'

'Cassie? That you, Cas?' Dad interrupts me.

'No Dad, it's me, Lizzie. Cassie is on the phone –'

Dad's voice is desperately faint but perfectly clear. 'Tell her, our song, remember our song,' he whispers. 'Me and her and Connor. And Bob,' he adds.

Confused I relay this message back to Cassie who is once again quiet for several seconds before eventually breaking the silence. Her voice is pained but somehow, I detect a smile in her tone.

'Okay Mum, I get it. Tell Grandad I love him.'

Cassie

Thank god for that policeman, Jeff. What a lovely geezer, as Grandad would say. Thanks to him, I think we drove through every red traffic light and every single speed camera in the entire city. We were flashed so many times it felt like the whole sky was alight at one point, very Christmassy in a way.

Maisy, now crouched on a bed, is half-dressed and soaked in sweat. Her lips are a purplish colour and her face is white, really white. She glances up at me and wears a look of fear, which makes my tummy flip. Grunting and puffing and panting, Maisy stretches her arm out towards me. I walk towards her, take her hand in mine and gently rub it. I wonder why we do that, rub people's hands to make them feel better? Suddenly my head starts to spin. For a minute, despite still holding her hand, Maisy feels like she's a long way away. At the end of a long, dark tunnel. Her grunts and moans, and even my voice, are muffled. I'm cold but I'm sweating at the same time and my legs keep bending at the knees, despite trying my hardest to stop them. I don't really understand what Maisy is saying any more but I feel sick and I know Mum is right. I need to get help. I also need to get away for a minute.

Snatching my hand away from Maisy's I rush for the door. I tell Maisy I'm going to get someone; at least I think that's what I say. The corridor is squeaky and my head feels like one big messy mush of Grandad, Luke, Hunter, the abortion and the rape. I'm not sure where I'd go but I have an overwhelming need to run away, disappear from everything. I start running, my eyes darting in and out of half open doors, looking for someone, anyone to help. Why isn't there anyone around? But now I've started running I don't want to stop. I think of Forrest Gump, didn't he run for three years or something? Maybe I can do that.

Just run and run and run, from everything and everyone. No more hurt, no more pain.

Someone starts screaming and I'm not sure if it's Maisy or some other poor woman. I can't believe women still have to give birth like this, you'd have thought they would have invented a better way to do it by now. It's actually barbaric. I hear more screaming. Shit. Maisy could be in trouble and I need to help her. I open and close doors and shout, loudly, for help. The lights in the corridor are so bright it causes my head to ache. I hate hospitals, they remind me of bad times. I yell out again and eventually a red-faced woman in a blue uniform appears.

She looks really irritated. 'Yes?' she asks. I explain about Maisy and although she seems annoyed I can tell she is listening to me and, thank god, is taking me seriously. She shouts something to the people in the room she's just come from then follows me to Maisy's room. She mumbles something about being short staffed, again, then flashes me a lovely warm smile and I'm amazed how less worried I suddenly feel.

The nurse in the blue uniform is in fact a midwife and tells me her name is Alison. Maisy really doesn't look good when we get back to her room but Alison completely takes control. She is so calm and matter of fact, she reminds me of Mum. Telling her it's too late for any other real pain relief, Alison props Maisy up into a more comfortable position with a couple of heavy pillows on the bed, then passes her what looks like a plastic tube with a mouthpiece. She says it's gas and air and tells Maisy to suck on it. Maisy takes it and sucks on it greedily. For the first time in forever Maisy looks relieved and I see the whites of her eyes when she rests her head back on the pillow.

Alison continues to move around the room. She looks busy but seems really calm, like she knows exactly what she's doing. Which she does, I suppose. I hover, helplessly watching, wringing my hands and chewing the corner of my mouth. I suddenly feel useless, like a spare part. I glance back at Maisy who, with the tube still in her mouth, seems a lot calmer. I stifle a laugh; suddenly reminded of the time Luke and I were drunk in Camden Town and decided it would be good to share a coffee and a shisha.

When I look back at Alison she smiles at me and winks. 'So, is this the first time for you two then?' she asks. It takes me a minute to understand what she means then I realise she thinks that me and Maisy are together, as a couple, and for the first time in a long time I start to laugh, so loud and so hard, it actually hurts. I explain that the loser in the bed is in fact my sister, step-sister, and that her stupid boyfriend is really going to be in for it because he's getting drunk in some pub somewhere, not answering his stupid phone.

Alison opens her eyes wide in surprise. 'Oh dear, like that, is it?'

I nod my head as does Maisy who, still sucking on her gas pipe, wears an expression that can only be described as pure anger.

Maisy pulls the pipe from her mouth. 'Ring him again, will you,' she asks.

I look at Alison who nods in agreement. 'Be quick though,' she cautions.

Swiping the screen on my phone I look for Crazee's number. I press call, desperate for him to answer but after a couple of rings it goes straight to voicemail. I don't even bother leaving a message this time. Looking up from my phone, I shake my head. Maisy looks like a puppy waiting for a treat that never comes and I suddenly feel as sad as she now looks. If Crazee were here I could say goodbye to Grandad. I'm about to ask Alison if I can nip off to the other end of the hospital for ten minutes when I see the look on Alison's face.

'Right Cassie, we haven't got much time. This baby is coming whether we like it or not but I think the cord is wrapped around its neck.'

Maisy pulls the tube from her mouth. She looks horrified and her jaw drops. 'It's fine, Maisy,' Alison continues. Her voice is calm but assertive. 'I've come across this a few times before and you'll be absolutely fine. I just need you to do as I say. Okay?' Maisy's face crumples and her eyes widen. She nods her head up and down. I don't realise, until Alison then looks at me, but my mouth is also hanging open. 'You too, Cassie,' Alison says. I close my mouth and also nod. I think of Grandad and what he told Mum to tell me. He was talking about "our" song, mine and Connor's and his, 'Three Little Birds' by Bob Marley. That was what he used to sing to us when we were little, telling us never to worry because every little thing would always be alright, in the end.

Maisy has another contraction and starts screaming again and I notice Alison pick up something silver in colour. She's quick to fold it into her hand to hide it but as she does it catches the light and sparkles like the star on Mum's Christmas tree.

With Maisy still screaming, Alison walks towards her and tells me to hold her hands. Head down, Alison pushes Maisy's legs further apart. I hear a ripping sound and for as long as I live I swear I will never, ever, ever have a baby.

Lizzie

Looking out of the window, I'm met with a car park the size of a small city. I watch cars pulling in and cars pulling out, willing one of them to be Simon. Where are they? Why the hell aren't they here yet? Dad mumbles something behind me. He is slipping in and out of consciousness now. Sometimes he wakes with a start, appearing completely lucid, at others he rambles and seems confused and disoriented.

My phone buzzes in my pocket and when I look at the screen I'm surprised to see it's a call from Scott. I press the green accept call button, and place the phone to my ear.

'Oh, hi, Lizzie, Scott says, his words stilted, his tone slightly agitated. 'Sorry to bother you on Christmas Eve and everything but I was wondering if you had half an hour or so?' Apologising, I explain my current predicament and that of Cassie and Maisy. 'Shit, yeah, of course. I'm so sorry Lizzie,' Scott replies. 'Do you want me to, what I mean is, should I come to the hospital. For the kids?'

I ask Scott what it was he wanted, what he had actually phoned for in the first place. When he tells me he is worried about Ruby, I feel a slight ripple of concern run through me and Scott clearly detects it in my voice.

'What do you mean?' I ask.

'Lizzie? Lizzie gal, that you?' I swing round to see Dad staring, eyes wild and full of fear, or is it anger?

'It's okay Dad, I'm still here,' I reply.

'Lizzie? Can you hear me, Liz?' Scott asks?

'Yes, Scott, I can hear you. What the hell is wrong with Ruby?'

'Listen to me,' Scott replies, 'it's honestly nothing. I haven't seen her for a while and I had a Christmas present for Andrew and I just thought if you came with me to see her, she'd be more likely to answer the door.' Realising I've been holding my breath I breathe a heavy sigh of relief. 'So, you see to your dad, and Maisy, and I'll pop by Ruby's then drive straight to the hospital,' Scott continues. 'Would you like me to tell Ruby about your dad, if I see her?'

'Lizzie,' Dad calls again.

'Coming Dad,' I reply. 'Yes, please do tell Ruby if you see her. Thanks Scott. I have to go.'

Walking back towards the bed, I resume my place beside my father. His voice is whispery but perfectly clear and once again I hold his hand in mine, squeezing it gently. 'Yes Dad, it's me, I'm still here.'

'You still got that card I gave you? Just in case, for Cassie?'

I nod and Dad starts coughing again. Spots of blood form a random smattering of crimson on the white bedsheet, as if someone had flicked a loaded paintbrush at it. 'Facking, lousy scumbag cunt.'

'Shhhhhh, Dad, it's okay, we've got it sorted. Cassie is, will be okay.'

Dad shakes his head violently and tries to sit up. His distress distresses me. Face screwed up, he continues coughing, struggling for air. Mouth open, he gasps and holds his chest. I stand up and the chair I'm sitting on rushes backwards, hitting the wall behind me with a thud. Bending over Dad in a bid to help him, I'm not sure what to do. He wheezes and gasps, his previous sickly white face now turning into a fury of red. I call for help and within seconds there are a flurry of people around us. Pushed out of the way, useless and helpless, I watch.

Please don't let this be it. Not like this, Dad.

Crazee

For a small-town pub, the atmosphere in here ain't half bad. I could get used to living here, for a while, if that's what Maze really wants. I mean, it's not the Gold Coast and I miss the surf. And sitting down to a huge roast dinner tomorrow for Christmas ain't exactly a barbie on the beach, but I guess I can get used to it. Maze needs her family, I get that.

'Nother pint?' Ajay asks.

I salute him with my half empty pint. 'Oh, go on then mate, may as well make the most it. Before the baby comes, eh?'

Ajay snorts. 'Yeah, too right. Soon as that little one pops its head into the world there'll be no more nipping down the pub for you for a while, just sleepless nights, dirty nappies and fuck all sex for a year or two.'

'A year, or two?'

Ajay laughs, grabs his empty glass and starts to push his way among the throng of people that now swamp the bar.

Thinking of Maze, I smile. Complicated as hell, but I love her anyway. Still find it hard to believe she and I are going to be parents in a couple of weeks. Me, a dad? It's just plain fucking crazy!

'Crazee?' someone calls.

Looking up I immediately recognise the face and the leather jacket. 'G'day mate. It's Luke, right?'

The poor bloke sounds breathless, as if he's been running. 'That's right, oh fuck me.' He bends over, holding his knees with his hands before taking a few deep breaths and straightening up again. 'I really do need to give up the fags.'

'Word of caution, don't ever say that in the States mate.'

He looks confused for a second before breaking into a wide smile. 'Right, yeah, gotcha.'

'Actually, come to think of it, I thought Cas said you were in the States? You and your band?'

'Yeah, I was, I mean I am. What I mean is, I fly on Boxing Day. The others have gone on ahead. I just, well, I just needed ...' he trails off, coughs and scratches his head. Looking thoughtful he rubs his chin. 'Well, the thing is, I need to speak to Cassie.'

Jeez, he doesn't have to look so bloody serious. 'Righto,' I reply. 'Fancy a pint?'

Luke shakes his head. 'I really do need to speak to Cassie, do you know where she is?'

'At home, as far as I know, well, I say home, I mean Lizzie and Si's house. Watching Christmas shit with Maze last time I checked.'

Luke shakes his head. 'Nah mate, she's not. I've been round and the house is all locked up. You can see no-one's in.'

'Really?' I reply, reaching into the back pocket of my jeans for my phone. 'They've probably gone to ...'

I'm about to suggest they are probably at Salocin's with Lizzie when we are interrupted by a loud voice demanding to be heard. Looking towards the pub door, festively draped in colourful, tacky tinsel, I spot a copper standing, legs apart, waving his hand like a stop sign.

'Excuse me,' he shouts. All eyes turn towards the voice of authority but the festive spirit is noisy, especially when set against Wizzard's 'I Wish It Could Be Christmas Everyday'. The man in uniform catches someone's attention at the bar and flicks his wrist in a turning motion. 'Can we just ... yep ... turn it down.' The music disappears and the copper gives the barman the thumbs up. 'Right,' he bellows, 'I'm looking for an Australian lad, goes by the name of Crazee?'

I feel my jaw drop and my cheeks burn. All eyes turn towards me and I suddenly feel as though I'm in the country pub scene from *An American Werewolf in London*. I pat my pockets in a panic. Nope, no weed. What the fuck is this about? A few people point and others nod in my direction.

At least I know who my friends are, my real friends, bastard snitches.

The copper follows the outstretched accusatory fingers and strides towards me, grinning like one of those insanely hideous laughing policeman trapped inside a glass prison, sometimes found at old funfairs.

'Crazee?' he asks? I swallow hard and nod my head. Opening my mouth to speak I find, despite drinking several litres of beer, not an ounce of moisture remains in my dry mouth. Any attempts to respond finds my fat, furry tongue sticking to the roof of my barren mouth.

The copper shakes his head and starts laughing.

'Are you ever in trouble, young man.'

Connor

Staring at the back of Si's head I have the sudden urge to punch it. Punch it and push him out of the way so I can drive, even though I don't know how to, yet. He's driving way too slow. Why can't he just break all the rules for once in his uptight bloody life. Okay, I'm not being fair. He's not uptight, well a bit, maybe, like most stupid adults. Except Grandad, of course. Grandad is the soundest man on the planet, especially for an old bloke. If Grandad had been driving, we would have been there by now. He wouldn't have been worried about a few speed cameras. I mean, so what if Si gets banned from driving for a year, he'll survive. Grandad won't though. Grandad is dying. Shit, he is actually fucking dying. 'One day soon' still seemed a long way off. Because he still looks the same, a bit thinner maybe, but still grumpy, still telling everyone to "fack orf," still singing as badly as ever, still playing guitar with me, still talking to me and making sense when no-one else does, still there for me. But 'one day soon' has arrived and it doesn't matter that it's now or if it was in a year's time or ten years' time, it would still be too soon.

My stomach twists and turns like the riffs on my drum and base tracks and I feel sick again. I look across at Uncle Sean. Leant forward, he has been back seat driving with Si for most of the journey. 'Oh, come on, mate,' he shouts as the car in front of us driving really slowly virtually stops. 'What is he doing?' Uncle Sean continues, throwing his hands up. 'Don't indicate then! Idiot. He's letting you go I think, Si.'

'How much longer?' Simon asks.

Uncle Sean buries his face in his phone. 'Twenty-three minutes,' he declares looking up. 'Twenty-three minutes,' he repeats, 'and we should be there. According to my phone, that is.' Turning towards the back of the car he mumbles something over his shoulder to Nat, who is cuddled up with a now sleeping

Summer. At least she's not crying anymore. I feel so sorry for her. I know she doesn't believe in Father Christmas but she should be thinking about Christmas stuff and presents under the tree. But instead, we are rushing to the hospital to say goodbye to Grandad, forever.

Looking out of the window I use the sleeve of my hoody to wipe away the hot tears that have taken me by surprise. My phone buzzes and it's a text from Alesha. I immediately put my finger to my lips; I can taste our kiss on my tongue. Smiling, I read her text;

I'm so sorry about your grandad. I read this and thought of you. "Goodbyes are only for those who love with their eyes. Because for those who love with heart and soul there is no such thing as separation" –Jalaluddin Rumi xxxxxxxxxx

When I look around again Uncle Sean is watching me. Winking at me, his face cracks into a smile and I realise how much like Grandad he looks. Leaning across, he ruffles my hair. 'How we doing, Rocky?' he asks. I can't help but smile. 'Do you remember how much Grandad laughed about that, with you and the chickens?'

I do remember and start laughing, a lot. Grandad looked sad that day, in pain, maybe. I wouldn't know coz he wouldn't say, not to me anyway. "Connor, you bleedin' plonker" he said when I reminded him about Sir Barks-a-lot and the escaping chickens. He almost couldn't breathe from laughing. Which made a change from the cancer causing him to wheeze.

The heavy, dragging feeling in my stomach lifts a bit. I'm glad I made him laugh that day, even though he was right, I was a plonker. But I didn't care. And I didn't care he was laughing at me coz it wasn't really at me, it was with me, there's a difference and Grandad taught me that.

Sean's face reflects mine, screwed up and ugly from laughing too much. Pointing at one another we take it in turns to re-tell the story. Behind me, I hear Nat start to chuckle and it must be infectious coz then I notice Nan's shoulders heaving up and down and I see Si's face in the rear-view mirror, also wearing a huge, equally ugly smile. Our loud, snorting laughter wakes Summer. I don't think she understands why we are laughing but she starts laughing too, anyway. Maybe our laughing is making her laugh. I love the sound of everyone laughing. Closing my eyes, I swear I can hear Grandad, too. I know it's probably my imagination but I swear down Grandad is here, in the car, with us.

My tears, just as hot and just as salty as they were ten minutes ago, are now tears of laughter, until I remember, that is. Then, just like a light switches from on to off, the laughter is gone again. The tears, still falling, come from a different place now and I feel as though a great cloak of doom has wrapped itself around me and once more I am unbelievably sad.

Looking at the back of Si's head again, I seriously want to push him out of the way.

Just drive you bloody idiot!

Leaning forward, Uncle Sean asks Nan if she's okay and once again Nan nods her head. Uncle Sean squeezes Nan's shoulder then turns to speak to Si. 'You're doing well mate, making really good time.'

'Thanks Sean. Doesn't feel like it though, what with all the fucking speed cameras. Sorry for swearing Ellie,' he says turning to look at Nan

Nan shakes her head. 'Fack orf,' she replies, 'I'm used to it.' This causes a ripple of laughter through the car, but nothing like the hysterics of a couple of minutes ago.

'No, honestly, you're doing all right mate,' Uncle Sean repeats. 'Festina lente,' he declares.

'What does that mean?' I ask.

'Make haste slowly.'

'Isn't that an oxymoron?' Si asks.

You're a bloody moron. For not driving faster.

I catch Si looking at me in the rear-view mirror. He smiles and … *what the hell? Why is he giving me the thumbs up? There's nothing okay about this situation, knobhead.*

Flicking my hood back over my head, I look out of the window again. Cars with bright lights rush by, as do twinkling towns and cities, all dressed up for Christmas. It doesn't feel like Christmas though. Suddenly angry for being angry, I glance at the back of Si's head again.

Why am I so angry? It's not Si's fault Grandad is dying. Simon has been pretty good to me and Cas over the years, better than my own dad. Who is, at least, trying now. But right from the start, before and after Dad left, before Si came along, it was always Grandad. Grandad was always there for me. One of the three little birds is dying and everything ain't gonna be alright and I don't know what the hell to do about it. There'll be no more Nicolas Flamel, no more being told to "fack orf" or "cheer up, it's not a life, it's an adventure." All of it will be gone, forever, and all I want right now is the chance to say goodbye.

Si's phone rings and straight away I can see it's Mum. Si's finger hovers on the accept call button as Mum's number flashes at us in neon green on the front display. Nan gasps and I swear everyone is holding his or her breath.

Why is she ringing again? Why?

Si's finger presses the accept call button. 'Hello, it's me,' Mum says. 'Can you all hear me?' Her voice is quiet and weird, crackly like the old vinyls I use to mix up the tracks on my DJ decks. We're too late, surely that's why her voice sounds weird and that's why she's ringing us.

We're too fucking late.

Cassie

Alison looks at me in the same way Mum does when she's pissed off at me for something.

I look down, sheepishly. 'Sorry, it's just that she's crushing my hand.' I point timidly to Maisy who is now soaked in sweat and panting like a crazy woman.

'Arrrrrgggghh, where the fuck is he?' Maisy screams.

I notice blood on Alison's rubber gloves and feel sick. This is barbaric, fucking barbaric. If men had to give birth it would have been outlawed years ago.

'Yes well, I'm not sure who was screaming loudest, you or Maisy,' Alison replies. 'And I really need your help Cassie, to keep Maisy calm.' Alison sees me looking at her bloody hands and shouts my name again. 'Cassie, look at me Cassie.' I do as I'm told and am met by Alison's steely glare.

Maisy squeezes my hand again and it's all I can do to stop myself from yelling out. 'Where the fuck is the fucking crazy bastard?' she wails.

'Don't worry about him,' Alison replies, 'you're doing really well.'

What about me! Aren't I doing well? I don't even want to be here. Maisy's right, where are you Crazee, you crazy bastard.

I quickly manage to swap hands with Maisy so she can crush that one instead and give my other hand a rest. Alison, who up until this point looked really calm, now looks concerned. She catches me watching her and smiles, like Mum does when she doesn't want me to worry.

'Cassie, you're doing a great job too,' Alison tries to reassure me, 'but I need you to help me stay focussed, okay? I need you to hold Maisy, let her know she's doing all right. Can you do that for me Cassie?' Alison talks slowly and calmly but Maisy doesn't hear her, Maisy is gone, lost in a world of pain, however, Alison says it in such a way it makes me realise this is serious and we're all in it together, all three of us are really important in this baby being born safely.

Looking at Alison I nod my head up and down, offering up both my hands to Maisy, like sacrificial lambs to the slaughter.

'Maisy,' Alison calls. Her voice is warm but official. 'Maisy,' she repeats, and Maisy, turning her head looks at her. 'Listen to me, Maisy, you're doing really well and the baby is fine but it's in a bit of distress because the cord is wrapped around the baby's neck. When I say push, I want you to push for as long and as hard as you can. Have you got that Maisy?'

Maisy nods like she understands but she is whimpering like a dog that has been left on its own all day. It's a pitiful, wretched sound and I just want to hug her and tell her I love her, so I do.

'Right Maisy,' Alison interrupts, 'after three. One, two, three, PUSH!'

Lizzie

God only knows how he's hanging on but thankfully Dad is still with me. More morphine has been administered and once again he is quiet and looks at peace. I'm watching my dad die and I can't quite work out if it's a blessing or a curse. His body is shutting down. One by one his vital organs are giving up until his heart will stop. And then what? Does he pass on from this world to the next? I used to think that was a load of old bollocks but now, with Dad so close to death, the idea that somehow he'll still be around watching us all is strangely comforting. I know Dad doesn't think it's the end; he believes some strange law of attraction and one that doesn't end with death. He says our bodies are merely vehicles that wear out with time and somehow, in this great circle of life, we all find our way back to one another. "What, even me?" Maisy had asked Dad. "But I'm not related to you, what I mean is, we don't share the same blood?" "Blood has fack all to do with it, gal" Dad had responded with a knowing smile.

Reincarnation? Is that what Dad was referring to? A ridiculous idea but again, strangely comforting. Except I don't want Dad to come back as someone else, I want him to stay here in the same body, wearing the same face I know, forever.

Bending forward, I rub my tired face with my very dry hands.

'I won't be far away, Lizzie.'

I look up and find Dad staring at me.

How does he do that? How on earth does he pick up on what I'm thinking?

I smile and Dad smiles back, although it looks more like a grimace, like every movement is now too much effort for his dying body.

I hold Dad's hand again. 'Shhhhhh,' I struggle to say but my voice breaks, as does my heart and try as I might, I really can't stop the tears. Hot salty water stings my eyes and burns my cheeks. I look down in some pathetic attempt to hide my grief. It is only when I look up once again my tears stop as abruptly as they started. For, although he barely makes a sound, I notice Dad is crying too.

'Oh god, I'm sorry, Dad. Please don't cry. What is it? Do you need more pain relief?'

'I'm frightened, Lizzie.' Closing my eyes, I can't bear to hear that my father, my big, strong protector is frightened.

'Don't be frightened Dad. It's okay, you'll be okay.'

Dad's voice is a whisper. 'I'll be fine, I'm not afraid of dying. It's your mum, Lizzie gal. Fifty odd years we've been together, I need to go but I'm afraid to leave her. You have to promise me you'll look after her?'

My thorax tightens and I struggle to find my voice, so find myself nodding instead, like an excited school child. Fanning my face like I've just eaten the world's hottest chilli, I gather all the strength I can muster to dignify my father's request with a response.

'Course I bleedin' will,' I say in my best cockney accent. 'Besides, you said it yourself; they don't make 'em like her anymore, tough as old boots, Mum is. She'll soon replace you, probably with some rich toy boy. She might even try her luck with Oliver!'

Although it's faint, Dad chuckles and a wonderful smile lights up his whole face. And there and then I realise, that's it, that's the smile I need to capture and hold onto in the months ahead of me.

I continue staying close to Dad as he drifts in and out of consciousness, sometimes rambling incoherently, at other times quite lucid. He mentions Cassie again a couple of times, stressing I ring the number on the card he gave me should the shit hit the fan.

Dad's voice is fading faster than I care to admit but yet, even now, so close to the end, it is a voice of conviction and one that demands to be listened to. 'I know people Lizzie,' he says, gripping my hand in his, almost crushing my fingers. 'And that bastard, with all his money and all his connections, thinks he is untouchable. But there's more than one way to skin a rat, believe me.'

Cassie

Maisy's scream is as terrifying as her grip on the hand I can no longer feel. I didn't think I did, but I must have screamed as well because Alison's head pops up for a second and she gives me her "shut the fuck up" look again. I smile, through gritted teeth, and Alison's head disappears back between Maisy's blood-stained thighs.

'Good girl Maisy, that's it, keep going. We're nearly there. I can see the head. One more big push.'

Shit! Did she really just say she could see the head? Part of me wants to rush down and look, part of me feels sick at the thought of it. As I'm busy thinking about it I realise my numb hand is coming back to life and is swinging by my side. Maisy has finally let go and as I turn to look at her I realise she is crying.

'Can't. Can't do it anymore,' she sobs.

Alison's head is back up. She rests one of her bloody hands against Maisy's knee and I feel sick at the sight of it.

It's not like this in the bloody movies, three screams and the baby is out and there's none of this blood and guts shit either. God, I feel tired. Like I've been partying hard at Glastonbury for three days and three nights with barely any sleep. Only this ain't no festival!

Maisy is still crying and her screwed up face is wet from tears and snot and sweat. 'Can't you just cut it out of me, cut it out of my stomach?' she says sobbing.

'Yeah, she's right. This is barbaric. Can't you just give her a solarium, or whatever the fuck the word is?'

For 0.2 seconds exactly, Maisy's face breaks into a grin while Alison just looks confused. 'It's called a caesarean, Cassie, you bloody idiot,' Maisy yells before falling into heaving sobs again.

Alison isn't impressed and the tone of her voice is crystal clear, stop messing around and do as I say, NOW. 'It's too late for a C-Section Maisy,' she replies, 'besides, one more push and the baby will be here.'

Maisy's voice is high and pitched with pain. 'You said that fucking ten pushes ago!'

I shake my head. 'This is crazy,' I add, but instantly regret my choice of words.

'And him,' Maisy screams, 'where the fuck is he, Cas? I'll be the crazy one by the time I've finished with him. If he ever turns up!'

Alison half smiles, as if she's pleased with the fire once again burning in Maisy's belly and uses it. 'C'mon then Maisy, let's show him. Let's get this baby out and let's show him.'

Maisy's tired eyes are bright and alert again. Her hand flaps about wildly at her side, searching for mine and once again I willingly sacrifice it to this woman's work, hoping and praying she doesn't cause any permanent damage to my piano playing fingers. Lifting her sweat soaked head off the pillow; Maisy wears a look of complete determination, a bit like a runner waiting for the crack of the gun on starters orders. She locks her fingers around mine, squeezing and crushing them like her life depended on it, and somehow, god knows how, I manage not to yell out, despite the pain. Maisy starts screaming again but it's different this time. It's a long, really low sound, demonic almost. It seems to rise from the pit of her stomach and pour out of her wide-open mouth.

'Aaaaaaaarrrrrrrgggghh,' she screams. I swear she doesn't even take a breath.

'That's it Maisy. Good, keep it going, keep it going,' Alison yells back from the bloody abyss I now imagine is Maisy's fanny. 'Good girl,' Alison continues. 'That's it, that's it.'

Hearing a gushing sound, I am shocked when Alison suddenly pulls out and holds up what looks like a bluish grey sack attached to a slimy looking rope. I realise it's the baby and I don't know whether to be amazed or appalled. From out of nowhere, it seems, there are suddenly other people in the room and lots of urgent rushing around. There are clamps and scissors and blankets. Maisy looks as confused as I feel. Looking across at the blue baby now being bundled into blankets, Maisy asks me what it is.

I look at her in disbelief. 'It's a baby, you idiot,' I reply.

'Would you like to cut the cord, Cassie?' Alison interrupts.

Swinging my head so abruptly my neck cracks, I look at Alison in the same way someone would if they'd just been asked if they'd like to behead someone. I shake my head vigorously until I feel sick and dizzy. Alison smiles, says something to another nurse standing next to her and they both look at me and laugh. I see the flash of silver from a pair of scissors and before I know it Alison is walking towards us with a bundled-up blanket.

'Right, who wants to hold him first?' she asks.

'A boy? It's a boy then?' Maisy replies, eyes huge, smiling like a wide mouth frog.

'He certainly is, and quite a big one at that, considering how early he is. Eight pound, two ounces.'

Maisy's eyes start filling up. She looks at me, and smiles, once again squeezing my hand. I flinch but this time, thankfully, her grip is much gentler. 'Thanks, Cas,' she whispers before turning back to look at Alison. 'Let Cassie hold him first,' she says.

Maisy beams at me, like her offer is the biggest honour of my life, but if truth be told, I'm horrified. Horrified by the bluish bulbous thing I've just witnessed being pulled out of Maisy's bloody nether regions and I'm not sure I want to hold it.

'No, it's fine,' I protest. 'Let Maisy hold her baby first.'

Maisy smiles and squeezes my hand again. 'No Cas, you've earned this. I could never have done it without you.' And before I know it, Alison thrusts the bundle into my arms.

I'm not sure what to expect but for some reason I imagine it looking like the thing that bursts out of that woman actor's stomach in the Alien films. I'm definitely not prepared for the perfect, now pink face, looking up at me. His searching eyes seem familiar and bore right into me, tugging at my heart in a way I never knew possible. His perfectly formed mouth matches his perfectly formed nose and two tiny hands, each with tiny fingers and thumbs, wriggle above the blanket. I lift one of the tiny hands and am amazed when it folds around my finger. I stare in amazement and can't quite believe the teeny tiny perfectly formed nails on each finger and thumb. I think of my abortion and a slight jolt of regret pierces my heart, but it only lasts a few seconds. Especially when I see how needy the baby is, how fragile and dependent. The truth is, I can barely look after myself at the moment, how would I ever cope with a baby right now. Being a parent is for life, Mum and Nan and Grandad have shown me that.

'I'm going to call him Nicolas,' Maisy says.

I look at Maisy, shocked. My throat tightens and I can barely get my words out. 'After …' my voice cracks so I cough and try again '…after Grandad?' I eventually manage to ask as hot tears stream down my face.

Maisy, who is also crying, nods her head. She holds out her hands. 'Yes,' she whispers, 'after Salocin. Now give Nicolas to me and go, Cassie, you need to go to him.'

Connor

Thank fuck. The huge hospital building comes into sight and thanks to Mum, Simon knows exactly which car park and which entrance we need. Well, she told Si to drop us lot at one entrance then park the car at the maternity unit so he can go straight up and see Maisy. Then they argued, Si saying he was going straight to Mum and Mum telling him to go straight to Maisy. Each of them going at it like fridiots, until I snapped. Told them both to shut the fuck up. I was surprised when they did and even more surprised no-one had a go at me for swearing, but no-one did. I feel a bit of a shit for shouting but what does it matter who goes where, just let me say goodbye to my grandad for god sake.

Nan has her glasses on. Sat forward, she is studying all the hospital signs and I know, even without seeing her face, she is squinting, desperate, like me, to see the sign, the one that says car park C, and the entrance opposite it. The entrance that will take me to Grandad. I have Mum's instructions seared into my brain. "Go to the entrance opposite car park C," she said. "Walk in through the automatic doors, past a smallish reception desk on the left then push open the big double doors where you see a set of lifts. Get in and press the button for level 2." Get out and run like hell. She didn't say the last bit; I added that, quietly, to myself.

Pressing my face against the car passenger window, I desperately try and look where we are but it keeps misting up from my cheese and onion crisp breath. I spot a huge sign shouting out the words MATERNITY UNIT. Nan points to the sign and turns to Si. 'You need to go that way, left, for the Mat Unit. Why don't you just drop us here and go straight to Maisy?' Uncle Sean and I look at one another. 'I'm sure we can find our way from here,' Nan continues. 'We just passed car park B, so C can't be that far away can it? Drop us here, Simon, and you go on to see Maisy.'

I stare at the back of Nan's head in disbelief.

What the hell are you playing at, Nan? I know Maisy and her baby are important, shit, I keep forgetting she's having her baby, right here, right now.

Quietly laughing, I can't help but wonder who is screaming more, Maisy or Cassie?

Shit, man, how can I laugh when Grandad is dying? I wonder if they got hold of Crazee? Wouldn't want to be in his trainers if he doesn't make it to the birth!

Turning away from the back of Nan's head I look at Uncle Sean again. Legs splayed, one arm resting on his jittery knee, he runs the other one through his floppy hair. His brow is knitted together in a frown and once again I think how like Grandad he looks. Uncle Sean and I wait for Simon's response, and god help Simon if he does drop us off here because if the look Uncle Sean wears, which is a lot like Romeow's when he's ready to pounce on something, all big black eyes, flat ears and arched back, is anything to go by, I think he'll dive over the front seat and punch Si's lights out.

Thankfully for Simon, although he doesn't know it, he

shakes his head. 'No, Ellie, it's fine,' he says. 'I'll drop you lot at the entrance then I'll park the car and follow you. I want to see Lizzie and Salocin,' he adds. 'Maisy will be just fine and I'm sure she wouldn't mind.'

Nan smiles and reaches out to squeeze Si's arm and that's when I spot another sign saying the car park to the Maternity Unit has been closed off due to a burst pipe or something, and all visitors should use the other hospital car parks instead. But as Si isn't going to bother using it, I don't see the point in mentioning it. Uncle Sean's uptight shoulders seem to drop with relief as he slumps backwards in his seat. He rubs his eyes with two balled fists for what feels like forever and I'm not entirely convinced he isn't trying to gauge them out. Looking away again, my eyes dart towards the window and I am met by the huge hospital building. I shiver. There's only one way this is going to end, badly.

I wonder how many other people here are dying, or having a baby, like Maisy. How many other people have also had their Christmas blown to rat shit, like us? Where the hell is car park C?

Simon is, for the first time in his life, ever, ignoring all the speed bumps and driving quite fast. We pass the main entrance and several other smaller entrances but none of them are the one opposite car park C. Then I see it, a blue sign with a white arrow pointing in the direction of car park C. I start shouting, as does Nan and I notice that like me, she has her hand resting on the door handle, ready to yank it open and fly out the minute Si stops the car. The entrance to my grandad's exit comes into sight and my heart starts thumping hard against my ribs. I've been desperate to get here and now I am; I realise how scared shitless I am.

Si tears round one last small corner and I swear he nearly tips the car up onto two wheels and almost collides with the police car that has literally pulled up in front of us. Si slams on the brakes and we are all thrown violently forward.

'Fuck me!' Simon shouts, 'sorry about that, everyone. Fuck me!' he shouts again as a tall, pissed off looking policeman gets out of his car. Only, as I take a closer look, I realise Si isn't looking at the policeman, he is looking at one of his passengers now climbing out the back of the car.

'Fuck me,' Si repeats. 'Is that who I think it is?'

Lizzie

I'm shocked how quickly Dad is deteriorating. His breathing is shallow and wispy and his grip on my hand waxes and wanes like the tides of grief washing over me. I'm watching my father slip away and my sorrow is insurmountable, rising within me like the molten ash of a volcano on the brink of eruption. I want to scream like a small child that can't have its own way. To rally at the world, at the unfairness of it all. I think of Tabitha's comments, that seventy years is not a bad run, all things considered, and I'm appalled at her thoughtlessness. Did she believe she was comforting me when she uttered such stupid words, or did she simply not think at all? Knowing Tabitha, it was the latter.

All things considered it's just as well she's not here, because if she says that to me again, I'm likely to claw her eyes out. But she isn't here so I claw at my chest instead. I seek out the soft flesh behind my festive red jumper and sink my nails into it, slightly alarmed at the strange satisfaction I feel. Anything, any physical pain is better than the heartache burning me from the inside out.

Looking round the room again for the millionth time, I am completely taken by surprise at the swiftness in the change of my mood. My grief is replaced by anger and its immediacy is as rapid as Dad's descent.

Where the hell is everyone. Why am I here on my own? Why is it always me? Why do I have to be the strong one? Is that what being a parent is, being the strong one, and if so, why is Dad giving up now? Why has he given up the fight? Fuck cancer, Dad is bigger than cancer but he's choosing not to fight any more. He's choosing to leave us all. It's his choice and I hate him for it.

I look at my phone with no messages and no calls. This isn't how it was supposed to end. Everyone should be here, not just me. Why am I catastrophically alone? My thoughts drift as incoherently as Dad's punctured speech, and I find my anger accelerating when I think of my nearest and dearest. I picture Simon's careful driving, at the designated speed limit, slowing down for the speedbumps. I think of Cassie and Maisy and wonder who, out of the two of them, is causing more of a spectacle. They always were a pair of drama queens, why can't they give it a rest? Give me a rest for a while. And why isn't Cassie here already?

'How long does it take to have a baby anyway,' I shout out loud.

'It's a boy,' Dad whispers in reply to my ranting. At least, that's what I think he says?

'What? What's that Dad?' I lean towards him to better hear but realise he has slipped away again. His mouth opens as if to speak but his shallow breathing appears alarmingly faster paced. There's an air of urgency around him and I know now, for sure, this really is it.

Reaching for Dad's limp hand, I cradle it in both of mine. Dad stirs a little and mumbles something I don't understand. I look up and stare at the limp bag of fluid, the contents of which are doing their best to keep him sleepy and pain free. Biting my lip, I look down again, my eye drawn to the thin, blood spattered sheet covering his skeletal body. He seems smaller than he was, even more so than a couple of hours ago, and his face seems different too. Puffier, and darker in places. Dad's eyes flicker open and he looks alarmed and tries to speak again. It's barely audible but I just about make out what he's saying. 'Connor, that you boy?' he asks. Closing his eyes again, hot tears blur my vision, and even though he can't see me, I shake my head.

'No Dad, it's me ...'

A shadow catches my attention at the corner of the door and I turn to see Connor filling the entrance. Standing a little over six feet now, I don't see the man, I see the boy. I see the six-year old grandson come to play with his grandad. Mouth wide open, he wrings his hands in dumb show. His expression is one of shock, afraid almost, to move any further forward. Standing up, I offer Connor my out stretched arm and, head down, he rushes forward. Ignoring my arm, he throws himself at me and engulfs me in his grief. Quickly releasing me again he looks at Dad, then back to me, then back at Dad again.

Connor's voice cracks and I hear my little boy speak. 'Can ... can he hear me?'

I nod my head, ashamed at my lack of words, I should be stronger than this. Connor wipes his nose on the sleeve of his hoody and gently shuffles past me.

'Grandad. It's me, Connor. I've come to say goodbye.'

Cassie

I look at the rabbit warren of white walls ahead of me and try and remember the directions Alison gave me to get to the ward Grandad is on. I pass two nurses wearing Christmas hats. One of them says something to the other and they both break into fits of high-pitched giggling. I smile back at them but they don't see me and I can't work out if I feel happy or sad. Is it possible to be both, very, very happy and very, very sad, at the same time? Passing a half open door, I hear a woman scream and a baby cry. Oh my fucking god, I've just helped give birth to a real life baby. Nicolas, baby Nicolas. I can't believe how tiny he is. Was I ever actually that small? Alison said, weighing just over eight pounds, he isn't actually that small. Alison said he is quite big for a first baby.

First? I wonder if Maisy and Crazee will have more babies? And Crazee, where the hell are you man?

Continuing along the corridor, I turn a corner and am shocked when, mid-thought, I'm suddenly thrown against the wall. 'What the f ...' I start saying.

A wild-eyed man stops and stares at me, hands raised as if I've just told him to put them up or I'll shoot. 'I'm, I'm so, so so-rry,' he stutters.

'Crazee! Where have you beeeeen?'

'Cassie!' he replies, wearing a look of complete terror. 'I ... I forgot to turn my phone on. Missed all your calls.'

I want to hear his explanation but at the same time I'm desperate to get to Grandad. 'Walk with me,' I reply. Crazee looks confused. I explain about Grandad and urge him to walk and talk. 'After all, a couple more minutes is hardly going to make any difference to Maisy now, is it!'

Crazee lowers his head, like Freddy does when he's been caught stealing food from Grandad's plate. 'Oh fuck,' he says, now speed walking alongside me. 'It was only when the police–'

'The police?' I interrupt. Crazee shakes his head and I can no longer keep it in, my laughter gushes forward like a spray fountain of spit. I want to be angry, almost wish I could be. But I can't. I laugh so hard my stomach hurts.

Crazee's look of terror has now morphed into something different. He looks slightly annoyed. 'Yeah, the policeman, the one that gave you an escort to the hospital–'

'You mean Jeff, Jeff Grundy?'

'Yeah, that's the one. He only came to the bladdy pab!' For some reason, Crazee's Australian accent seems more pronounced than usual, which only makes his tale of woe even funnier. 'It's not bladdy fanny, Cas, I think the whole pab thought I was some sort of bladdy criminal!'

This shit is too much and I can hardly catch my breath from laughing. Bending over I hold my hand out like a stop sign. I laugh for what feels like forever but is barely a few minutes and I start to wonder if maybe it isn't that funny? If maybe it's just relief at the normality of it all? That's all I want, normal, whatever the hell that is!

Wiping the tears from my face with the back of my hand I don't really give a shit when I see the black smudge marks from my mascara. Crazee tells me how he saw Simon and Nan and everyone but that he didn't hang about to speak to them because he wanted to get to Maisy. 'I stupidly thought they'd all come to see her.' It's a little awkward, but Crazee pulls me towards him. We hug for a few seconds and I can smell beer on his breath. It feels good to be hugged. I sense his restlessness though. He's as desperate to get to Maisy as I am to Grandad and quickly pulls away again. 'I'm sorry,' he says, 'I hope Salocin is okay, really I do. But I have to go. I have to get to Maisy. She'll never forgive me you know, Cas, for not being there.'

'She will, she loves you,' I reply, smiling. But Crazee is already half way down the corridor. I watch his retreating back; jealous of the happy place I know he is going to, frightened of the one I'm heading for.

'By the way Cas,' Crazee shouts over his shoulder, 'what did we have? What did Maisy have?'

Folding my arms across my chest I can't help screwing my nose up in confusion.

'What do you mean?' I reply. 'She had a baby, you bloody idiot!'

Lizzie

In between shuddering gulps of grief, Connor tells me the others are behind him. He also mutters something about Crazee and the police, and although a wave of concern crosses my tired mind, I decide now is not the time to quiz him. I watch as the abandoned grief pours from my normally reserved adolescent son. Gone is any fear of showing emotion here. His sobs are wretched and the sound fills me with an overwhelming sense of helplessness.

Slumped forward, in the same uncomfortable chair I had been sitting in minutes earlier, Connor grips the wet sleeve of his hoody and drags it down each sodden cheek before crossing it above his mouth. He looks at me. 'Mum?' he says. He's not addressing me though, it's a question, a cry for help and a deep-rooted need for me to make it better because one way or another, as a parent, I usually can. But not this time. This time I have no say in the matter. Fleetingly, my thoughts turn to Cassie and I'm reminded again how fallible I am and just how much I have let my daughter down. Everyone, even Cassie, agrees that the violation of my daughter by that vile man had nothing whatsoever to do with me, but why doesn't it feel like that? Dad would have fixed it for me but now, just when I need him more than ever, he's leaving me.

My thoughts are interrupted by more movement at the door. A drawn looking Sean walks in followed by a tight-lipped Nat and awestruck Summer.

'Well …?' Sean asks, his eyes darting towards the bed.

Biting my lip, I shake my head. 'He's still with us … just,' I whisper.

Sean closes his eyes and hangs his head for a few brief seconds. When he looks up again, his eyes are open and he takes a deep breath. He reaches for Summer's hand and leads her towards the bed.

'C'mon,' he says gently, 'let's say goodbye to Grandad.' Summer sniffs, but places her hand in Sean's and moves towards the emaciated body of my father. Effortlessly, Sean lifts Summer up and places her next to Dad on the bed. Summer cocks her head to one side, studying her dying grandfather. Without hesitation, she begins to stroke his arm.

'Shush … shush,' Summer says gently. 'It's okay Grandad. It's not a life, it's an adventure, and now you're going somewhere else to have a different one.'

Connor

Uncle Sean, Nat and Summer have just come into the room and Uncle Sean has placed Summer on the bed next to Grandad.

'How we doing, Rocky?' he asks. Swallowing the lump in my throat I shrug my shoulders. A lone tear runs down Uncle Sean's cheek and I have to look away. Taking Grandad's hand in mine, I close my eyes and my ears. No longer in the hospital, it's ten years earlier. I am six years old and Grandad is fit and well. His face is filled out and his grey hair is thick and curly. Everyone says he is grumpy, but he is funny grumpy, always laughing and always shouting "fack orf" especially at men in suits on the TV.

One minute it's hot, the sun is shining and Cas and I are helping Grandad trim the rose bush in his and Nan's garden, stopping for a minute to eat strawberry split lollies; the next it's winter, cold and miserable and Grandad and I, mug of hot chocolate in hand, head out to his laboratory to read stories. It's not really a laboratory of course, it's just a converted garage with lots and lots of books, a library really. I recognise some of the writers of some of the books but others, whose books wear old, brown or red, leather jackets, I've never heard of, or can't even pronounce. In fact, some of Grandad's books are so rare and so precious he actually has them locked up in glass display cases. Tattered looking, with yellowy, brown pages; you can tell they are very old.

There is one small corner filled with laboratory equipment, though. A Bunsen burner, clamp stand and test tube holder all sit on an old wooden bench along with other weird instruments like forceps, crucible tongs and dropper pipettes. There are also a couple of shelves with neatly stacked glass beakers and flasks, as well as watch glasses and test tubes. Hanging from a few rusty nails banged into the wall are some protection goggles and on another, higher up shelf there are lots of different coloured glass bottles with lids, some containing what look like powders, others have liquids. Some have labels with writing on and some have no labels at all, whilst others have a yellow triangle with skull and crossbones and the words DANGER, TOXIC HAZARD underneath. "Just for show" Mum says, "in homage to his namesake." Wish he was Nicolas Flamel, then he wouldn't be here, dying.

It was a place where magic happened, though. Grandad, who has always been a rubbish singer, made up for his terrible singing by being a brilliant storyteller. I suppose that's where Mum gets it from. Grandad's characters are the best, though. Damon, the ditsy do-gooder was one of my favourites, as was Freddy the farting fuddleduff. And Nicolas Flamel, of course, my absolute favourite. Whenever I was upset Grandad always made it better by helping me to escape. Sometimes it was just me and Grandad, sometimes Cassie was there too, the three little birds disappearing into far off lands and magical places where anything was possible.

The real stuff didn't matter then.

Lizzie

Mum walks in with Simon. Her face is ashen and she looks very old tonight. I smile but she doesn't smile back. I can tell from her tight-lipped stare she is angry with me. She blames me, like I knew she would, for persuading her to go away. Opening my mouth to apologise, I find the words get stuck at the top of my throat. Swallowing my worthless words back down again, I can't believe my thoughtlessness. How would I have felt if Cassie had persuaded me to leave Simon when she knew his days were numbered? Why did I let Dad talk me into it?

Feeling my legs buckle at the knees, I grab the back of a chair for support. I listen to the pitiful sniffling of my son and wonder if Maisy has had her baby yet, how Cassie will get past all that has happened to her and how on earth I am going to live without my cantankerous old man. Suddenly light headed, the room begins to close in on me. The weight of life is a heavy one at the moment, and one I seem incapable of carrying. I've failed everyone, Simon, my best friend, my son, my daughters and now my Mum.

As Mum's angry eyes bore into me I want to scream that it's not my fault, that Dad made me do it, as a test, to show her she can survive without him. Only, I realise the insanity of it all now, and I still can't believe I let Dad persuade me to do it. For the mere briefest of seconds, before the sound of Connor's sobbing brings me back with resounding immediacy, I no longer wish to be here. Life feels terribly painful and the thought of joining my father is strangely comforting.

Hot tears stream down my face and I wonder if I haven't cried enough to fill a river. 'I'm … I'm so sorry Mum,' I whisper. And then, true to a mother's love, the anger filling my mother's eyes has gone. All I see now is love and forgiveness. Walking quickly towards me, Mum wraps her arms around me. She holds my head as gently as a new born baby's and tells me to shush. I love the familiar smells of my mother, the same soap and shampoo she's used for the past god knows how many years and the floral bouquet of her favourite Chanel No.5 perfume.

Still stroking my hair, Mum continues telling me to shush, reminding me everything is okay, even though it isn't, until my heaving shoulders shudder no more. Reluctant to move away from the safety of my mother's love, I eventually look up. 'He's frightened Mum,' I say. 'Dad is frightened, of leaving you. He's scared you won't manage without him, so he's hanging on for you. You have to let him go, Mum.'

Mum looks up at me through watery eyes and forces a smile.

She raises her hand to my forehead and brushes wet, matted hair away from my eyes, tucking it safely behind my ear. Taking several deep breaths, Mum nods. 'I know love,' she replies. 'I know.'

Straight backed and determined, my mother walks towards the bed to bid goodbye to the man who has shared more than fifty years of her life. "Gawd and Bennett, that's two bleedin' life sentences" Dad had said on their Golden Wedding Anniversary, and I can't help smiling at the memory of it.

'That's better. Your dad always says you have a smile that can light up a whole room.' Turning towards the door, I realise Simon is here. 'You do know the old bugger has threatened to haunt me for the rest of my living life if I don't take good care of you.'

Still laughing, I immediately burst into tears again. Simon holds me in his arms. We sway from side to side as he kisses the top of my head. For the first time in hours I feel relief. Suddenly the thought of my father's departure is not so bad. Not with everyone else here. I know the love and strength between us will sustain us.

Simon asks me if I've heard from the girls. Shaking my head, I insist Simon leave at once, and head for the maternity unit. He argues with me and I argue back. 'You have to go,' I insist. 'Besides, Cassie is with Maisy because they couldn't find Crazee and–'

'I know,' Simon interrupts, 'the police were bringing him in when–'

'The police?'

Simon grins and rolls his eyes. He tells me what the nice policeman, Jeff Grundy, told him and I make a mental note to seek him out and thank him. Simon then walks towards Dad's bed. He coughs and Sean looks up and steps aside. Mum, holding Dad's hand, is now sitting on the bed on the opposite side and Connor, Summer and Nat hover helplessly towards the end of the bed. Simon gently places his hand on Dad's shoulder and leans forward.

'Don't worry Salocin, I'll look after them all,' he says. Mum forces a smile then covers it with two balled fists. Simon nods at Mum, smiles, then fondly looks back at Dad. 'Gawd and Bennett, Salocin, you've certainly given me a run for my money over the years, but it's been a pleasure and an honour.'

He lingers no more than is necessary then, with a reassuring pat of Dad's shoulder and a gentle kiss on the cheek for me, I watch Simon's retreating back as he heads towards the other end of the hospital, in search of new life. Still holding Dad's hand in hers, Mum starts to talk. 'Salocin. I'm here love. Can you hear me?' she says. Dad's eyes remain closed but there is movement behind the lids. A frail smile lifts the corners of his dry lips as he attempts to speak. Mum puts her ear to Dad's mouth and smiles. 'Everlasting love? Course it was. Always will be.' Open-mouthed Connor merely stares, Sean hangs his head and Nat and Summer openly weep. 'I'll always love you, you silly old fool' Mum continues, 'but it's time to go now. You hear me, Salocin Lemalf? I'll be just fine and when the time's right we'll see each other again.'

Then, leaning over, Mum gently kisses my father good night.

Cassie

Shit, I'm not entirely sure I haven't taken a wrong turn. It seems to be taking for-bloody-ever to get to the other end of the hospital. Most of the corridors are empty and they have those automatic lights that come on as you enter and go off as you pass. It's a bit spooky, actually. I feel like I'm on a horror movie set, half expecting some axe waving maniac to jump out on me from the shadows.

A light clicks on up ahead and I see a man walking towards me. His jacket looks familiar and the more I watch him the more

I recognise his walk. Stiff backed and serious, I realise it's Simon. I wave and shout his name and he seems to hunch his shoulders, like he's cringing. He waves back at me then puts a finger to his lips, which if I'm honest pisses me off, a bit. But it doesn't last and I start running towards him.

I'm not really sure why, but when I reach Simon I throw my arms around him and hang on for dear life. After a few reluctant seconds, I feel his arms fold around me and for the first time tonight, I feel as though I can actually breathe again. I start crying and once I do, I can't stop. Somewhere in between all the tears and the snot I tell Simon about Maisy and me, and our trip to the hospital and I'm more than a little surprised to hear he already knows about our police escort. I ask him if Grandad is okay and feel sick when he shakes his head.

'You should go to him, now Cassie,' he says, 'time is running out.' Pulling out a clean tissue from his jacket pocket, he hesitantly offers to wipe my black mascara stained cheeks for me before kissing my forehead and thanking me for looking after Maisy. I smile and shrug my shoulders and tell him "anytime", although I'm not entirely sure I mean it. Simon's smile is warm but his voice urgent when he tells me again to go.

We head off in our different directions and I only look back when I hear Simon call my name.

'Cassie! Cas, what did she have? Maisy, what did she have?'

Not for the first time tonight, I feel myself frowning, wondering if everyone has gone mad. 'A baby, Simon. She had a baby,' I reply. 'You bloody idiot,' I mumble under my breath.

Continuing my never-ending journey I am pleased to see lots more lights and noise and people up ahead. I spot another sign for the ward Grandad is on and know I'm close now. Doctors and nurses, some wearing tinsel scarves, others wearing Christmas cracker hats, pass me by, as do patients and visitors. The huge, whitewashed wall abruptly breaks into a corridor of glass, displaying a naked winter garden outside. Someone is in the garden, a patient, I think, bent over, looking at something. Flashes of red catch my eye and I realise the patient is admiring some beautiful red roses.

I didn't know roses bloomed in the winter?

I don't know why, but I feel compelled to stop and look out of the window. I can tell, mostly by the type of dressing gown and PJs sticking out underneath, the patient is a man. Still hunched over, he reaches around and places one of his hands in the middle of his back and straightens up. His dressing gown looks a bit like the big blue one Grandad wears. He seems old like Grandad, too, and when he turns away from the flowers, towards the window, I'm shocked to see it is Grandad. Spotting me, he smiles and waves his hand. His face seems fatter than it was a couple of days ago and his grey hair looks thicker and curlier.

What the hell was Simon talking about? Grandad looks well, really, really well. Simon must have got it wrong. Or, perhaps he's taken a turn for the better and we will all be together on Christmas Day after all. Yesss! Thank you, god, even though I don't believe in you, after all the shit this year; this is the best Christmas present ever. Grandad will get to see baby Nicolas after all. Jumping up and down like a six year old, I wave back at Grandad. Laughing, he points to a door. Stretching my neck to see, it's pretty obvious Grandad came through a door I don't have access to from here. Holding my hands up, I shrug my shoulders, wondering how he expects me to get around there. Grandad then points upwards and I suddenly get what he is saying. Mum said the ward Grandad is on, is on the second floor, so he must be telling me to meet him back there. I nod, giving Grandad the thumbs up and, throwing his head back laughing, Grandad does the same.

Stuff Hunter, stuff the abortion, stuff Honey and even stuff Luke for that matter. None of that shit matters right now because Grandad is okay. Grandad is okay and we have a new baby in the family, which I helped give birth to. Ugh ... never again, though. I still think it's barbaric. What idiot came up with that idea for giving birth? Pressing the button on the shiny metal door of the lift I catch my reflection and realise how rank I look. Dark circles around my eyes and bags under them big enough to be suitcases, I look like a walking zombie. And tired. Shit, I really do feel sooooooo tired. Happy, though.

Terribly tired but hilariously happy.

Simon's text says Cassie is on her way and he and Crazee, who was being verbally roasted alive upon Simon's arrival, are now with mother and child, who are both safe and well. I wonder what Maisy has had, if it's a boy or a girl, Simon hasn't said. Looking across at my grief-stricken son, whose painful sobs are being rocked into submission by an equally distraught Nat, I am grateful for the respite. Holding Connor to her chest, Nat strokes his hair and tells him to shush while Sean does much the same with Summer. Nat looks at me and somehow forces a smile. I smile back then wave my phone at the door mouthing the word CASSIE. Still stroking Connor's hair with her many ringed fingers, Nat nods at me and releases one of her hands to wave me out of the door.

I slip out, shielding my eyes from the intense light of the hospital corridor. I feel slightly disorientated and weak. My tummy grumbles and I realise it must be hours since I last ate. I think of all the prepped food and the pre-basted turkey sitting in Mum's fridge and wonder if it will all go to waste. How can we celebrate Christmas now? My tummy growls again but the thought of eating anything only adds to the seasick nausea washing over me.

"Whachu need is a nice strong cappa," I hear Dad whisper in my ear, "plenty of sugar to give you some energy, gal." I laugh and the nurse passing me in the corridor mistakes it as a smiling salutation to her. She grins back at me with mock suspicion. 'Someone's happy,' she states. I close my eyes for a second and nod in agreement. I'm too tired to explain that my already broken heart has exploded into a million tiny pieces and I'm fearful of it ever mending again. I ask her where I can grab a quick coffee and the nurse, with the wide-mouthed-frog smile, points to some doors towards the end of the corridor where she says I'll find a vending machine. Thanking her, I head towards the double doors up ahead as my thoughts turn to Cassie. Not entirely sure from which direction she'll come, I look over my shoulder, worried I'll miss her. When I look round again, the double doors swing open and I'm completely taken aback when a red-faced Ruby walks through them. Scott, who is carrying Andrew, follows close behind and both Ruby and Scott look like victims of a car crash.

Raising my hands to my mouth I gasp as I try to take in Ruby's black eye, split lip and somewhat more disturbing, bruised neck. Scott's face is a pulped bloody mess. The smell of blood lingers, like water from a rusty tap reminding me of Amber and the huge fist that bloodied and cracked her nose as she tried to defend herself from the bully that called himself her boyfriend. I shiver and wonder where she is, why she and her daughter have gone missing and if the police are still looking for her.

'Lizzie. Liz. Are you okay?' Ruby asks, concern etched into her beaten face.

'Me! What about you? What the hell happened to you?'

Ruby shakes her head. 'I'm sorry I haven't been a good friend lately, haven't been there for you.'

Raising my hand to her chin, I gently turn her face to the side to get a better look at her neck. Some of the bruising is new but judging by the varying colours that bleed and overlap into one another, it's obvious some of the marks on her neck are weeks, if not months old. 'I think it's me that hasn't been a good friend,' I reply pulling my oldest friend into a tight hug.

'How's Salocin?' Ruby whispers in my ear.

Biting my lip, I shake my head. 'Gone,' I reply.

'Shit!' Scott interrupts. 'And the kids? Where are the kids, Lizzie?'

I point up the corridor in the direction of the room containing my recently deceased father and explain about Cassie and Maisy. 'Cassie's on her way over now, apparently. I want to be the one to tell her. Prepare her before she …' Unable to continue speaking, I find myself sobbing and my ex-husband, who is still holding Andrew, comforting me in a welcome embrace.

'Don't cry Wizzie,' Andrew says, stroking my hair. I look up and am met by a wide-eyed little boy who gently runs his hands across my wet cheeks. I take his soft squidgy hand in mine and kissing it, I smile. 'I'm sure Connor would appreciate you being here,' I say turning to Scott. He lifts his eyebrows questioningly then winces as he raises his hand to touch his very swollen eye. 'And I strongly recommend you get that looked at,' I suggest.

The doors behind us once again swing open and Cassie crashes through them.

'Mum!' she shouts. She's a little out of breath, but laughing and I'm suddenly reminded of Cassie, my vulnerable but headstrong, pigtailed six year old, desperate to show me something. 'He's okay then?' she continues, waving her arms and running like her once younger self, more of an awkward hop-skip than a full-on sprint. Within seconds, though, she reaches us and is suddenly throwing her flaying arms around me. 'Oh shit,' she declares as if she has only just realised her dad, Ruby and Andrew are with me. 'What the hell happened to you two?' she says, looking from Ruby to Scott.

'Erm … think we'll go and see Connor then?' Scott suggests. 'See you in a bit, Cassie.'

Cassie watches their retreating backs and pointing, her nose wrinkling in confusion, asks again what happened. I shake my head and tell her I'll explain later. 'Okay,' she replies shrugging her shoulders. 'Anyway, I'm so glad Grandad is all right. I thought it was waaaaay more serious when I spoke to you earlier on the phone. God, that seems like days ago. Well, it was hours and hours ago I suppose–'

'Cassie, Grandad has gone.'

'What, home already? That was quick? What a shame, I was gonna ask if we could borrow a wheelchair and take him down to see the baby.'

I'm puzzled as to why Cassie thinks Dad is okay but can only imagine she misunderstood what Simon told her. She still appears mildly confused but her smile is gloriously intact. I didn't think it was possible but I hear my fractured heart break just a little more because I know I'm the bitch about to wipe that smile clean off my daughter's face.

'And, oh my god, I am never, EVER, going to have a baby. It's positively barbaric, Mum. If men had had to have babies they would have invented some other way to do it by now! And you did it – twice! Jeez, it's just wrong. It was pretty amazing too, though, I suppose. Although, look at this, for god sake.' Cassie waves her hand in front of me. 'Look, see, Maisy did that. Almost crushed my hand to death, she did!'

Pulling Cassie's hand down and holding it in mine, I look directly into my daughter's eyes. 'Grandad's gone,' I repeat.

'I know. You said but–'

'He passed away, about fifteen minutes ago.'

Cassie's mouth falls open and the light from her eyes drains away as quickly and as surely as it did from Dad's.

'No! No! He didn't, he's not. I saw him …'

Cassie pulls away from me, jerking her head violently back towards the double doors she just came through, pointing. 'But … but, I saw him! I saw Grandad, in the garden downstairs. Looking at the roses.'

I shake my head and realise Cassie is confused; roses don't grow in bleak midwinter. 'It must have been someone else, love, someone who looked like Grandad?'

Cassie's lip trembles as her tears fall silently, unashamedly down her cheeks. She shakes her head again. 'No! It *was* Grandad. He pointed upwards, telling me to ...'

Cassie trails off and slaps her hands across her mouth, one after the other. Rocking from side to side, she shakes her head releasing a muffled pitiful cry. 'It was him,' she says earnestly, as her hands fall by her sides. 'Oh god, it's all Crazee's fault. If he'd actually turned his stupid phone on he would have seen we needed him, and ... and ... I could have ... would have been there ... to say goodbye. And now it's too fucking late.'

Cassie takes one giant step forward as if to run, then stops. Her crumpled face is wet from tears and I feel as mortified as she looks. Movement up ahead catches my attention. A young man is walking purposely towards us and as Cassie swings round, her grief-stricken face morphs into one of complete surprise. 'Luke!' she shouts, throwing herself at him. He pulls her to his chest and wraps his arms around her. 'He's gone, Luke. My grandad, has gone, and I was too late to say goodbye,' Cassie sobs, burying her head into Luke's worn leather jacket.

Luke, who doesn't say a word, simply kisses Cassie's hair before pressing his cheek against the top of her head. In response, Cassie moves in closer and slowly they start to turn, him guiding her into a tight circle until eventually, Cassie's sobbing stops.

Part Three

Chapter 49

"WE SHALL HAVE SPRING AGAIN"

"Wrong will be right, when Aslan comes in sight,
At the sound of his roar, sorrows will be no more,
When he bares his teeth, winter meets its death,
And when he shakes his mane, we shall have spring again."

Lizzie

It's 6.00 a.m. and a crisp, cold morning. After weeks hidden away writing, I felt the need to escape. To walk along familiar ground and replay treasured memories without fear of upsetting anyone else; just Dad and I walking together along the riverbank where yellow daffodils dance and renascent wild crocuses and snowdrops weave a carpet of colour among a pulp of dead leaves. Spring has sprung. Writhen, gnarly trees, once absent of colour, are beginning to breathe again and small buds, with the tiniest hint of green, sprout amongst their branches. The blossom trees are in full bloom though, including the huge one opposite Mum's house, once again a beautiful pink cataract of blossom, serving as constant reminder that nothing endures but nonetheless life goes on. It feels strange to say Mum's house, to me it is and always will be, Mum *and* Dad's house.

It's just a little over three months since Dad passed away, and it doesn't get any easier. Christmas Day celebrations were postponed and it was agreed we would mark it several days later, once Maisy and baby Nicolas were home. I don't think any of us felt much like celebrating, not really, but we all conceded it was something Dad would have wanted. And so somehow, amongst the grief and tears, glasses were raised to commemorate the passing of one old life and toast the arrival of a new one.

We staggered, we stumbled but two days late we made our way through our Christmas Day celebrations.

It was a strange day, all in all. Bittersweet. Tears of pure joy quickly spiralled into moments of sadness until, coming full circle, we found ourselves smiling again. Much alcohol was consumed and much food prepared, although little was eaten. Every time a fond or funny memory of Dad was resurrected, glasses were raised and ceremoniously chinked. It was both exhausting but liberating at the same time. And, in between all the merriment and grief, baby Nicolas, a tiny bundle of pink wrinkled skin, snuffled and slept and cried along with us.

Nicolas has proved to be a marvellous distraction, though, especially for Mum. Although a very contented baby, Nicolas is very colicky. I'd quite forgotten how tiring a colicky baby is. Cassie was just the same. I remember those blurry weeks of exhaustion, trying everything to ease her pain, which often included pacing the floor for long hours or laying her, tummy down, across my knee and rubbing her tiny back. I tried it all with little Nicolas, too, but to no avail. However, Mum appears to have the magic touch and, much to her delight, seems to be the only person who can settle Nicolas during such moments. It was during one such episode, whilst gently carrying little Nicolas across her shoulder, a couple of weeks after Dad's funeral, Mum offered her spare room to Maisy, Crazee and Nicolas. Said there was more room at her house than ours and they could stay there until they decided whether they were going back to Oz or not. When I protested, Mum also pointed out that it was better for me.

'How can you possibly expect to write with all the noise of a new-born in the house?' she'd asked.

I wasn't too sure at first. Wasn't convinced my devastated mother needed a crying baby to interrupt her grieving. Happily, I was wrong. Mum is like a different person around Nicolas. Her dull eyes quite literally light up in his presence. My only fear is

Mum will become too dependent on Nicolas, replace him for Dad. 'Dad,' I say the word out loud, a tiny word with mammoth meaning. I still can't say it without experiencing a painful jolt to the heart. I thought I was prepared. Hoped, rather naively, that having time to get used to the idea of his leaving us would make it easier when he did. It didn't. His last breath quite literally took mine away too. I'm left feeling winded and wounded with such a colossal gap, such a vacant void, I'm afraid it will never be filled.

Sat on the same favourite orange, paint peeling bench I sat with Dad just before Christmas, before he left us, I suddenly feel colder and fold both my arms across my chest to hug myself.

Fuck. Fuck. Fuckity, fuck fuck!

Knowing my propensity to share my internal ramblings with the world at large I look up, nervously scanning my surroundings to see if anyone has heard my expletives. Thankfully, save for a few dog walkers in the distance, I am very much alone. The words *carpe diem* spring to mind and I immediately seize the opportunity to blaspheme as loudly and proudly as possible.

'Fuck. Shit. Fuck. Wank. Bollocks. Tossing. Fuckity fucking and FUCK!' I shout. It doesn't make me feel any better but I am resolved to stop worrying about Mum. What's the point? It doesn't change anything. Besides, I have other, more pressing matters at the moment, Cassie being my main concern. Connor too. My little-big man has once again regressed into a grunt in a hood, which was only to be expected, I suppose, and yet I find his quietness worryingly disconcerting. I know he misses Dad dreadfully, but other than that I have no idea what is going on inside that head of his. Which is how he appears to want it. He is polite enough but it's painfully obvious he is keeping me at arm's length.

A beautiful golden retriever, nose to the ground, lopes past me, quickly followed by his leash-swinging owner. 'Good morning,' she smiles, 'lovely day.' Returning her smile, I nod. I can't disagree, it is a lovely day but my dad is dead and his passing will forever taint my lovely days. Twelve weeks on and my grief is as raw as the first. Not that I expected any deliverance from it, not yet. Not ever, perhaps? And what with everything that has happened to Cassie, it feels as though my world has tipped on its axis. I have lost my balance and will never, I fear, regain it.

My phone buzzes and it's a text from Ruby asking to meet for coffee later. I smile. I never saw that coming, the day my best friend ended up with my ex-husband and me being totally cool with it. I still can't believe what a bastard Harvey was, how controlling and how completely taken in by him Ruby was. How we all were, in fact. And he emptied her bank account, eighty thousand pounds gone.

'In the words of the late, great Tommy Cooper, "just like that!"' Ruby joked.

At least she managed to laugh about it, although it's obvious she is still terribly traumatised, not least by the fact she trusted her child with this man. 'I was compliant,' she said, 'compliant in my abuse and Andrew's.'

'How so?' I replied.

'By keeping quiet and submissive. By begging Andrew to be good, to do as Harvey said so Mummy didn't get hurt. Oh god, what kind of mother am I?' she wailed.

'A good one,' I replied, 'who was hoodwinked by a very charming man who gradually, over time, convinced you, through fear, isolation and abuse, you were worthless. In a way, your compliance was about survival. God only knows what he may have done if you hadn't been compliant. You did good, you bought time for you and Andrew. Don't you see that?'

Ruby said she sort of understood what I was saying, in a way. I'm not sure I believe her, though, and it makes me angry because I know that's how Cassie feels too. Compliant in the assault she suffered, merely because she agreed to go to the said event in the first place, compliant because she drank alcohol, compliant because maybe the black lace dress she treated herself to in the sales was a little too tight and a little too short; in short, she asked for it. Are we really living in the twenty first century? When are attitudes towards women really going to change?

Known to the police, Harvey has done a runner, of course, probably under a fake ID, the police say. So, it's highly unlikely Ruby will see that money again. Thank god, the house was paid off; at least Ruby hasn't lost everything. Her recovery is proving to be pitifully slow, though, not unlike Cassie, for although both women are determined not to let these monsters define who they are, there's a fear in their eyes that never leaves them. Hopefully time will do its work, lessen the memory, the damage. Dad always said time was a good anaesthetic to our bad experiences.

Harvey hasn't completely knocked the stuffing out of Ruby, though. Somewhere, amongst the fear and the pain, old Ruby is resurfacing, and I was never more aware of that than when she started smoking again. Previously annoyed by her smoking habit, purely for health reasons, I must confess to feeling a strange surge of relief the first time I witnessed Ruby lighting up again. Even if her brightly manicured fingers did shake as she held the glowing cigarette to her mouth. She doesn't know it, but I quietly champion the return of my voluptuous, gregarious, chain-smoking best friend.

Smiling, I message Ruby back agreeing to meet her, just as my phone buzzes with another text. It's Cassie and my heart sinks. Reluctant to open her text for fear of its content, I eventually stab at my phone and open the message I've been dreading. After expecting to find me in my study, she asks where I am and if I'm okay. She goes on to say Luke has found them a flat in London and she'll be moving out at the weekend. I want to cry but I feel too stunned. I'm torn between wanting to let her go, again, and keeping her home, safe from harm. My only consolation is that I know Luke loves her and has promised me faithfully he'll look after her.

Taking a deep breath, I look up and sigh. I hate myself for thinking it, but sometimes I hate being a parent. It's relentless. And the worry never, ever ends. For god sake, why? Why must Cassie go back to London? Hasn't she been through enough? Haven't I been through enough? What's wrong with staying close to the ones you love? I understand London is where the music industry is but can't she do something else?

'Kids, who'd have em?' I shout out as a rather startled, heavily-pregnant, young woman marches past me. Sheepishly, I meet her scowl with a half-smile before quickly sticking up two fingers to her retreating back. I chastise myself for my childishness, quelling my desire to once again burst into tears. Not that I could cry, even if I tried, that well has truly run dry. My grief for my daughter has moved on from shock to anger and there it remains, festering like an infected abscess, gnawing at my black heart like poison. Why couldn't it have been me? Somehow the thought of me being assaulted is far more palatable than that of my child. I know I could live with it, better come to terms with it, if it had been me. Knowing someone hurt her in such a despicable way is almost too much to bear.

But, being a law-abiding citizen, it is out of my hands. I find myself having to rely on an antiquated judicial system that is, quite frankly, still appallingly flawed. Where the conviction rate for rape is far lower than that of other crimes, with only a little over five per cent of reported rape cases ending in conviction. If it ever gets that far, in the unlikely event he is charged, Hunter Black's appointed solicitor will then hire a private detective to dig up anything and everything on Cassie that will help his defence. This will include internet searches, interviewing friends and family, tracking down her sexual history via ex-boyfriends, naked or provocative photos and no doubt abortion clinics. Anything, frankly! Anything that sullies my daughter's reputation and restores her perpetrator's. And, living in a society where being drunk still works against women and where a third of the population still believe women who flirt are partially responsible for being raped, once found not guilty, which is highly probable, I will have no other recourse than to accept this as justice. I'm resigned to the fact that I'm left with little choice in the matter. I will just have to kill the bastard.

A lone blackbird hops onto the branch of the tree opposite me. Watching me intently, he jerks his head in swift, almost robotic fashion before releasing the sweetest bird song I believe my ears have ever had the pleasure to listen to. My thoughts turn to Dad and I can't help but wonder if it's a sign. I shake my head and although I do my best to fight it, a wry smile lifts the corners of my mouth.

'It's okay, Dad,' I shout out loud, 'I wasn't planning on doing it in person.'

That's the good thing about being a writer, I get to kill whomever I want in whatever inhumane, barbaric way I want. Thank god for my writing. It has proved to be extremely cathartic. Virtually hidden away, me, my grief and I, the words have poured from me. It's only a first draft but I've completed my third novel. Inspired by Dad, it's not what my publisher was expecting but everything Michelle wants. This is a work of fiction based on facts about a young lad growing up in post WWII London. Homage to one of the greatest raconteurs I have had the pleasure to call Dad.

Chapter 50

THE HAVES AND THE HAVE NOTS

Lizzie

Simon immediately lowers his newspaper and looks at me. It's the same vexed look as it always is of late. 'Go on then, what did they say?'

I stop pacing and turn towards him. 'In a nutshell? He's going to get away with it!' Simon closes his eyes then slowly re-opens them again. I look away from him and start pacing the room again. 'All those women, girls really. All those girls that had the courage to come forward, and it counts for nothing. Like Cassie, apparently,' I continue, waving my arm like some overzealous music conductor. 'Course, Honey hasn't helped matters. Quick to put Cassie down, she won't have a wrong word said against Hunter.'

'Well, she's not going to, is she. He's made her famous. Given her everything she ever dreamed of. She's hardly going to sabotage that, is she?'

'What, and you think that's okay?'

Sighing heavily, Simon folds his newspaper away. 'You know that's not what I'm saying.'

'She's evil is what she is. How? How could she do that to her best friend?'

Simon leans forward and looks directly at me. 'I'm so sorry, love. What can I do? What else can we do?'

My thorax tightens and hot, angry tears stab my eyes. 'Nothing!' I reply. It seems there's nothing more to do when you're a "have not."

Simon's tired brow creases into a frown. Patting the sofa with one hand, he extends the other, beckoning me to sit next to him. As I sit down he wraps his arm around me and asks me what I mean.

'I miss Dad,' I reply, changing the subject. 'Miss him terribly.'

I don't say it for effect or to make Simon feel sorry for me, but this statement seems to soften him somewhat. His steely stare is replaced by one of concern. He reaches for my hand and places it between both of his. 'I do too,' he replies. 'Grief's a bastard.'

I pull my hand away and point to my nose. 'I inherited this hooter, this bloody Roman nose from him you know?'

Simon grins. 'Humph, so did, much to her annoyance, Cassie.'

I smile and nod my head. 'However, I also inherited his irrepressible belief in the basic goodness of people. A naïve optimism that will not be extinguished, despite significant evidence to the contrary.'

Simon nods his head. 'I know you did, babe, that's why you'll get through this. You're still grieving for your dad and you're grieving for what happened to Cassie. But we'll work it out, between us we'll work at it and–'

'And what?' I snap. 'Justice will prevail? Because we all know it won't. We all know the bastard is going to get away with it? But never mind, eh? Because it could have been worse! Do you know that's what people say to me? What Tabitha, that stupid cow next door said to me.' Anger forces me to stand up. 'It could have been worse, she said! She could have been gang raped, or worse still, murdered.' I turn and pace the room again. 'Stupid idiots. Why don't people have the decency to keep their fat mouths shut? How would she feel, if it was her daughter!'

Simon bends forward placing his head in his hands and mumbles something about Tabitha meaning well. He reminds me of all the free hair appointments she's given me.

'Only because it's good for business to have a D List celebrity as a client,' I snort.

Simon shakes his head and looks disappointed. He also reminds me of the free haircut and make-over Tabitha gave Cassie to make her feel better, and how good she was with Mum, when Dad passed away. He also points out that it was hardly fair to berate Tabitha's comments when Cassie herself says exactly the same thing. And it's true, she does. "It could have been worse, Mum," she said, quoting the young medical student Jyoti Singh, the poor girl in India who was gang raped and later died from her horrific injuries. "Or what about all the young girls trafficked from war torn countries and forced into sexual slavery?"

I shake my head. 'She speaks like a victim trying to make sense of it all. Don't you see? Cassie was right.'

'About what?'

'She once said to me that our parents fuck us up.' Raising his eyebrows, Simon smirks. 'And although I have to concede there is some truth in what she said, in relation to her life, I never felt like that about my parents. But now I realise she was right. Our parents do fuck us up because my dad was wrong. He was so wrong. He should have warned me about life, because nothing has changed.' Simon's eyebrows knit together in a quizzical frown. 'There's the "haves" and "have nots",' I continue. 'Two distinctly differently worlds living side by side, each governed by different rules. In a nutshell, the "have nots" have to abide by the rules, whereas the "haves" don't. There are no rules for the "haves". As long as you have the money, the cold hard cash via legitimate means or otherwise, you have the power to buy just about anything you want, be that property, land, art, your own football team, child labour, trafficked girls, homeless boys; I mean, sod it, you can even steal the pension fund off your employees and pay it into a savings account in the name of your wife. Oh, and don't forget tax evasion, that's always a good one.

And then of course there's rape, as a "have", you can always buy your way out of that slippery sucker, especially when she's some low-life piece of white trash "have not". The stupid bitch should be grateful you fucked her, not feel violated.'

Simon sighs heavily and mumbles something I don't quite catch.

'What? What did you just say?'

He looks up again, his expression one of tired resignation. 'I said, here we go again.'

The rising anger surging through my tired body races through each pulsating vein until I hear the violent drum of my own heartbeat between my ears. 'That's easy for you to say. She's not your daughter. If it had been Maisy, you would have –'

Simon jumps to his feet and strides towards me. 'I would have what?' he yells. 'Go on Lizzie, tell me. I would have what?'

He's so menacingly close I can actually smell the recently drunk cup of tea on his breath. I flinch a little and step back, reaching for the scar on my head. I lower my voice: 'I just think you'd feel differently if it were Maisy?'

Simon steps forward and gently touches my cheek with his hand. 'It's true, I may love Cassie and Connor differently to Maisy but I love them nonetheless. They mean as much to me as Maisy does.'

'Then why won't you help me? You heard what that policeman said, off the record …' I trail off because I don't actually know what I expect Simon to do, any more than I know what to do.

Simon's voice is soft, quiet even but it's laced with anger, threaded with the intonation of a man at the end of his tether. 'What do you want, Lizzie? What do you want from me?' Deflated he sits down again and runs a tired hand through his floppy hair. Funny, I never noticed how grey it was until now.

'I just want some sort of justice. Some sort of closure for Cassie so she doesn't have to keep living in limbo like, like a victim.'

'I don't think she is.' Gobsmacked, I look at Simon. I open my mouth to speak but Simon holds his hand out like a stop sign. 'Let me finish, please. I know she's struggling with it, that she wants and should get some sort of justice but she's not living like a victim. She speaks like a woman who refuses to let this define her. Look how well she handled the media. And those excuses for human beings, otherwise known as internet trolls, I'm not sure either you or I would have handled that with as much dignity as she did. She's still living in London, with a man who clearly adores her and she has an amazing group of supportive friends. And okay, she's a bit of an outcast in some of the music industry circles and isn't necessarily doing the work she trained for but she's working on it and getting by. I wouldn't call that the behaviour of a victim, I'd say she was a fighter, like her mother.'

And it's true. I realise everything Simon has just said is true. I suddenly feel very tired and very weak. My legs turn to jelly and I long for my father, to make it all better. With my head in my hands I fall to my knees and sob uncontrollably. Simon sits down beside me. Wrapping two strong arms around me he holds me tight until I stop crying.

'I just don't want that bastard to get away with it.'

Simon kisses the top of my head and promises me he won't. I want to believe him, I truly do but I also decide to root out the card with the handwritten name and telephone number on it that Dad gave me just before he passed away. Dad said I should only ring that number if things became desperate. I decide now is that time.

'You, okay Mum?' I turn to see Connor behind us, hovering nervously by the door. His sandy hair purposely stands on end, held in place by some gel like styling product. The slight stubble sprouting around his chin makes him look so terribly grown up it brings a lump to my throat and I wonder where all the years have gone. He wears a look of concern, not unlike he did as a boy when the girls and their teenage angst was my biggest worry in life: if I only knew then, what life had in store for me.

Chapter 51

WARRIOR QUEEN

Cassie

I'm standing on the north-east corner of Westminster Bridge looking at my favourite statue. Framed by a drizzly, grey sky, in the shadow of Big Ben with the London Eye looming up behind her on the opposite bank of the Thames stands the 'Warrior Queen' Boadicea and Her Daughters. Tall with long flowing hair she is driving her carriage, with lethal blades sticking out from the wheels and her horses rearing up. She wears a crown on her head and holds a spear in her right hand, both daughters behind her. She is a fierce, angry warrior and looks every bit ready to defend her people and her territory. I vaguely remember her being mentioned during a history lesson at school but my teacher pronounced her name Boudicca, which both Mum and the counsellor scoffed at, so I'm with them and prefer to think of her as Boadicea, despite the on-going arguments about how to name her correctly.

Defeated by the Romans, who were basically down on women, who had no rights whatsoever under their rule, Boadicea came from the Iceni tribe that practised equality between men and women. Can you believe that? Men and women treated the same, all those years ago. And it was the Romans that messed it all up. Another bloody good reason to hate my nose. My counsellor says we should honour the statue of the woman who reminds us that there was a time in history when men and women in this country had equal rights. I must admit I didn't really notice her before and because her statue has a souvenir stall and fast food stand alongside it, I'm not sure how many other people miss her, don't even see her.

Big Ben chimes, reminding me to get my shit together and make my way to the pub we all agreed to meet at, and my phone buzzes at the same time. I smile. It's a text from Luke to say he'll be there soon. It's great that we're all here in London, on the same day, doing different things, of course, but all able to meet up. Except Nan and Maisy, that is, who are looking after baby Nicolas and getting stuff ready for Christmas day dinner, which will also be Nicky's first birthday and the anniversary of Grandad's death. I can't believe it's almost a year since Grandad passed away.

It's been a long year but at the same time it feels like no time at all. I miss him as much as I thought I would, more, if I'm honest. It's the moments you don't see coming that completely blindside you, those brief spaces of time when you have forgotten your shit and your sadness and all feels well with the world. And then something reminds you, a song on the radio, his coat hanging in the hallway because Nan can't bring herself to move it, the sound of someone's voice that sounds similar to Grandad's, small, insignificant things to the rest of the world, but nonetheless so significant, to you at least, they quite simply take your breath away. Not being able to speak to him is the worst, not that that stops me. If you carry a phone connected to a pair of earphones no one bats an eyelid if you have conversations with the dead. He isn't gone, though, not to me anyway. I swear, late at night when I've drifted off into troubled sleep, somewhere between dream and nightmare, Grandad is with me. Telling the bad guys to "fack orf" then chuckling and reminding me "it's not a life but an adventure" and "what doesn't kill ya only makes ya bleedin' stronger, gal."

Chapter 52

BIG BROTHER

Lizzie

A quick tube ride on the District line, followed by a brisk ten-minute walk and here I am. One of the "have nots" standing outside the house of one of the "haves." SW3, Chelsea, where the average price for accommodation is anything from one million pounds upwards and can be as high as seven million. Bordered by Knightsbridge to the east, Kensington to the west and the River Thames to the south, this area forms one of the most affluent residential portions of central London. Chelsea's populace, including the red-suited pensioners, appear to be an eclectic bunch, boasting a mix of old landed gentry, new Russian entrepreneurs, London City Bankers, rock stars, pop stars, movie stars, footballers and various wealthy businessmen and women, not to mention several privileged politicians. And who knows, there may even be one or two writers amongst them.

I stand on the opposite side of the road and look at the house I now know to be his, Hunter Black, the man residing in the same country as me and mine and is therefore, supposedly, governed by the same laws. Only he isn't. This man, due to his wealth and position, is above the law. This man can use and abuse whomever he likes without fear and without consequence. This man is untouchable. And in the same sense, he has made my daughter untouchable, but to her detriment. There are still those in the music industry who will not go near her. It's as if she's been marked by some terrible disease and is consequently being punished. It broke my heart when she told me what they said to her at her last interview.

"Look, we know you're good Cassie, you come highly recommended, but off the record it would be bad for business. Hunter Black is a big noise and, well, it would look as though we've sided with you. He could finish us over night."

And I'm supposed to do what? Accept it? Feel grateful that Cassie's experience "wasn't too bad all things considered."

Starting from the ground floor up, I study the beautiful building before me. One of several, I believe, that Black is lucky enough to call home. Standing proud and perfectly groomed, this striking feat of Georgian architecture boasts four floors and is, I suspect, every bit as immaculate on the inside as the outside. Even the brickwork shines. The second-floor balcony, containing a heterogeneous array of green foliage in weather worn, expensive looking pots set against beautiful sash windows, is made of the same black iron bars at the helm of this great house. Prison bars, in fact, to protect the "haves" from the "have nots" maybe?

A stone's throw away from this beautiful house, you can walk along the Kings Road where you'll find boutiques fashioning stunning clothes, but only, of course, catering for those that don't have to ask prices. Trendy nightclubs and pubs are filled with the festive spirit of raucous, alcohol fuelled hilarity and five star restaurants serve exquisite but exorbitantly priced poetry on a plate, costing more in one sitting than most people earn in a week.

No sign of austerity here, then. A stark contrast, in fact, when juxtaposed to the towns and cities I visit on my book tours. The same places where ex-servicemen beg on the streets, where defunct buildings, once small, family-run businesses, vibrant with life, are now boarded up and hauntingly empty, where pensioners ride the No 10 bus on a loop every day in order to remain warm in the winter, where charity shops and discount chains do a roaring trade, where yet another public library closes its doors or reduces its opening hours, and where overworked, under-funded GPs would rather dish out antidepressants to patients waiting two weeks for an appointment than deal with the problem at large.

These are the same people of the same towns and cities whose residents bailed out some of the largest banks on the point of collapse during the 2008 financial crisis. We were, of course, hoodwinked as usual, by those in power, those with the money, into believing that (despite awarding themselves above average pay rises or outlandish bonuses) in order for the country not to spiral into chaos, public services would need to be slashed and benefits cut because we've all been living beyond our means anyway and we're all in this together. Really?

It's three days before Christmas and, like my mood, there's a tangible chill to the air. I look up into the same sky shared by everyone. Cloud-covered and already darkening to a deeper grey, I realise it's getting late. However, regardless of the dirty dishwater coloured skyline, I understand that here, where cold hard cash can buy you just about anything, the sun always shines. Everything and anything is possible, even rape. Perhaps even murder.

My dark mood is interrupted by the arrival of a dark car with blacked-out windows. A burly, uniformed individual opens the driver's door and steps out of the car. Looking from left to right, he scans the quiet road. After watching several passers-by his gaze falls on me. I am being watched and not just by Hunter Black's burly bodyguard. From my short walk here just now, to my tube journey earlier and my train journey prior to that, I am uncomfortably aware I am living in a surveillance state. My every move will have been privy to some of the six million cameras operating nationwide. Then, of course, there are all the other details of my life circulating via texts, emails and social media, available to be harvested, should someone wish to do so, just by a few simple clicks.

I pull my newly acquired baseball cap down as far as it will go. Wearing baggy jeans, trainers and a nondescript dark jacket, I stab the screen of my phone with my finger in feigned confusion, praying I have pulled off the lost tourist look.

The driver walks around to the back-passenger door of the car and opens it. A well-dressed man, slightly grey and slightly balding steps out and heads towards his shiny, black front door.

Hunter Black is home.

Chapter 53

PRIMAL INSTINCTS

Cassie

I chew my nails nervously. Festive lights wink on and off and the pub is busy and loud, mainly because it's almost Christmas but by the looks of some, especially the large group of lads at the far corner of the bar, any excuse will do. I feel slightly panicky, but there's a buzz about the place and it's infectious. Despite the shit storm of the last year, I still love London and I like all the noise.

Startled, I look up to see the boys in the corner taking part in what sounds like some sort of tribal chant. Some bang their fists on the bar while others smack their hands together. They've formed a large circle around one of their own, demanding he "down it, down it," whatever 'it' is. Some god-awful toxic alcoholic cocktail by the looks of it. A mixture of anything and everything, judging by the black syrupy liquid running down the sides of the boy's mouth. He'll be hoofing his guts up by the end of the night. I laugh because it reminds me of some of the messy nights that took place at uni and I'm pleased with myself for not feeling frightened by these noisy boys and their drinking games. At least, that is, until one of the lads from the group catches me watching. He smiles and raises his pint to me and I'm disappointed to see how quickly the fear takes hold again.

I turn away and pretend to look at my phone as my tummy flips and my fingers shake as I try to swipe the screen. Not daring to look back up I stab at my phone with my finger. Fuck. Everyone told me not to read the comments at the time. And now I can't get them out of my head. And even though I was entitled to anonymity, it didn't stop the trolls finding me.

Die cunt

I put my hand to my forehead and rub it, hard.

Racist lying bitch

Think Cassie, think. "Try and think of nice things," the counsellor said, "when unpleasant memories or thoughts come to mind, replace them with nice thoughts, Cassie," she said.

I hope you die of cancer

Easier said than done. Easier said than done.

You deserved to be raped

Did I? Did I ask for it? Remember the song Luke wrote for you. Remember when the band performed it for you, for your birthday.

Gold digging bitch

Think of fat faced baby Nicolas with his dribbly chin trying to say Cassie, but it coming out as "Assy" or his squidgy fat-fisted demands for a "beagle" which means, according to Maisy, boiled egg.

He should have stuck a bag over your head and finished you off

Think of Connor and how he made you laugh over and over again with his hairy fanny and escaping chicken stories.

Lying lesbian slag

It doesn't matter. It doesn't matter what these people think. Sticks and stones will break my bones but names will never hurt me.

Ugly skanky bitch

Not true. Not true at all.

Lying whore

Words. Just words Cassie. It doesn't matter. They don't matter.

Sticks and stones will break my bones. Fuck. Off. Fuck. Off. Fuck off out of my head. I can't do this. I need to get out of here. Promised I'd hold the table for everyone though. Where are they? Where the hell are they all? I can't do this. Stupid,

stupid bitch. What was I thinking? Reaching inside my jacket I feel my heart hammering against my chest. I feel winded, like I can't catch my breath. Like I'm six again and I've done a belly flop in the swimming pool and as the water fills my ears and the chlorine stings my eyes, I can't breathe. I can't breathe. I'm drowning on dry land and there's nothing I can do about it.

I look round and expect to find everyone staring at me, pointing and laughing. But no one is. Not even the boy who raised his pint to me. He's now busy looking at the arse of the leggy blonde with her back to him. Anyone who does glance my way just as quickly looks past me again. They probably think I'm some kind of loony talking to myself. A loony or drunk. One or the other. No one gives a shit. I could keel over, right here and now and no one would notice. Everyone is too busy getting pissed. Feeling slightly calmer, I take a deep breath. Count to five, Cassie, like the counsellor said. One. Two. Three. Four. Five. Breathe out. I shouldn't have come here today, not on my own. How? How is it possible that words remembered cause my body to twitch and jump? I still find it strange how we always remember the bad shit above the good stuff. It's because we're hard wired to. At least, that's what the counsellor told me. Something to do with going back to our primal instincts and the need to focus on the bad crap for survival, the fight or flight thing. It takes me a minute, as it takes time to retrain the brain to remember the good shit over the bad stuff. But I do remember:

Don't worry. We've got your back, girl

Stay strong. Keep moving forward

Love is the answer

Remember, you're a survivor, not a victim

Karma will have its day

Thank you. Your courage has given me courage

You are a flash of light in a world of darkness

You are woman. You are strong. Always be proud

At least I found out who my friends are. Who my real friends are. I know some people blame me, or worse, don't believe me. They say they don't understand how I could go back and work for the bastard for all those months afterwards if he actually raped me. And if I'm honest. I don't really understand it either. I suppose the thing is, I didn't actually want to believe it myself. Pretending it didn't happen meant I didn't feel weak and useless. It meant I hadn't lost control. It's not the response people expect, though. And I'm starting to understand that people don't like things they don't understand. I was in denial, the counsellor said, and people don't really believe that either. Like they don't like the fact that eighty per cent of rapists know their victims. It's easier for people to believe that these shit bags are faceless strangers, but it's just not true. And instead of blaming the bastard that does it, people blame the victims.

A flickering TV above the bar catches my eye. The sound is turned down but it's clear to see it's another story about fleeing refugees. A few onlookers watching the TV screen roll their eyes and look away as terrified looking people with little ones, kids, with snot covered, tear-stained faces scramble to get off a battered looking boat, only to be met by the screwed up angry faces of others pushing them back. Some people are even spitting at the refugees, including the kids. One of the bar staff points a remote control at the screen and the tormented faces of the refugees are quickly replaced with some band from the seventies strutting around in flares and platforms, covered in fake snow and silver tinsel.

I didn't want to but I feel sad. No wonder Mum's heart is hard.

I wish Grandad were here.

♥

Chapter 54

SUSPICIOUS MINDS

Connor

I look at Uncle Sean, confused.

'What d'ya mean you're not coming? You told me you loved Indieknot?'

'I do, it's just we, Simon and I have something, someone we need to see.' Simon coughs and Uncle Sean looks at him. 'Like I said, it's a business opportunity,' he continues. 'I promise we'll be as quick as we can.' He nods at Dad and Dad nods back.

I let out a heavy sigh and Dad looks at me. His craggy face cracks into a huge smile and he pats me on the back and laughs. 'Looks like it's just you and me then, kiddo. Bit of father and son bonding time, eh?' He nudges me and winks, but inside I cringe.

It's great that things are better now with Dad, although it still seems weird that he's seeing Ruby. And I suppose it's pretty peng that I'm sat here on the train with both my dad and my step-dad but, if I'm honest, I haven't got a clue why Si and Dad wanted to come and see Indieknot in the first place. Uncle Sean, yeah. He knows the band, even went to see them with Nat when they did a few gigs in Cornwall a couple of years back, before they started to make a name for themselves. And, even though he's old, like Dad and Si, Uncle Sean is just, well, different. Sounder, somehow. Whereas Dad and Si, in their grey T-shirts, boring jeans and trendy *brown* shoes, just look, well, proper old! They're proper gonna stand out at this gig, and for all the wrong bloody reasons! And now Uncle Sean isn't even coming, least not straight away, so I'll look like a right knob. I mean, who goes to an Indieknot gig with their dad for god sake! I can already see the boys pissing themselves laughing when I tell them! We haven't even got there yet but already I can feel my cheeks burning with embarrassment. Fuck this, I'd rather be on my own.

'I don't mind going on my own, Dad, if you wanna help Si and Uncle Sean?' I suggest, hopeful, looking from Si to Uncle Sean and back to Dad. Dad's smile vanishes. His mouth hangs open as if to speak but he doesn't make a sound. He looks at Si and Uncle Sean, who both then look at each other. Si raises his eyebrow and Uncle Sean chews his bottom lip. 'I'll be fine on my own, honest,' I add a little too enthusiastically. I see a flicker of pain dance across Dad's eyes and I sort of feel bad, but still not bad enough to go to an Indieknot gig with him on my own. 'Then all three of you can catch up with me after?' Shoving both hands into the pockets of my hoody I cross all my fingers.

Please say yes. Please say yes!

A freaky silence falls between us all. I look out of the train window and see a grey sky sitting on top of bare fields and every now and then I notice a cluster of dead looking trees with gnarly branches waving at me. Sleety rain hits the window and I'm suddenly glad I brought the bigger, bulkier jacket Mum nagged me to bring. I hope her meeting with her agent goes okay today, that they tell her something to make her smile. She never really smiles much any more. Not since Grandad passed away. God, I miss Grandad. And all this crap with Cassie doesn't help. I swear I thought Mum and Si were gonna split up over it at one point. And it looks as though the bastard is gonna get away with it. Cassie said she doesn't care, but I know she's lying.

As if on cue my phone vibrates and it's a text from Jake, telling me everything is set. My stomach flips and I suddenly feel really nervous, both about the deed itself and the fact I am now in debt to some criminal friend of Jake's uncle. Someone had to do something, though, coz no other fucker seems to be. Well, actually that's not true; Mum, Si and Dad have been trying to sort it out legally but it seems the law doesn't give a shit. I wish Jake's uncle's friend hadn't planned it for today, though. I know they can't trace it back to me coz I'll be at the gig, but what if the police get involved and think it's strange that I'm in London on the same day?

The naked fields give way to dull-looking industrial buildings and ugly tower blocks, which eventually morph into the last but one platform before Kings Cross. It's only been a few minutes but the silence between us all hangs heavy. Si's slightly bushy eyebrow is still arched with the same annoyed look he gives Mum when she's screaming at him, saying he doesn't understand.

'Well?' I ask. My phone vibrates again and it's another text, this time from Alesha wishing me a happy Christmas. My tummy flips for a second time but it's a different feeling, both painfully happy and sad at the same time. Happy coz she texted me, sad because she won't give us a chance. She says I need to go out and live, meet other girls, but I don't want other girls, I want her. Although it was pretty sound touching Hayley Patterson's boobs, until I thought of Alesha, that is, then I felt like I was cheating on her. Even though she isn't my girlfriend. I'm pretty sure Hayley would have let me go all the way, too. It was me that said no, and ever since then she's done nothing but chase me. If I'd known, for all those years at school, that the best way to get a girl to like you was to ignore her, I could have had loads of girlfriends by now!

'Well?' I ask again. Still chewing his lip, Uncle Sean responds to Si's raised eyebrow with a firm shake of the head. My heart sinks and I slump back into my seat.

'No. I think it's best if your dad goes with you.'

Dad closes his mouth and lets out a small sigh. He seems sort of relieved and nods his head in agreement. 'Yep. Good call,' he mutters, nodding his head up and down like baby Nick does when he's excited. 'Absolutely. Someone needs to stay with

Connor in case …' trailing off mid-sentence he throws Uncle Sean a concerned look.

'In case, what?' I ask.

Uncle Sean's eyebrows knit together. 'In case things run on a little late and we don't get back on time. It wouldn't be good for you to be stuck at the venue, on your own.

Again, Dad nods his head in agreement. He coughs to clear his throat. 'Yep, yes. If you don't make it back, we, Connor and I, will go on and meet the others and tell them you'll catch us up.'

I'm pissed off but I can't help feeling sorry for Dad. His voice sounds weird, almost robotic. I realise he doesn't want to be at this gig any more than I want him there. He's doing it for me.

'Oh, and Connor,' Uncle Sean adds, 'don't forget, as far as everyone else is concerned, we,' he points to Si then waves his hand back at himself, 'have been at the gig with you two all night. Like we discussed earlier, it's important you stick to that. Okay?'

I shrug my shoulders. 'Okay, but Mum won't like it if she finds out we've been lying. And besides, you still haven't told me where you're really going.'

Uncle Sean pretends to smile. 'Lets just say, it's a surprise.'

Chapter 55

RECONCILIATION

Cassie

Looking up from my phone, I glance at the TV screen again and freeze. Honey's face fills the monitor. She's singing her new song, released in time for Christmas, which has, of course, shot straight to number one in the music charts. It's quite good, a bit poppy for my liking, but Honey always had a good singing voice. She could probably make anything sound good. I feel sick and sad and betrayed all at the same time. I still can't believe she sold out and sold me out, too. I trusted her. Really trusted her. I want to but I can't take my eyes off the screen as I watch her strutting her stuff. A voice to the side of me says hello and when I look round I almost choke on my drink. It's Flippity. I feel my mouth open but I'm not sure if any words come out. It's been over a year since I last saw her, just before Luke dumped her for me.

Panicking I look around for help. I can't do this. Not now. I can't take any more shit. I've had enough for one year, for one lifetime, actually. To my surprise, though, Felicity is actually okay. She says she sees now that Luke and I are better suited for one another and as she glances up at the TV screen she says she's truly sorry for what I've had to go through. Says she's disappointed with Honey and it's bloody awful how she betrayed me. I thank her and ask her if she'd like to stay have a drink with us.

'Luke's coming,' I say.

Felicity smiles, or smirks, I'm not really sure which it is, and shakes her head. 'That isn't going to work, is it?' she replies.

'You don't deserve what's happened to you Cassie but that doesn't mean I suddenly want to be friends with you. Besides, if I'm honest, I'm still in love with Luke. Even though I know now I'd have been no good for him. Take care of yourself Cassie and tell Luke I said hi, will you?'

Slightly shaken but not necessarily in a bad way, I nod my head and watch her leave, just at the same time Mum walks in and makes her way towards the overcrowded bar. Wearing a 1950's style skirt and tight-fitting top she looks as beautiful as ever. She seems a bit flustered, though, smoothing down her hair with her one free hand whilst carrying a huge plastic bag in the other. A group of rowdy lads stare at her with drunken approval and make way for Mum to get to the bar. She smiles at the boys and, with a bit of playful nudging, they smile back at her. Still feeling numb at seeing both Honey and Flippity, I'm grateful when I get the opportunity to laugh when a pretty girl, wearing loads of make-up, clearly trying to get the boys' attention by flicking her long, blonde hair flirtatiously, wears a look of both disgust and surprise as they turn their backs on her and start talking to Mum.

Mum spots me and holds her glass up and points. I nod just as Connor and Dad walk in, quickly followed by Luke and Useless. I wait, expecting to see Si and Uncle Sean but I don't see them. Luke makes his way towards me and I'm gobsmacked to see he has a black eye and split lip.

'Shit! What the hell happened to you?' I ask.

Luke grins and says that he and Useless were just messing around when Useless accidently hit him.

'Really?' How does someone accidentally hit you?'

'Luke did not duck,' Useless, who has now joined us, replies, laughing. His Polish accent still as strong as ever.

After about thirty minutes or so, Si and Uncle Sean turn up, apologising for being late, saying something about needing a piss then getting lost.

Once we are all present and correct, each with a glass in hand, Uncle Sean proposes a toast, to Grandad.

'And to a better year next year,' Mum suggests.

Uncle Sean winks at Mum. 'I think it will be, sis. I think it will be.'

'Count back from three?' Si suggests.

'Three. Two. One. It's not a life, it's an adventure!'

Chapter 56

HAVE YOURSELF A MERRY LITTLE CHRISTMAS

Lizzie

I look around at contented faces and smile. Locked hands cover full bellies and I'm grateful to have my family around me. Not everyone is here, though. Aunt Marie, who will join us later, has chosen to spend Christmas Day with Uncle Teddy. He barely knows who she is these days but she says she can't bear the thought of Christmas dinner without him. Ruby, Scott and Andrew have decided to spend their first Christmas together, which is understandable. My ex-husband and my best friend, together, who'd have thought it? And then there's Dad, of course. I can hardly believe it's been a year since he left us. Sometimes it feels like a lifetime, at others mere seconds. The gap he has left in my heart is huge and just when I think I feel better, that I am coming to terms with my loss, something will set me off. It can be anything from an old song on the radio, or a favourite film on the TV, the other day it was the smell of Old Spice aftershave on a man passing me on the street and it was all I could do to stop myself from following him. Even the automated voice on the London underground makes me think of Dad. "Mind the gap. Mind the gap," the soulless voice repeats. I'm trying, Dad, I really am, but the gap never seems to lessen.

This morning it was one of Dad's books from my study, a rather battered copy of *The Lion, The Witch and the Wardrobe*, of all things, which Summer chose to read. The sight of its worn jacket brought with it such an abundance of memories that I found myself reluctant to part with it. 'Please be careful with it,' I implored a rather bemused looking Summer, as I thumbed its shabby, yellowy pages, my eye instantly drawn to the words of one line in particular "Always winter but never Christmas." How apt.

'Tell me something else, Dad?' I found myself saying out loud before the book slipped from my hands. 'No!' I shouted as a somewhat startled Summer made to rescue the book from its crash landing. She jumped back as I tentatively reached down towards it. Jacket face up, it had of course fallen open. 'The first words you see, Lizzie,' I whispered as I flipped the book around. And the first words I saw were; "All shall be done, but it may be harder than you think."

'Why are you crying, Auntie Lizzie?' Summer asked.

'Oh, I'm sorry Summer, I just miss Grandad, very much.'

'Me too,' she replied.

As if on cue, baby Nicolas calls out to me. 'Nan nan nan nan nan,' he declares. Chubby, outstretched hands point to me as he rocks back and forth on Maisy's knee and I can't help wondering if Dad has heard my rambling thoughts. I smile and hold my hands out in response to my dribbling grandson. Maybe the gap is not so wide after all. Grateful to give her aching arms a rest, Maisy passes Nicolas to me. He eagerly shows me one of his new toys. Life is super-exciting for a one year old, and for a few brief seconds I'm completely swept away with his enthusiasm. As Nicolas guides my hand to large buttons that, when pressed, release an amusing array of animal sounds, I look across at Cassie who is snuggled close to Luke. I remember when she was Nicholas's age and how overwhelmed I felt at the time. How desperately tired, desperately afraid and desperately happy I felt. I also remember how vulnerable I felt, too, and how I swore I would do anything to protect her.

I failed.

Common sense tells me, as others have repeatedly reminded me, it was out of my hands. I'm no more responsible for the attack on my daughter than she was. But as a parent that doesn't cut it. As a parent I want to protect my child at all times and at all costs. However, short of inventing a time machine, there's sod all I can do about it. However, as Dad always said, there's more than one way to skin a cat, or I should say, *rat*, as Dad preferred to say.

'Cat!' Nicolas shouts pointing to Romeow. Looking slightly alarmed, our tired old moggy spots the fat fingered, pointing baby. His look is one of mild exasperation, no doubt at the thought of once again being manhandled by the manically laughing, small person, so, despite his advancing years slowing him down of late, he pegs it. Nicolas begins to wriggle and squirm on my knee. For a one year old he's not particularly light and I feel the tired relief in my legs when Maisy nods at me to let him down, no doubt in search of the cat, who by now will be well out of the way.

When I look up again Cassie is looking directly at me. 'Thanks. I love you,' she mouths. I smile back at my beautiful daughter and wonder if she will still love me as much when she discovers what I've done. I know, deep down, it was the right thing to do. Despite her insistence that she is moving on and putting this whole horrible year behind her. 'Let karma do its job,' she'd said. Unfortunately, I'm not prepared to wait for karma and I hope to god Cassie understands that.

After all, as I have now discovered, there's nothing quite as ruthless as a bitch of a mother frightened for her children.

Connor

My phone buzzes. It's a text from Jake and when I open it I find he's attached a photo of Robbo, hugging the bouncer from last night. I'd almost forgotten about it and can't help pissing myself laughing. What a knob. He was so drunk he thought the bloody bouncer was putting his arms out to hug him, not frisk him. Luckily for Robbo, and us, the bouncer saw the funny side and still let us in. This being eighteen and legal to drink thing is good, except I never have enough bloody money. That's why I'm not sure about going to uni. Maybe I'll get a job when I finish college. I could even move down south, perhaps live with Uncle Sean for a while. Maybe then, if Alesha saw me every day, she'd feel different about giving us a chance.

But then again, would I want to leave everyone? I say everyone, I mean the lads, mostly. Cassie is always in London, which is great when the boys and I can afford to visit. Nan's obsessed with baby Nicolas, which is fine, I understand it stops her thinking about Grandad, and he is pretty cute, for a baby. Maisy and Crazee are in the middle of selling up their tattoo business in Oz in the hope of setting one up here, and they move into their new house in January. Still can't believe how mumsy Maisy is, never would have believed my Goth of a sister from a few years ago could be so soft. Think she's surprised herself, too. Then there's Dad, of course, who has proved us all wrong and is still here for Cas and me. He and Ruby are even talking about selling her house and buying a house together, but Dad did say it had to be big enough to include a room for me and Cassie to use, in case we ever wanted to stay, which is nice, I guess. Then there's Mum and Si, either busy working or back and forth with solicitors and barristers and police and shit, for Cassie. Again, which is fine, I understand, it's just that (and I feel bad for thinking it) sometimes I feel as though I'm invisible, especially to Mum. Maybe, now the deed is done, Mum will find some sort of closure and she'll go back to being, well, my Mum again.

Oh god, Summer is calling for everyone to play charades. Suppose I could join in, for a while. Groaning, I roll my eyes then something outside the window catches my attention. It fills me with a warm, fuzzy feeling and I kind of feel sad but really happy at the same time. I look round the room in search of Cassie and when she looks my way I nod at the window.

Like me, she smiles.

Cassie

I watch Mum as she gently lowers baby Nicolas off her knee. Nicolas catches me staring at him and looks straight back at me. I experience the tiniest of flips in my stomach as his face breaks into a huge grin. He reminds me of Grandad. He has no biological link to Grandad so it's not actually possible. But nonetheless, at times, I swear I see Grandad staring back at me through my nephew's big, brown eyes.

I miss Grandad. More than I ever imagined. Wish he were here with us right now. I don't know how, in what way he could have done more than anyone else has, but somehow, I think Grandad would have sorted this shit. I look at Mum and smile. 'Thanks. I love you,' I mouth. She smiles back but she looks so tired. And here comes the guilt again. I've spent this whole year feeling racked with guilt, and yet people tell me I did nothing wrong? Maybe I shouldn't have told Mum? Maybe I shouldn't have told anyone? Maybe, just maybe, it was my fault? But what about the others? Was it their fault too? He, him, it, I can't bring myself to say his name, is not going to be prosecuted for what he did to me, anyway. Not enough evidence, apparently. So, what has telling solved? Fuck all, that's what.

Oh great. Despite all the self-help books, despite the counselling, the bastard is here again. Will I ever have a day when thoughts of him don't invade mine? How long will this creep stay inside my head messing with my thoughts? Hot tears well in my eyes and I quickly look down so Mum doesn't see me. It's been a lovely day so far and I don't want to be the one to ruin it, again. Haven't I done enough? I quickly swat the bastard from my thoughts then just as quickly dry my eyes. Luke leans over. He whispers in my ear and asks me if I'm okay.

'Just had a bit of a wobble,' I reply. Luke's face hardens and I can't make out if he's pissed off or disappointed. Clearly, when I told him the other night that I'd moved on, he believed me. I put my hand up to his eye and gently touch the cut around it, and even though I barely touch it, he winces. I'm surprised how sore it still looks and can't believe Useless caught him with such a blinder. 'I was thinking about Grandad and how much I miss him.'

Luke's face softens. 'Of course you do,' he replies before kissing me on the nose.

I wrinkle my nose and smile. 'Love you.'

Luke takes my hand and stares at me for a few seconds. 'I love you too, Cassie. You do know that, right?'

He suddenly seems very serious which makes me giggle. 'Are you pissed?' I ask.

'I mean it,' he continues.

I nod my head. 'Okay, thanks babe,' I reply.

'Let's play charades,' Summer shouts which is met by lots of groaning and eye rolling, especially from Connor but nobody means it, not really. I smile at Connor and I'm glad to see he smiles back. Sometimes I can't make out if he's still upset about Grandad or if his quiet moments are because he resents me, and all the time I've sucked out of everyone this past year. I wouldn't blame him if he were angry with me, not really. Even Mum forgets she has a son at times. Connor nods towards the window behind me. I turn to see three birds sitting on an empty tree branch. Three little turtle doves I think; bunched together looking in on us. I feel my throat tighten and once again the tears are threatening to fall. Everyone knows turtle doves mate for life and you only ever see them in pairs. It's Grandad. Grandad is still with us. Connor knows it and so do I.

Several rounds of charades later and the room is ringing with laughter, so much so, in fact, my tummy hurts and the tears rolling down my cheeks are happy ones. Uncle Sean, who is sat next to me, throws his arm around my shoulder and squeezes me tight.

'How we doing, Cas?' he asks.

I try to shrug my shoulders but Uncle Sean is holding me so tight I can't actually move and I realise, again, just how much physically stronger men are than women. 'I'm okay,' I reply.

Uncle Sean turns to look at me and I can smell the beer on his breath. 'C'mon, really. Tell the truth. How are you, really?'

'Honestly, I'm getting there. It could have been worse.'

Uncle Sean runs his free hand through his hair and sighs. 'Mum said the police are not going to prosecute?'

I shake my head. 'Nuh-uh. Well, it's not actually the police, it's the CPS but no, they're not going to prosecute. Not enough evidence. And there's not really a case now some of the other girls that came forward have withdrawn their statements.'

Uncle Sean mumbles something I don't quite catch. His vice-like grip makes me anxious so I ask him to please let go. His expression changes to one of confusion and he immediately lets go. 'Shit. Of course. Sorry Cas.' He holds his hands up in surrender. 'I didn't mean anything. I … I was only trying to give you a hug …'

He looks mortified, and once again I feel guilty for upsetting those who love me. I gently place my hand on his shoulder. 'I know. Thank you, Uncle Sean.'

My mood has dropped like a lift out of control and all I want to do is get it back again. As I didn't get much chance to ask Uncle Sean about the Indieknot concert the other night, I decide now is as good a time as any.

'Yeah. Yeah, it was, they were, very good,' he replies waving his empty glass towards Simon. 'Sorry Cas but I need a refill. Simon. Oi Si,' he shouts as Simon turns towards us. 'Cas wants to know about the concert the other night.'

Uncle Sean disappears and Simon scratches his head and smiles. 'Err, yeah. They were very good.'

'Really? I honestly didn't think it was your kind of thing, or Dad's for that matter. You know, with Indieknot being a bit trap, a bit dubstep?'

Simon smiles. 'I … suppose they were … are, a bit. But you know me … happy to go with the flow.'

'Have you seen Nicolas?' Maisy interrupts.

'Shhhh,' Mum shouts, waving her arms. 'What's that noise?'

The chattering room goes deathly quiet and everyone looks at one another. I listen hard. I swear to god I can hear Grandad, and someone else? Maisy and I look at one another other. 'Nicolas,' we both say at the same time.

'In the living room?' Mum suggests.

We all quietly turn and head towards the direction of both voices. As we draw closer to the living room I can clearly make out Grandad saying: "it's not a life, it's an adventure" and above his voice I also hear Nicolas. As we enter the room, Grandad's face fills the TV screen and dancing in front of it is Nicolas, holding the DVD remote. He somehow has film footage of Grandad on a continual loop.

"It's not a life, it's an adventure!" Grandad declares. Nicolas laughs and does his level best to repeat it back.

'Naw naw life, v v venture!' Nicolas declares, thrusting the remote triumphantly into the air.

Nan, who is now stood beside me, has tears in her eyes, as do Mum, Maisy and I. Everyone gathers behind us to watch Nicolas who seems to be totally unaware of his audience. Simon makes some joke about Grandad not wanting to be left out even though he's dead, and eventually Crazee swoops down and gathers Nicolas up in his arms. He passes the remote control to Maisy who, randomly stabbing all the different buttons on it, aims it at the TV. I turn to look at Nan who is being comforted by Mum and as I turn back towards the TV screen, Grandad's face disappears.

However, a woman reading the news quickly replaces it. Her face is solemn with a voice to match.

'Now,' she states. '*Police have confirmed that the body found at the London home of millionaire music producer Hunter Black, is in fact, his. We now go over live to our news correspondent, Ben Parsons, who is outside the famous music producer's home. Ben, have the police released any more information?*'

The image on the screen switches from the newsroom to outside Hunter Black's house. A well-spoken, serious looking man with a comb over and a microphone starts to speak.

'*Thank you, Philippa. No, not much. As you can see, I am in Chelsea, standing here,*' he points to the shiny, black door of the house behind him, '*outside the London home of millionaire music producer, Hunter Black and police have confirmed that the body found here earlier today is that of the man himself. Apparently the alarm was raised by friends and family when Black failed to turn up for Christmas Day celebrations as planned.*'

Although he is some distance away, the news correspondent stands directly in front of the black door, now decorated with crisscrossed yellow and black crime scene tape flapping manically in the wind. The familiar clicking sound of news cameras can be heard in the background and their flashes of bright light dance around like the blinking fairy lights on our Christmas tree. Stern faced police men and women guard the area and other men and women, covered from head to foot in blue plastic overalls, can be seen disappearing through the same black door.

'*Of course, as many of you will know, Black is no stranger to publicity, mainly due to his work within the music industry. However, he has, of late, been at the centre of public news for very different reasons,*' the newsman continues, '*namely the alleged rape and assault of at least ten young women. Something*

Black has always denied. Now, the police have also stated that although his body was found several hours ago, it is their belief he actually died several days ago and they are, for the moment at least, treating his death as suspicious. Back to you in the studio, Philippa.'

'Thank you, Ben. Now, let's take a look at other news ...'

Someone turns the TV off. I feel numb, completely devoid of all emotion, except shock, maybe. I take a minute to observe the faces around me and quickly realise everyone is wearing the same wide-eyed look of disbelief as me. Mouths open and close as if to speak but except for a few muffled gasps, the room has fallen deathly silent.

To be continued...

♥

Acknowledgements

This book is dedicated to my amazing family, and wonderful friends – old and new, you know who you are. I thank you all for your unwavering love and support, as always.

I would particularly like to thank Lisa Bainbridge, Jane Green, Michelle Ryles, Alexina Golding, Helen Neale, Philippa McKenna, Tracey Peel-Ridealgh, Nina Kirby, and Louise Auckland, as well as all the wonderful friends I have made on various Facebook groups including writers, readers and book bloggers. Your encouragement, support, and words of wisdom are always truly inspiring.

I would also like to thank my children, Jade and Callum, and their lovely friends for being honest with me during my research, and for making me laugh.

Special thanks to my editor, Emma Mitchell, and my proof-reader, Theresa Shiels. And for the poetry of James Whitcomb Riley – *Away* appears on page 216.

And last but not least, I would like to thank Matthew, my publisher, for his continued belief in me.

Eva Jordan, born in Kent but living most of her life in a small Cambridgeshire town, describes herself as a lover of words, books, travel and chocolate. She is also partial to the odd glass or two of wine.

Her career has been varied including working within the library service and at a women's refuge. She has had several short stories published and currently writes a monthly column for a local magazine. Eva also works on a voluntary basis for a charity based organisation teaching adults to read. However, storytelling through the art of writing is her passion and as a busy mum and step mum to four children, Eva says she is never short of inspiration!

As well as writing, Eva loves music and film and of course she loves to read. She enjoys stories that force the reader to observe the daily interactions of people with one another set against the social complexities of everyday life, be that through crime, love or comedy.

It is the women in Eva's life, including her mother, daughters and good friends that inspired her to write her debut novel *183 TIMES A YEAR*, a modern day exploration of domestic love, hate, strength and friendship set amongst the thorny realities of today's divided and extended families.

183 TIMES A YEAR

£7.99
ISBN 978-1911129813
368pp

'I really enjoyed this book. It really grasped the nature of mother/daughter relationships very well, in a way that was funny but also at times, touching and poignant' – **Jill's Book Café**

Mothers and daughters alike will never look at each other in quite the same way after reading this book – a brilliantly funny observation of contemporary family life. Lizzie – exasperated mother of Cassie, Connor and stepdaughter Maisy – is the frustrated voice of reason to her daughters' teenage angst. She gets by with good friends, cheap wine and talking to herself – out loud. 16-year-old Cassie – the Facebook, tweeting, selfie-taking, music and mobile phone obsessed teen – hates everything about her life. She longs for the perfect world of Chelsea Divine and her 'undivorced' parents. And Joe, of course. However, the discovery of a terrible betrayal and a brutal attack throws the whole household into disarray. Lizzie and Cassie are forced to reassess the important things in life as they embark upon separate journeys of self-discovery – accepting some less than flattering home truths along the way. Although tragic at times this is a delightfully funny exploration of domestic love, hate, strength and ultimately friendship. A poignant, heartfelt look at that complex and diverse relationship between a Mother and daughter set amongst the thorny realities of today's divided and extended families.

Urbane Publications is dedicated to
developing new author voices, and publishing
fiction and non-fiction that challenges, thrills and
fascinates. From page-turning novels to innovative
reference books, our goal is to publish what
YOU want to read.

Find out more at
urbanepublications.com